I0824518

# Prince of MidWest

Abigail Linhardt

A SpaceDragon Creations book

This book is a work of fiction. Names, characters, places, and incidents either are the product of the author's imagination or are used fictitiously. Any resemblance to actual persons, living or dead, events, cultures, or locales is entirely coincidental.



Edited by J.H. Flemming. Cover art by SpaceDragon Creations. Chapter font *Carnival Freakshow* designed by Living Hell.

Also available in audiobook and ebook.

Paperback ISBN: 978-1-957175-03-4

Hardback ISBN: 978-1-957175-05-8

Ebook ISBN: 978-1-957175-07-2

# Acknowledgments

Special thank you to K.N. Nguyen for beta reading what must have been the fourth draft of things and still finding great ways to make it better. And thanks to Katelyn for her help in polishing it as well.

Special shout out to my editor, J.H. Flemming, who caught a massive flaw that I had not picked up on for over five years. Thanks for reading my monstrous books and making them shine. You are invaluable.

# Prince of MidWest

Abigail Linhardt

# Dedication

For Anna and Luke.
Two of the most fabulous vampires I know.

"Fool that I am," said he, "that I did not tear out my heart the day I resolved to revenge myself."

— Alexandre Dumas, *The Count of Monte Cristo*

# Contents

## Part Two
## Pirates



## Part Three
## Le Grande Marquis D'Noirpierre

# PART I

# THE CHATEAU D'OUBLI

# Prologue: The Journal

I sat in the long grass, facing a great lake just beyond the prairies filled with royal buffalo. Not any of the Great Lakes, now full of the French navy, but big by Kansouri standards. The flatness of the land forced me to duck behind a boulder and lower my over-plumed hat to protect myself from the sun. It would be rising soon, turning me to ash. Far behind me, the new king of MidWest—the central and high throne of the American Empire—took his oath pledging to protect the people and uphold the laws. Tradition placed the ceremony at sunrise, to be followed by day-long revels.

"Dear Ezra," I wrote in the front of a large, leather-bound book. "Félicitations on your coronation. I hope you are prepared to defend your title as king just as your grandfather did. They say after the Revolution, the French had no business curating our monarchy, but, as they say, c'est la vie. You're a king because the French diplomats wanted an empire, but calling you a king sounded more demarcated. In 1778, France aided young America in its fight against the Europian Empire. Once the new world was victorious, the French aristocrats stayed and built the monarchy we have today. But you, my son, are king for a whole different reason."

I stopped and tapped my pen against the page. This shouldn't be a history lesson. Ezra knew his own history in respect to how the empire was founded. I wrote, "I suppose I used that opening line to avoid the real story I need to tell. It's a good one, though. It's about adventure, love, pirates—and best of all—revenge."

I looked up, distracted by the festive coronation going on inside the castle walls behind me. Should I divulge every secret, every sin? What did the boy need to know? Did anything I had done in the years leading up to this moment matter enough? Did I matter to Ezra?

Determined, I set my hand to the page. Everything poured out. Every evil action, every dark thought.

"Dear Ezra," I began again. "The man who raised you is one of the greatest this sorry world has ever produced. He saved me, and because of that, I sacrificed our life together. I want to tell you about him. This won't be easy, and there are things I will tell you I wish you didn't have to know. I will write everything down, up to the minute I died, which will be soon.

"I want to start with the underground—The Château d'Oubli. I had a life up till then, but it might be better if I don't start with my birth and how I grew up. No, it gets interesting a few years after I was thrown in The Château d'Oubli, the underground hell our ancestors created as a place to hide the bearers of secrets. The prisoners of The Château d'Oubli were not guilty of anything that would get you swinging from the gallows in a town square. No, their crime was knowing things they shouldn't. Or being the wrong kind of person. It's a place where people are sent to be held, to be watched, hidden away, but not killed. Just in case. That's where *he* came into my life. But before that, he came to America looking for something I can never give myself: redemption."

I shook my hand out, then gripped my pen again.

"I have his memories locked away inside my mind as well. I've treasured them these last eighteen years. How I got his memories inside my head is quite a story as well. I'll get there, telling his story along with mine so you can see how we came together. His name was Cecil, and he landed on our western shores one wild, stormy night…"

# Welcome to America

I can say with confidence what Cecil's first day on our shores looked like. More on that later. But just know you can trust my accounts of his actions. Before this, he spent a significant amount of time in the dark places of Europa. America must have been quite a shock for him.

He stepped off the train in the dark of night, pushing his red sunglasses up his alabaster nose. His keen eyes shot right and left. The messenger said to go to the first post office he found outside the train station. Looking up, he checked the huge clocktower perched atop the green metal of the train station: midnight. Checking his own pocket watch, he found that meant it was five in the evening back home in London. Not that time meant anything to Cecil. Unless it was high noon when the sun blasted down. But he liked to keep track of his home's hours. He had kept the watch running on London time for the last several decades. He buttoned the silver clasps of his greatcoat and smoothed the front down, then fluffed the lacy cravat at his throat.

"Giddy up, foreigner," a cowboy behind him grunted. The ranch hand carried a huge saddle over one arm and a small piece of baggage in the other. "Move off the walkway or get run over."

"American hospitality at its finest," Cecil replied, tipping his top hat. He scooted out of the tired man's way. "Excuse me, sir," he called, falling in step with the cowboy, his ruby-handled cane clacking against the green metal flooring. "I was wondering if you knew where the nearest post office is?"

Glaring up at the stranger the way he might inspect a cow stuck in the fence, the cowboy pointed directly to his left. "Right there, under the skydock with all the fancy airships hoverin' over it. Or can't you read English?"

Squinting, Cecil inspected a large, hand-painted sign above a glowing window. It didn't say anything in any language. A crude, simply painted image depicting a sealed envelope splashed over the wooden sign. It was almost impossible to make out through the clouds of moisture from the various steam-powered contraptions around him.

"Ah, the translation must have been off," Cecil smirked, but the ranch hand had vanished into the rain on the other side of the muddy street. Above him, lightning cracked across the black sky like a whip. A swarm of aircraft hovered over the much higher docks above the train station.

As he pushed through the other travelers on the deck, he found a sign that said he had reached the Karaho Territory. This was where he had been told to pick up a letter, the first step in his long overdue quest. Reaching the post office window, ducking against the cold wind, he knocked on the glass. A golden clasp on the inside locked it against the torrents of rain. A notice board beside him gave him a small taste of the American Empire he'd landed in. There was a wanted poster for some aeronaut pirate dripping with fresh ink, a notice about a cabaret that just came into town, a bounty on a coven of vampires, and a poster stating the queen of MidWest was going to host some Independence Day rodeo later in the year.

*Queen and rodeo in the same sentence,* Cecil thought, tapping again on the post office window. *What a place the west is.* He'd been warned by his correspondence in the American Empire to come at night and lay low. Where vampires might be more feared in Europa, here in America, they were hunted by all classes of citizen.

While he waited for the older woman inside to shuffle to the window, he looked out over the train tracks to the town. A single muddy street reached between two sides of shops, a saloon, a corral of heifers behind a black smith, and a few other amenities people needed to survive in this "wild west," as they called it. The only thing with warm light in its windows was the saloon across the way. Next to it was a kind of blacksmith shop with a huge wooden sign that read "Mancer-forged: Trust the magic." At the end of the street, a decently sized white church with bright red double doors and a large bell tower glowed.

"What?" the woman inside shouted, cracking the window just enough to let her gruff voice out.

"There should be a letter, registered mail," Cecil replied, leaning a little too close to the window, "for Cecil Corbeau."

"Corbeau?" the woman repeated, squinting with only one eye through her spectacles. "Haven't gotten anything from France in over three weeks," she finished. "Even if we did, it'd not come through here. You might have to check with the RMS."

"RMS?" he repeated.

She moved to close the window. "Royal Mail System. Everything from France has to go through Palais Kansouri's sorting system."

"The palais," Cecil repeated, looking down the tiny one-road town. "Kansouri is miles east. And I'm not here about any of the five kingdoms."

The American Empire was divided into five kingdoms, each ruled over by monarchy: MidWest where the high king sat, SouthWest, NorthWest, FarWest, and the ever-confusing EastWest.

"Wait!" Cecil pressed his long fingers against the glass, stopping her from shutting the window. "It would be sealed with the Creed's mark. A cross and chains."

With the mention of the religious Creed—the system of holy men and women who worked the churches—the woman blinked, taking in his black hair, sharp jaw, and deep-set eyes. She turned away and shuffled back to a wall made entirely of wooden slots, laden with mail. Looking up, she spotted a black envelope with a golden seal. Sighing, she climbed up onto her rolling ladder and grabbed it. Reading the front and squinting back at him, then back at the envelope, she decided he must be who he said he was and climbed back down.

"No signature required," she mumbled, sliding it out to him. She watched him carefully as he picked it up.

The glossy envelope slid between his long fingers like silk. A wax seal of a cross closed the back flap.

"Thank you, ma'am," he said in his posh accent. Her eyes bored into him as he walked away. Tucking the envelope into his flouncy greatcoat, Cecil ducked across the muddy street to the saloon for some shelter from the freezing weather and gushing rain.

The inside was like no place Cecil had ever been. An out of tune piano tinkled a quick melody for a trio of dancing girls up on a stage. A group of empirical guards with long muskets lounged in one corner, their heads engulfed in cigar smoke. Exhausted cowboys and businessmen alike dotted the other round tables. Girls in frilly, low-cut dresses served beer and fried food. A few eyes turned to him as he entered, and he realized he'd stood too long in the doorway.

Tipping his hat, he retreated to a side booth, his cane clicking on the wood floor, and sat down in an isolated corner. After a quick scan and a sniff, Cecil broke the religious seal of the envelope with a hiss of pain as it burned him. Inside, a letter on creamy, gossamer paper waited.

The letter read:

*Monsieur Corbeau,*

*After much consideration, and seeing as you have followed our steps to the letter (or else you would not be reading this), the Creed have decided to heed your plea for redemption sans vindication. You will find Brother Sylas in Harkness, the town in the Territory you have no doubt found yourself in. It shouldn't take much thought to know where he waits for you (we cannot say, should this letter fall into the wrong hands). We will know if you succeed or not. Once you have, visit Brother Sylas and he will absolve you. As previously stated, we cannot know what will happen once you are ash. We can only have faith.*

*Best of luck, and may God bless your endeavors.*

*Arch Father X*

Quickly folding the letter again in case anyone was spying over his shoulder, Cecil stood up and marched to the swinging double doors. A pretty automaton in an apron tried to ask him what he'd like to drink, but he pushed past the clumsy machine and re-entered the cold rain. Looking around, he frantically checked each end of the single road. Lightning kissed the rain, followed by an uproarious thunder crack as his eyes alighted on the church behind him. With his keen violet eyes, he could just make out the flicker of a candle deep inside the sanctuary through one dark window.

Running down the street, water and mud splashing over his fancy clothes, he hammered against the red door when he reached it.

"Sylas!" he shouted into the wood. "I was told to find you. My name is Cecil Corbeau and I seek redemp—"

The crack of a pistol shot through the night—and the wooden door —straight into Cecil's chest. The force of the bullet shoved him backwards several steps. He stumbled, clutching the wound in his chest. Blood seeped between his fingers.

"Come in," a gruff voice called from behind the door.

Panting, Cecil shoved the doors open. Inside was a typical MidWest church: wooden pews, large stained-glass windows, and a pulpit raised up on a sprawling stage. On the left side sat an ornate wooden desk with a red, wing backed chair behind it. A single candle burned on the desk, illuminating the face of the man in the chair. Black hair framed the gruff face. A few scars pulled flesh in odd directions. The man wore a wide-brimmed black hat, even in the church, and a matching black duster. A pearly-handled gun etched with silver sat longways across the desk. Its barrel was long for shooting from a great distance. He held a pistol in his hand and blew the smoke away from the barrel.

"Welcome to America," he mumbled, holstering the gun.

"Brother Sylas?" Cecil asked, shaking the blood off his hand onto the church floor. It hissed and sparked into a tiny flame like a candle when it hit the wooden slats.

"Just Sylas," the man said with a sigh, sounding exhausted. He dropped the pen he'd been writing with and gestured for Cecil to take the seat opposite him. "You must be Cecil. Sorry I shot you, but I can see by how disturbed you are by the wound that you're the man I've been waiting for."

"You didn't use silver," Cecil mused, taking the chair and smoothing his hair back. He leaned his ruby-hilted cane against the arm of the seat. He sat so straight his back didn't touch the chair.

Sylas's cheek twitched in mild amusement. "I don't want to kill you, I hear."

"Father Xavian told you I was coming?"

Sylas nodded.

An unwarranted silence fell between the two men. Cecil glanced around the church.

"Thank you for inviting me in," he said softly. "Makes it so much easier to bear."

Sylas nodded again. "I'm not sure how to do this," he started, finally taking his hat off and dropping it onto the table. "But I have an idea."

"Anything," Cecil said, scooting forward on the chair with anticipation.

The man in black raised a finger, stopping Cecil from promising something out of desperation. "Don't do that, bucko. Leads to all kinds of bad oaths."

Cecil nodded, waiting.

"Here's the proposition." Sylas stood up, flinging the flourishing folds of his duster behind him before planting his hands into his hip pockets. He looked out the floor-to-ceiling window behind the pulpit. "Save the American Empire."

Cecil followed Sylas's gaze out the window, then looked back at the tall man. "I don't understand. I'm not an American. How can I…?"

Sylas turned around halfway, leaning against the pulpit. "The empire is doomed. We've not fared well since the French implemented their ways after the Revolution. The kings in NorthWest and SouthWest fear a second revolution if the High Throne is not secure. If you can save it, you might be able to redeem your soul."

Lightning cracked across the window, lighting up the sanctuary and the man's scarred face.

"What's going on in the empire?" Cecil asked. His fingers touched the delicate lace around his throat.

"The French," Sylas said with a touch of dark humor.

Cecil still didn't understand. "France is your ally."

"Just because the country is doesn't mean the people who run it are," Sylas advised darkly.

"Queen Whatever-Her-Name-Is should be keeping the peace with her countrymen. I thought the point of marrying a princess of France was to unite the countries."

"You'd think." Sylas paced slowly behind his desk. "The Creed has worked in the shadows of the church to keep the monarchy steady, but we lost our footing some eight years ago when High King Markus was killed."

"Killed?" Cecil asked. "I thought he died."

Sylas frowned at Cecil. "What the hell's the difference, bloodsucker?"

Cecil inclined his chin up at the tone. "Killed is when someone else makes one die," he said smugly.

"Damn right," Sylas mused. "He was killed. And his son as well."

Nodding, Cecil stood up to match the man's height. "How do I start, then? I assume you have something specific in mind, or you wouldn't ask."

"Sit down, vampire," Sylas groaned, annoyed.

Cecil slowly obeyed, keeping his eyes on the towering Ecclesiast.

Sylas went on, "Xavian thinks you're the man for the job." He lit a cigarette and took a long inhale. "I don't know anyone else who could do it. You're tough." He indicated the hole in Cecil's chest with the lit end.

"Something like that," Cecil agreed with a cocky grin. "So?" he asked, closing his coat up in the front to stop Sylas from staring at his wound.

Taking one last drag of the smoke, Sylas said, "Find the king's son, the prince. Put him on the throne and soon enough a good man will rule, bringing security back to the empire. This will save your soul."

At this, Cecil couldn't stop the scoff that escaped his throat. "How prophetic."

Sylas glared at him.

"King Markus's son died eight years ago, as you said," Cecil explained, spreading his hands wide. "The whole world heard that. The king died, the prince died, and the Duke of Dakota—originally the eldest son who abdicated the throne—swooped in to rule for the time being. A steward, if you will." He smirked. "No doubt comforting the French queen."

"Mhmm." Sylas nodded, dropping his cigarette and stamping it out with a great black boot. "Find him. It's the only way."

"Find the dead prince," Cecil repeated, nodding sarcastically. "Right on it, boss."

Honestly, I loved that side of him.

"Put him on the throne and soon enough a good man will rule," Sylas repeated. He looked over his shoulder for something Cecil couldn't see before seating himself behind the desk again to write.

"Where do I start?" Cecil asked, doubt creeping into his dead heart.

Sylas's pen stopped scratching the rough paper. "Sometimes, a person of high repute, or even a political spy or bounty hunter, goes missing. Or someone says they found them dead in a gorge, but there's no body and no one knows who found the supposed expired victim." He tapped the brim of his hat with his metal pen. "When that happens, the people say, 'He went down to The Château d'Oubli.' "

Cecil readjusted in the seat, trying to follow the vernacular of the Ecclesiast. "Is that an American saying? What's it mean?"

Sylas started writing again. "It's a place no one thinks exists."

"Does it?"

Sylas signed his name and started to fold the letter.

Enraged at the churchman, Cecil leaned over the desk to get into his face. "Listen, preacher," he growled. "I have no time for games. I've lived long enough to know that—"

"You are no longer welcome here," Sylas grunted, flicking his hand towards the big red doors.

A lurch grabbed at Cecil's back. "Oh, no," he sighed.

With an invisible jerk, he flew back down the aisle, hitting a pew on his way out, and slammed into the doors. They burst open, releasing his soaring body back onto the street with a muddy splash.

"Preacher!" he shouted, staggering to his feet. He ran to the doors, but an invisible barrier kept him out. Roaring like a lion, he flailed his arms uselessly towards the church. "You have to help me start! Where do I begin? I don't even know the damn royals' names!"

"Find The Château d'Oubli," Sylas's voice called out. The inside of the sanctuary went dark, but Sylas appeared, walking towards the doors. He gripped them to close them.

"How do I start? Give me something," the vampire begged.

Sylas looked out towards the town. "Find trouble. Ask about the dead prince. That ought to get you started. If you get caught, you're headed in the right direction." He slammed the church doors shut.

Defeated, Cecil sighed and looked up. "Did it have to rain?" he screamed to the sky. "My nicest clothes are wet now. And muddy." He moaned despondently and pulled open his coat to inspect the bullet hole in his silken shirt. "This will cost a fortune to fix, preacher man!"

No sound came from inside the church.

"Fine," Cecil huffed, fluffing his cravat as best he could despite the rain. "Where the hell do I find a little trouble? And get caught?" he repeated.

# 2
# The Search Begins

With little to no leads, Cecil went back to the saloon. If he'd been mortal, I imagine he would have drank and slept the rain away. As it were, he was an immortal with no patience left.

"Hello, there," said the pitching voice of a female automaton. She angled her metallic hips against the bar and blinked her genuine sapphire eyes. Curling her jointed fingers, she rested her clicking head against her fist. "My name is Guinevere, and I am here to ensure you have the best experience possible. How may I be of service to you?"

Cecil leaned over the bar and looked at her back where a great golden key slowly rotated, churning her clockwork gears. Her silver metal skin gleamed in the yellow light, stenciled over with golden swirls and flowers up and down her arms and legs. Thin golden chains like that of a pocket watch made up her hair. It wiggled in tiny waves with each click of her internal machinations.

"You are a beautiful piece of craftsmanship, Guinevere," Cecil said, arching one brow as though wooing a flesh and blood saloon girl. "What happens when you run down? Do certain activities take more power?"

"I am not run on electricity," Guinevere said, her voice cracking in her pitches. "I am not steam-powered, nor was I created by a metal-mancer. I am pure clockwork, wound up by the key in my back and run by the perfection of the craft. My master says I am of old-world art."

Cecil nodded. "You are." He slung his arm around her waist and spun her like a music box. "I often love women, Guinevere, but not like you."

All around them, the air whirred with the clinking sounds of more clockwork machines that wasted more men's gold than living girls ever would. The motel squirmed with life, ticking, breathing with the steam generator and glowing lights.

"I have many moods." Guinevere stepped back and unlatched a little leather purse at her side. Inside were what looked like music box disks. Each one was a unique gear shape with indentations and knocks of metal. "Choose one and I will change to suit your needs."

Cecil leaned in and kissed her cold cheek, inhaling deep. "You smell of oil and metal dust. I like blood."

The womanly automaton tilted her head, clearly confused by what he'd said. She froze and did not move, processing his words. Cecil wasn't stunningly clever, but he assumed the thing wouldn't tell anyone.

"I know how you can help me," he said. "Tell me where I can play a card game. Sloshed gamblers are great for conversation, and I need a chat. I'm lost, you see."

Recognizing the command, Guinevere showed him into the game room with the stage. A great red piano stood in the middle and a woman sang melancholy tunes to entertain the guests. The gloomy darkness in the room made it perfect for his way of playing cards. Fried food and imported spices heated the air. The electric vibration of the card players' brains buzzed around him. He found one table near the center of the room where elected officials in top hats and aeronautical pirates in exotic clothing were just starting up a game.

"Perfect, Guin," Cecil praised the clockwork machination. "Nothing like fat politicals to get the rumors flowing."

He approached the table, fluffing his cravat and polishing the ruby on his cane. "Deal me in, gentlemen," he said, taking a seat next to one of the officials.

They looked him up and down, just as confused by his garments and accent as I would soon be.

"I say," the bowler-hatted official huffed, waving his hand through the air, trying to dispel the powerful fragrance of dust, flower petals, and amber that Cecil always had hovering about him. "Whom do you represent?"

"Cecil Corbeau is the name. I am a hired gent, sirs," he said, taking the cards.

"Corbeau?" the official asked, mentally sifting through French names he knew.

This comment made all the other men glance at each other. Hired men were never good news. They all took turns shuddering and checking each other out now: which one of them warranted a hired man's talents? Of course, Cecil was just trying to stir the pot. Get the rusty gears in their heads cranking and their tongues wagging.

Cecil shuffled the cards and dealt each man one facing up and one facing down. "Blackjack, gentlemen. A simple wager. For every round I win, I get to ask a question and you tell me the answer. No lying, though. I can tell when a man lies." He smiled and his violet eyes sparkled in the dim light.

"And what about us?" one of the aero-pirates asked, pushing his goggles further up his bald head.

Cecil shrugged and fluffed his cravat again. "What do you want?"

"Gold is always good." The pirate took a swig from his tankard with a sloshy grin. "Those skydocks ain't free."

"Of course." Cecil smiled. "Onward, then?"

I don't know every detail, as I can only remember what went on in his head. But I know Cecil lost the first hand. I can't decide if he did it on purpose as part of his plan or not. I suppose he wanted to show a weakness, draw them in.

He lost the first one and handed the pirate a velvet draw-string bag with a ruby inside. It wasn't gold, but the pirate took it. The officials noted it as well. Men didn't typically carry around chunks of shine like that.

The next hand, Cecil let the victory go to one of the officials. You know what they say about the third time. On the third hand, Cecil got dealt a perfect twenty-one, taking no extra cards.

Sad their luck ran out, the official asked, "So what is it you want to know, foreigner?" His palms moistened as he gripped his new hand, waiting to hear what the foppish rogue wanted.

"You may all be calm. Though my accent is from Europa, but I am not here on government money. You won't offend anyone should my corpse end up in the gutter." He eyed each of them with a twisted grin. "The smell of your fear is vexing me and I'd rather we clear that up." He smoothed his long black hair. "I'm looking for a place I've never heard of," Cecil said simply. He took a shot glass of the black liquor from the official and threw it back, not even wincing. "And also some trouble, if you know what I mean. Or rather, those who deal in trouble."

Perhaps for the first time in history, the pirate and the official looked at each other, confused. The aero-pirate took his chances. "I can get you all kinds of trouble and take you almost anywhere," he said. "You looking for…employment?"

Cecil smiled in his delightfully crooked way, shuffling the cards again. "I have a job." He dealt the next hand and played smoothly. Perfect twenty-one again.

The official dropped his cards in defeat. "Twenty-two. How did you…?"

But the pirate stopped him from speaking. "Again, foreigner," he snapped. His eyes glinted in the dim light. He'd caught on to Cecil's way.

He trained his eyes on Cecil's hands as he dealt the cards. The pirate's weasel eye did not catch the trick, but that didn't stop him from believing he saw it. Cecil slipped the cards he needed into his elaborate sleeve, dealt the rest, and then slyly flipped out his hidden cards when dealing to himself. I've seen him do such things, and I can tell you, it is hard to catch happening.

I can't say what made the pirate not draw his curved sword then or blast Cecil away with his chemical gun. But it probably had something to do with pirate greed, wanting to know more about the fancy stranger, or curious to see how deep his pockets were and if he could separate anymore of the gold from Cecil. Pirates are a strange lot, and aero-pirates even more so—and I've met a few. They spend too much time with their heads above the clouds, and I think it dulls their wits.

"Again!" The official loosened his necktie and his fellows ran their hands across their pale chins. "What else do you want to know, foreigner?"

"Tell me about the Duke of Dakota." Cecil ran his fingers through his black hair and cocked his head to the side. "How is he these days?" Rather than asking about The Château d'Oubli right away, he danced around the details, wondering what he needed to know before barreling ahead.

A far more well-fed official took this answer for himself. "He does the best he can, foreigner. No concern of yours. With the king and his only son long gone, the Duke of Dakota took office with the queen by his side."

Cecil narrowed his eyes. "How do you like that? I heard in Angleterre that foul play might be at hand."

"Rumors," the officials said quickly.

The aeronautical pirate ran a blade over his bald head, nicking at growing stubble. "Rumors like the ones of the French vessels docking at the Deleon place?"

The bowler hat's jewels quivered. "I paid you to keep your trap shut about that." His eyes danced to Cecil. "I have nothing to do with what goes on at the Deleon estate. It's under royal protection these days. I'm a businessman, you see. I like to know what goes on in the territory."

"American business?" Cecil asked, smiling.

The bowler hat sniffed haughtily. "You Easterners always want to taint the American Empire with your false reports. The Duke had no hand in it," he said, deflecting the conversation back to Cecil's initial question.

"Shakespeare disagrees," Cecil said, leaning back in his chair. Behind him on the stage, the woman began to play a slow, haunting melody while a man accompanied her on a violin. "How many times have you seen a king and a prince vanish and the Duke weep? Spilt family blood is never, oh, negative to an evil Duke." He smiled widely at his own stupid sanguine pun.

At this, the three officials narrowed their eyes and prepared to breathe fire, as officials did when cornered.

"To speak thusly of the Duke and steward of MidWest is ill advised, my good sir. And as you are a foreigner, I can only assume you are here to stir up trouble. Tell me, what is a man dressed in a Europian coat doing in the American Empire? This is very far from your home. We have nothing here to please you. Your emperor saw to that."

"On the contrary. I love the rodeo," Cecil said lightly.

A girl with a glittering cyborg eye attending the bar came by and refilled their mugs, setting down another large platter covered in fried mushrooms, pickles, and a medley of other vegetables. Cecil took her hand and pressed his lips to her knuckles, kissing her deeply and making her giggle. He inhaled long into his throat and closed his eyes as she walked away.

"I am also here for the local cuisine, of course," he said with a smile. "The western empire is so full of variety. It is the best place to satiate my ever-hungering pallet."

The pirates and the officials were simply out of their minds at that point. This man had a way of being far too mysterious for my liking, so I can only imagine how their simple minds felt about him.

"What do you want?" the over-fed one stammered. "Spit it out already! Are you a spy? Why are you asking about the High King and the dead prince?"

Sensing his time had come to depart, the pirate burst out, "Barkeep! Come quick! This man cheats!"

Taking the cue, the official barked out, leaping from the table, "This man is a spy! Guards, come quickly! Send word to the Duke that a spy has come!"

As was the way with bar-rats, when one man shouted and threw a deck of cards and another pulled out a yellow-glowing chemical blaster, they all followed suit. Shouts of "Cheater! Treason! Danger!" went up all across the room, and some idiot fired at the pirate with his drawn gun. That was all it took. The guards rushed in, tables turned, the piano woman screamed, and bullets flew. Someone had a steam powered gas gun and took it upon himself to launch the foul stuff into the air after pulling on a gas mask.

With a curse, Cecil slipped between the brawls to find the exit. The gas, not being of silver alloy or any other harmful substance to him, did not affect him. He needed to vacate the area before his vampiric nature was found out. Disheartened that he still had no leads, he ducked past the bowler-hatted official.

"Guards!" the official screamed, pointing.

With their hook-shot arm cannons (something only found in the west where roping animals with a rocket strapped to your back was considered a sport) the guards lassoed Cecil and pulled him down. He didn't put up any fight, thinking he could escape at any time. They bound him in chains and marched him to the Big House, where he would be instantly brought to justice.

# 3
# The Duke

The Big House lived up to its name. Well known as the house of justice, it stood to be a pinnacle—a beacon—of warning. It could be seen from any hovering dirigible, any clocktower, and any high top in MidWest. All you could see was the great greying dome with Lady Justice atop it, blindly doling out her scales. Farther down, the real danger appeared. Spikes, turrets, and designs from the dark *Allemegne*-era tore their claws at the sky, creeping up the white Big House. The doors and hinges were all made from specially fortified wrought iron. Caged in by yards-high wire fences that would cut the hairs from your arms, the House and black-clad guards with their electro-spears stood watch.

This sight greeted Cecil as he quaffed his hair and said, "This place looks like it could use a little life running through it. Something has sucked it dry."

His stupid joke did not amuse his escorts. If it had, they would have known his bloodsucking ways and wondered why he hadn't killed them then and there, leaving their husks behind. Cecil later told me that each man handled the discovery of the vampire differently. Some wanted immortal life with them, begging to be killed, and others ran away screaming. I often thought which kind of man I would have been had we not met in the circumstances we did.

In the black of the night, the oil lamps painted dark dancing figures on the walls. Cecil's passive facade melted away once inside the fence. The great doors opened and pulled him in like tendril arms, languidly delighted to have a new victim. The walls and the floor were all made from smokemarble to keep things dark and hidden. Blood never showed up on black. Huge and gross above the empty, cold fireplace, an obsidian cross stood erect, judging down on those who dared look up at it. Cecil felt his vampire blood shiver inside him. The symbol was there to terrify those who still had any kind of faith. But for Cecil, it boiled his blood and froze it at the same time.

"Inform the High Judge that we have a matter of a spy that needs attending to," one of his captors said to a pale secretary wearing an old lace vest and cold eyes.

"Lucky for you, he's in the House," she said just as coldly. She reached up to the copper horn above her head and pulled it down on a squeaky crank. "A spy, Judge Marthon," she said into it as if nothing could be more boring in the entire empire. "Your favorite."

Seizing the opportunity, Cecil quipped, "Tell his honor that I am here on behalf of his highness the Prince of MidWest." His eyes glittered as he spoke, like gems in a dark cave. But in his mind, he thought, *What the hell am I doing?* and hoped he'd not gotten himself in deeper than he could swim.

The secretary frowned so deep her eyebrows touched her wired spectacles. "The perpetrator says he has something to do with…the late king's son," she said breathily into the horn again.

Somewhere high above them, the monster copper bell that signaled a high court in session thumped its large, cavernous thunder down the tower and through the black marble halls. Cecil's ears perked up at the sound and his maniacal grin spread, his sharp, charming teeth showing in the dim light.

"I feel so magnanimously important right now," he said, shifting his shoulder to lay the little wrinkles in his coat to rest.

The guards pulled his chains and led him by his wrists into the hall of judgment. They marched to the pillory in the center of a marble arena. Surrounding this place of guilt were rows of cold steel pews, all raised up to ensure that the audience looked down on the criminal. Cecil's dark eyes took in every corner, sniffing out a small hole he may escape through should the need arise. But here there were none. There were no holes one may slink back into in the daylight.

"Oh, dear," he mused softly. "I may have gotten in over my head." He glared around, wondering what he *should* have done. Doubt at his mission began to creep into his dead veins.

Once in the center, they locked a wretched iron collar around his neck, chaining him to a post on the pillory. He hissed at the guards as they snapped it shut, the tiny spikes on the inside biting at his neck and crimping his luscious hair. The shackles around his wrists were also locked to the post. He'd have to have been very strong, or perhaps one of those cyborg-men, to break himself free. Cecil had greater strength than any mortal, but he was weak with hunger. I would later find out that being near silver sapped his strength too. He wasn't monstrously strong or tough and could feel pain.

He didn't need windows to know the night had worn on. It had to be nearing three in the morning—the witching hour. Surrounded by all the hot-blooded men, he realized hunger—starving almost—made his legs weary. But his spirits were never dampened. He watched the great black door behind the judge's seat, knowing any moment now a man in a great powdered wig would burst through, ask him some questions, and have him sent somewhere he could do no more damage.

The doors slammed open and a man with white gloves, a tall, muscled body flounced in a blue military uniform with golden lapels and medals enough to sink him, marched in. He wore half of an ornate armor set as though he had been interrupted during changing. Two pistols at his side, more for decoration than firing, glinted in the lamp light. His stark-white, ten-gallon hat covered his head. His hair had been gloriously brushed to a shine and his beard perfectly trimmed around his jawline. Jethro, the Duke of Dakota and self-proclaimed protector and steward of the MidWestern throne, had arrived.

"My king!" the judge called, coming in just behind him. He was a tiny, round man. "Er, I mean, my lord. I said someone mentioned the prince, not that he had appeared." Behind the military glory of the Duke, the judge looked like a bumbling idiot. A pig in a wig.

Behind these two came a flurry of witnesses, scribes with little typewriters falling out of their arms, and gossipy journalists. All of them appeared in an explosion of papers, skewed top hats, and loose corsets. All the voices shrieked and pointed and questions lobbed off the walls. The Duke glared down at Cecil.

"Shut up!" a voice bellowed from behind them all. Another tall man swaggered to the front, his fur-lined duster sweeping behind him. A set of axe-like blades clinked on his hips, dangling from long, shiny chains. His scarred face probably could have been handsome, but the scar over his left eye just made him look permanently raged. Cecil recognized him from the covers of penny dreadfuls: Don Mateo of San Muerte. The bastard brother of the Duke of Dakota from a wealthy lady in Espagne. He was popular for his glorious executions in MidWest and the stories the tall-tale authors wrote about him killing criminals, but he had spent most of his life in Espagne. His infamous singing blades hung at his sides. They were long and curved at the ends, hanging from thick, silver chains. Images of him spinning them like a lasso came out at least once a month in some newspaper.

The people went silent. The Don ran his fingers through his shiny black hair, relaxing into a pose that made a young female journalist snap a picture before peeking out from behind her lens with a deep sigh that popped one more corset grommet loose.

"Now, what have we here?" the Don said in a gravelly southern drawl.

The Duke watched Cecil with a mixture of fear and apprehension.

Silence.

"Speak, vermin!" the judge raged, his face turning purple with nerves. The cockade on his lapel shivered with every word. "We were in the middle of practicing for a ceremony. We are anointing the new Arch Father for EastWest church and deputizing the Wardens. The press is here! Who are you? What have you done, and why is it so important?"

Cecil's hawk eyes watched the Duke as he let a smile pull his lips across his face.

"We have witnesses?" the judge said. He motioned to one of the guards. They opened the doors to admit one of the aero-pirates and the fat official who now sweated into his handkerchief.

"We can make anyone talk," the Don said, lying a hand on the looped chains of one of his blades. The silver within the singing steel glittered.

Another moment of silence. I don't think Cecil meant to meet the ones he was suspicious of.

*So, this is them,* he thought to himself. *The Duke and his bastard brother.* Had they killed the High King? Why had the mention of the dead prince landed him so swiftly in the House of Justice in their presence? He realized now he had waited around so long, chained here, because the Duke had to be summoned from *Palaise* Kansouri several miles away.

He wasn't sure what to say, and what he had said had gotten him into the shackles he now found himself in. So, he let the fat man and the pirate do the talking for him.

"Please, your majesty," the official blubbered with a stupid bow that almost toppled him over. "Er, your highness… I can tell you what he said."

"As can I!" the pirate shouted up to the audience. "But I feel if you need a story so bad, we should get a little something out of it, too."

"Idiots!" Judge Marthon called down. "Do you not know who this man is? What did he tell you?"

"If you will allow me—" the official began.

"Strap it!" the pirate cut in, hitting the official in his great chest. "I want a deal, judge." He planted his feet and crossed his arms. "I came here against my better judgment, and I want a deal."

"The only deal you will be getting is my blade," the Don said softly. The camera girl sighed in a high-pitched gust of air, her eyes glued to him.

"I feel very left out," Cecil finally said. "Isn't this *my* trial?"

The audience cranked the levers on their tripods, shooting their cameras into the air over each other's heads, and began a hurricane of typing and a storm of flashes once the prisoner spoke. They all shouted questions: Who was he? What did he want? Who sent him? What did he know about the dead prince? Was this a sign of intercontinental war again? Cecil's eyes grew big at the sudden commotion and he mimicked locking his lips, shrugged, and smiled.

"He has nothing to say for himself," the pirate said, silencing the audience. "If I tell you what he told us, I want a free contract with the empire."

The Duke glared down at the pirate, his medals reflecting in his eyes like sparking fire. He listened patiently. "A privateer contract?"

The pirate nodded sharply. "That's right. I will be contracted as a privateer of the skies, but under no man's orders. I hunt who I will, when I will. I pray on any foreign ships and aircraft I want and get to keep eighty percent of what I gain. For other pirate vessels, I am allowed to turn in the men, keep the ships, and ninety percent of what I receive from them." He spread his hands, smiling. "Sound fair, your Dukeness?"

"The cheek," Judge Marthon gasped.

"I could swing this blade so fast your head'd be spinning into next Sunday," the Don mumbled with a smirk. He lifted a blade off his belt. "See this blade? It's made of singing metal—banshee metal, as you lot call it. So, when they hit their mark, especially bone, it makes a right pretty song. One that drives a mind mad. A little nonconsensual geomancy, if you will."

"And I," the official jumped in, emboldened by his new acquaintance's guts and the thinly veiled threat from the Don, "want a free election next year. I want my position in the royal court to be maintained by default. No elections, no registration—simply to remain in my post with an added bonus of being first in line for the promotion to judge."

"Vultures!" Judge Marthon shrieked. "This is an outrageous—!"

"Let them have their way," the Duke growled, speaking for the first time. No one saw him speak; his movements were too subtle, too small to be seen. "I do not care." His eyes never left Cecil's. He glared at the reporters. "We will pay to have nothing printed of this incident. Nothing."

At this, there was a huge gasp, followed by an apocalyptic silence.

"The queen cannot know," Jethro mumbled. "We must keep this from her."

"Better speak now." The Don smirked to the men down below, running his strong fingers over his blades.

The official swallowed hard and continued to grasp at the brim of his bowler hat. "He was asking questions. Suspicious ones!" he babbled when the Duke frowned. "We were playing blackjack, and nothing was suspicious until he won."

"Imagine you losing at cards," the Don said in a low sing-song tone. His eyes twinkled.

"It wasn't like that!" the pirate cut in. "He made a wager, see? But he didn't want money."

"No one wants money but you," the official said through tight lips. "He wanted information, your grace. For every hand he won, he asked one question. As I am a man of honor, your grace, I simply had to abide by his rules."

The Duke's eye glinted. These weak-willed officials would be the death of him.

"But things got interesting," the pirate went on. "He asked about you, your high and mightiness. And then about King Markus and his dead son. And he was cheating!"

"A capitol offense within the city limits!" the official shouted, pointing his finger to the heavens as though giving a sermon. "He's..." the man fumbled for his words. "He's a foreigner. With a French name." He tapped the side of his nose. "Why is he here, asking questions?"

A moment of silence passed in which Cecil, still smiling, looked from his star witnesses to the Duke. The Duke seemed unmoved, but a three-pronged vein throbbed in his lordly temple under his perfectly elegant hair.

"Leave us," he snapped to the reporters. A small cry of protest went up, but between a glower from the Don and a few legal threats from Judge Marthon, they filed out, snapping some last-minute pictures.

Once they were alone, the Don running his hand lovingly over the edge of his axe, the Duke glared down at Cecil.

"King Markus's death was a tragedy," the Duke said with finality. "As was the death of his only son and heir to the throne. Queen Camille has worked tirelessly to heal MidWest and the other four kingdoms within the empire. We want no conflict with your country, sir."

"And I don't want any either," Cecil started. "I had no idea inquiring about a dead prince would cause so much havoc." He narrowed his eyes at the Duke. "Are you hiding something, your highness? Everyone seems a little peeved, and I meant no harm."

Judge Marthon cut in. "We can't be too sure, Jethro," he whispered. "Why stand around inquiring? Send him to The Château d'Oubli."

The Duke, Jethro, looked up.

"If we need him, we'll know where to get him," the judge added.

The Duke shifted at this, his shoulders tensing. "That may not be a wise decision."

The judge smiled. "No one has ever escaped. We have ways of keeping the prisoners inside. A whole network, in fact. Duke." He picked up his gavel and eyed Jethro. "Trust me, as you once did. No one gets out. *It won't matter what he finds inside,*" he said with obvious emphasis. "The château has done its job since time immemorial. Have I —or it—ever let you down?" He raised his brows into his powdered wig. "It's been eight years. No one his age could last that long."

The loaded conversation caught Cecil's attention. That was it! That was the place the churchman had told him to find. But it sounded like a prison. How could getting locked in a cage help him find the dead prince? He wondered if he should run now. But no. His desire for redemption held him.

Finally, the Duke took a deep breath, the metals on his chest glinting. "Very well. Take him to The Château d'Oubli."

# 4

# The Chateau d'Oubli

"Years of bat and mole-glider shit. Wet floors, rust, black lung, and murder for a drop of water!"

The mournful chatter of fellow convicts on the underground train drove Cecil mad. New prisoners always cried, sweated, and screamed for death. The underground prison had been designed to make one feel helpless. Created by prisoners, what had started out as a mine probably two hundred years ago now served as an underground city of murderers, thieves, treasonous pigs, and all manner of other offenders. And of course, the ones who believed with all their black souls that they were innocent. Most of them were right. This was where the politicals sent people to be safe and held, should they ever need them again.

Once they put you on the train to The Château d'Oubli, if you had any sense, you watched out the window until the very last. Arrested on a cloudy day, I don't even remember what the sun looked like for my one last glance. Fortunately, the same thing happened to Cecil. He didn't know to watch out the window, though. He couldn't be bothered to glorify the sun, busy fluffing his cravat and laced sleeves one last time to notice when the tunnel swallowed him like that Jonah from long ago. But I remember. I so wanted to watch as the sun vanished one last time, eaten up by the tunnel and the underground.

Cecil remained calm for some time before the screaming of the other prisoners grated just enough on his nerves. *I'm in the right place,* he told himself. There were about a dozen of the lowlifes all shoved into a train car with no light and three guards. This special train went too fast for one to leap out of. I saw a man do it while being brought down. The speed smeared him on the cave walls like country jelly before he even stopped screaming.

"You better have sent me down for a good reason," Cecil mumbled to no one in particular. The deeper the train dived, the more he believed the judge; even for him, there might not be a way out.

The guard beside him flicked his wrist, letting all the links to his electro-chem spear click out and lock into place, making a six foot long, hissing beam with a large spike at the end. It sure did its job in keeping me in line.

"Time to hush up, foreigner," the guard said.

"Please," Cecil huffed, shrugging to let his elegant coat relax onto his tense shoulders. "A man such as myself does not belong in such a place as this."

"They all say that," the guard grumbled. He reached out and touched Cecil's ear with the electro-chem spear. Cecil shouted out as the electricity vibrated his nerves. I've often wondered what that felt like to him—his heart being so cold and still. He panted and fell down, clutching his chest.

"I say, that was something!" He counted the beats of his dead heart until it pattered out again. He felt his cheek. For one moment it felt warm and rosy. "So Frankenstein was right after all? I don't think I've done enough to deserve that."

The guard raised the spear threateningly again. "You all deserve it."

"They never tell you your crime," a quiet prisoner beside him said. "The best way to survive is to make yourself useful."

Cecil sighed and leaned against the dirty crate wall, listening to the tracks clank past as he went deeper and deeper under the living earth. He let his eyes feast on the colorful figure who had spoken to him. He looked like an Egyptian nomad, of sorts. His beard was sharp and small, his eyes just as keen. His mottled clothing dangled with decorative coins, glinting like the golden hoops on his ears, hidden behind glossy black hair. Around his neck on a thick chain hung a cruel-looking medallion that gently ticked like a pocket watch.

"I like your style, vagabond," Cecil said. "Don't you get robbed with all that shine hanging off you?"

The Egyptian shook his head. "Useless down here." He touched a large copper coin on the chest of his coat. "From my homeland."

Cecil smiled. "Glad I am not the only one in this place who takes pride in his looks and aesthetics. It's all one has in this long life. Does the money come in handy, or is it just a statement?"

The nomad cocked a half smile. "You think money is worth something down here? First time?"

Cecil scoffed through his nose with a secret smirk. "Not the first time I've been buried alive. What is this?" He casually pointed to a ticking medallion hanging from the man's neck.

The nomad smiled, showing white teeth, and tapping the medallion in time. "Something special. Keeps me alive. When you're convicted without a crime, you do what you can to survive," the nomad said. "We are sent here to be kept hidden. We know too much." He narrowed his eyes and tapped the bridge of his slender nose.

"What do *you* know?" Cecil asked simply. "What do *I* know?" he challenged the guard who had shocked him. "Hm? Sir? What do I know? Nothing, that's what."

"And you lie." The nomad sighed, twirling the scarf around his head and slapping a roving hand of someone reaching for one of his coins.

"How do you know?"

"Like I said, you wouldn't be here otherwise. What *do* you know?" His eyes took in Cecil's posh garments. "Not our normal country fare."

Cecil quickly felt his jovial defenses weakening. "What have I done?" he murmured. *Is it too late to escape?*

The nomad leaned back, closing his mysterious eyes. "I did as I was told. That's how I landed here. Again."

Cecil felt his cheek one last time as the warmth drained away. "Again? I was informed by a very rotund small man that no one gets out."

The nomad smiled crookedly. "No one *escapes*. This is a place designed by the politicals, my gaudy friend. If they want you, they will find you. If they want you to disappear, but not die, you will. If they want you dead…" He ran a bronze finger across his elegant neck. "Nothing will stop them. As I said: find a way to be useful." He gave him a knowing stare.

Had the churchman fooled Cecil? Had he sent him to die? No, someone like him could just kill a vampire. That was their job. "I'm so confused," Cecil finally mused.

"All right, wimp rats," the guards shouted, taking out their electro-chem spears, which sparked in the darkness. "Stand up and make a line. We're about to come into the station. You will be tagged and taken to your first day's work immediately."

"They like us too tired to try escaping on the first day," the nomad added in a low whisper as they all stood and filed to exit. The train jerked and the steam hissed as it slowed. "Makes us less aware of our surroundings and all."

He lifted his hand to his ticking medallion and touched the center. With a whirring sound, the gears, barely visible beneath the intricate design, stopped and began to wind backwards.

Cecil stood, smoothing the wrinkles out of his coat and fitted trousers. All the wretches around him showed signs of fear and agitation. Faces paled and their hearts beat like nervous insects. Their loud panting sounded like the panicked flapping of a moth to a source of light, desperate for something to reveal their fate.

"There is no way I am letting this place get in my way," Cecil hissed through gnashing fangs. "But this is not going to be as simple as I had imagined."

The doors slid open, loud and like a dragon roaring in the caves. Tiny yellow lanterns lit the roads, bobbing in the darkness on the ends of long poles. A train station loomed into view; a horde of buildings reached up into the dark heavens. Watermills spun alongside large manors where the officials and guards must live. It all came together to create a small port, all underground. Some would call it home, but for the prisoners, it would be their grave. The Château d'Oubli hid hundreds of men buried alive, walking corpses, making the men above them rich and powerful: a graveyard metropolis.

"Dear God, save me," Cecil whispered. "How am I ever to escape?"

"Know the right people," the Egyptian replied. "If you ever have doubt or if fear takes your mind, ask for Khalil."

The nomadic Egyptian, Khalil, smiled and winked as a guard grabbed his arm. The man shoved the mottled sleeve of the coat up, seeing something marked on the nomad's arm. Then, checking the ticking necklace, he nodded and led him away with a few other separated men.

"Where are you going?" Cecil called after him, unsure if he should follow.

"No," a guard snarled, poking him with the tip of his spear. "You and your friends come this way."

*He said he'd came back,* Cecil thought. Khalil was just the kind of man he needed. Unsure if he was supposed to be looking for the dead prince or was just here to be taught a lesson, Cecil made up his mind then that he wanted out. But it wouldn't be as easy as bursting into flying and muscling his way out. Vampires had weaknesses, and in MidWest, they were hunted on the regular. The sooner he got out, the better.

Unsure what to do now that he had found the place the Ecclesiast had told him to find, Cecil let himself and the rest of the prisoners be rounded up, surrounded, and marched down the underground road of lights.

Silence didn't exist in The Château d'Oubli. Trains and mine carts rattled all around them. Track covered all the walls, moving with clattering and shaking carts and small trains. Calls from deep under the ground rose and echoed off the walls and up into the darkness. Steam machines run by coal-faced men and women hissed and dripped their boiling liquid beneath them. The huge claws of the machines scratched at the walls like trapped beasts, digging for precious stones and metals. Every few meters, an ignored vein of some kind of metal glowed in the walls and floors. Cecil tried to understand the machines that kept the people alive, pumping air and water down to the prisoners.

The guards made the new prisoners queue up outside a small version of a ramshackle town hall, surrounded by a tall, turret-guarded, black metal fence. They were taken inside in large groups rapidly. Cecil merged with the crowd, shoved into a group of a dozen men and women. The guards clamped shackles on their ankles, linking them all together. Not so much as one man put up a fight. They were miles under the earth with no way out but to walk. And in these dark halls lurked creatures that had not yet broken onto the surface of the earth. The prisoners learned to stay and live out a life in the underground rather than to run and parish as a monster's meal, or worse, become one of the stalkers in the darkness.

Letting himself be led into the town hall—really just the entrance and offices of The Château d'Oubli—Cecil marveled at the savagery of the place. The floors were stone like the roads. Nothing had been laid down to make them more welcoming. All the lights were dim and dirty, and the sound of dripping water echoed from every vent and dark hole. The place dripped with constant moisture. Humid and cold, the distinct black smell of mold wafted on the air. To the left in a great room, a forge with shackles glowing inside added to the rank air. Inside, men were being marked as prisoners, and that was where Cecil waited.

Forced by the guards into the room, four guards held down the first prisoner as the smith, a fellow prisoner, picked up the tools of his trade. The smith reached into a cauldron of smoldering metal lengths and pulled one out. When he disturbed the hot metal, a stench came up from it that even Cecil could not bear. He clapped his hand over his nose and listened to his fellow prisoners moan. The man on the ground screamed.

The smith placed the metal length along the side of his neck and melded it together into a collar, burning his hair and searing it into parts of his skin. The smell worsened to include burning flesh. At this, some of the prisoners twitched as if to run, but were reminded to stay put with a jab of electricity.

Think of what's out there, some of them seemed to be saying. This could not be as bad as that, right? Doubt and fear reached inside the new clan. Cecil smelled it as it changed the scent of the prisoners.

Slowly, the first few prisoners were marked and branded by the rotlead. Then Cecil's turn came. The guards took each of his flouncy arms and ripped his jacket from his back. Then they pulled him over the table next to the forge and removed his shoes.

"Is this necessary?" Cecil grunted as they held his head and arms.

"Checking for gold and shinies." The smith smiled, reaching into his oven. "It's extra booty for me if rich men like you come bearing gifts. A nice bonus."

"I have nothing." Cecil looked at the hot, black forge, its pipes snaking up the walls like a giant centipede. It went up out of the roof and no doubt spit its black vomit up into the never-ending darkness.

The smith pulled out a thick, bent piece of metal that reeked of burning eggs. Cecil gagged as they brought it up to his face. "Rotlead," the man sneered. Every one of his teeth were replaced by sharp screws, drilled into his gums. "It smells and will rot in actual sunlight, like acid into your flesh. Keeps you all here. The base metal is silver with a distinct mancer quality."

"Mancer quality?" he asked, unsure if that meant the silver would be worse than normal.

The man shrugged, gripping the glowing orange collar with a pair of tongs. He grabbed his hammer. "Some might call it a magical quality. But that sounds more like fairies and unicorns, don't it?" He stepped towards Cecil. "Don't struggle or it'll get ya."

Cecil screamed as the red-hot metal seared into his flesh, wrapping all the way around his neck. His head ached and his skull felt like it would explode from the center out from the heat. The smell pushed him over the edge. His last meal bubbled up in his gullet. He lurched off the table. The men released him and he spewed hot blood across the floor and into the forge fire.

The guards and the smithy stepped back, groaning in disgust. "Get him out. Let's finish!"

Cecil let his fellow prisoners lift him and pull him along with them. He had never heard of rotlead, but realized it affected him the same as the mortal men. The silver crackled ever so slightly, burning him just enough to leave a tiny red ring around his neck.

"My jacket," he panted. He pointed with his elegantly clothed hand. "Do not leave it."

"Forget it," one prisoner hissed as the guards herded them away.

He pushed away from the horde in two strides, took up his jacket and shoes, and rejoined his fellows.

The prisoners were shackled together again and marched out the back door of the jailhouse. Cecil, ever the dandy, put his blue jacket back on, puffed his cravat and smoothed his long black hair. When his hand touched the rotlead collar, a slight tingling hissed against him. But Cecil was brave. He smoothed his hair one more time, not quite soiled, and marched with the others into the mines.

As I said, on the first day, there is no one to show you to your bed. No one tells you where the food is, or the shelter. It rains in The Château d'Oubli, too, making that first twenty-four hours miserable. The humidity accumulates from all the steam machines and gathers in these clouds higher up where it's cool. Then they get too heavy and rain back down.

Once deep enough into the tunnels, the guards unshackled the new prisoners and let them loose.

"You will man the machines today," a man in a shredded green greatcoat with brassy trim shouted at them from behind his red beard. His voice easily carried over the grinding and screaming of the claws and tracks. "Housing and food is up to you once your shift is over. Forget about that for now."

Some men looked around as the guards left. Could they run? No, the prisoners already working dragged them into a line and set their hands to work. Cries of relief went up from those who had been working all day as the new recruits entered. Not only the relief from work pleased the men of the dark. Fresh faces, not dirty from coal, and familiar and fresh stories and voices to be heard in the forever dark enlivened their spirits.

Redbeard, the man in the green coat, looked to be the man in charge and let no one rest. The swap of tired men for new, terrified prisoners was swift. Swept along in the throng, Cecil's dead heart began to doubt his redemption.

# INTRODUCTIONS

"You! Keep the coal coming," Redbeard shouted at Cecil as an older prisoner pried off his shackles. "We need it. If this machine stops, we don't get air down the tunnels." Shouting to the rest of them, he called, "We've got froststeel down there, boys!"

The dirty men and women cheered with glee. Froststeel glowed and felt cool when touched. It did something to the air, too, making it fresh and giving one the feeling of happiness. It was a precious metal-quartz hybrid to the prisoners of The Château d'Oubli. But to the rich above, its only value lay in being a home decoration.

"I don't know what to do," Cecil started, but shut up when the man handed him a shovel. He understood quick enough.

Lines of carts rolled past with little lanterns attached to them, illuminating the wall's lines with steel beams. The carts rolled out of the mine empty. Cecil got the job of filling them all as they rumbled past. Then they rolled deeper to a huge furnace where some of the other new prisoners tipped them into the fiery hell that kept the huge pumps moving. These pumps gave air to the men deeper beneath the earth's surface. A dozen or so openings spidered out from where they had landed, mine shafts and tunnels leading under the ground.

The heavy shovel strained Cecil's back. Every lump of coal he scooped up made it near unbearable. He stumbled over the rocky ground, cutting his ankles on the rocks, and quickly grew blisters on his palms until he finally dumped the first shovel-full into the empty cart. He huffed and leaned on the shovel after doing this twelve more times in quick order.

*These wounds won't heal until I drink,* he thought bitterly.

Despite the massive shovel with its huge lip, it still took thirteen scoops to fill one cart. He could not imagine doing this all day. There were other prisoners working with him, but none to relieve him or give him a rest. He examined his minimal wounds, gauging how much blood he would need to consume to heal himself.

The hours dragged on, and he began to wonder how much time had passed. Not so much as a watch could be heard ticking in any man's pocket. The hunger started to bring out the weakness in him. He felt faint. But he wouldn't even feed on one of these wretches for fear of giving himself away. The darkness closed in on him, reminding him of a close shave he'd had with being locked in a coffin. Unlike other vampires, Cecil didn't like being locked away.

"Look out!" a woman screamed.

Cecil flung himself around to watch. A huge crane with a dumpster trailer on the back tipped over, its load too much. In horrid slow motion, the machine toppled. The men inside screamed, and others ran out of the way, but not far enough. The machine completely overturned, sliding down a narrow cavern, resting in a large pile of dirt that had been freshly dug.

"Get them out!" Redbeard shouted. "They'll be crushed or suffocate!"

Cecil noted the lack of guards rushing to the scene of the accident. In fact, the only people around were other prisoners. He looked on in awe at the scrambling men and women. Shovels and picks were tossed to one another and lanterns were lifted up and carried to the accident.

"Help us. We need smaller ones to go under first," Redbeard said. "You!" He spotted Cecil right away. "Take this lantern and go under there. Tell them we are on the way. Get a tunnel open!"

"Here!" a woman shouted, pointing to a quickly dug hole that she and another had just made with wild effort. "We can go."

"No, we need your nimble hands here," Redbeard said.

Cecil couldn't stop. Everything moved so fast around him. Rolling up his lacy sleeves, he knelt and peered under the huge dumpster trailer through the small hole they'd dug. A small glow shone on the other side. "I see them," he called. "Give me the light."

The lady struck a match and lit the little mirrored headlamp on her own head before doffing it and handing it to Cecil. "Fire will burn air. Move quick," she added. Her dark eyes glimmered upon catching his face.

Cecil fought to muster his bravery. The closed walls and a suffocating ceiling looming just seconds ahead of him made him claustrophobic. He hated the small, enclosed spaces. That was something we had in common.

Shaking, he lowered himself down onto his belly and thrust his head under the side of the dumpster truck. He hesitated. Underneath, the dense darkness made it so he could hardly see beyond his own halo of fire. With urges and shouts from the people behind him, he took a breath and pushed himself through, ripping his fancy shirt and smearing it with dirt. Once inside, he hesitated. He didn't move, his vampire eyes adjusting to the darkness quickly. But this didn't help ease the unnatural fear.

He could feel the enclosure moving in on him. The truck's floor, now his cage's roof, seemed close, as if it slowly descended onto him. The wet, slimy ground made him slip. The air hung so stiff he couldn't breathe it in. His mind played mortal tricks on him and made him believe his damned soul would die in this small place. His hands grew clammy for the first time in years. He wrapped his arms around himself and swept the place for survivors.

He struck a match before him, lighting up the grimy, skinny face of one of the worst people to ever exist: me.

Cecil's eyes roamed up and down my body, taking in my scars and assessing my strength. Skinny, pale, and looking like I had not slept in a decade, his fear of me dissipated. I knew he could smell my long, dirty hair under my pinch-front hat. I lit a cigarette I had taken off the body of a man.

"I worked next to this rat for about three years," I said casually, kicking one of the dead prisoners. "He grew the best stuff. Not sure it's safe to smoke, but hey." I coughed.

Cecil stared at me, his jaw hanging open. "Did you loot all the dead already?"

No ceremony, Cecil, thanks. I shook out the match and tossed it aside. I inspected the dead man's wrist and found the bracelet I had coveted for years: a froststeel bangle. I pocketed it. "You can only safely loot a dead body down here, sunflower," I said dryly. "Otherwise, the rest of their gang come after you."

Cecil looked around and saw at least five other dead men. "You did this in the time it took me to crawl under that hole?"

I glared back with my dull, blue eyes. "Oui, monsieur. I'm a safe killer. Only getting those I know I can. Get me out," I ordered. "I can't breathe in here."

"I'm beginning to think there should be no survivors," Cecil snarled, taking in the quick carnage.

I owe my life to how unappetizing I looked. He didn't want to pounce on me and drain my blood right then and report all the men dead. This side of him made me stare at him. Looking back, I don't know why he decided not to kill me. Of course, I had no idea the dangerous presence I was in.

"Nice ring," I said, eyeing a plain gold band on his thumb. I casually sauntered towards him. He frowned, confused, but didn't move to hide the ring in his hip pocket. I dodged behind him and made to snap his thin neck, eager to loot his corpse, too.

"Hey!" he roared, grabbing my wrist from behind and throwing me over his shoulder with one arm. "Animal! What the hell is your problem? I've come to get you out." He removed the ring and shoved it into his pocket.

The men outside heard us. "You got them?" they shouted.

The wind shot out of me when my back hit the rocky ground. I lay on the earth, half glaring at the indignity of being tossed so lightly and in awe of it at the same time.

"You're strong," I groaned. The fall cracked my new froststeel bangle.

Shaking his head, he leaned down to the hole to call out. "Only one survived."

He was going to spare me.

Watching him like a predator, I went to the hole and slithered out like a snake. He followed me through.

"Ah, it's you," Redbeard said with a sigh when he saw me.

"He killed the rest," Cecil said quickly, still shaken from being in the small space.

I saw his paleness. His veins. The way his eyes and even his pupils glinted in the lights like diamonds. He had damned blood inside him. I knew it the instant I saw him. His strength made sense now. Like most in MidWest, I'd never seen a Europian vampire in person. I'd seen drawings of them on wanted posters for the hunters of such things, and even a picture of a dead one in a coffin, a stake in its heart and a mouth full of garlic. Looking around, I saw the others hadn't caught on like I had.

"New prisoner doesn't know how things work around here," I sneered. "Keep him away from me."

I left. I felt Cecil staring after me, probably not wondering who I was, like I had hoped he would. But Redbeard took care of that for me.

"Don't get your lasso around Ezekiel," he told Cecil. "He's already spoken for. And I'd hate to have to take him out."

Cecil cocked a brow. "Why's that? He just killed five men."

Redbeard huffed a dry laugh and turned away. "He's not as menacing as you think. And I have my reasons." He turned back to the rest of his workers. "Let's go! Three more hours and then back to San Sous-terre."

A small cheer went up at that. Cecil went back to where he had left his coat and gloves, but they were gone. Silly man left his nice things unattended in a place full of thieves and criminals. No doubt sad about that, but knowing he had no choice, he went back to carrying coal while others upturned the dumpster truck.

He fought off fainting again when the lady who had given him the headlamp came back to him. She had her thumbs hooked into her denim overalls. Her boots, which were too big, made clomping sounds as she came nearer.

"Can I have my headlamp back, hey?" She had deep brown eyes that smiled even though her lips didn't. She was beautiful: her dark skin tone blended into the shadows perfectly, her hair woven with blasts of colorful shreds of fabric, beads, and even nuts and bolts she had picked up.

"Oh, of course." Cecil took the lamp from his head and gave it to her. "Thank you, as well, Miss…?"

She thrust her hand out happily. "Jacquline, but Jacque is just as good. I thought that was brave of you. If Redbeard sees it the same way, he owes you. Ezekiel is his property."

"I highly doubt he will." He took her delicate hand, which was engulfed in an oversized working glove. "Cecil, if it pleases you."

"It does," she smiled, replacing the helmet on her own head. "You going back to San Sous-terre in three?"

"San Sous-terre?" he said, grimacing sarcastically. "What a bastardization of two beautiful languages."

"Yeah." Jacque smiled. She had the slightest Cajun accent. "But I was also thinking, do you want to go get a drink in town, hey?"

The invitation took our vampire by surprise. He scoped Jacque up and down. He had no reason to say no. "I'd like a little company while I try to decide my next move," he said.

She grinned, clasping her hands joyfully. Her energy, smiles, and sparkling eyes took in most people. Cecil wondered how she could be so bright in such a place.

"Great," she said, tapping her light to make the flame brighter. "Don't wander too far off. I'll find you when the shift ends."

# 6

# SAN SOUS-TERRE

The workday ended when it ended in The Château d'Oubli. The clocktower chimed high noon twice within a workday and our hearts were in rhythm with it. Whether the clock was correct or not didn't matter. That chime meant it was time to change shifts. When it sounded, striking nine times, Cecil didn't know what to expect. This was the time no one worked. Our "nighttime," if you will.

The men and women simply dropped their picks, their steam-engines puttering out, leaning cattywampus on their sides. The air stopped flowing to the lower levels. Some of the lights vanished in a puff of smoke as the haunting exodus began. Like zombies, the prisoners trudged, feet dragging, away from the mines. No one spoke. The only sounds were the shuffling of feet in clodhoppers and boots and the screeching of the last of the picks and shovels being dragged just a couple of steps before being loosed from calloused hands. This march showed a new humanity: no one pretended to have energy, to not be sore. Any thoughts for anyone who didn't make it up from the deeper shafts stayed behind. I think it showed mankind at its best.

Confused, Cecil followed them, not willing to put up a fight or ask questions. Once you were so exhausted from digging your own grave, you followed almost anyone away from the work. And you followed them anywhere because if they were all going in one direction, it must mean some kind of comfort ahead. In this case, it meant light, music, and food. It wouldn't be until late in the "night" that the prisoners would be liquored up enough to engage in human activities again. We lived for those few hours. In fact, that had been most of my life.

"Where are we going?" Cecil asked a man who seemed to be walking in his sleep. To no one's surprise but the foppish vampire, the man did not answer back.

Used to a kind of silence, Cecil followed them out and up a little higher until the air felt less full of steam and the black dust no longer clogged their lungs. They walked past offshoots into other mines, all lined with metal beams leading up into the un-seeable ceiling of earth. They passed through a large cavern covered in a meadow of moss. The walls were thrown back and every rock shimmered purple. The ground quickly turned moist and Cecil noticed a kind of long, soft green and blue moss growing. Marveling at the living plant, he knelt and touched it. It suddenly felt like he had not laid hands on anything so soft in all his life. That's how you know how dark and unforgiving it was down there. Even a vampire marveled at the tiny plants. He froze where he knelt and looked up. The tunnel slithered on, then down into a huge, alveolate darkness. In that moment, he wondered if he could run, escape, make it out.

"Don't even think about it," said a familiar voice behind Cecil.

He turned and saw the mottled garments of Khalil. The Egyptian spun his pendent around his index finger. It no longer ticked.

"I wasn't going to think *too* long about it," Cecil admitted. "I almost shot off like a jackalope just now. I fear I've made a terrible mistake in coming down here."

"Oh, of course," Khalil said, nodding sarcastically. "Because you chose to be buried miles beneath the American Empire and enslaved for the rest of your life."

At this, Cecil narrowed his eyes at the nomad. "You all but let on you were brought *back* down here. How did you escape?"

Khalil shook his head. "I didn't escape. I was let out on a temporary pardon to work for my father. He's very close in with a few politicals topside, but I still remain his greatest displeasure." He shrugged half-heartedly. "No one ever really leaves The Château d'Oubli. And no one gets out by their own cunning."

"Why not?" Cecil asked, finally standing up. "I see very few guards."

With a handsome and wicked grin, Khalil curled his finger, indicating for Cecil to follow him. "I'll show you, my obtuse friend. It's not that complicated."

The walk back to San Sous-terre inclined entirely uphill. If one digs farther and farther into the earth, where you started seems to run away from you; hence the town, the home, always crawled farther away. The men were dedicated to it, though. A few years back, a steam engine started to be constructed with rails going out to the all the main digs. In the fifteen years I'd lived in the Château, San Sous-terre had fallen nearly five miles farther away.

Anyone in The Château d'Oubli when San Sous-terre was just a few ramshackle sheds would be a well-aged bone by this time. It really wasn't just a town like you see in those penny dreadfuls, with one road leading down a line of shops on either side with a chapel at the end. No. San Sous-terre was a living city, a metropolis of man's inventions and dreams of a world they longed to return to.

Khalil stopped at the top of a dirt hill where the steam engine unloaded cars full of dirty miners from deeper down. "May I present to you, Cecil of the finer things, San Sous-terre. Any place you want is yours for rent, or of course you could kill the occupants and take it. I suppose you could build yourself a home. Not like anyone will charge you for tools or lumber. Take it; it's yours."

Other men and women had returned home before them, and even more with differing shifts were just leaving. San Sous-terre lit up with life and movement like firegold. From the hilltop, one could look down on our Frankenstein metropolis. We had created a generator that sent electricity to certain areas like the saloon (the one place we all loved) and The Red Mary motel—not really a motel, though. Well, you could sleep there, of course, and they served food and drink. Lush and silken, dimly lit and run by a nun, calling it a motel was generous. You can rightly guess what happens when a nun starts a "motel" in a place where she thinks she'll never see her church topside again. But the girls who worked for her were nice. They were also paid to not go to work on any shift. People paid good prices to have a fresh, clean, frilly girl in their room at night. The place glowed with red lights and golden walls.

Cecil stared, his violet eyes wide. "Man will survive," he said softly. His keen eyes scanned the whole town from their perch. Towers that flickered and belched up steam cranked the life of the streets. Near the center of the city, a large, round reactor generated the huge amounts of electric steam it took to light up the streets. It glowed a kind of green and sparked in the darkness. Large rubber tubes slithered out of it like a pot full of serpents.

"How?" Cecil managed as they started the trek into the inner streets.

"I suppose," Khalil offered, "when one realizes they will never leave, they make it as comfortable as possible."

Cecil backtracked. "I mean, how does this town run goods and services if we are made to dig all day?"

"We call it the honor system," Khalil answered, waving to a man lurking in a dark alley. "Someone *will* tell on you if you don't go to your shift. Usually another prisoner. You met Redbeard?"

Cecil nodded.

"If we had a mayor, it'd be him. He's a prisoner just like us, but he's got his fingers in all the proverbial pies."

The vampire frowned lightly in thought. "He said he owned that little rat I saved," he mused.

"Most likely," the Egyptian agreed jovially. "Some people are information gatherers, weaklings who take a beating from one just to spill their secrets to another."

Cecil scoffed in doubt. "Everyone down here knows this and just goes along with it?"

With a crooked grin, Khalil said, "Just like topside, my elegant friend."

Once inside the town streets, everything changed. From far away, the city flashed golden, bright, and looked exciting. The buildings rose up impressive and awe-inspiring. Like most things, the inside contrasted sharply to the glitzy package. The steal walls were cold and dirty from the inhabitants urinating on them. Vomit coated the gutters from exhausted workers dehydrating themselves on liquor. Discarded scraps of mine carts, machinery, and tools littered the streets where homes were being built or taken apart for scrap. One shop had heaps of metal horse parts in a dumpster out front. A huge plank of wood read "Geomancy" over it. Cecil even spotted a corpse, white and soggy, in a puddle of oils and liquids.

"To the bank first, I think," Khalil said. "I need currency if I'm to show you a good time before you go back to work."

He looped his arm over Cecil's shoulders and steered him towards a two-story building with Grecian pillars out front. The pillars swirled in various colors, almost like dozens of different stones had been melted down to mold them. Khalil pushed the barred door open and led the way in.

"What's hot, wheeler?" Khalil said casually to a man behind a barred desk. The man stood in front of little more than a wooden box-like building with crates upon crates of goods out back surrounded by jagged, make-shift fences. The sharp, unclean barbed wire could kill you with the diseases lingering on it if you cut yourself.

The man behind the desk wore a top hat balanced on his head rather than pulled over his crown. It looked like he had sat on it at some point; the ribbon around it wrinkled so much it looked like a prune. His brown, patchy coat smelled, and his glasses had been turned into thick-lensed goggles to be held onto his face, giving him huge, round, blue eyes.

"Snakes! What do you want, you bedazzled punk?" he snarled, touching his many necklaces and golden earrings, fearing they may disappear if Khalil got too close.

"Now 'punk's' a nasty word, sir," Khalil said with a laugh, his offense perfectly hidden. "I wouldn't let you touch me for all the froststeel in these mines."

"It's not froststeel tonight," the banker said with a smile. "So, if you were planning on trading for it, you're going to have to really bring it. It's not valuable right now."

"Bartering?" Cecil asked, crossing his arms and trying not to touch any of the odds and ends hanging off the walls. He gathered his long hair up and braided it to keep it away as well. "This place is disgusting."

"I like your pants," the banker said in the likeness of a cooing pigeon. "Those will be worth something. And your boots. My, my, my! Snakes, what a fine dandy we have here!"

Cecil took two very fast steps back when the banker leapt out from his perch and came around the bars to touch and prod his legs, feeling the fabric.

"Very nice, very expensive. Not even that soiled from work. Silk, twenty-four karat gold trimming…"

"Get off." Cecil kicked at the man, but fell over when the banker seized his booted foot to inspect the materials.

"Oh, animal skin, ruby studs. All natural."

"We have a gold mine!" Khalil cried triumphantly. "What do you say, Moriart?"

"Is this what you wanted?" Cecil glared up at the other prisoner. "To bring me here so you could go get a drink tonight once you've bartered away all my clothes?"

The nomad smiled and shrugged. "We are all animals trying to survive." He turned to the banker. "What is hot tonight? Hmm? What can I get for these britches and boots?"

"Nothing," Cecil shouted, swatting away the banker one last time.

"Dark lenses and glowgems," Moriart replied. "That's what's hot." He rubbed his hands together, eyeing Cecil's pants still. "This would complete the set."

"The set?" Cecil asked.

Moriart nodded, his rat-like nose bobbing. "Little Ezekiel brought in a coat."

A personal rage at me boiled up in Cecil's gut at this. He couldn't find it after coming out from under the upturned truck and realized I must have pilfered it.

"You do stick out in those clothes," Khalil offered. "You'll want something hardier."

"Fine. Take them. But." Cecil glared at the rattish banker. "You give us twelve lenses for the fit of any pair of goggles and two dozen glowgems. And give me clothes in return."

"You raising snakes?" the banker gasped, adjusting his own goggles as though not seeing Cecil correctly. "I'll give you ten glowgems and you'll be grateful."

Khalil smiled, slapping Cecil on the back. "I need to take you more places."

After a humiliating change into old boots, used pants, and a long duster, Cecil counted what they called the shinies twice only to find Moriart had given them nine. Cecil held his hand out for the last one. Rolling his eyes, Moriart handed over the missing gem. Cecil, in turn, passed them off to Khalil.

Khalil pocketed the lenses and the gems, and led the way back out into the streets. "To The Red Mary!"

# 7
# Rat, Lady, Vampire

The short walk between the bank and The Red Mary didn't leave Cecil time to primp and preen as he would have wanted. Khalil went right from one door to the other, his glowgems eagerly waiting to be spent on some of the foulest liquor America has ever birthed.

The Red Mary motel and saloon had been added on to, adjusted, and altered over the years. Now towers and boxy turrets grew out of its original body, mimicking The Château d'Oubli itself in its eternal, mutated growth. Added-on upper decks stuck out like cancerous limbs, awkward and unsure of their footing. Two round lamps blazed on either side of the double front doors, which were painted the brightest red. Cecil smelled the electricity in the air and felt it buzzing in his veins, foreign and strange. The cobbled road led directly to the front doors and above it hung a sign with chain-linked additions swinging in the vibrations reading: hot baths, paid toilet, dancing girls, and a list of house rules—none of which mentioned leaving your gun with the barkeep like the saloons topside did.

They were about to push through the saloon doors when Jacque's melodious voice cut over the din.

"I thought you were trying to ditch me," she shouted to Cecil, running to catch up. Her too-large boots flopped, and loose overalls swung as she dashed across the dirty street to them. "Hey, you," she said to Khalil with a tiny frown. "Been a while since we've had one of you down here."

"That's rude," Khalil said with a smile, winking at her just the same. "But I cannot outrun the Syndicate's business. *Hey*?" he added mockingly, but it rolled off the hardy engineer. He led them to a round table near the center of the saloon, which was covered in fake, dirty felt.

Jacque shoved her way between Khalil and Cecil, forcing him to sit next to her. "Careful with this one, pretty boy," she said cautiously. "Topside, the likes of him are not of good repute."

"Why's that?" Cecil asked, allowing himself to be lured in by her sweet tones and shining eyes.

She leaned forward to look at Khalil as the three of them made their way to the bar. When he didn't stop her, she went on, "Politicals pay the nomads—of all places of origin—to do all kinds of horrid things." She nodded to a tattoo on Khalil's lithe forearm. "See that?"

Cecil had noticed the mark before on the train. The nomad quickly pulled his patchwork sleeve down over it. It was made up of the same nonsensical, cruel looking lines that adorned his now silent pendent.

"It's basically a letter of marque the Syndicate uses," Jacque went on. "Each faction of the Syndicate has what they call a patriarch, the man in charge. Usually he has many spies, bounty hunters, assassins—you know the type. That tattoo allows them to do a lot of, shall we say, shady things, and get away with it."

"Like ending up here," Khalil quipped, signaling for shots to be brought over.

With this reminder, Jacque relaxed a little and even deflated apologetically. "You're right. So, what happened? Rat on the wrong bowler hat, did ya?" She took her shot and raised it up.

Not wanting to give himself away, Cecil took his and eyed it. Somewhere between a putrid green and shit brown, the liquor sloshed in the glass. The fumes from it made even Cecil's eyes water.

"I highly advise against putting this in your body," he said around an involuntary gag.

The other two laughed and clinked their glasses. Simultaneously, they threw the liquor back and slammed their glasses down. They shared some joke Cecil didn't understand and then called for another.

"Again?" he asked despondently. "You all must be made of pure iron."

They repeated their little ceremony, then called for something less vile.

"How long you been here?" Jacque asked Khalil, cheering him with the beer.

Khalil blew his cheeks out and spun around to lean against the bar. "Some time. Maybe ten years. I get brought up every now and then to, as you say, do some shady work."

"So you do get out," Cecil mused.

Khalil shrugged with lackluster enthusiasm. "It's worse than staying. They rip the collar off and put it back on. It's not worth it. Nothing I do will reduce my sentence here," he added in a dark mumble.

Jacque scooted closer to Cecil, tapping his untouched shot. "Go on," she said to him, smiling. To Khalil she asked, "Then why go up? Isn't it torture to see topside and then come back down?"

He nodded, eyes vacant. "Harder every time. But I keep hoping one day the patriarch of our Syndicate will relent and keep me above ground."

Cecil had heard of the nomads before. They were not near as used in Europa as they were here in the American Empire. "Organized crime?" he asked, interested now. "There are rules, factions or chapters, families, and one patriarch who dictates what jobs will be done and who will do them?"

Khalil nodded. "One such patriarch is my father. He got a sweet deal some ten years ago." He aimed his finger like a gun and made a soft sound, mimicking a bullet. "Then here I stand."

A moment of silence between the three fell. Jacque took it to gaze at Cecil, cocking her head. Turning, she ordered six more beers, packed them up and said, "Let's go to the quartz chapel."

She slid off the chair and Khalil followed her. Cecil watched them go, the weakness from starvation making his mouth water the more he thought about sinking his teeth into both of them.

He followed them out.

The chapel, it turned out, was a huge, vaulted cave with veins of quartz lining it. Khalil and Jacque sat down and started to drink again, comparing life stories and who had suffered the most. Cecil stepped away from them, not sure how long he could control the hunger. At the back of the chapel, a sudden drop off stopped Cecil from going too far. Below, he heard trickling and swore the soft pad of bare feet flitted up from the shadows. He sniffed the cold, stale air but didn't catch much. He was too weak.

Annoyed at his hunger, agitated by his regret, he rejoined the other two. He listened, deciding whether to eat them or use them. Khalil's story intrigued him, and Jacque's brown eyes made it hard to imagine eating her.

"My whole family was sent here," Jacque said, plunking down a tin box. She opened it to reveal some sort of fried meat, covered in breading. She handed Khalil one. When she held one up for Cecil, he politely shook his head. Even if he were mortal, he wasn't going to take his chance on mystery meat.

"That's not unusual," Khalil offered her. "Were you…" he narrowed his eyes, scanning Jacque, "a noble family?"

At first, a quick panic flashed over Jacque's face. Probably too quick for Khalil to catch. But then she smiled coyly and said, "That'll cost me, hey, nomad? I know to guard my secrets around you. I came here when I was thirteen. Five years ago. My family was in hiding for some time before."

"What had you done?" Khalil asked.

Again, she shook her head and smiled. "Nothing. As always. My grandfather, Jafa, gathered us in the night and we disappeared. Eventually they caught us. All rounded up, we landed here."

"They always do catch you," Khalil agreed, taking a long drink of the beer. "Politicals are always fighting each other. Offering assassins all kinds of pay to off one another. This prison is practically civilized compared to the topside."

Jacque agreed and toasted Khalil before taking another long drink.

"Aren't you starving, Cecil?" Khalil asked.

"Famished." He sighed sadly. "You've no idea. But I'd rather not—"

"Can it!" Jacque snapped, going stiff. Her eyes bulged and her head slowly turned to the drop off behind them. "Don't move," she hissed, stowing the meat quickly.

Khalil, understanding, snuffed the lantern they'd brought. The chapel plunged into almost pure darkness. The glow from San Sousterre lit the place in a dim, hazy yellow. Now Cecil smelled it. He stood up, sensing the predator that was climbing up the drop-off.

"Don't!" Jacque hissed, grabbing the back of his duster.

He held his hand up cautiously, warding her off. He could see better than them and smelled it now, too. A sort of wet, rotting, fleshy scent. He took one step deeper into the darkness and saw it. Outlined against the sooty background crouched something pearly white with huge, orb-like eyes. He watched it blink. The snuffling sound told him it sniffed, too. It took two more loping steps towards them. It looked like a man on all fours. When it spotted Cecil, it stopped. It made a clicking sound and four other sets of eyes he'd not noticed before blinked over the edge, turning to each other.

Knowing he was by far the more dangerous predator, he opened his mouth and let his fangs drop. A low, rumbling growl reverberated in his throat. The thing noticed and cowered backwards. In a moment, they were gone. He listened for the fleshy feet retreating then turned back to the others.

"By the rougarou, that was so brave!" Jacque gasped, lighting the lantern again. She held it up and reached to Cecil with her other hand.

"That was impressive," Khalil acknowledged. "Not everyone can stand up to an underman."

Exhausted, tired, and starving, Cecil plopped down, not even caring what an underman was. "Are there other creatures in the caves?" he asked.

They both nodded.

Good. He needed to feed. Badly.

"You've had a wild first day in The Château d'Oubli," Khalil mused, grinning broadly. "How about you come back to my place and sleep? You'll need your strength."

That night, Cecil went out to hunt down small rodents and drink as much blood as he could find. Without fresh blood, he'd grow weak, not heal from wounds, and lose his other vampiric gifts. With renewed strength, he didn't mind the day's work so much.

Khalil and Jacque worked beside him and showed him how some of the larger machines worked. He allowed it for the sole purpose of getting closer to Khalil and trying to convince the nomad to show him the way out. It wasn't that he didn't trust Khalil, but that the man had a sneaky way about him that Cecil picked up on. He couldn't decide whether to stay in The Château d'Oubli and seek out whatever the Ecclesiast sent him to find, or look for a way out. But that meant eternal damnation for his soul, and Cecil wasn't ready for that. But he was ready to get out. And how long did he have until the unknown doom Sylas had mentioned came to fruition? Not knowing made him anxious and eager to leave. He might have been immortal, but a dead —or possibly lost—prince wasn't. And according to Sylas, neither was the American Empire. He couldn't wait forever.

Several days into working the mines, after getting the two mortals comfortable in his presence, he finally asked, "Show me why no one escapes."

Jacque wiped her brow, smearing a black streak of oil across her forehead. "Give it a year, Cecil, and this desire will melt away. You have to try to accept that this is where you live now."

*That's the last thing I want,* he thought, and a small panic took seed in him. Eternity in The Château d'Oubli would appeal to no one. A thought did arise in him, though: more than likely, there were no other vampires in this place. He could possibly slaughter the lot of them in a few months, changing a few. He'd done something similar before. But that was what he was trying to put behind him.

"Khalil," he called, pulling the Egyptian behind a large digger. "Say I wanted to get out, just check the perimeter. Could we?"

The nomad sighed, rolling his amber eyes. "You are not going to give up until I prove there is no way out, are you?"

Cecil smiled saucily. "I have a very hard time giving up."

Chewing his lip in thought, Khalil eyed Cecil before replying. "There are only two actual tunnels out of here. The one with the train, covered in topside guards as you saw. And the one with the skydocks. If you go out and look for another way out, you end up like our pale friends from the other day. Lost, wandering until you're a rabid animal. Cannibal, too."

"Is it guarded?" Cecil asked. "The tunnel out?"

"Something like that," Khalil replied. "But I think what comes in and out might interest you more."

Behind him, Jacque shook her head and put her hands on her hips. "We should get Ezekiel. He's good at this."

Khalil hissed cautiously. "You know he's under Redbeard's boot. He'll rat on us if we leave for a shift."

She nodded and shrugged. "That's to be expected."

Cecil followed them as they moved from the dig site to the entrance of the mine where a group of prisoners were unloading the mine carts into a larger train. Cecil spotted me, the one he'd dug out of the wreckage. His guard went up instinctually. Khalil reached into his hip pocket and pulled out one of the lenses he'd bargained for the other day.

"What's good, Ez?" he said casually, leaning against the mine cart that had just come to a stop before me.

Cecil watched me look up, eyes dead, back bent. What little flame flickered inside me died. At some point in my eight years in the The Château d'Oubli, I had become this snitch. I didn't do it on purpose. One day, someone told me a secret plan of skimming off some rubylead. I'd let it slip to Redbeard, and that was that. Next thing you knew, I had everyone's secrets, got them beaten out of me, and then got real good at picking up new ones to tell to get back at those who tortured me. It was more complicated than that, but that was the haft of the shovel.

"What do you want?" I asked, propping my tired body against my shovel. I spotted Cecil and Jacque behind him. Something in me sparked at seeing them. "If it ain't the sunflower," I said to Cecil. "Come to take my loot?"

He scoffed and rolled his eyes. "I'm not interested in your contrivance. Khalil thinks you can help us skip out today."

Khalil spun the goggle lens between his long, lithe fingers. "Far-sight quartz," he said, indicating the lens. "Would go great in those goggles you're always tinkering with. Polishes up so good you can see through it."

Cecil caught me looking at it eagerly. He added, "We'll give you four if you cover for us."

I smiled at him. "You catch on quick, sunflower. But..." I looked him up and down. Had Khalil not figured out yet that he was a vampire? His blood was more valuable than anything in all the mines of the American Empire. If you knew how to alchemize it. "You got anything else more valuable? You know what's going to happen to me if Red finds out."

Cecil smiled at me, took the lens from Khalil and held it out to me. "Then don't get caught. You'll have the other three when we get back."

I swiped it and shoved it in my boot. I watched them leave, wondering what they were doing. There was only one way I could find out.

# The Perimeter

Once far enough away from all dig sites, the three of them walked more easily. "Right," Cecil said, fluffing his hair and instinctually going for a cravat that was no longer there. "How far out do these mines go?"

"Far," Jacque said. "Let's get a crawler and head to the border tunnels."

Crawlers lay all over in The Château d'Oubli. Some ran on firestones—geos we mined and were plentiful in the earth under Kansouri—some ran on water and steam, and some ran on animal carcasses. We'd gotten pretty creative with fuel down below the earth. Crawlers looked like pedal bikes, but had massive wheels made of strong steel. Controls on the handlebars caused the wheels to grip vertical terrain, making them able to crawl up steep walls, over rocks, and other such surfaces.

It took them a few minutes to find three, but soon they sped down the tunnels with loud, rumbling motors.

"Won't we get caught making all this noise?" Cecil shouted.

"These can't cut above the roar of a digger," Jacque assured him. "But we'll have to walk once we get farther out. We don't want to attract anything living deeper in the earth."

The caves of the The Château d'Oubli might have been beautiful every once in a while—glittering with aquamarine, red, and yellow gems—but that beauty was long lost on us prisoners. The trio cut through some abandoned sites, dilapidated living quarters, and a tiny ghost town before Khalil signaled that the time for walking had come. He led the way up a rocky trail.

Cautious, Cecil suddenly got the feeling he was being led somewhere specific. "What are we doing?" he asked.

"I want to show you the one thing that does go in and out," Khalil mused. "Since you're so keen."

"Watch out!" Jacque hissed, ducking behind a large rock. "Prisoners."

Cecil craned his neck to look at a long string of fellow prisoners heading around a bend. They marched in sets of three. "Are they watching for escapees?"

Khalil nodded.

"Will they rat on their fellows?" he asked.

The other two sighed, exhausted. "Yes," Jacque groaned. "We've said that. There are very few guards here because we guard ourselves. No one wants one prisoner to have something they don't. If you skim off a haul, someone will tell. You try to break free, someone will tell."

Cecil eyed them darkly. "So, what you're saying is, I've said too much to you?"

She touched his shoulder gently. "Not me. I won't rat on you." They both turned to Khalil.

He raised his hands in surrender. "I know too much to rat on anyone else. And if this topsider thinks he's getting out, I want in on that. Follow me." Running in a crouch, he ducked around the cave corner the prisoners had vanished behind.

On the other side was a little more of an ascent, then a steep drop-off that opened up into a huge dome of earth. Skydocks and a lower dock along the river below indicated this was an exit. A barge slowly floated into the darkness. A tiny airship hovered above them. It bore no marks or standards, but Cecil's keen vampire eyes caught an empirical messenger ascend the gangplank onto the ship. Shaken, he quickly glanced at Khalil.

"You see," Khalil whispered so softly Jacque couldn't hear. "This tunnel is guarded even more. Some who come to this one, hoping to slip out, never come back." He nodded to the ship. "Royal ship. Something has happened." He tilted his head. "The royal topsiders only come down once a year, and it's always the Don. For bloodshed." Putting on a sarcastic tone, he asked, "Now why would a royal messenger be coming down now? And at the same time a strange, foreign prisoner shows up, asking for a way out, saying he's looking for something." He locked eyes with Cecil. "Or *someone*?"

"It's not like that," Cecil snapped, moving away from the skydocks. "Why is everyone in this empire so terrified of foreigners? Is something going on between the countries they're not telling us?"

"Always," Khalil offered, falling in step with him. Jacque hurried to catch up.

"That river lead underground?" Cecil asked.

Khalil nodded.

"And the tunnel goes up and out, above the skydocks," he mused out loud.

"So, Cecil, who are you looking for?" Khalil asked, cutting his thoughts short.

The one thing Cecil had picked up on in his days underground was that no secret was safe. "I don't know if I can tell you," he said cautiously. "Every tongue seems to be a leaky pipe down here."

Cecil dodged around Khalil and walked next to Jacque. He slipped his hand around her waist, making her smile.

"You really mean it, don't you?" she asked. He noted the tiny hue of hope in her voice. "Will you try to escape?"

He and Khalil met eyes in the darkness again as they found their crawlers.

Sitting in the leather saddle, he sighed, defeated. "I doubt I can do this alone. I'd rather not drag you two into my affairs."

The nomad revved his own engine. "By all means, drag, Cecil. Most of us will rat on you for a gem or an extra day of sleep. Those things are temporary. Freedom can be eternal."

"We just need to know," Jacque added, "if you're serious."

The point of no return came to Cecil. Letting these two in would make or break his quest for redemption. With little to go on, not knowing what the right thing to do was, he nodded. "I'm serious as hell itself."

To himself, he thought, *The prince isn't dead. He's here.* He replayed the royal-clad man on the skydocks in his mind. *Yes, that's for certain. And they're looking for him. Or checking in.*

He glanced one more time towards the heavily guarded area. He might be able to slip out by himself. But he couldn't get a clumsy flightless mortal out with him. Maybe if he had an airship and somewhere down river to launch it from.

When they returned to the dig site, the shifts were preparing to change within the hour. They'd been gone for maybe three hours with travel time. I waited for them, dumped into an empty mine cart. I was just coming back to consciousness when they appeared. Cecil looked down at me with a kind of pathetic pity. He took in the bruises on my face and how I cradled a fractured hand as I climbed out.

"What happened?" Jacque asked, reaching down to me as I tumbled onto the earth in a destroyed heap. She took my good arm in her hands and hauled me up.

"Red," I spat, blood coming out of my mouth.

"You told him we left?" Khalil growled.

"Hello?" I indicated my aching hand and the shiner. "But I have one for you; he said he's fixing the rencounter this year."

Jacque and Khalil both gasped and made indications that they did not want this information. "Why tell us?" Jacque cried, clamping her hands over her ears.

I snorted. "He told me so someone else could beat it out of me. It's a trap. Now you know, too." I shoved passed them, knocking into Cecil. His alabaster body hurt, like running into ivory. That just confirmed my suspicions.

Cecil watched me go, gauging my steps. "We should have just left," he said with a sigh. "Now one more person knows we've been up to no good. And by the sound of it, Ezekiel is the last one I want knowing my secrets."

# 9 Black Assassin

Cecil let a few days pass, keeping his eyes and ears open for any sign that I had ratted on them to anyone else. I think the wait made him paranoid, and that's what drove him to enter The Red Mary one night. He didn't tell Jacque and Khalil, but he was looking for me. If he couldn't find me, he'd settle for any loose-tongued snitch.

Khalil maneuvered his way through the tavern like a snake, with grace and ease, past each jam-packed table. Inside, the darkness and dim lights couldn't hide the machinery churning away, ticking and grinding to keep the place alive. At each round table, a single socket was drilled in the center with one rectangular light poking out to brighten up the place. Dice rolled, cards flapped as they were shuffled, and something that resembled pool clicked and clacked near the back. Off to one side on a tiny stage (really just a large crate with a piano on top of it) a young lady in what we considered fine clothes trilled out a song about a drunk maid and her pious husband. The bar glowed green with colored electric lights and the tap never stopped running that greenish-brown liquor.

"We may be out of luck, gents," Jacque said sadly. "Every table is full."

Cecil could already feel the saloon churning with information: he couldn't miss this opportunity of drunk, tired tea-spillers.

"Let me." He strutted over to one table where two men glared darkly at each other over a game of Black Assassin. "Boys, I'm sure it's fun, but I have business."

"Crank off, glowgem," one wearing his hat over his long oily hair snapped. He considered the cards laid out in front of him. "We're in the middle of a game."

"I will make you crank off," the vampire snarled, his voice turning into the dark growl he owned so well. "I don't have time to—"

"Black!" the man on the other side of the table shouted through an entire set of wooden teeth.

A woman screamed and glasses crashed as the man's hand streaked to his knife, ready to stab the oily haired man in the hand.

"Stay back!" Cecil cried, grabbing the stabbing man's wrist and pulling the oily haired man back to safety at the same time. "What is this? Not fair play, is it?"

"You dirty snake!" the man with the knife screeched. "That's how you play the game. You've ruined it all!" He pointed down to the card, which Cecil's movements had overturned. "Card's shown. Game over. Bastard!" He yanked his hand away and tried to bury his cold steel in Cecil's chest, but the vampire dodged aside, and the drunk man fell over.

"Now get," Cecil said to the oily haired man. He locked eyes with him. With me. "You!" he gasped.

"Me," I growled, picking up the cards and shuffling them as lazily as I could, trying to show him I didn't care how scary he might be. "What business you got that's so damned important you gotta go and ruin my game of Black Assassin?"

Cecil narrowed his eyes at me, his thin lips hardly moving. "You would like a game where you kill the other man."

"How else am I gunna keep all these men in line?" I spread my hands to include the whole saloon.

I saw the light dawn in Cecil's eyes. He pushed his hat back onto the crown of his head and looked hard at me. "We both know that's not true, Ezekiel. We need to have a talk."

I laughed, letting the cards fly from one bandaged hand to the other in a perfect arch. "You think it's that easy, sunflower?"

"I'll make it that easy," he challenged. He picked up the drunk man's chair, spun it backwards, and sat down, resting one arm on the back of the chair. "Deal me in. I win one, you give me information. You win one..."

"I slit your throat," I offered. I bit down on my thumbnail, waiting for his reaction. Somehow, it didn't have the effect I thought it would. I suppose I'd just assumed all vampires knew the price their blood carried.

"Fine," he shot back. "You disgust me."

This gave me pause, and sadly, I couldn't keep the mixed shock off my face. I covered it with a quick, sharp sneer. "Fine."

"Rules?" he asked.

The nomad and Jacque sat behind him, their eyes on me, not saying a word. Khalil supplied the necessary advice.

"There are three phases to this game. Watch your hands." He winked at Cecil, wiggling his fingers like a magician. "You deal out like blackjack and all the cards have the same value: face cards are ten, each number is the value shown, and aces are eleven or one. Each player gets one card face up and then one more face down. The player may split if they want, making two hands. You may only split during phase one. No splitting after being dealt a third card, though, so watch it. If you do, you cannot take a third card, or split and just stand. That is phase one, called the setup. Your cards need to be close to twenty-one for you to win, and that's where phase two starts.

"The second phase is called the deal. Each player bets for each hand they have that's closer to twenty-one than their opponent's. Lies ensue. That's my favorite part." Khalil smiled but stopped when he saw my bored face. "Now, go back to phase one in order to acquire another hand if you want.

"Continuing with phase two, jacks are the assassins. If you have the jack of spades, you may make a move at your opponent's hand to see his cards. If your opponent calls "Hearts!" then you may not look at his card as the jack of hearts protects against the assassin. This means he has the jack of hearts in one of his hands, though. This gives you an advantage anyway for having the assassin, but you do not know where the heart is. However, he also knows you have the assassin now.

"Something to watch out for are the black aces. If you see one in your opponent's hand or yours, it's called a hidden assassin. The ace can be equal to one or eleven. Remember that when you know where the heart or the assassin is. That's a natural twenty-one and a victory. You won't want to bet against that hand.

"Phase three is the time of truth. Roll the dice to tell who shows their cards first, assuming you get to that point. The lower number must go first. If the black assassin is in play, then he may refuse to show any of his hands until all other hands have been shown. The hand closest to twenty-one gets every hand and must shuffle them into a new deck, separate from the house's deck. The one who collects all the cards in the end wins."

I loved seeing Cecil think. His eyes would go dark, hard, and genuine. It sounds weird, but really, he had a great mind. His years of un-life had been well spent acquiring knowledge, tact, and an unhealthy obsession with fashion.

"Be careful with that assassin, sunflower," I said. I spoke quietly to try to send a shiver down Cecil's spine and relieve the one crawling down mine when I looked into his pale face. "If you look and I don't have hearts, I can still win."

Cecil frowned, thinking. His slow methodical way of looking at the simple game intrigued me.

"You could have twenty-one already and I might surrender," he said evenly. "Then what?"

Khalil pursed his lips. "Then he'd get your cards and have the assassin in his deck somewhere. You'd have to be careful. You don't want him to have the heart and the assassin."

"What happens if I take a third and go over twenty-one?" Cecil asked, picking up two cards and reading them.

"Bust," Jacque offered, touching his shoulder with her long fingers. "You lose then, too."

Cecil smirked, nodding. "There are a lot of ways to lose this game."

"And only one way to win," I replied coolly.

He drew himself up, nodded, rolled up his sleeves, and delicately picked up a set of dice off the table. "Then let's get started. This is how I do most of my business anyway."

"Oh, yeah? You a law breaker, sunflower?" I taunted, trying to get things shaken up a bit. I hated boring games. This life had been monotonous for years. Cecil was new. Shiny. "I somehow doubt that. Watch your hands." I put my silver dagger on the table and smiled when I saw his nose twitch into the slightest of wrinkles. "When I 'go for the hand' as the assassin, I really go for your hand."

He nodded. "Now I see. Good thing I lost my gloves. I'd hate to have them ruined."

"You should be more afraid than you are."

Cecil's head bent down to look at his first hand, but his eyes snapped up to mine, his dark brows casting shadows over his violet eyes. "Don't think you're the first man I've seen kill another, boy. You may feel tough, but you have no idea what you're dealing with."

Name calling always ground my gears. But I pretended it didn't. I couldn't let him get to me. I wanted to stay in control. But he *did* start to get to me. I didn't know him at the time, but looking back, I cannot fathom why I thought I could take him on. I thought my boots were bigger than they were. I used to be the only shark in my pond, but not anymore. And I couldn't do half of what a driven vampire could do. Or *would* do.

"What happens when the house is out of cards?" Cecil asked, peaking at his second card.

"You deal from your own deck," Jacque said, looking over his shoulder.

"So the house can't win?" He chuckled.

"One needs a house in order for the house to win," I snapped, taking a third card. I couldn't stop myself from glaring. I had gone bust on the first phase of the first hand! "Damn!" I shouted.

Cecil smiled, but tried to hide it—such a good sport. "We skipping phase two and three, then?"

"Spade you, fop."

Cecil raised his eyebrows. "That sounds like a nasty word, boy. Your mother wouldn't want you talking like that in her home."

He took the cards and set them to the side, not saying anything else as the nomad dealt us our second hand.

"I won't make that mistake again, sunflower."

"I'd hope not," he said, checking his second card. "I'll split and take another, please."

Khalil nodded, calmly handing Cecil another card, eager to see if it was a good draw or not. The vampire nodded and laid his card down. I tried to read his face, but it hardened like glass as he caught me searching. His eyes were marbles in a handsome doll's face, unblinking and not even trying to lie.

"Split," I parroted. I had two hands of twenty now. He could not have two hands of twenty-one.

"Do we bet now?" he asked. He ran a finger over each of his elegant eyebrows.

"Careful, Cecil," Jacque said quietly, her fingers now interlocked like vises in her lap.

"Another hand?" Khalil asked us.

Cecil rubbed his fingers and thumb together, eyes unfocused. "Another, please."

The dealer handed him another card: the jack of spades. But he didn't smile, smirk, or do anything to let me know he had it. Remembering his stony façade now still impresses me.

We drew once more each and then began to gamble. He took Khalil's bag of shinies and used the lenses and gems they'd gained by bargaining his clothing.

"This is my currency," Khalil moaned, handing over the bag to Cecil.

"Contrary, my gilded friend," Cecil said in a flat tone, eyes on the cards. "My clothes got you these shinies." He went completely monotone.

"You owe me three more lenses," I snapped, glaring at what was rightfully mine.

He tried so hard to hide everything that he showed nothing. Suddenly, he transformed again, not human at all. Flat and robotic like that automaton on the piano, a machine. Emotionless. I wanted to achieve that level of humanlessness. Being cruel would be so much easier. And being cruel made life's hard choices simpler. In that moment, I admired him. However, this was his tell. I knew what was about to happen.

"You are good," I said.

Cecil decided to hit me with a scare tactic. He reached up to my face and pushed my long, greasy hair behind one ear, revealing the black eye I had been hiding behind the oily curtains. "Let yourself see first."

A shiver involuntarily ran from where he touched me all the way through my spine to my toes. I shook his hand off. I hated being touched. I looked at my last card, jack of hearts, and pressed my lips together trying to stifle a smirk. My hand would not lose, even if he did have it.

"I win," he said softly. "Twice now. You owe me information."

"Show me!" I bellowed. "Two hands of twenty!" I flipped my cards over, grabbed my silver knife, and stabbed at the table with all my might. "Beat that."

A tinge of relief waved over Cecil's face. "Two hands of twenty-one." He showed me the jack of spades and the ace. The other hand a queen, an ace, and a ten. Two perfect hands. No way.

I narrowed my gaze and tried to poison him with my glare. "How did you do that?"

He smiled now and took my cards, my jack of hearts with it, and shuffled his now growing deck. "Luck. It's how I do business."

I leaned back, crossing my arms. "What do you want?"

Cecil's eyes went to the silver dagger, to my nice shiner, then to the saloon around us. These were the things I thought he'd ask about. Fortunately for me, he had more questions than I had losses. But two wins in a row made him confident.

"I was sent here," he started. "I'm not sure why. But I think I'm supposed to find someone."

"Tch," I spat. "Who cares? We are here, they are there, we don't bother them, and they make sure we stay."

Cecil sighed ever so slightly at my vague reply. He bit his tongue. "I don't care what you think of those above you. I need to know if there is royalty in prison here."

I stopped breathing, going still. Cecil noted the change.

Beside him, Khalil and Jacque stiffened.

"Rich people don't go to The Château d'Oubli," I mumbled almost inaudibly. "That'd be the day we know the world has gone to pot. When they start to kill their own and take more of the land than they can handle." I couldn't stop the bitter tone that dusted my callous words.

"Why would a royal be down here?" Jacque asked. "Nobles, sure." She sighed sadly. "But a royal?"

"That's what I need to know," Cecil replied. He looked back to me. "How can I find out? You seem to be the one into secrets."

I shifted in my seat, heart hammering. "Did you come down to find the prince?"

Even if he said yes, I wouldn't believe him.

His eyes widened, then quickly returned to their normal, soulless gaze. "Of course not," he said flatly. "The prince is dead."

That was a mistake. I'd said prince. He'd never said who. I'd put a target on my back for the vampire. He hid it well, but I was able to read Cecil somehow. I saw renewed interest in me behind his stony eyes.

Khalil twirled his long black hair around his finger, eyes flicking between Cecil and me.

"What if we *could* get someone out?" Cecil asked urgently.

"Lies," I scoffed. "You have to be a special kind of steamed brain to tell *me* this. I may not govern any firms, but they know I harvest information. I could go to anyone now and tell them you're planning a breakout. And anyone looking for a dead prince is truly mad."

"Listen," Cecil said, leaning in. We all stupidly followed his lean, looking like children about to exchange marbles for secrets about the town drunk. "I am here to find out about the dead prince and get out. If you help me, I can personally guarantee you the best, longest life you could ever imagine."

His charisma would have manipulated a raja out of his riches. But me, I needed to know I was right about him. Most people didn't have a chance of getting out. If he was a vampire like I thought, we might stand a chance.

"You've told me a lot." I gripped the silver dagger, but he didn't flinch. "Don't tempt me with escape." My eyes watered and a tear shook at the edge of my eye.

Jacque wrinkled her nose. "We may have done the wrong thing in telling him."

Cecil's violet orbs bored into me, searching. Finally, he said, "You may be right. We can't let him go, knowing what he does."

I snapped, jerking the knife out of the table to attack. Cecil tried to dodge, but he had been lulled into a false sense of security. That was his biggest flaw: too trusting for a vampire. I seized his throat in my own iron grip and plunged the dagger into his heart. Everyone screamed, Jacque leapt back, and Khalil pounced on me. Cecil cried out and clutched his chest, bloody tears instantly streaming from his eyes.

He fell backwards, writhing in the pain. I had hit my mark.

# 10 SPIES

I flipped off Cecil and grasped Khalil's throat, trying to strangle him off me. I landed some marvelous punches on his face before Jacque pulled him off me and begged him to help carry Cecil out.

Together, they pulled the bleeding Cecil to his feet and rushed to the swinging doors of the saloon. No one interfered. Some cajoled us, encouraging us to fight.

"Let them go," I laughed as some men tried to chase after them. "He's a goner." But I knew he wasn't.

Cecil panted, choking on his own blood for probably the first time in his life as Khalil pulled him out into the street, leaving the saloon behind. Jacque ripped her outer shirt off and put pressure on the wound once they laid him down in a slightly more secluded alley. He coughed and spattered his blood on their faces.

"I'm sorry," he said through bloody lips. He grew paler than before, almost translucent. "I hadn't planned on that rascal to be so rash. Oh, dear." He touched the tear in the shirt. "So sorry about your acquired raiment, Khalil. I'm afraid I've ruined it."

"Shh," Jacque cooed. Her hands were strong and held his leaking blood at bay. "Khalil, what can we do?"

Khalil watched almost curiously as Cecil's eyes fluttered open and closed, his panting like the gurgling of a clogged drainpipe. His gentle fingers pulled Cecil's shirt open to see the wound. The poisonous silver let his secret out. Black veins pulsed into his chest from the dagger's buried tip. Khalil jerked his hand back.

"Get him out of the streets." His voice took on the steel tang of an alarm. He grasped the handle and jerked it out of Cecil's chest. The vampire shouted and grabbed at his wound, panting. Seeing he didn't seem to be getting worse, Khalil threw the dagger with all his strength away down the alley.

Jacque shook her head, worried tears still in her eyes. "He won't survive. We have to get him to Mother May-bell. She'll know what to do."

"No, we don't," he snipped.

"Why not? He's dying, Khalil. We have to try!"

Cecil coughed and cleared his throat. "Not so much dying as tired. That was a lot of blood to lose."

Cecil sat up with a moan. Jacque gasped and fell back, eyes wide. Her brows went up and she covered her mouth to stifle a scream. He pressed onto his wound, but the bleeding had stopped. He moved to raise his shirt up and inspect the scar, but the nomad stayed his hand and spoke a command with his eyes to not reveal his poisoned flesh.

"How?" Jacque gaped.

"Missed my heart," Cecil said, patting his chest. "Damned hurt, though. And that knife—"

"Was made of silver," Khalil cut in, "and Ezekiel probably didn't want to damage it when he stabbed you, hitting a rib instead. He'll come looking for it. You'll be just fine, though."

Cecil eyed Khalil cautiously. His eyes flitted to the silver dagger farther down the alley. Unsure how much danger he'd be in if the prisoners knew he was a vampire, he let it go.

"I need to rest," Cecil said evenly. He let his tone drop down to a serious, more dangerous lull. "Khalil, take me somewhere I can rest."

"B-but," Jacque stammered. "Are you all right? Mother May-bell is practically a witch. She's a great mancer and can cure anything."

Cecil took her chin between his forefinger and thumb and smiled at her charmingly. "Thank you, pet. But I do not need medical attention. Not yet."

A shy smile tugged at her lips as she gazed into his eyes, his hand on her face. "Cecil, he stabbed you."

He dropped his head in defeat. "If there is an infirmary here, go and find some bandages, will you? Bring them to Khalil's digs."

"West side," Khalil offered her as she stood up to run. "Know the wagon trail?"

Jacque nodded.

"I'm the two-tiered boathouse where the river used to be."

"I know it," she said, and dashed into the streets.

Cecil nodded and motioned for Khalil to help him up. He waved to Jacque when she glanced back, helping her to leave them, as the two started off between buildings to wherever Khalil called home.

Once they were properly alone, Cecil used all his leftover strength to grasp the Egyptian's tender nerves between his neck and shoulder. He dug his vampiric claws into his skin. Khalil gasped and froze in pain.

"Listen now, for I will only say this once," Cecil hissed through his elongated fangs. "I am no longer a man of violence, so do not tempt me. Hide nothing from me and you will not be harmed. You have played the mystery with me long enough. It is time for you to tell me all I want to know." He squeezed again and heard the young man inhale sharply. "And we start with keeping my sanguine ways under lock and key. I have not made it this long as one of the children of the night, as that depraved Irish man called us, just to be snuffed out by a vagabond buried miles under the American Empire. Do I make myself clear?"

Khalil nodded quickly. "I'm your man, if you like. I see in your eyes you mean business."

*I don't know what I mean,* Cecil thought. *But I'm not ready to be hunted down in this darkness yet.*

"Let's get back and we can talk," he said in a soft, dangerous growl.

Khalil wasted no time in leading them to his derelict boathouse tucked away behind abandoned furnaces. It looked like the boat had once floated in some river long gone. He'd built onto it—like most structures in The Château d'Oubli. It had gotten out of hand and transformed into a long, rounded rectangle made out of every piece of garbage and scrap imaginable. His door opened when he solved the clockwork puzzle that stood in for a lock and a pushed it.

The nomad stood back as Cecil made his own way inside. He took the blanket off the bed just inside the door and wrapped it tightly around himself. Then he collapsed onto a rocking chair and breathed a moment, one eye still on Khalil. He looked nervous.

"Get me a pint of milk and whiskey," he ordered Khalil. "Now," he added when the man didn't move right away.

"I've got milk." Khalil poured some into a large tankard from an ice chest. "But all I've got in the strong department is rustwash."

Cecil wrinkled his nose. That did not sound good at all. "Does it have minerals in it?"

Khalil shook his head. "Made from white wheat that grows here in the caves. We just call it that because it looks like rusty water, and tastes like it, too. Does the trick, though."

"Give it to me."

Cecil took the gross mixture and sniffed it. The foul, greasy smell made him gag and pinch his nose. "This is not cow's milk, is it?"

"Where am I going to get a cow?" Khalil's kohl-lined eyes mocked him from across the room.

The first sip proved bad. It tasted worse than wash water and the milk was somehow worse. Sour, dry, and the taste filled his mouth all the way up into his nostrils. But the warmth spread into his fingers and his healing wound tingled.

"It will have to do." He sighed, downing the rest before shouting outrage at the taste. "Spades, that is bad!"

Khalil didn't reply. He had his hands in pied pockets and his eyes fixed steadily on Cecil. Cecil could smell the nervousness pulsing with every beat of Khalil's heart. "I'm not sure my guess is right," he started, "but I swear, whatever it is, I won't tell a soul."

"No, you won't," Cecil replied, finally getting over the smell. The house reeked of stale, wet cloth and the rusty smell of disintegrating metal. He took his hat off and smoothed his hair back. "I meant what I said. I used to take on missions like this all the time. Well, not like this. I was a mercenary. It was easy for me. Missions brought me money. Money gives me fine clothes, a place to stay, and all the pleasures in life." He paused for effect and narrowed his eyes at Khalil. "Can you guess why I need so much of these things?"

The nomad's face could not hide the answer. He knew, but he didn't want to say. He swallowed hard. "I suppose after the first hundred years you get bored and need more stimulation." He raised his black brows. "I don't like being threatened," he added. "I can be of use to you."

Cecil smiled at the humble offer. "I am not threatening you. But I really didn't want anyone to know. Being hunted makes jobs like this so much harder." He stopped and looked around the sad house and listened to the chugging sounds of the outside world. "I am willing to take you with me if you help me."

Khalil's fear dissipated just enough to let him frown a little. "In exchange for what?"

"Simple. Keep my vampirism a secret. Help me out. You've gone out before; you know the royals. Consider yourself a diamond in the rough."

A small scoffed escaped Khalil's lips and he tensed. "But vampires are strong. You don't need me."

Cecil nodded, his eyebrows raised. "Of course." His voice grew low and croaky. "I could get rid of you. But I won't yet. I don't have as much time as I'm used to. So, I need someone who knows how this place works, where the information is. Someone to teach me Black Assassin." He winked, then tapped the tips of his fingers together and narrowed his eyes in thought. "I supposed we have to do something about that little weasel, Ezekiel."

Cecil hoped freedom would entice the nomad. Especially one who had tasted freedom recently and had been brought back underground.

"I could offer you gold, too," he added. "Enough to leave the American Empire. You could go anywhere."

Khalil didn't say the word out loud. A green flame of desire struck like a smoking match behind his eyes. Cecil caught the gears whir in the nomad's head. His defense went up. He couldn't read

Khalil's mind, but the light of an idea nearly blinded him in the darkness.

"Do we have a deal?" Cecil reiterated.

"Of course." But he didn't take Cecil's proffered hand.

"What is it?" the vampire asked. When Khalil didn't answer right away, he added, "You know my secret. We'd be even. What's stopping you?"

Khalil gripped a lock of his black hair, absently spinning it around his finger. "I may be in too deep elsewhere to be making new deals. But..." he dropped his hand, hesitatingly reaching for Cecil's. "This may be my last chance to get out for good before things go too far."

They shook on it. Khalil's grip wasn't as firm as Cecil thought it would be.

Khalil asked, "So, what's the story? We don't have long before Jacque comes back. Tell me what I need to know so I can keep my ears open."

Cecil snuggled up in the chair and pulled the blanket up to his chin, closing his eyes. Taking a deep breath, he said, "Tell me about the line of Markus Aurelium, High King of Midwest, Protector of the Colonies, Emperor of the Hawaiian Whatever, blah blah blah." What he wanted to know was how finding the dead prince would be worth his soul.

Kahlil absentmindedly traced the tattoo on his forearm. "Did someone send you? Is this a political affair?"

Cecil cracked his eyes open a little. He sighed. "I miss my cane. And no, it's a...spiritual affair. A personal matter."

The confused nomad didn't know what to say. He'd only dealt with politicals and businessmen. Or underhanded syndicates. "Well," he started slowly, "there was supposedly a plot in the palace and court. The rumor was that Jethro, Duke of Dakota—who previously abdicated the throne to his brother Markus—had a change of heart."

"Naturally," Cecil mumbled, signaling for Khalil to give him more of the disgusting liquid concoction. He threw it back quickly. "Evil Duke—what?—kills his brother and heir?"

Khalil nodded.

"How simple," Cecil noted, sitting up a little. He tapped the edge of the shot glass in thought. "Who was the queen again?"

"Really?" Khalil asked mockingly.

"I'm not an American, my pied friend. I don't worship your politicals and royals like the rest of the world." He squinted with one eye. "Didn't he marry a French woman?"

"Yes," Khalil said with a nod. "To strengthen our ties with France, King Markus took the third daughter of one of the most influential kings in France as his wife. Camille."

"Hmm," Cecil mused, only slightly interested. "Why would the Ecclesiast send me down here, then?"

"The Creed?" Khalil asked. "A vampire running an errand for the holy church?"

Cecil laughed, darkly amused. "The church is not the strangest thing I have sought help from," he assured the nomad. "So, American king married French princess. Duke changes his mind, wants to be king? Kills his brother..." Cecil stood up now and paced the boathouse, rubbing his chest. "One of them is here." He suddenly stopped. "By my blood, one of them *is* here!" He turned and ran towards Khalil.

As anyone would with a vampire running towards them, Khalil backed away into a corner. "What are you saying?"

"How can you not know?" Cecil said, turning on his booted heel and pacing again. "You worked in the ranks of the royal families with the Syndicate, yes?"

Kahlil stumbled over his words. "It's complicated. MidWest is a big place. We weren't all nestled under the palace's roof. Some Syndicate only work in the towns, with the mayors or railroad barons. I had other jobs." His long fingers fiddled with the pendent now under his mottled coat. "I'm sorry, I'm still distracted by the vampire factor." He shook his head. "*How* could I not see it?"

"Why would you?" Cecil asked.

Khalil swallowed, eyes unblinking. He turned away and started a fire in his makeshift grate.

"I see," Cecil said, only slightly interested. "Well, first things first. I am famished, and there is a weasel out there who knows about my bloodsucking ways *and* what I am looking for." He settled back down into the chair. "Sometime soon, we find him and either use him or eat him."

He snuggled back into his blankets by the fire now. Cold and weak from blood loss, he had to fight to not feed on Khalil. Not killing someone after feeding on them came with dire consequences. "Tomorrow, though," he said with a sigh. "I'm tired now."

"It's not tomorrow," Khalil said, facing the fire. "It's only not now. There is no sun and no tomorrow."

Cecil allowed himself a smile. "No sun. My kind of place. If Jacque comes, tell her I'm fine and will see her later."

# 11 SAVIOR SERVANT

A few days of searching for me took Cecil, Khalil, and Jacque deeper into The Château d'Oubli where the machines dug fresh holes we'd soon inhabit. Blazing veins of strange elements and metals lined the walls all around them. Redbeard and his cronies stood by, watching over our every move. He glared down at us whenever we started a new dig, eager to get his share of whatever lay inside.

"Stormsteel, solar adamant, maybe some kind of ensorcelled crystal, and, oh! Rubylead!" Jacque squeaked the last one like a child at Christmas time. She jumped into the monster drill and slipped her goggles back on. "Watch out! I need four more inches, hey?"

Cecil put his mask and goggles on, getting his thick rubber gloves stuck in the strap and swearing even over the drill as the strap stretched and sprang back, slapping him hard in the face. Khalil laughed and Jacque's white teeth shone in a visible grin.

"Four inches!" another engineer shouted from a catwalk yards above them. "Engineers ready!"

"Keep the coals hot," Jacque shouted back to Cecil and Khalil, who shoveled large, glittering coals into a furnace the size of a dragon's belly. "Open the valve and let her rip!"

Cecil breathed hard through his mask as he cranked the opening valve, letting the heat hit the water tank. Still weak, the physical labor tried his strength. The work didn't break his back as it had before, but the lack of feeding sapped the last of his tenacity. Paler than he had been in years, his hunger made his mouth ravenous for relief.

"Watch the gauge!" Khalil shouted, ducking from a sudden release of steam that boiled over. "That boiler isn't the kindest of ladies."

"Here we go!" Jacque shouted at the same time. The massive drill plowed into the corner of the foremost wall and the ground. The rocks screamed against the iron and the entire cavern shook. "Forward ho!"

Cecil grew slightly nauseated trying to keep track of the five gauges in front of him and the pressure tube where a little lead ball rose and fell according to the engine's need. Learning all the workings of steam-powered mining had never been a desire of his. It cramped his style in every way: not gloriously fashionable, made his hands dirty, and didn't allow for sleep on silken linens. Worse than that, he didn't have access to easy, healthy, or even tasteful food.

The drill whirred to a halt. The engineers grabbed their night vision goggles (made with lenses crafted from an element that allowed them to see in the dark) and gathered around the new hole. Cecil didn't bring his and peeked in over Jacque's ear at her hands where they were pressed against the rock. Her gloved fingers stroked a deep, glittery red vein just visible in the dim light.

"Rubylead," she said. "I'm compatible with it! Let's get this out."

"We don't have time for personal gain. I'm sorry," the lead engineer said. "Underneath there is solar adamant, and that's what we're after. Hot seller topside."

Jacque's face fell. She looked back into the glowing red hole and sighed.

"Mancing is dangerous, anyway," the engineer warned her. "Won't last to thirty if you put that stuff in your body."

"We can get it," Cecil said behind her. "We need to go through this wall anyway. Let's drill and I'll get what I can when we start to gather. You can still drill and do your job with the solar adamant; I'll get your jewels."

Khalil watched Cecil's coy chivalry from the corner of his eye. Cecil knew he didn't have to convince Jacque to work with him like he did Khalil. That girl would have followed him to the grave. This was the quickest way to earn her loyalty.

"Why go after the rubylead? It's a common gem," Khalil murmured to Cecil.

Cecil put his goggles back on when the drill started up. "I need friends, Khalil. Ones who aren't scared spades around me." He stopped mid-step and added, "Mancing?"

Khalil hissed at Cecil to be quiet. Redbeard watched them from his perch on a crane, his eyes boring into the Egyptian. Cecil cautiously glanced up.

"Why does that man look at you like that?"

Khalil took Cecil's upper arm and led him away from the drill, back up into the engine room. "Remember when I told you I was in too deep?"

Cecil nodded. "I will die of shock if you divulge a secret right now, my covert friend."

Khalil cast about, licking his lips, trying to think of a way to spill the oil without breaking some other deal. He picked up a piece of coal and a silver stone that had been discarded on the floor.

"Geomancy," he explained. He rubbed the element between his fingers. "Coal is a mineral, yes? Made from other organic material." He held up the silver and Cecil flinched. "This is darksilver. See how it's darker than whitesilver?"

He laid it on the control console and smashed the darksilver with a hammer. Taking a small knife off his belt, he made a cut on the tip of his finger. Gently, he placed his finger into the dust of the smashed silver. Wincing just a little, he waited.

"Watch now." Squinting, Khalil's once brown irises turned to a dark, almost inky grey—the same color as the darksilver. He gasped, and grey veins pulsed out from the cut under his skin. Cecil winced as grey tears dripped down from Khalil's eyes.

"Touch my hand." Khalil held it out.

Hesitant and still grimacing, Cecil touched Khalil's forefinger with his own and hissed as the silver burned through his skin.

"Snakes, that is disgusting!" he cried out, shaking his pained hand.

Khalil sat down near the fire, his eyes clearing up a little. "That was just a little darksilver. Take in—as you saw— something like rubylead and other properties arise, including being able to see in the darkness without the lenses. But it's not very compatible with me." He wiped the tears and smiled. "That little prick was nothing. Some mancers open their flesh to powder their veins. Makes the magic stronger and take effect faster."

"That must be what mancer-forged means," Cecil realized. "When I was topside, that seemed to be the selling point of some wares. Saw it attached to forges that made automatons and weapons."

The Egyptian nodded. "It's not outlawed yet. To preserve the empire, the royal family discourages those who can from using it. They have their Ecclesiasts and Wardens and others to keep mancers in line. Until recently. Last time I was topside, I'm pretty sure I saw an organized lot of mancers in royal regalia." Khalil shook his head. "But the power is not endless. There are many drawbacks. Addiction, sickness, poisonings—magic is not free. But sometimes they use it for experimental weapons and…augmentation." The nomad said the last word like a curse he feared. "That's one of the things Red does. Augment prisoners for experimental weapons."

Cecil eyed the silver stone on the control panel. "I never considered it. In all my years."

Khalil brushed the remaining silver away. "Well, we didn't discover it until after the revolution. It was used, but not understood in Europa for years. But I know gold is used in the Central Eastern Empire. How have you never seen it?"

Cecil smiled dryly as he tended to a spiking gauge. "I'm not a thousand years old. Not all vampires are centuries old with a tragic past."

"How old are you?"

"Not old enough." Cecil kicked the silver rock away. "Keep *that* away from me. And you."

"Afraid I'll protect myself with it?" Khalil sneered. "You can't touch me then."

Cecil smirked. "Spades, no. I'm afraid you'll poison yourself, of course. Can't have my only friend rotting from the inside out."

He went back to the boiler and glared into the inferno inside the metal walls. No vampire had ever mentioned that humans could ingest silver, practically turning their skin into armor. If every human did that, he and his fellow nosferatu would starve. Perhaps some things were better left buried in the darkness of The Château d'Oubli. He turned to ask Khalil about the exact deadliness of geomancy, but the nomad was gone.

A few hours later, the hole turned into a new cavern and the rubble sparkled with tiny dew drops of rubylead. While Jacque and the other engineers went into the new cavern to measure for beams and stays to keep the cavern aloft, the other workers began to pick through the rocks and dirt to test for what lay beyond. The rubylead could be easily seen, as it shone brighter amongst the others and had the most colorful dust Cecil had ever seen. But the stench of rotlead overpowered even the bright red dust. They knew it must be mined, and if it somehow didn't appear in storage, a supervisor would be sent into The Château d'Oubli to find out why they were running low on the most torturous metal known to man. Cecil took a long inhale and wondered if humans used rotlead in their blood, too. The thought made his too-empty stomach churn. He touched the band on his neck and remembered the pain.

Calls for lamps, steel stakes, track supplies, and mortar were passed back and forth. Soon every worker donned a mask, goggles, and a pick. They had to sound the walls to find the tiny pockets where the solar adamant would be growing. Cecil didn't understand why the walls had cavernous rooms or why the adamant grew in them, but he had to distract himself from his hunger and moved along the wall, looking for the pockets.

I came up behind him and swung my pick with a savage shout. He cried out and dodged to the left, raising his own pick, thinking I'd come in for a kill. I laughed darkly at his fear and drove the sharp end into the wall with a hallow clunk.

"You've been looking for me?" I chuckled. "Don't go in there," I warned. I tied a cloth around the rotlead encircling my neck. Rotlead melted into acidic poison on contact with sunlight. Harvesting solar adamant was dangerous work, but so worth it to see some rays in your long, dark days. "I'm getting first dibs before the others come. Solar adamant is a valuable commodity to these prison rats."

"Where have you been?" he asked.

"Watching you looking for me," I replied. I screamed, driving my pick in again and pulling it out with an animal shriek. "I'm very interested in how you shook off my attack."

"I'm sure." Cecil braced himself and put his booted foot through the wall with one powerful kick. It crumbled away to reveal a small, dark, hollow chamber. I quickly hid my shock.

"Ha! No solar adamant for you. I suppose you won't mind if I go in first, then?" He smiled cheekily and lowered himself onto his belly to slither in.

This time, the maniacal grin crinkled my face. "By all means, sunflower."

Cecil pushed himself through the small opening, knocking a few more sections down, and entered the chamber on the other side. The space opened enough for him to stand up in. He squinted and reached for his headlamp, but too late. Solar adamant was triggered to glow around movement. It was the underworld's only security light. That made it valuable to the guards who ran The Château d'Oubli. Giant pillars of it were all over the outskirts so that no one who lived there even bothered to go there anymore. So, it was a waste. All that shiny cash sitting around us. But still, the unspoken rule was to mine it on sight.

I waited outside, smiling, thinking he would just be blinded by the light and that would give me a small laugh. No. He screamed like a man on fire. I heard him drop his pick. The adamant, ignited by his movements, shot bright beams of sunlight into his vampiric face. I didn't know it at the time, but spades, the time had come to learn that it had the same effect on vampires as the sun itself.

He screamed, shielding his eyes with the burning flesh on his hands and backed away into a wall. You'd think he'd never been touched by the sun. His starved, weak body ignited instantly. He backed away and slinked up the wall like a lizard to get away from the light. That was how I found him. At first, my eyes were shining with the greed of the adamant, but then I spotted him writhing and screaming on the ceiling, covering himself with his arms and duster. Flaming flesh dripped down on me.

"Snakes from hell!" I shouted.

I rushed to the adamant and threw my own ratty jacket over the largest spear of it piercing up from the earth. The last two little ones, I buried quickly in dirt. I essentially saved his life. But I also scored a great dig.

After I covered them, Cecil panted and slid back down the wall, too weak to grip it properly. However that worked…

I ran to him and took the canteen from my belt, emptying it, then held it to his burning body. His singed blood dribbled into it. He kept pushing me away, yelling when his sensitive skin came in contact with mine. He squirmed too hard for me to properly fill the canteen with his precious blood. He made a frightful sound in his throat, a kind of gurgling roar. He finally landed a blow to my face, knocking me back.

"Shut up and hold still!" I demanded, gripping his scalp and pulling his head back.

He suddenly froze, his voice gone. He glared up at me with one terrified eye as though confused as to why he had obeyed me. He tried to scream again, but no sound came from his wide-open mouth. Confused but glad, I took out a new silver knife and made a small incision on his throat to let more of his blood out. It trickled into my canteen. I smiled and licked my lips.

"Your blood is worth more than this adamant," I explained. "Bloodstones are not common. I've never seen what they do, but I know people will kill for them. One time, there was this guy here—or so I hear—who was a vampire hunter, and he…" I stopped. "Never mind, it's not important. Someone down here has to know how to alchemize this."

I felt him struggling against me again. Whatever spell I had over him began to wear off already. "Don't move!" I ordered again and he went stiff. I didn't understand, but I didn't care.

"Saved…me," he gasped. I had forgotten to tell him to shut up again. "Impossible." He choked.

Digging deep, he said again, "You saved me. From the adamant." He looked angry, scared, and confused all at once.

I grimaced. "Not for much longer. There." I corked my canteen and let him fall forward, limp. "That's all I needed from you. No one will care that you're dead. And I will have this adamant and your blood."

He blinked, still not moving, my spell still active. "Why my blood?"

I stood up and shrugged. "They pay a lot for it." Turning to leave, I lashed the canteen to my belt again.

Cecil began that deep, rumbling growl in his throat again. He lifted himself up onto his hands and knees and prepared to spring. I froze and turned to command him again. Instead, I screamed a high, horrified yelp. Where once the dandy had been in his old duster, there now crouched a fierce monster with fangs and two enormous, bat-like wings arching over his head. Yes, I screamed.

He pounced on me like a viper, his extra strength nearly breaking my arm as he pinned me to the ground. He snarled, his fangs dripping with hungry saliva. He sniffed at my hair and something like a purring roiled up his throat.

"Be my master, will you?" he moaned softly. "Save me to make me your slave? Clever." His voice rose in terrifying anger. I didn't know what he was talking about.

"Get off me, you—!" I shouted. But I couldn't finish the sentence. Cecil's teeth flashed as his jaw popped open and his eyes burned fiery in the darkness. He'd meant to kill me before for just knowing his secret. But now that I had unlocked some ancient vampire law by saving his life, he had more reason to devour me savagely.

My own mouth jerked open in a silent scream as his four fangs popped through my flesh and into my veins. I tugged at my arm, but he held me tight. I could hear him swallowing before I felt it. He pressed his nose against my throat and his ravenous breath puffed on me. I suddenly felt all of him, like I was him; his legs holding my hips down, his hands tight on my wrists, his panting chest against mine. His lips on my neck and his teeth inside me. My own heart thumped louder and faster, fearing for me. My face pulsed like a swelling bee sting. He wanted to drink me dry. Kill me. I felt his every emotion and his recent memories flooded my head.

I gasped feebly, almost gone. The world turned black. His once cold body heated up against mine, my blood warming him. Giving him life.

Strength. He purred against my throat, slaking his thirst and lust for blood.

In the darkness, I saw his wings retract into his shadow.

"Enough!" I screamed hoarsely, hoping that mysterious bond still held. "Get off me!"

Instantly, he sprang away. On all fours, he hunched like a monster finishing his meal. He licked his lips and then wiped his mouth with his dirty sleeve. He cackled in the darkness.

"Lie down!" he shouted.

Terrified, my body froze and fell stiff to the floor. My eyes fixed on the ceiling.

Cecil stood up and walked to me, towering over my prostrate form. Rage filled me. Somehow, the roles had reversed. "Thank you for not commanding me to not bite you." He crouched down and pressed his bloody finger to my lips. "Do not speak."

Even in the flickering light from our discarded headlamps, I could see he had completely healed from all the previous wounds and bruises. His white flesh turned to a healthy glow. His hair glossed over, turning silken, long, and black. Before my eyes, my blood had brought him back to life. He'd transformed into the elegant man again.

"What you did was foolish," he said simply, as though giving a mathematics lesson to a boy. "When a mortal saves a vampire, that vampire is in debt to that mortal. Doesn't happen often, but I don't like it." He smiled and took my face in one of his strong hands, pinching hard. "I am my own master. I choose what I will or will not do. To make it fair, I have taken all but the last of your blood, making you *my* servant. You're familiar with this kind of story, yes? They call it a tether. Terror tales to tell around the campfire. Vampire bites you, controls you, makes you his slave."

I tried to move, but his spell did not lessen as mine had on him.

"Vampires tell it differently. Having a mortal pet can be a weakness. We are warned away in our covens from keeping our victims alive after we bite them because of the tether that binds us. I've known vampires that have fallen in love with their tethers, making foolish choices to save them. It's a complicated place between the unnatural, ravenous love vampires are capable of and mortal friendship. Something new, strange, and even perverse. This will not happen to me, understand? Have no hope of that, rat.

"I came to kill you today, as you could expose me to anyone. And now, make me do things I'd rather not do. But know that my power over you is stronger, slave. I will use it and you will not like it."

I blinked, anger boiling in me hotter than the steam-powered furnaces that dictated our lives. The more I felt my loss of blood, the more something else began to happen in my mind. I started to see flashes of memories that were not mine. They started as a gentle trickle, but the longer he talked and the deeper I looked into his eyes, the more I saw. They were his memories. I saw him with Khalil and Jacque. Saw him standing trial in the Big House. Saw him speaking to an Ecclesiast. Saw him disembarking a train in MidWest. Felt his pain and agony. His fear for his immortal soul. Everything that was him filled me.

"Now, no Black Assassin required." He stood up and lifted me easily in his arms, carrying me to the hole I had caved in. "Tell me why you wanted my blood so badly. Speak."

"To alchemize into stones," I said instantly and against my will. I clamped my mouth shut. "This is like a curse from hell. Release me!" I demanded. Forgetting my own powers over him, he dropped me instantly onto my backside. "Snakes! You bastard." I gnashed my teeth.

"Well done, mortal!" Cecil praised, clapping his hands before crossing them over his chest. "Who was the brave mortal who learned that vampire blood could be alchemized into stones? Who does that?"

I scoffed. "You don't know what a dangerous world this is for vampires. You think you are the monster? The predator?"

At this, Cecil's lips spread into his darkest, most dangerous smile. "Oh, no, little man. You humans are far more the monster than I will ever be."

He didn't say it, but since I had access to his every thought at the moment, I knew he wasn't going to kill me. But he wasn't going to let me go, either.

# 12 AUGMENTATION

Jacque ran to Cecil when we reemerged, eyes wide under her goggles. "I heard shouting," she gasped. "I was distracted, though. Some thugs came and took Khalil. I'm so sorry. I couldn't stop them."

Cecil's face paled and he cast about, looking for his pied friend. "Oh, no," he breathed. His mind spun, wondering if Khalil had left to rat on him, or if what he mentioned about being in too deep before had come to fruition. His emotions permeated me as well. He didn't seem to notice that we shared a mind. Weak and tired, with him distracted, I was able to slink away.

"Where's Redbeard?" he asked. "He was a little too keen on Khalil earlier."

Jacque shrugged. "I knew we shouldn't have trusted him. The way Khalil looks at you gives me the shivers."

Cecil hadn't noticed. He looked around for me, but I was long gone.

"Redbeard's gone to prepare for the rencounter." Her tone dropped with disdain. "That's the event we do once a year to 'thin us out.' A series of tasks and duels. Winners get perks, pardons, rewards—anything Redbeard can swing. Turns this place into a madhouse. Firms form, supporting their favorites. Self-proclaimed authorities like

Redbeard back certain contestants. It's just a bloody popularity contest."

"Sounds like an opportunity," Cecil mused. "When will this rencounter begin?"

Jacque held up a piece of rubylead to her eye, inspecting the clarity. "Hard to say. If you want to know, we should frequent The Red Mary often. That's where he'll announce it."

A day or two passed without Khalil reappearing. Cecil kept his eyes on me as we worked but didn't so much as approach me. His aloof manner towards me, after trying to eat me, made me realize he didn't know we shared a mind. His past popped in and out of my dreams in nonsensical images and feelings. At first, I stayed away from him, but the random thoughts and emotions I felt made more sense if I kept him in my line of sight. I thought he might want to finish the job, so I stayed hidden. But then I got wind of Khalil missing. The rencounter was due to start as well, and I thought I could prove myself to them. Especially since I knew he was looking for a way out. I wanted in on that.

While Jacque was chatting up one of Redbeard's engineers for information about the rencounter, I joined Cecil in sorting genuine froststeel from a faux stone. His eyes glared down at me before sweeping the area and seeing too many witnesses around.

"Bold of you," he mused softly. "Come to offer me the rest of your blood?"

"Actually, I had something else in mind." I curled my fist around a chunk of the cool stone and almost sighed in relief. "Sponsor me in the rencounter," I spat quickly before I lost my nerve. "Help me complete the tasks, show me off in the nightly soirées. I'm a social skunk—you can help me interact with the people. You're pompous and flashy."

A twisted smile lightened the lines of his frown at my backwards compliment. "Why?" he asked. "If I needed to be involved in that, I'd do it myself."

"Because they know me," I cut back. "I've tried before. I've never won. The rencounter is huge down here. It'd be a prime time to gather information and break out."

He locked eyes with me. I'd lost most of the connection to his mind now, but the way his eyes narrowed ever so slightly told me he considered it. "You are disposable, I suppose," he said with a sigh. "And you'd be wanting something in return?"

I nodded. "Take me with you. Get me out of here."

He took in all of me at that moment. I must have looked pathetic. Something in him changed as he stared at me.

Jacque came skipping back up to us. "First meeting is tonight," she said once Cecil signaled her that it was safe to speak in front of me. "Redbeard has something to show us all."

We got back into the heart of San Sous-terre an hour later. With Khalil missing, I led them back through the stinking, dark streets, past the buildings and homes that spewed oil and rank steam into the air. The glowing lights were dim, as always, the only bright spot being the loud saloon. Piano music spilled out of it once again, a singer trying desperately to make the people forget their lives were nothing but digging in the dirt for gems to feed the world above them.

Once inside, Cecil spotted Redbeard in his evening wear. He asked about the finery, but I made him watch the events rather than answer him. This kind of thing was what people like me lived for and others dreaded.

"Welcome to our calendar event!" Redbeard shouted from the stage, where he had thrown the piano man from his seat. He wore a red greatcoat with golden trim and shiny white stockings. "Tonight marks our dungeon's one hundredth anniversary. We will hold our rencounter as we do every year to count our days here and bring life back to us."

"Or death," Jacque said, sighing. "I'd never do it. It's suicide."

"What exactly is it?" Cecil asked as people lined up to sign up. A great ruckus rose as the queue grew. Some people refused to sign up while others tried to force them.

"My favorite thing," I said. "Those who wish to win a place among the politicals go out to face off against nature and the other cunning minds of men. A test of iron will."

"Spades, are you all mad?" Cecil shook his head. "Why? This is The Château d'Oubli. You don't need even more useless bloodshed."

"It's a real shame when a political comes down here, looking for a certain prisoner," I said mockingly, "and they're dead. You see, now? I killed two men ahead of me last time, sunflower," I boasted, and Jacque covered her ears. "Redbeard won. Once, about two years ago, and now he…" I stopped, about to divulge a valuable secret.

Cecil glared at me and held out his hand. "All right, Ezekiel, have it your way. I'll be your spokesman, help you navigate the social side, if you risk life and limb for a few whispers." He smirked. He knew it wasn't an even trade, but he didn't care enough about me to question it.

I shook his cold, ivory hand. "So, Redbeard wins. The next year after that, he sponsors the winner. As these things go, word gets out to the topsiders. So then the Don starts to show up. He slaughters a few prisoners, but also makes a deal with Redbeard. You seen his hoard?" I asked.

Cecil nodded. "He seems to have a nice little operation on some docks near the perimeter."

"Exactly," I went on. "Red makes inventions for the topsiders, special orders. Tests them out on prisoners. Augmentation."

A shadow of doubt passed over Cecil's face. "And everyone knows this?"

"Didn't use to," I corrected. "But over the years, it's gotten out. Now a lot of them try to win his favor. Red's been moving faster these last couple of years. Something is happening topside." And it was killing me that I didn't know what.

"Why do you want to get back up so badly?" Cecil asked. "You seem pretty at home here."

I leaned away, taking a drink of my beer. "I'm not sure we're at that point yet, sunflower. Let's start with this."

A sudden outcry arose from all around us. "You take the wells in the mines!" a young man shouted. "You take all the wells we have saved up. Every well, of every currency. What's next?"

"What I do is for the best," Redbeard shouted over the masses. "That is why the banker has entrusted me to run his wells, too."

Outbursts exploded from the enraged prisoners.

"You cannot take all the currency in The Château d'Oubli under your control!"

"You will take control of our very lives?" one woman shouted, her fist raised.

Redbeard smiled with gold teeth. "I promise you!" He had to shout over the rage once again. "I swear I only have our best interests at heart. I can bring in new tools and machines with this treasure. *Our* treasure. We can invent new technology. Our clockwork has gone beyond the limits of The Château d'Oubli. Trust me. We create. We enhance."

He glanced over the prisoners and saw they were still not convinced. Deciding to strike fear into them, he snapped his fingers and two men in bowler hats hoisted up a pale and shaking body clothed in a pied coat. His handsome face was covered in sweat and grime and his jewelry was tarnished. Khalil.

"I need willing bodies to experiment on for a very notable client," Redbeard went on. "But it doesn't have to be you. Don't make yourselves my enemies. Stand by me and bask in the wealth I can bring us all. Regardes vous!" Redbeard called, pulling a green cloak off Khalil's shoulders. The people gasped and Jacque covered her mouth, her eyes popping in surprise and abhorrence. She gagged.

Where once had been a strong, muscular arm at Khalil's side, there now hung a cold and twisted array of machinations and gears. There were many different alloys making up the automatonic arm so that it seemed to glimmer and change shade as he shifted. It moved with a mysterious and complex grace, covered in switches and little things that clicked into other positions, but it was still grotesque. A part of him had been torn off to make way for the mechanical member.

"Mother of pearl," Jacque finally whispered like a curse. "What have they done to him?"

Part of my stomach churned.

"How?" Cecil said, finally finding his voice. "Why?"

"Your shock is disturbing," I pointed out. "I'd have thought a killer like you would wonder at such a mechanical miracle."

"I'll leave that to you, Ezekiel," he snarled.

"But why him?" Silent tears rolled down Jacque's dark face.

"He wanted out," Cecil said, eyes still glued to Redbeard's demonstration. "He said he knew he'd gotten in too deep."

I could read the concern on Cecil's face. He worried Khalil might have ratted on him. He worried it might be too late to escape now.

"Damn it," he hissed. Cecil made his way to the front slowly. "We have to get him," he said over his shoulder to Jacque. She nodded and ran past him up to the front where Redbeard finished off the signups for the contest, gloating about the piece of machinery as well.

"This is just a small example of what we can build," he said, from the stage above the table he'd planted Khalil at. "This is why I need those wells. What I do is for all of us."

"Khalil," Cecil cooed softly, taking a seat at the table among more men in fancy greatcoats who drank and looked over the events for the rencounter and the signups. "Can you hear me?"

"Snakes, Cecil, I'm in pain, not deaf," he replied, his voice strained, parched. The beautiful clockwork tech ran up his neck to the side of his head. Ornate metal plate with a small, green, glowing tube ran along one side of his head. Blood still seeped out from underneath it where they must have cut his into his skull. The rotlead band around his neck shone more than ours, no soot or dust: it was new. "Jacque," he said softly, "I know you hate menial work, but would you be a dear and fetch me some water?"

She didn't even arch a disapproving brow at him. She got up and came back in a matter of seconds. "Used some of my own shinies to get you some ice, too." She handed him the metal tankard and he chugged quickly.

"Slow down." Cecil took the tankard away from his cracked lips. "Why did this happen to you?"

Khalil's chest heaved as he gasped after the long drink. "Part of my time here, Cecil. Just...part of the sentence." He leaned his head back and closed his eyes, clutching the ticking medallion around his neck. It hadn't been ticking the last time Cecil saw it.

"Let's take him home," Jacque said. "Get him settled before the next shift."

# THE PRINCE OF MIDWEST

I led them through narrow alleys, behind the stinking backs of the inner city to where Cecil told me Khalil's boathouse sat. We had to wake Khalil long enough to get him to open his puzzle lock, but once inside, he drifted away again.

"Go upstairs and see if you can find any kind of medicine to stave off the infection," Cecil instructed me. "Jacque, get some water boiling and find any kind of cloth we can use to lay over him to ease the pain."

I flew up the tight, metal spiral stairs into the upper level of Khalil's shanty house. None of it looked familiar, so I know Cecil had never been up here. Makeshift glass cabinets lined one wall and other steam-powered and chem-powered devices lay on shelves. An old trunk rested next to one hutch with chains wrapped around and through the wrought iron handles. Curious, I pulled the chain off and looked inside. Jars of different geo dust, knives of various metals, and sharp pendants of colorful quartzes lined the shelves. A few other instruments were scattered among them. The last object that caught my eye was a brass cauldron—the one absolutely necessary component to alchemy. Empty vials surrounded it. The smallest bit of liquid purples, greens, and some reds lay in the rounded corners of the vials.

Khalil had an entire arsenal of geos. The brass cauldron was clean, and I could see in the dust prints under it that it had been moved recently. What was this little rat getting ready to alchemize?

Flipping open the trunk next to it, I froze. Not out of fear, but out of fascination. Inside were all the tricks and tools of the trade usually reserved for the Wardens above: a large pewter cross, wooden and silver stakes, partially empty crystal beakers of holy water, and a few other bits and bobs. None of them looked recently used and were covered in a soft layer of Château dust.

Closing the lid softly, I went to another cabinet and pulled out some cleaning alcohol and a few bottles of herbs for pain. So Khalil had a past of alchemy. Then he had to know what Cecil was. But he hadn't killed him. Or harvested his blood. Yet? I wasn't sure. Was he waiting? Or did he really not want to take Cecil's precious vampire blood?

Before I went back down, I thought about snatching the hunting box and forcing Khalil out into the open. But I stalled; if I did that now, I'd ruin our escape attempt. And I wanted out bad.

When I got back, Cecil and Jacque were administering aid to Khalil.

"I can't believe you let him do this to you," Jacque hissed, pulling his long hair up and tying it off his neck before dabbing at his clammy flesh.

Cecil looked at Khalil with a little less sympathy and a little more suspicion. "Did you tell him anything about us?" he asked.

"Spades, Cecil, this had nothing to do with that," Khalil said with a sigh, leaning back as Jacque guided him. "Redbeard tests his augmentations out on lots of people. It's part of his bargain with the politicals above. You'll see once the Don is down here for the rencounter."

"The Don?" I snapped, coming to attention. I'd hoped he wouldn't come down this time.

"Scared to face him?" Cecil asked me. He spoke genially, but I caught the taunt in his tone.

"Everyone is," Jacque reasoned. "Every time he participates, he wins. No one wants to kill royalty."

Cecil sighed, finishing binding Khalil's gruesome wound. "We may need to rethink our plan, then." His eyes drifted to me.

I felt his intentions more than saw them this time. I was just a loose screw in his plan. I was in danger.

With Khalil's augmentation, Cecil took some time to let him rest and I made myself scarce. A few days into waiting, Cecil grew anxious.

He and Jacque worked on the grand mechanics of the walls. Some of the older walls were covered in gears and belts to pull the trains along. This made an entire wall into a great face of a mechanical mountain. Just as hunger hit Cecil, Redbeard came by with an entire entourage of royal guard. Cecil froze and pulled his hat low over his face.

"The Duke's guard." Jacque nodded to Don Mateo. "That one there with the adventurous mustache and keen eyes? That's the Dukes's half-brother."

Cecil nodded. "I've seen him before."

"I'm shocked Redbeard didn't come up with some excuse to keep him out of The Château this time around."

"Why's that?" Cecil asked. He eyed the Don like a raptor. It would be so easy for him to slay the man. Make his life end, therefore making his whole plan easier. He licked his parched lips.

"Because Red skims off the top of the gemstones we send up top." She nodded towards the perimeter. "I figured that'd make the topsiders mad."

Cecil nodded, agreeing. "So he'll participate in the rencounter? Or just watch? Are there bets and wagers? Is it fixed?"

Jacque adorably bit her tongue between her teeth as she coaxed the machine back to life with her loving touch. "It ain't fixed. Darn near about the only thing down here that ain't. No need to. People are foolhardy in this contest. It's our way of keeping life lubricated with adrenaline. And for Red to get his due and snuff out people who might peach on him or who think about taking his place. Also to show off his augments."

"That's what I mean," Cecil interjected. "How does he do that?"

She shrugged and pursed her lips. "Assassins, pays off another contestant, pays some to bow out. Always backs the Don. I don't know."

Plans were about to start ticking in the halls of the great Château d'Oubli, and it might be an opportunity to put his own in motion. Cecil slinked back into town to find Khalil in his own home, organizing what looked to be a metal chemistry set. The Egyptian jumped when Cecil entered but quickly caught his breath.

"I thought you were the guard," he hissed, shoving his beaker and things away into a cabinet with one clumsy, shaking hand.

"They are here to watch the contest." Cecil peeked out the window. He didn't see anyone; the other prisoners were sleeping or out at work. He heard the clicking of Khalil's mechanical arm. "Tell me what happened last time. Ezekiel didn't win?"

Khalil shook his head. "Lost on the last task."

"How many are there?"

"Three. Each one requires proof of completion."

"To Redbeard?" Cecil rubbed his clean chin, then went on to fiddle with his long hair. "Why do I get the feeling he just works down here for the topsiders?"

Khalil unclenched his robotic fingers and his eyes glassed over, as though reliving the moment his arm was torn from his body. "Probably because he does. He does everything to please the Don. The Don is pretty much the only contact the politicals have with this place, so Red does what he can to impress him."

He clenched his jaw tightly. *We have too many moving pieces,* Cecil thought. *I need to get rid of some.* "Where is Ezekiel?"

Khalil pointed out back of his house. "The first task is to go out and hunt an underman. He will be miles from here now. He's been out for hours."

Cecil dashed out the door, his legs pumping madly and faster than any human. Ignoring the gasps around him once he left the city boundaries, he leapt and latched onto the wall, climbing up and down into the tunnels. His fear of losing a contact and ally to the underground pushed his limits. In a matter of an hour, he was deep underground. He stopped when he came across the glow caves. They were not full of solar adamant, but instead alive with the crawling lunar bugs that we all called loonies. Softly white moongems peeked out from the dirt. These geos grew in perfect orbs out of the rock. Like pyrite, but spherical and glowing. He spotted me gathering up some in my satchel to take deeper underground.

Cecil licked his lips, deciding to follow me. Digging his claws into the rock, he pulled himself closer to the ceiling and into the darkness. He sniffed the air only to have a foul, sour stench rise up his nostrils. In the darkness, his eyes showed him two cold figures with crude spears in their hands. They crouched, eyes trained on me. I had no idea they were stalking me. I had walked miles out, but thought I was still far from the nearest underman settlement.

The pale undermen had three limbs on the ground, one arm raised above their heads, holding spears. Their eyes glimmered with the moongems, devoured in the hopes of gaining heat-sight in the darkness. Chunks of their own skin had been cut out of their legs and arms. They did this when food grew especially scarce, feasting on their own flesh. This, and with the solitude and black water, made them mad. With no language, they were less man and more animal. And they bred in the darkness. The first task had been implemented as a way to minimize their numbers and keep them at bay.

The undermen were ready to pounce and devour me alive when Cecil leapt down. With his animal-like shriek, he bared his teeth and showed his claws. With a guttural yap, one underman heaved his spear at Cecil with deadly force. But the point never struck flesh. As easily as catching a baseball, Cecil caught the spear out of the air. The angry underman took out a knife carved from rock and leapt off all fours at Cecil while the second came at me.

I saw them now and did what any coward would have done: I ran away. The screams of the undermen followed me down the dark passages until finally they stopped with the cracking of bones and the twisting of necks. I skidded to a clumsy stop and looked back, one moongem still clutched in my fist. I saw nothing, everything silent and cold.

"You are the best coward I have ever met."

I screamed and jumped back from the shadow behind me that had spoken into the silence. "Show yourself!" I demanded.

Our tether forcing him out, Cecil stepped into view, licked his lips, and then spat a great stream of foul blood from between his lips.

"They taste wretched," he said simply.

"Snakes, you monster!" I tried to sound defensive and angry, but my heart pounded with hot fear.

"Fool. I saved you."

I saw his white fingers tense up, desiring to strangle me. A tiny sliver of his thoughts came to me again. He was here to kill me.

"But I shouldn't have," he went on. "The Don is here, and Redbeard is preparing to add to his horde again." He took a breath and spat again, making a face that hinted at vomiting. "You are useless to me, Ezekiel. And I've told you too much."

I stepped back. The dandy suddenly grew quite terrifying. I could almost reach out and touch his anger, like a curtain over him.

"I can still help," I stammered. "You can trust *me*. Just let me finish this task."

I turned to leave, but he flashed around me, blocking my path. I swallowed.

"You are nothing. You can help in filling my belly, though." He did his dark half-smile and locked his eyes with mine just under the brim of his black hat. "I'm done being underground. But I can't leave loose ends."

I leapt away, running back the way we had come, back to the two dead undermen. I gasped when I beheld their heinous forms. Their eyeballs poked out of their drained faces. I could see the outline of their teeth under their empty lips, like sheets laid over bones.

"You know you can't run from me," Cecil said in his dangerous sing-song voice. He blinked before me again.

"You'll regret this!" I yelped.

"Yes," he snapped. "I hate to go back on my vow to never take a life, but I think the powers that be will make an exception for a rat like you."

He gripped my hair and pulled my head back painfully to my shoulder. I put my hands on his chest and tried to shove him away with all my strength. I pushed so hard I felt my arms would break.

"Stop! Stop!" I commanded. But too late.

The familiar puncture stopped my voice. His teeth popped into my neck like sharp knives. I couldn't even feel the pain until a moment later. My blood struggled to keep flowing, but the force of his hunger sucked it back up and out. My face tingled and my brain spun for lack of air.

Cecil jerked back with a cry of pain, his hand clasped over his burning lips. "Silver? Really, fool?" He spat again, his face blackening from the burning. The veins in his neck glowing like cinders, flickering. "Very well. I'll rip your heart out instead."

He flew at me, his claws dug into my chest like writhing knives, and I cried out with him in harmony as my silver-tainted blood burned him again. He raised his other hand to claw me.

"Don't!" I screamed. "I'm the one you're looking for. I'm High Prince Ezekiel Aurelium of the American Empire!"

# 14 The Teather

"Liar," Cecil hissed accusingly, but he stayed his clawed hand. "I don't know the damned prince's name. But I know you're no royalty."

A drop of my poisonous blood trickled down his chin, sizzling the whole way. He licked his lips and let go of me, wiping away the blood. "Clever, that. The silver in you."

I scrambled away from him once his grip slackened, planting myself between the dead undermen where I could take up their weapons if I needed to. "If I'm so weak, why kill me, then?" I asked, my voice low to stop the quaking. I could feel my heart pulsating like a butterfly in panic under my chest. "Why not let something else finish me off?"

"It's not you I want," Cecil replied, not meeting my eyes. "I don't care who you say you are; you are no prince. How many mothers name their children after royalty? You must be one of a hundred Ezekiel's your age—if that even is the name of the prince."

"I can't prove it to you, can I?" My neck tingled and a coldness started to inch over my skin.

He didn't move, pace, or show any sign that he considered my words. Neither of us spoke, me from fear of what might come next and him from disbelief. His blood boiled underneath the surface of his white skin and my words did not shake him. He stood like stone. Not even a furrow in his brow from thought. His face glassed over to a mask of defense I could not see through. A tiny tinge of his doubt entered my mind through our blood bond. But he also searched for why I would confess to being the prince he sought.

"You can prove it, Ezekiel," he said suddenly.

"High Prince Ezekiel Aurelium," I corrected him. "Born September 10, 1850 to King Markus of the American Empire and Queen Camille, a princess of France."

Cecil snorted and smiled falsely. "I assume everyone in the colonies knows who the royal family are and their birthdays. You Americans only celebrate them every year. In excess. Try again. You like games. That was try number one; you get two more. If I'm not convinced, I finish you off."

I wet my dry lips and nodded. I only had one thought: I didn't want to die here in this place with his lips fixed to my neck like a perverted lover. If there was even the smallest chance that he could return me to the surface, then I would take it.

Having one's blood drained sure does put a new perspective on things.

"The Don!" I stammered. "He'll recognize me."

Cecil laughed darkly and licked his sharp teeth. The bond between our minds let me know he liked my blood. A lot. With him feeding on me again, our minds had linked up strongly once more. He wanted to eat me. He liked the salty taste of my blood.

"I doubt he would," Cecil supplied, squaring up to face me again. "They told me you were dead."

I gulped. I was dead?

Cecil took in my startled expression, and I felt his fervor melt just a little. He narrowed his eyes at me, considering.

"You've been gone from Kansouri for eight years," he said steadily, measuring my every breath. I saw his thoughts: *His surprise is genuine. Doesn't matter.*

"Why not?" I asked. "Why doesn't it matter? I can't prove it to you. Take me back to San Sous-terre. Show me to the Don."

His face fell into an annoyed glower. "The tether. You can see into my mind, hear my thoughts."

"You can't see mine?" I asked.

He shook his head. "Damn it!" he growled, punching the air. His duster twirled around him in rage. *I should finish him off,* he thought.

"Don't!" I said again. I almost thought about falling to my knees and begging. "Help me bring back the undermen for the first task. Let me do the next task. We can still get out of here. I *am* the prince; I'm the one you're looking for. How is this not a good thing?"

He whirled on me and bore down until I cowered under him. "Why didn't you tell me that the first night, when we played Black Assassin?"

I steadied myself before replying. "Because I want revenge."

*Oh, I see,* he thought. "I'm not sure that aligns with what I need," he said out loud.

"Exactly," I replied. "Your intentions are so noble, and I am—"

"A rat? A liar? A coward?" he supplied a little too quickly. "Eager to kill if given the chance?"

"Help me," I bargained. "All you have to do is get me out of here." With something like a posh vampire on my side, could I really lose? He was strong. He would be good cover. And despite him trying to kill me, I liked his sarcasm and wit.

With a scoff, Cecil leaned against the cave wall, crossed his arms, looking down at the mangled undermen. "It won't be that easy. Let's say I do believe you, *your highness,*" he said mockingly. "I still don't know how to get out."

I smiled. This was my area. "Make me popular. I have to be to go up against the Don."

He cut me off. "Spades to the rencounter. We need to get out."

I shook my head. "The more popular I am for the rencounter, the more people down here will help me out." I shoved myself up and paced around the corpses. "We need an airship to get out those tunnels, and the more people I have giving me support, the easier it will be to get supplies. They'll be distracted by the show I'll give them, going up against the Don. We can take Redbeard's hoard, too."

"What for?" he snapped.

"For me. For my revenge."

Cecil tilted his head, listening.

"Once we're out of here," I went on, "they won't just let me back into the palace. Especially with the Duke in control."

Cecil rubbed his chin. He almost smiled at me, as though he might have found something inside me to be fond of. "I suppose this won't be the quick jaunt I thought it was. There's too much we don't know. But, for once, you are right." He shoved himself off the wall and made his way back down the tunnels. "I still don't believe you," he called back. "You have one try left."

The only way Cecil would be convinced would be for me to face the Don, the man who'd killed my father. He would recognize me. I knew he would.

Cecil and I were in sight of Khalil's boathouse when he and Jacque came sprinting up from a side street, ducking as they ran. When they saw us, they waved for silence. Jacque grabbed Cecil's hand, pulling him into a crouch, and the four of us bolted away. Jacque led us down some twisting old streets with leaning buildings and out-of-commission steam engines. Tracks long unused lined the road. Once we were a good distance away, she stood up, gasping for air.

"Redbeard was there," she panted.

"Looking for me," Khalil added through a large puff of air.

Cecil moaned and rubbed his temples.

"Don't worry," Jacque said, smiling. "I have a place we can make our headquarters."

The vampire winced but looked quizzical.

"We need a headquarters, right?" she asked, beaming. "A place to lay our plans, build our getaway?" She clapped her knuckles together. Her enthusiasm was adorable. The engineer in her came out. "I've been prepping the top floor at my place. Follow me."

She guided us through the abandoned slums to a place long forgotten by most of The Château d'Oubli. A few tall, dangerously leaning homesteads dotted the dark cave. Jacque's home surprised me more than anything else I had ever seen in The Château d'Oubli. It was an actual house, made after what they called the Victorian style of

Angleterre. It had sweeping turrets and a vicious-looking pointed fence all around it. Almost as though it had flown from Angleterre and landed in The Château d'Oubli by mistake. Even a little garden grew outback where she raised a strange variety of herb I had never seen. It was lined with dim solar adamant.

Pillars rose up in front of the double door entrance and the inside held even more splendor. Red velvet stairs (moth-eaten, but what wasn't?), chandeliers like spiders hanging in every room (covered in spider webs), a piano in a room off to the side with a dim fireplace, marble floors (cracked), and gas lamps throughout the house. It was the grandest thing I had seen in fifteen years. Cecil ran his finger along the elaborate wooden railing leading up a swirling staircase, his fingertip getting covered in a thick, grey layer of dust. Looking around, we saw mansions built by spiders and that dusty blanket all over.

"Jafa!" she called once we were all properly inside. "Grandpère, où es-tu??"

A door above us on the second floor opened with a creak and a groan. An old man with midnight skin and long, white hair looked down at us through a set of goggles. His too-big overalls hung off a thin body. He held a soldering iron in one hand.

"Greetings," he said slowly in a deep, rich timber. "So, you are the ones come to take my granddaughter away."

Khalil and I both pointed to Cecil.

The vampire snapped his head to each of us in turn, stuttering. "It's not like that," he defended in his posh accent.

"I don't care what it's like," Jafa said, sighing sadly. "Take her. Free her. Giver her the life that was taken from us." His eyes shot to Cecil for a hard minute. He pulled at his goggles and turned back into the room he'd come from.

Cecil turned back to us. "What a charming man. Now, let's decide how we want to play this rencounter. You all have seen it before. What would be best, considering our final goal?"

Khalil flexed his automatonic arm, calculating our options. "Depends on how visible you want to be."

"Just enough," Cecil answered, eyeing me. "We want some on our side so we can gather supplies. Jacque, airship?"

She smiled so broadly her eyes watered. "Can do!"

"I'll work with you on that," I interjected. "I have an idea for getting away with Redbeard's hoard, if we can."

Khalil bit his bottom lip. "Why?"

"For after," I said flatly. "Once we're out. Cecil's mission doesn't stop there. Right?" I glared at him.

"Unfortunately," Cecil mumbled, running his hand over his chin. "And I think you're right, Ezekiel. Once we're out, we will need a leg to stand on."

Jacque perked up. "I thought the plan was to get out?"

I locked eyes with Cecil. "Tell them."

The vampire crossed his arms, considering me. "Ezekiel here claims to be the one I seek. I don't believe him." He looked to Khalil. "Tell me, Syndicate spy, does he resemble the royals?"

Jacque's mouth fell open as she stared at me with wide eyes. "Why? How?" she stammered.

I turned to face the nomad and opened my arms. "I swear I am Prince Ezekiel. I was sent down here when I was ten years old. Just after my father died."

To my surprise, Khalil tilted his head and nodded a little. "I might be able to see it. The timeline is right, too. But who would have you sent to The Château d'Oubli? Or who would have you sent here rather than kill you?"

The constant discussion of why I wasn't dead started to grind my gears.

"Something we might be able to answer sooner or later," Cecil mused, still taking me in. "I want proof before we go too much farther. So, we're introducing him to the Don."

Jacque gasped and almost took my hand in concern. I wish she would have. "He'll kill him!" she cried.

"Maybe," Cecil replied. "The Duke of Dakota knew I'd mentioned the supposed dead prince. He sent me down here. If he killed King Markus, then why didn't he kill Ezekiel, too?"

I audibly groaned and rolled my eyes. Was I the only one glad I was alive?

Cecil turned to Khalil. "Well? Any ideas?"

The nomad shrugged. "Unfortunately, no." He looked me up and down one more time. "I don't see it. Sorry, Ez." He smirked. "Not sure I'd want the likes of you on the throne anyway."

I made a pitiful scowl and balled my fist. I could have outed him right there, but I was just as guilty of wanting Cecil's blood.

Jacque must have sensed the tension because she stepped between all three of us, hands out. "Stop now, hey? We need to deal with the rencounter first." She looked at the bloody bag at my side where I'd stowed the head of one of the undermen Cecil had killed. "Let's get some things under our control."

God bless Jacque and her collected, calm engineer brain. "Right." I hefted the bag over my shoulder. "Sunflower, you and I are going to the bank. Need to put some fear into Moriart so I can access some funds to give to my soon-to-be adoring firm."

"Don't forget to go to The Red Mary tonight," Khalil called after us. "Present your underman head to Redbeard."

Cecil opened the door for me and made a mock bow. "And meet the Don, *your highness*."

I shoved past him.

# On Top

Cecil's thoughts rang in my head as we made our way to the bank. Work slowed to an all-out slog as the rencounter picked up steam. Soon, it would stop all together. The prisoners who partook prepared for whatever task Redbeard might dream up. Some made vehicles, others tried their luck at creating chem-tech weapons. We also spotted a few roughly made banners and arm bands in similar colors.

"Firms," I informed Cecil. "They support certain contestants."

"Do we need one?" he asked, eyeing the gang.

"Wouldn't hurt." And the bank was a good place to start.

The banker, Moriart, grimaced upon seeing me.

"No tricks today, Ez," he said, sighing and eyeing a gem through a glass with varying colors of lenses. "I want none of your shady spades or shinies. Redbeard paid me a chip of time-platium to cut you if I saw you sneaking around here. But it's been a while since I've cut you for the fun of it." He stopped and looked over my shoulder at Cecil. He narrowed his eyes, flipping the lenses up to see more clearly. "Why are you back here?"

"To stop you from cutting Ezekiel," he said smoothly.

Moriart blanched. I emptied the small pouches of my belt onto the counter and spread the glinting jewels out. "What's in, Moriart? I need currency."

"So does everyone else," the grimy banker replied, setting aside his lenses. "Until the first task is finished, I am not allowed to trade. Redbeard's orders. I'll be whipped just for letting you go without a scratch."

I took the opportunity to act like the badass I'd told Cecil I could be. Something like the spirit of a wild coyote rose up in me. I leaned into its rabid nature, emboldened by Cecil's presence. I reclined onto the bar with all my weight and tilted my hat down, shaking my head.

"Moriart, sir, I'm in the rencounter. I have bagged two undermen. I'm good for it."

Moriart smirked, but rubbed his two oily hands together, licking his lips. "Enticing, Ez. But where's the proof? You're nothing but a con and a cheat. And a liar. I've not forgotten what you did on the riverboat."

"The foolishness of a young cowboy." I picked up a lasso from the pile of junk nearest me and gave it a couple twirls around my head. Moriart's eyes were bored, wandering over the things on the bar. I waited until he reached for a shiny emerald.

With a snap of my wrist, I brought the lasso down around his neck and pulled, instantly cutting off the scream and burning his neck. I pulled him over the bar and leaped on top, winding the rope around his arms and placing my spur against his neck.

"Don't move," I hissed. I took a leather sack from my back. "Here is your proof, sir." I slowly tipped the bag down over his face. A thick, black stream of blood trickled out and splattered his face, making smacking noises as it covered him.

"Blah!" he gagged, trying to wipe the thick blood away.

I shook it one last time and the two severed heads of the undermen fell out, plunking onto Moriart's chest. One rolled off, but the other knocked the breath out of him and stared him right in the eye.

He shrieked like a scared mouse. He flailed his free hand, knocking the head off the bar and across the floor to the door. "What the hell you need those damned spurs for down here?" he choked when one cut him on the surface.

"As you see." I dropped the bag and took out my revolver. "Cheat's a nasty word, and liar's just a false way saying I know shit you don't." I dug my heal into his neck a little harder. "These spurs aren't just for show." I ran it slowly over his neck, making it spin. "It's immorta," I said. I chanced a glance up at Cecil. The vampire had turned to stone, watching me. "Some of the strongest alloy we've ever found. Also gives wicked dreams." I dug my heal into Moriart's neck again.

"Stop it!" the banker shouted, trying to twist out of my grip. "Redbeard will hear about this, Ezekiel!"

"I have a friend here," I said, indicating Cecil, "who watches over me, Mor. I strongly suggest not upsetting him. See, not everyone is willing to do what I am to protect myself. You're vulnerable. Now, you've stolen quite a lot from me, Moriart. Cheated me out of some nice trades, given me less than what was worth at the behest of other men, and given me a beating just 'cause Red said to. I'd say that warrants a hand." I pressed the barrel of my revolver into the soft underside of his wrist and drew back the hammer.

"No!" the banker screamed. "I'll trade. I know you, Ez; you're good for it. You're good for it." He said it twice to convince himself. "Here." He reached up to his neck and took the bronze key from around his oily head and handed it to me. "The vault's behind that wall of bars."

"Thank you, sir." I tucked the key into a pocket inside my vest. With a grunt, I brought my heel down over his bound wrist. I had to press down harder than I thought to crack through the bone. And I didn't expect his screaming and wailing to be so loud, either.

Moriart shouted curses and vile words and made animalistic noises as I went to withdraw what I wanted from the vault. He didn't bother me as I filled my bag and pouches with whatever suited my fancy. I needed currency to pay my way and to encourage other to lay heavy bets me. I needed people rooting for me as soon as I could so they'd be willing to show me where I could get the supplies we needed. Cecil didn't budge and followed me out silently.

I'd never felt power and authority like that before. Never had someone have my back. On the high from crunching Moriart's bones, I went out and traded for some finer threads. I wanted to change before going to The Red Mary.

"Do we have time for this?" Cecil asked once we were back at Jacque's home.

I flipped one of the coats I'd bargained for onto my shoulders. "I thought you'd appreciate this. Isn't fashion one of your passions?" I grabbed a black cane with a red ruby atop it and held it in front of me.

"Snakes," Cecil swore, grabbing the cane from me. He stopped, noting another coat in the heap I had. He reached down and snatched it up, polishing the buttons. "This is mine. And second, nothing down here can be considered fashion." He eyed me in the mirror. "Though I suppose it won't hurt."

"If you think no one here cares about clothes, why are you polishing those damn golden buttons?" I glared hard at him, having to turn my head around to see him behind me; he had no image in the mirror before me.

"This coat was given to me by the queen of Australia," he replied, as if that settled it. "I thank you for retrieving it, though."

"Of course it was."

He glared at my tone. "You might want to think about presentation, *your highness*. Especially once we get out of here." He went to the second button. "The Ecclesiast said I have to get you on the throne. Seems like an impossible task."

"Stop polishing those stupid buttons," I ordered.

His fingers faltered and his face twisted as he tried to throw off my command. Our tether was still strong. His hands shook against my will until the coat finally dropped to the floor between his fingers. His eyes slowly came up from it to my eyes, his head still bent low, making him look like a hunting cat, his brows arched sharply.

"So, it has come back to that game has it?" he whispered.

I turned to face him, no longer trusting him to be behind me when I could not see his reflection. "I'm not afraid of you."

"You think a little silver in your blood will stop me from killing you if you push me too far, *your highness*?"

I stiffened my knees to keep them steady. "No. I believe that title will, though, *vampire*. I am valuable to you."

Cecil sneered. "I'm not sure you're worth my soul right now." His hand stopped halfway through smoothing his hair. "I'm done with this game." He glared down at me with his violet eyes, his black brows casting darker shadows around them. "I command you, tether, to never order me to obey again."

"But it's my favorite game."

I drew my revolver, but his hand clamped around my neck, his whole body smashing me against the mirror. Shards and glittering powder rained down on us. He wasn't sure what kind of bullets I had in the gun and was taking no chances. His face contorted again into the snarling monster he had been in the caves. Even with yards of velvet, lace, and silk covering his body, I could feel the transformation occur. His fangs elongated before my eyes. The pressure built in my head as he squeezed. I had a way of making him snap. Vampires are volatile.

"Give me a reason, High Prince Ezekiel of the American Empire, to not kill you and be done with this episode of my life." His spit flecked my face, his words hissing through his teeth. Where bits of the silver backing of the mirror landed on his skin, it sizzled. "Why do you tempt this monster?" he murmured.

I realized my toes were not on the ground. I reached, but my boots couldn't find the hardwood floor. "You need me," I gasped, channeling my full fury into my voice. Cecil exhaled in a dark laugh and ever so slowly shook his head.

He might be able to find another way to redemption. He had forever. I didn't. Choking, I looked into his eyes and told the truth. "I—I need you." I couldn't stop the pathetic whimpers coming out of me. Through our tether, a wash of powerful emotions emanated from him at my confession.

His black eyebrows twitched and his violet eyes softened. His cold fingers loosened and I fell at his feet, gasping and coughing. I blinked and took deep breaths, trying to stop the world from spinning. His shiny boots didn't budge.

"Ezekiel, your highness, it is imperative that you look your best this evening. We cannot risk the Don not recognizing you." His voice whispered softly, the monster in him retreating.

I rubbed my neck and stood up. "It's been eight years underground, miles beneath the surface. I doubt he will know me. However," I added quickly, seeing the glint in his eye, "I will do as you advise."

He nodded. His mind faded from me, his thoughts and feelings with them. The tether between us weakened when he did not feed on me. I was curious, though: I'd heard stories about how it was the other way around. Vampires could read the minds of the mortals they were tethered to. But the roles were flipped. If only he could see my mind, he'd know who I was.

"What if he tries to kill me?" I asked. I hadn't had the courage to stand up yet. The feelings of being on top for just an afternoon melted away like froststeel in a blazing forge. I had felt bold and unafraid for the first time in eight years and Cecil took that feeling just as fast.

Cecil smoothed the front of his coat before heading out the door, looking back at me with just his eyes. "I won't let him harm you, your highness."

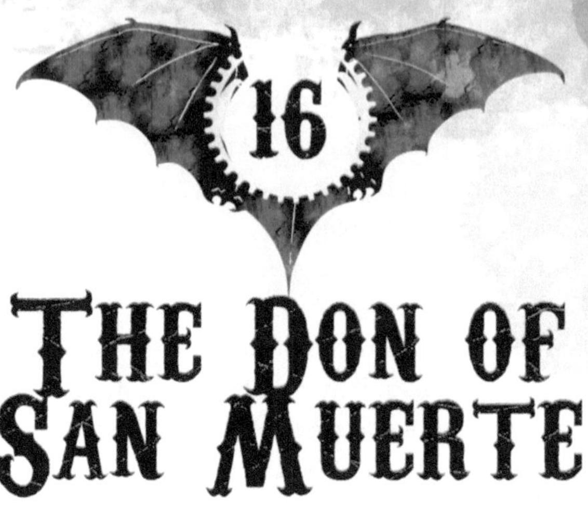

# 16
# The Don of San Muerte

I lashed the two severed heads of the undermen to my belt (much to Jacque's disgust) with the lasso I'd stolen from Moriart. I bargained with a stall near the saloon for two special pistols he had hidden under his cart. When I asked to see his best, he had laughed and said no one could afford them. I had the best shinies from the bank, though. Eventually he gave up a custom pair of long-barreled revolvers he'd had commissioned for some other up-and-comer Redbeard had offed. They were thicker than regular ones, shot larger bullets, and had ornate designs welded into the butts.

I kept taking them out and twirling them, trying to land my finger on the trigger every time as we walked to The Red Mary with the rest of the masses. I felt Cecil watching me out of the corner of his eyes and smirking. When I finally got it right, I smiled. I tried it again and this time flipped them straight into my holster, but got the trigger guard caught on the many belts of bullets I had slung around my hips. I quickly slipped the gun away, along with my embarrassment.

The lanes all around The Red Mary lit up with colored lanterns in red, white, and blue, showing their false appreciation for the America above them. Flags and cockades adorned the windowpanes, and extra harlots gathered around the door to tempt men. From the number of armed men and flocking women, I realized the Don was already inside.

I pulled my hat low, not from a desire for mystery, but out of a fear of seeing him. I knew I would recognize him, but I prayed he did not see me. I gripped my pistols tightly. Behind me, I felt Cecil push Jacque out of the way and take her place just beside me. His arm touched mine lightly. He'd said he wouldn't let my uncle harm me, but he'd also intended to force me to face him to prove I was the prince he sought.

"Spades, stop shaking, you dolt," he hissed.

I rolled my eyes, sighing.

"You are—will be—the victor of the rencounter. At least act like it."

I hadn't realized I was shaking. Knowing I had to show myself to the man responsible for my father's death, coupled with Cecil's violent outburst before, rattled me.

"You are the rattlesnake king," Jacque added. I could hear her smile as she thumped my shoulders hard. I liked it. "Your words are poison, your smile is sharp. Your eyes know every secret. Your ears hear every vibration." She giggled.

My heart slowed and my steps got stronger, the heels of my boots digging into the ground. With the best wicked grin I could muster, I pushed the swinging doors of the saloon open hard enough for them to bang into the wall behind them. When they swung back, Khalil and Cecil caught them, holding them open for me. I stood akimbo, hands in belt loops, head turned down, my prizes in the light on my hip.

All the eyes fell on me. I froze.

"Walk to a table, Ezekiel," Cecil hissed after a little too long of posing in the door like fools.

I started and they followed. The eyes slowly drifted away from me. We all sat down, Cecil pulling the chair out for me. I put my big black boots up onto the table and ordered beers for us all.

"Well played," Cecil said, swishing his coattails out and seating himself down on the edge of his chair.

"I think this wench should dress the part, too," I said, aiming a finger at Jacque like a gun and winking. I expected her to frown at me, chide me with her eyes. But she blushed and scooted closer to Cecil.

"Don't you wish," she smirked, immune to my jibes.

Cecil scanned the place and spotted Redbeard on the upper level making his way down. His blazing red greatcoat swished around his over-polished boots. At the bar, sitting with his back against it, sat Don Mateo. He wore a black leather duster framed with white fur around the front and shoulders. His black hair was brushed back and shone like fresh ephemeral adamant in a full moon. Since I had last seen him, he had collected scars on his face that he had turned into war-like tribal tattoos. At his side were his famous ringing blades. Whenever he threw one, it landed with a thud and hummed a tone, triggering kinetic vibrations. If memory served me, his in particular were tuned to harmonize.

I swallowed hard and Cecil heard it. "Don't worry," he said. "I won't force you over there yet. First, we turn in our heads, make sure you pass this task."

No sooner had Cecil said this than Red's voice rang out. "My fine dungeon rats!" He leapt up onto a crate atop the bar. "Bring your prizes forth and be judged."

This prompted a mix of outrage and cheering from the people as they realized they'd have to march before the Don. Fortunately for them, Redbeard could not distinguish who cheered and who shouted.

"Curse the Don!" a man with a yellow beard shouted. "No one topsider should have a sponsor, Red!"

A few around him shouted their approval. After all, it most likely had been some form of political who had sent them here. Why would they want one of them down below?

"He has to play by our rules!" Cecil shouted. He leapt up onto a table and raised his glamorous arms out to the people, his back to Redbeard. I rolled my eyes. He was such a whore for drama.

"Don Mateo," Cecil began, turning to face him. "Do you remember me?"

The Don didn't move from where he lounged. Slowly, he took a drink of some dirty whiskey in an even dirtier glass. His eyes remained calm. "I do," he said in his soft, deep voice. He took another drink, indicating he wouldn't say more in front of all these people.

"Good." Cecil turned to the crowd. "I'm no rich Don. I am one of you. *He* is one of you." He pointed to me and I ducked my face down, hiding it. "We know we are not the loyalest of folks, but this is our home. Which is why I urge you, fellow citizens of San Sous-terre, to give your support—in all the ways you hard-working folks know how —to my contestant. Not some rich Don here to be entertained by your blood."

Even Khalil had his face in his hands, shaking his head at this point.

"We are for the people of The Château d'Oubli, and will see to it that no one from the topside—especially a rich, spoiled brat from the palace—takes your glory and your chance at a better life!"

A tumultuous roar of approval did not follow, but a few nods and a few scattered, "Aye, that's it," and, "The Château is for the Château," encouraged him.

I went rigid while people turned to look at me, craning their necks to see the people's champion. I'd kill him for that later. "Subtle," I mumbled.

Redbeard shoved his hands into his hip pockets. "Fine," he said with a dark grin. "Challenge me, will you?" His eyes fell on Khalil. "You don't know the fight you've picked, dandy."

"Thank God for that, or I'd never have done it." Cecil raised a glass to Red and then the Don, and sat down, swallowed up by the throngs as they started to present their trophies to Red's judges.

We waited a little, checking out my competition as they filed up one at a time, but I never got a chance. A girl in frilly garments and a bare corset came to us. She had an automatonic eye like Khalil's arm. "You've been summoned to the back," she said, eyeing Cecil.

As if expecting this, Cecil stood up, buttoning his coat. "It's time, Ezekiel."

"Should we come?" Jacque asked.

The girl shook her head. "Just this one." She pointed to Cecil.

"Trust me," Cecil replied to the girl, gripping my arm and yanking me up. "This one, too. You two stay out here. Keep an eye out."

Khalil and Jacque exchanged looks, but stayed.

Cecil forced me to follow the girl down a dark hall behind the bar. This area was lined with doors with soft, orange light coming out between them and the dirt floor. She snaked her way down a few more halls and stopped outside a more ornate door. Inside, someone spoke loudly. Not quite shouting, but upset. She opened the door after knocking.

Inside, a huge circular seating area sprawled out under a chandelier made of scrap. A smaller bar with an automaton waited in the corner. Redbeard had his back to us, speaking harshly to the Don, who sat on the red velvet.

"I just think it'd be better if you waited," Red was saying. "I need to report back to the Palais that I have a successful full-limb augmentation. It's imperative, Mateo—"

Red stopped and turned to glared at us.

Snapping back to the Don, he growled, "You never mentioned any of this to me. How can I help you if you don't let me in?"

"Get out," the Don retorted, almost looking bored. His eyes shot over Red's and Cecil's shoulders, landing hard on me.

That rabid coyote inside me from before shrunk away and another, shriveled with fear, replaced it.

"Don't do it, Don," Red growled dangerously. "I can't control every soul down here. They didn't give explicit directions—"

The Don stood up, drawing one of his ringing blades and letting it hang from the clinking chains. "Shut the hell up, Red, or you'll need your own augmentation to piss when I'm through with you."

To my ever-loathing shame, I cowered behind Cecil, the new, scared coyote taking over fully. Red snapped his plumed head from me to Cecil to the Don before clicking his heels and marching out. He slammed the door, making me wince. The Don slid his blade back into its holster, wrapping the chain around a small horn above it. He tossed his duster out and sat back down, lounging with his arms on the back of the seat.

"So, you *are* still alive?" he mused, signaling the automaton to bring a canister of whiskey over. To Cecil he said, "How did you know?"

Cecil stepped cautiously forward, taking a seat opposite the Don. I followed. "I didn't, actually. I told the truth topside. I'm not a spy. But I assess you are here for him."

Finally, the Don looked me in the eyes. I hadn't seen him much growing up as he'd spent most of his time in his homeland of Espagne.

I had very few memories of him. My father had hated him as he was a bastard. My uncle Jethro, the Duke, often had to stand up to my father to defend his half-brother. I remembered one time in particular when I was small. Grandfather had thrown his fists at Mateo, only for Jethro to stand between them and take the beating. Markus, my father, had stood by and let it happen, shoving me behind him.

"I hardly recognized you, Ezekiel," the Don said lightly, swirling his drink. "And yes, my astute friend. I was not sent so much to kill him but to see if he was still alive after your appearance in the Big House."

Cecil relaxed a little next to me. Curious, I looked over at him.

"You weren't sent to kill him," he thought out loud. "They don't know if he lives. Well." He looked over at me and removed my hat. He gripped the back of my neck and shoved me forward a little.

I dropped my head. My murderous coyote melted quickly in these early days of working with Cecil.

"As you can see," he went on, "he's alive. Are you sure this is your nephew?"

Despite my fear, I finally looked up at the Don. Even though he might later murder me, I needed him to recognize me now. If he did, and if Cecil kept his word and got me out, soon enough, I'd have my revenge. I'd get that coyote back.

Mateo's amber eyes observed me. He nodded, lips downturned. "I do. He looks like his mother. Has his father's eyes, though." He pointed at me with one finger released from holding his whiskey. "That is indeed Ezekiel."

Cecil nodded as if finishing a business transaction. "I see."

"I'm going to fight you, though," the Don interrupted, glaring down at me now. "If you perish…" He shrugged. "I didn't have the guts to kill you as a child. I've gotten over it since then."

"You've not been told to execute him," Cecil reminded him. "Surely your brother would be furious if you took matters into your own hands."

The Don stood up, throwing back the last of his whiskey. "I'd do anything for my brother. Even take care of things he missed eight years ago. But you're right, as well. I won't do it here. Not now Red knows who he is. But…" He shrugged again, opening his palms. "Should you happen to die in the one-for-all, so be it."

I stood as well, not wanting Mateo to walk past me while I sat.

Cecil quipped curiously, "Do you *want* to kill him, Don?"

Mateo scoffed hard through his nose. With two long-legged strides, he cut across the seating area and checked me with his shoulder. I stumbled into Cecil.

"I'll challenge you," the Don promised. "Be ready." He went out the door.

I turned to Cecil, face pale. "What do I do?" I asked. "He wants to kill me."

Cecil looked at the dark doorway where the Don vanished, chewing the inside of his cheek. At length, he said, "We need to find a way for you to beat him."

"He's huge!" I pled. I held my thin, pale arm out for Cecil to see. "He could choke the life out of me with one hand."

There was only one thing I could do that the Don would never see coming. Something I'd done a handful of times. "Geomancy?" I suggested.

Cecil smiled. "My thoughts exactly."

# 17 GEOMANCY

Cecil and I studied an assortment of geos Jacque had collected for us, wondering which ones I should infect myself with to test the magics they would give me. Khalil came in the front door, a scroll clutched in his automatonic hand. "Got a quick drawing of Red's hoard and the connecting tunnels done," he panted, having run to avoid being seen. "He's moving a lot of loot into metal containers."

"Perfect." I smiled, thinking of the magnet idea I had offered Cecil earlier.

"And," the nomad went on, tossing his drawing onto the table of geos, "Micah Morgan challenged the Don in an all-for-one."

"Let me get this straight," Cecil said, examining a spike of quartz. "All-for-one is *not* one of the tasks?"

Khalil and I nodded. "It's like a little extra flex," I said. "To get more support. Also takes more people out of the thunderdome. The final task," I supplied when Cecil raised his perfect brows. "Any idea what the second challenge is?" I asked Khalil.

The nomad nodded slowly. "Flaxen coral."

"Shit," Jacque and I said together.

"Hard to get?" Cecil asked.

"Very," I said, nodding. "First, let's hit up Micah's fight. I want to watch the Don in action. See what I'm dealing with."

"And we could stir the firms up a bit," Jacque offered. "I need people more willing to give me supplies for the ship. Jafa and I are ready to build, but we need construction materials. If we can get some firms on our side, we'll have more hands giving us things we need or at least hunting for them."

Above us, the older man's slow stride could be heard pacing back and forth.

"All right." I grabbed my belt, fixing it around my hips. "Khalil, with me. We'll go down to Main. Cecil, Moriart has a small shipment for us. You and Jacque pick it up and see if you can get that engine running."

Khalil and I rounded an old, western-style strip of shops that reeked of slaughter and followed the leaking blood out from under them to Main Street. Every light possible blazed in the open street. Everything previously in the street was pushed out of the way to the sides. Carts, carriages, and all manner of wind-up animals and other scraps were heaped into the gutters. Striding authoritatively down the middle of the street, his arms around four women in bright frocks, came the Don. The sides of his long black hair were braided against his scalp. One girl pushed all of his hair to one side and kissed him passionately on his jawline. As we broke the front line, the Don spotted me.

His dark eyes roamed me up and down, then checked the people around us. He couldn't cut me down here. The rules of the rencounter were the one set of rules no one in The Château d'Oubli broke without suffering the consequences. I scowled and bared my teeth at him, then flicked my head to Khalil and we moved to the side of the street that supported Mateo.

Some of his supporters had braided their hair to match his. They screamed for him to win, to stomp the mine rat. A screamer behind me shouted his support for the Don, splitting my ear.

Micah Morgan came out just after the giant clocktower struck twelve. He stood at one end of the street, a few supporters calling his name, but not many. He put his hand on his whip and the other on a large-barreled, quartz rifle at his side. He had a tank of fuel attached to his back, and a hose ran over his shoulder and into the gun at his side.

"Burn 'im, Micah!" someone screamed.

"Show him who we are!"

I watched as the two fighters moved closer together to shake hands. The Don reached out his gloved hand to Morgan. I saw it first. Morgan smiled for not even the breadth of a flea before he raised his gun and pulled the triggered at the Don's face. With a strange crackling and a blue flash, thin white fingers reached out, grasping the Don's face, clutching him hard in their serpentine dance. The crackling grew louder, and we all heard the Don scream.

"Electricity!" Khalil shouted in mixed admiration.

The Don's firm screeched in rage, urging him to get up. We all watched as he stumbled back, away from the evil device. His hands shook but he laughed darkly.

"You should have mentioned you wanted to play dirty," he said in a deep voice.

"Come get more," Morgan taunted. "I have a little something for ya, courtesy of your experiments."

Morgan flexed his arm in front of him and little jointed prongs came up from his legs and met with his hand, connecting his limbs together. Morgan stomped his foot and a blast erupted from his joined limbs, blowing the Don head over heels. The impact shredded Morgan's clothes to reveal an automotonic arm and leg. Where they connected, a faint yellow shield wavered, fizzed, and then vanished.

"Gifts from above," Morgan sneered. "You topsiders are going to have to answer for what you do to us down here, one day."

"Cheat!" the screamer behind me squealed. "For the Don!" he shouted, raising a chemical scimitar with a bottle of the acidic stuff attached to the handle. Those things were never nice to be cut by. Singed and burned for hours.

I faced the screamer, signaling Khalil. To the screamer I said, "He doesn't know you exist, bat shit."

"And you are?" the screamer sneered.

I slid my fingers across my hat's brim. "You'll know me better after this." This would be an opportunity to stir the pot a little, get me on people's minds. We needed to start our own flow of support.

Behind us, I heard the Don charge at Morgan and the crackling of Morgan's device in reply. I took my lasso off my belt and Khalil launched himself into the Don's firm, metal fist balled.

"Teach the topsider the meaning of Château loyalty, boys!" I shouted. I lassoed the screamer and pulled him to me just to blacken his eyes.

The Don's firm scattered as a few followed Khalil's and my lead. Men and women ran across the street, into the crowds—all colliding in their frantic effort to join the fight.

"Drive them across the road!" I shouted over the uproar we had gloriously created. It felt like herding cattle back on the estates.

Khalil clawed, broke, and frightened the tar out of the rats of The Château d'Oubli. I watched in awe as a man drew his fist back and tried to punch Khalil in the face. The Egyptian raised his mechanical arm and grasped the flying fist easily, the assailant shrieking in pain as his bones were crushed to powder in the strong metal. Then Khalil lifted the man, his face shining from the effort, and tossed him—with the help of his metal gears—across the road, where the man skidded to a dusty stop.

I saw a group of five or so underground rats watching us battle, neither cheering nor running in fear. "It's me or the Don, boys," I said to them. "Think what we can do if we beat him; who will it be?"

"Freedom?" one of the men in over-sized overalls stammered. "I find freedom would be the life for me. I'm no friend of Redbeard."

"Then do your worst!" I shouted, kicking a spear up off the ground to his hands. "Let none out without bloodying them well."

They only hesitated for a second. When Khalil took off again, they followed. Somewhere, the Don and Morgan were still fighting. I couldn't even see the road anymore. Each firm shouted, raged, bloodying each other too densely for me to see.

Far away from our tussle, Cecil and Jacque followed old man Jafa out behind their home and down into a network of tall caves. The old man tapped his headlamp, making it brighter so he could see. Jacque followed suit, but Cecil did not. The old man's eyes roved to Cecil only slightly as he touched a gold cross around his thin neck.

"These caves run the length of the river," Jafa said cautiously. He pointed to a redness in the walls. "You can see where the water has run here, leaving its rusty wash."

Jacque turned to look farther to the softly flowing red river. "Is this the same river that comes around to the perimeter?" she asked. "Towards Redbeard's skydocks?"

"The very same," Jafa mused. "You will need something that can go from the river to the air."

"Something big with high potential for maneuverability," Jacque mumbled, thinking.

He rubbed his chin, nodding. "Something to fly underground, hey?" he asked, his accent thick with the south. "C'est magnifique, my child, but I have never built such a thing. Your father was the one who invented such things." He smiled sadly. "That thing your mother used to drive, what was it? All over the country. Everyone called it *The Louisiana Queen*. He made that."

"Oui, grandpère, but you helped. You drew the designs. If you can imagine something up, I can make it. I'm my father's daughter, hey?" She winked at the old man.

"Your father should have spent more time perfecting your skills than forcing you to take tea lessons," Jafa growled.

Jacque sighed in a girlish fashion and tilted her head. "You know I sneaked out to build things."

Jafa grunted with a smile. "Seems long ago."

She sighed again, loudly this time. "Ugh, Jafa, please. For me? I can't finish it myself."

Jafa turned his deep eyes to her. "You don't want to let him down, do you?"

Cecil snapped his head away, realizing Jafa was referring to him. To save Jacque some embarrassment, he meandered down the riverbank, looking towards one of the drop-offs ahead.

Jacque froze. "Hey now?" she hissed at her grandfather.

Their whispering argument drifted softly, swallowed up by the sounds of the river as Cecil got farther away. He caught bits of it. Jafa didn't trust him. He called him a démon de sang. Khalil's name came in a harsh snap, too.

"You are welcome to come with us," Cecil offered the old man, calling back over his shoulder.

The two stopped arguing. Jacque took her grandfather's hands in hers. "See the sun again," she said softly. "Don't die down here."

"Oh, ma belle," Jafa winced like he was in pain. "Very well. I know where to find the hull of a ship that will do just fine for your expedition. But we must hurry. The rencounter is half over. Contestants are slaughtering one another in the one-for-all. The second challenge will be over soon as well." He glared over at Cecil. "We don't have much time."

We had to keep an eye on who had gone out to search for the damned flaxen coral over the next few days. We used my few supporters and ties with Moriart to not only find but haul a great reinforced ship's hull to the river, where Jacque and Jafa started to work on it. I waited for Khalil and Cecil to join us with a selection of geos for me to try for geomancing. I wasn't strongly keen on the idea, but I knew in a one-on-one fight with the Don, he'd squash me.

I watched Jacque work, looking like a huge bug under her goggles and too-big clothing. She was intense when working. She'd shout orders to Jafa in their southern French then laugh with a deep, feminine joy when something went right. The ship was small, with a lower level just tall enough for me to stand up in. It had solar sails and an engine that ran on steam. Above the main mast, a huge balloon soon to be filled with hydrogen waited to lift it.

Jacque caught me staring at her. She looked up, smiled, and gave me a thumbs up. The point of getting out was, of course, my revenge. But I'd be getting her out. Rescuing her. Maybe she'd thank me…

Cecil appeared with Khalil, holding a pack filled of geos. My stomached turned as the vampire upturned the pack, spilling the contents out onto a work table.

"If you are not compatible with some of them," he asked, "will it kill you?"

I rubbed the back of my neck, anxiety eating away my insides. "One time, this guy who worked for Moriart got some geo in him that his body didn't like and he sprouted a third arm, then a second head. Died pretty soon after."

Cecil pulled a disgusted face. "Well, we know for a fact that silver is just fine with you. What about something like..." His long fingers flicked the gems, metals, and rocks around lightly. He grasped a small sapphire. Eyeing it closely, he found tiny, smokey veins inside.

"Smokesapphire," Khalil supplied. "A gem that only works when in the blood."

Cecil raised a brow at him while smashing it in his hands and handing me a small shard. I took it begrudgingly.

Khalil added, "Some geos can work if you put them inside you and use them externally at the same time." He reached down and grabbed what looked like a rainbow kind of quartz. "Ephemeral. Mind control. Sort of. If you put it in your blood *and* look through lenses made of it, it can make it more powerful on whoever you look at."

"Mind control?" Cecil asked, skepticism drowning his tone. "Why doesn't everyone use it?"

I twirled the shard of sapphire in my hand, unwilling to stab it into myself just yet. "It's more of a suggestion. It opens up thought pathways that already exist in the targets mind. So, say I wanted to kill you in your sleep."

Cecil smiled.

I swallowed. "But obviously I'm not going to do that for reasons of self-preservation. Khalil could use it, look me in the eye through the lenses, and suggest I do it. I already wanted to. So I probably will now. Afterwards, it's as if it was my own idea. Since I already wanted to."

The vampire nodded and set the ephemeral aside.

"Other geos need catalysts," Khalil went on, also picking through the pile. "We've developed catalyst machines that can activate the dormant properties of some goes."

Cecil pointed to the sapphire in my hand. "Go on."

Sighing, I turned my arm over and cut myself deeply with the jagged gem. When it touched my blood, something electric shot through my brain. I pushed back against it and shoved a whole stack of metal beams to be used for the frame of our ship. Jacque cried out and spun around, a protective mask of glass and metal over her face.

"Who the hell is using sapphire?" she shot at the three of us.

"Telekinesis," Khalil said, smiling and helping me up.

I groaned, gripping my arm. I dug my finger in, trying to find the piece of the gem that had broken off with my fall. As I did, a flash of Cecil's thoughts sliced through my still electrified brain. He wanted to bite my bloody arm. I turned away, finding the piece and tossing it to the ground.

"How about this?" he asked, holding up a metal ingot. He carried it to Jacque's work bench and shaved off some flakes on a spinning stone wheel.

Khalil examined it. "Magmagold," he answered. "Ever seen a mancer toss a comet of fire?"

Cecil shook his head. Khalil stood back as he handed me the flakes.

Reluctantly, I pressed the flakes into my wound. A rush of hot lava poured up my arm. My brain exploded in a sea of fire and red.

"Get it out!" Khalil's voice called. He sounded far away, under water.

My whole body erupted into painful flames. Sweat instantly trickled down my neck and back. A pang of fear from Cecil was the only other thing I could feel outside the burning. The next thing I felt were his teeth in me, clamped onto my arm. The flakes slipped out, taking the fire with them.

When the red cleared, I saw Jacque and Khalil looking down with concern. Jacque held an empty bucket that I remembered had been filled with ice water for her work a moment before. It dripped empty now. I was soaked.

"Good thinking, Jacque," Cecil mumbled, spitting my blood out to the side.

"I could smell him burning," she panted, resting the bucket on her hip. "Close one."

"I'd not recommend anything fire-related," Khalil said matter-of-factly. "Doesn't seem to be compatible."

"That's an understatement," I mumbled. Steam rose off me from the water Jacque had dumped over me. I looked down at the bite marks around my wound.

"Or if you insist," Khalil suggested, "maybe something more gentle like firequartz? Quartz tends to be easier on those not compatible."

After some looking, he found a small crystal of the orange quartz. Taking caution, I squeezed it into my palm. It cut into me and the heat surged through me again. It didn't burn nearly as bad, but still brought hot pain. Focusing on a tiny candle on Jacque's work bench, I snuffed it out.

Cecil hummed, interested.

Unable to hold it much longer, I dropped the bloody quartz and fell onto my knees. I suddenly wanted to jump into the deadly, but cold, rivers of the prison.

Cecil picked me up. "Perhaps we should take a break. You've had a rough day."

I didn't argue. Besides, sooner rather than later, I'd have to go into the dark parts of this prison and find that damned coral.

# FLAXEN CORAL

"You have us at your back, Ezekiel," a man smelling of fish told me as I guzzled a third shot of some of the worst vodka this side of the west. I had never needed so much liquid courage, and The Red Mary had plenty. But like most things when taken in excess, it turned from courage to poison and a false sense of aplomb after a while. I hoped that if I set my head already spinning, it wouldn't spin in the darkness of the tight, pressured waterways where the coral grew.

"Got solar adamant?" I asked him. "I need light."

Fish-man dug in his bags, nodding. "Whatever you need. But, uh," he paused. I should have known. "Rumor says you may be leaving us soon?"

I froze, slowly raising my head up to meet his eyes. My heart leapt into my ears, pounding. He grinned grotesquely.

"That's right. Someone ratted on you," he sneered. "Hasn't gotten back to Red, though. But it might." He shrugged, trying to be coy. "I've been looking for ways to climb the ranks down here. Moriart has such a tight hold—"

I jumped up, startling the man, lassoed his neck and kicked him onto the bar, putting my spur on his throat like I had done before. My rabid coyote came back. "Who the hell told you that, fish?" Spittle dripped from the corner of my vodka-numb mouth onto his brow. "Has anyone broken out before? You think I'm crazy enough to try?"

"Ease up there, son. It was just a rumor from The Red Marry. Someone saw you in the back with the Don." He chuckled nervously. "Doesn't mean you're getting out. He coulda just been threatening you, making a deal, maybe? Spades, take your boot from me."

He pushed on me and I let him shove me away. So he hadn't heard about the break out. Just saw me enter a private room with the Don and Red. "Sorry, no deal, fish. Nothing you can beat outa me." I inhaled in relief. "I'm off to the coral caves. Give me light." I glanced around to count how many people were gawking at us. Only a few.

He dug in his pockets right quick and handed me a little pouch.

"Much obliged, sir. The coyotes may not feast on your bones yet."

"M-may you not be b-be buried on the lonesome prairie," he called after me in an old, superstitious blessing.

"Vote Ezekiel," I said in reply like a numbskull, tripping over my own feet.

I heard others toast me as I left.

I walked out of the stinking bar into our stinking streets. A robotic dog ran through the garbage on three and a half legs. Its bark pierced like the twang of a rusty spring. It ran between the legs of a tart looming in a doorway to a house with no lights on.

"Hey there, Ez," the tart said through red-stained lips. "Take me on an adventure tonight?" She rubbed the inside of her thighs. "The red fairy is for everyone."

I had work to do. But it had been a long while since I'd had a decent shag.

"Not tonight," I barked at her instead. She rolled her eyes and took a flask from her white thigh garter.

I walked alone down the muddy, mechanical-ridden streets, out of town. I needed something from the bank first. At the border, I went to the machinist Moriart owned. I supposed I owned him now, too, since I'd dominated Moriart.

The machinist called himself Sven. His thick accent made me realize just how unrefined my knowledge of the overworld's countries was. "I need a bike," I said. "I can pay, but I'd rather not."

Sven's face barely reached over the wooden countertop. A defector from the Russe Empire, he had come to America seeking fortune like so many before him. He hadn't made it.

"Moriart told me about you," he said through narrow lips. "Said you'd be coming around. But I got news for you: I'm easier to persuade than him."

What a coward. Or he thought I would bring business if I won the rencounter. Either way suited me just fine. "I have a rare alchemy ingredient," I said. "I need goggles, too."

He sneered, hopping up on a crate to get his book of inventory down. "The Don's been in and gone near half an hour. Took a breathing apparatus."

"Give me the bike," I commanded. "I need to get there fast."

"You could grab anything from the tunnels," Sven said. "Three from the north side of San Sous-terre took off on street crawlers about a day ago."

I nodded in faux sadness. "They won't be back. I need something I know will run, Sven."

"Show me something shiny." He looked up through his misshapen brows at me.

I reached into one of my pouches and pulled out my old canteen and unscrewed the top. It smelled rather rotten. "Ask me no questions, I shall tell you no lies."

Sven narrowed his eyes at me. "Sounds like a rough deal, Ezekiel. I have ideals and faces to uphold. I have deals with many, you see. I'm what you call a neutral man."

"I'll take the bike."

I grabbed Sven's shot glass, dumped out his liquor, and poured just a bit of Cecil's blood into it so he could see it. The vampire's blood was thick with glinting veins of ectoplasm in it.

"Holy Hades," Sven mumbled, chucking a thick pair of lenses over his eyes. "Is that… Where did you get that? *How* did you get it?"

"Not so neutral now, are you?" I smirked.

"Aye, sir. One bike and goggles coming right up. They're out back. Take your pick. Need anything else? An engine? A convection counterweight?" Sven prodded at the blood gently. "Any chance the specimen is still alive? Do you know where—"

"I'll be in touch." I grabbed the gear and spun away from his prying, greedy questions.

I raced through the tunnels on the magnificent bike. The wheels gripped the walls for a short while to climb rocks and debris. I couldn't help but smile as I revved the engine, gliding over every bump and rut with its highly sensitive steam-powered shocks. Such a wonderful bike. Worth a bit of Cecil's blood, anyway. Anything from a vampire could buy you something shiny. Just had to make sure they didn't come knocking for more than I could give.

I swung around the caves like they were a paved trail. I jumped when I could, ramped off edges and soared around sharp rocks. I enjoyed it a little too much and ended up laying it down at one point. From then on, I took fewer risks. I had to get back before Mateo.

Before I knew it, the purple coral caves shimmered in the distance. I skidded to a stop at the gaping black hole that served as the entrance. Flipping some switches, the wheels clicked and the gripping spikes and chains were equipped. I slammed the goggles onto my face and lurched forward, revving the engine and praying the shocks were solid.

The initial fall felt the worst. My stomach flipped when I went over the edge, and I gripped the bike with my thighs so hard I felt my bones bruise. I heard the wheels grab the walls and my fall stopped. But the force jerked me forward, off the seat, and nearly over the handlebars. I hit my groin hard on the gas tank and my stomach hit the bars. I clutched for dear life as I spiraled down the black hole. Panicking that I couldn't see, I screamed as I fell, sometimes attached to the wall, sometimes not.

I spun, losing control of the handlebars as they bucked and jerked out of my grasp. They twisted and nearly snapped my wrists, so I let go. I held on now with just my thighs as I careened down. I didn't have enough strength. I felt my legs slip, my head smacking the stone wall, and the next thing I knew, I plunged into freezing, rushing water. The bike splashed next to me, spun in the current, and the wheel hit my head, knocking the remaining breath out of me. Panicking, I kicked in all directions, looking for the damned surface.

A bike spoke, broken on the way down, caught my belt and pulled me down. With a hard tug, I got the stupid spoke out. I kicked and kicked, clawing at the water until I broke the surface. But the current still rushed too fast for me to gain control. I came to a sudden stop, my head smacking a rock wall, the water leaping up into my face to gag me. It didn't stop, flowing with the current, trying to drown me even as I clutched the sharp crags. I reached down and pulled the bag I had taken from Sven from my belt and opened it, careful to hold my hands above the water.

I choked over the water filling my lungs and searched madly for the rubylead I'd bartered for. It would keep me warm and let me see in the dark. I didn't have time to think. Reopening the cut in my forearm, I dumped a small handful of the powdered gem into my wound. A significant portion of it washed away in the water before it took effect.

The stones were foul. A sickness roiled in my veins, down into my gut. I thought I puked, but realized the warmth spreading down to my toes and up to my head came from the stones. Suddenly, every hint of light and shadow became a sharper, vivid red. The tiniest glisten grew too bright until everything shone either pure, solid black or red. My head rang from the duo tones of blinding color. I blinked, the new vision startling me. Soon, my eyes started to burn. It seemed this geo and I were not as compatible as it was with Jacque.

But then I saw a tiny shoreline that led into the narrow caverns. I blinked. Bright red, like a flaming light, splattered the shore and some of the cave walls. I hoisted myself out and walked to the suspicious stuff. I didn't need to touch it to see it was blood. I could see signs of struggle on the ground now, too, the shadows and lighting playing off the tiniest detail. Handprints clawed their way away from the river. They were being dragged by something with bare, human feet.

"Undermen," I breathed. Great.

I threw myself onto my belly and slid into the narrow opening. I could not raise my head in here. If I did, it bumped the low top. When

I inhaled deeply, my chest got caught between the roof and the floor. The panic instantly settled in. I closed my eyes and crawled forward. Shallow breaths. The rubylead warmed me. Calm. I didn't used to hate closed-in spaces. The fear took me by surprise; something inherited from Cecil and our tether.

My hand touched water and went under. I gasped and my back hit the ceiling. I couldn't breathe, the air too close and compact. I imagined it turned stiff from the pressure of all the earth above us. I opened my eyes, but everything had gone black. Not a drop of light for the rubylead to pick up. The water got colder. I crawled on.

Soon, my head struck the rocky ceiling with every crawling step; the water deepened the further I went in. If I kept my head down, I would inhale the stale water. Damned coral. But this was the point of the contest: to prove your guts. Was I strong enough? This had nothing to do with talking my way out of something or sharing a secret to earn my way into someone's good graces. I couldn't threaten the rock into letting me go, and I couldn't barter with the coral to come to me. It came to guts this time.

I came to a fork in the path. I only knew a fork had appeared because I could feel the water trickle off to my right. I felt with my hand and realized that the ceiling went higher there. I crawled into that space and regretted it right away.

I plunged down into a well of freezing water that reeked of sulfur. I screamed and paddled back to my narrow passage. I clung to the wall even though the current in the river moved far gentler. But the water didn't smell right. Like dead animals and rotting eggs.

Crawling back up, I hit my head harder this time as I shook and felt hot blood trickle down the back of my neck. I stopped. No air. Blood leaking. My breathing getting shallow and fast. Dizzy. The world spun even though I couldn't see. A flash of Cecil's mind shot through my head. He was hungry. I suddenly got the urge to go back and let him bite me. The tether pulled at me against my will.

A wild shriek sounded behind me, followed by the banging of spears. Undermen. Panic kicked me. I crawled as fast as I could along the narrow passage. Soon I had to hold my face under the water and breathe less as the passage lowered too much to hold my head up. I stopped to take breaths until I couldn't handle it anymore.

The fear drove me to puke into the water. The stress had nearly clamped my jaw shut, but the bile seeped between my teeth. I pushed through it to finally feel tiny, tentacle-like flesh against my fingers.

"Damned coral!" I shouted into the suffocating darkness. I ripped at it with my hand and shoved it down my pants, missing the pouches on my belts entirely. I didn't care. I couldn't feel anyway. The rubylead had worn off, so I pulled out the solar adamant. The small chunk blinded me in the darkness. I gagged as I held it between by teeth and crawled forward. It dimmed every time it went under the water. I hadn't used it earlier, afraid to alert someone—*something*—to my presence. Didn't matter now.

I reached the part where the fork branched off when I stopped. The dim sunlight showed me a hazy purple shadow. The shrieking of the undermen started again and they banged their weapons. They must have smelled me coming back. The water splashed from the other side. They were coming. I froze. I couldn't breathe, my vision blackened from fear. My blood flowed back to the monsters, giving me away.

A tumult of splashing and screaming reverberated down the tunnel, hungry cries and banging sticks. I stared ahead, tranquilized by fear and cold. Something blocked my way. An underman on all fours stared at me.

"Mon infant?" it whispered. Then it screamed and charged towards me.

I dodged to the left and plummeted into the freezing, rank water. I kicked and pulled, not knowing the first thing about swimming, trying to propel myself wherever the water wanted to take me. A huge hand grabbed my ankles and pulled me backwards. My lungs filled with water as I fought back. I coughed under the water, the blackness taking my vision again as the solar adamant fell into the river. The current pulled the underman into the water with me. I felt it let go as the current picked up, tossing us around like a baker beating dough. Its spear flew free from its grasp and found its home in my side. I tried to cry out, but simply didn't have the breath or strength.

Closing my eyes, I kicked out one more time. I tried to shoot, but my revolver wouldn't fire, so I grabbed a hunting knife from my boot and slashed wildly at the underman. I made contact with what felt like his face over his eye. The spear and it were either carried away or retreated down a black side path after I struck.

Clutching the spear wound, I floated and let myself be carried back out. I opened my eyes for what I thought would be the last time and saw light. Not the solar adamant, but something else. I used all my strength to put pressure on my wound and swam to the light. The water sucked my blood out, weakening me. With every stroke, a cry like a lost dog escaped my desperate lungs. No one could hear me.

The first cavern came into my blurry view and the light came through the well where I could see my crashed bike on a narrow shoreline. Someone stood over it, facing me.

I thought for one horrible second that another competitor had arrived, but then I saw the gaudy frock coat run towards me and grasp my wrist, pulling me out of the water in one sweeping motion.

"You took the long way, didn't you? You stupid bastard," Cecil said. He stood me up and looked me up and down. "Khalil found out you can use a back well to—"

"Cecil," I started to cut him off, but my voice froze in my throat and my chest constricted, bound with immovable chains. I couldn't finish. Pressing my hands to my spear wound, I fell forward. I expected to fall face-first onto the rocky ground and probably break my nose. Instead, he caught me gently. After a moment of him listening to my shuttering breaths, he lifted me up and carried me away out of the wretched tunnels.

# 19 The Catalyst

Cecil and Jacque leaned up against a wall across from an arena, scoping out the machinations being corralled there while I rested back in her home from the coral escapade. Cecil didn't notice how close she leaned toward him, taking any chance to touch his arm or press up against him. Jacque had spied the machinations while out sourcing for the last parts we needed for the airship. She'd told us and Cecil wanted to find a way to get me an edge.

"Do you see anything that could help us?" he asked.

She tilted her head to the left. "The thunderdome," she said, her voice hitching a little. "The last task. Looks like Red got some fine machines. Automatonic gyro-arachnid. He's going to have to fight one." She slipped her goggles over her eyes and flipped down a few lenses to see farther. "Oh, see how they vibrate?" She handed Cecil her goggles.

The vampire put them on and focused on what he could see of the thunderdome. Ginormous, metal, steam-powered creatures loomed in a corral behind it. A handful of engineers tuned them up, tested their joints, and fixed up the engines. They had a certain stuttering, shivering movement to them even as they stood still. "I see," he mused. "This means…?"

"Telemantium," she explained. "Telekinetically charged metal. But you need the catalyst alloy to control it."

"Geomancy," Cecil confirmed. "He can do that. But why not just use smokesapphire? Sapphire gives telekinetic powers. He'd make quick work of this mechanical monster with that kind of power."

Jacque nodded, but said, "Because telemantium only responds to more telemantium. You could eat all the sapphire in the world and it wouldn't budge telemantium. I think in the future, a lot of military ships will be made of telemantium if mancing gets popular."

While he thought of ways to get our hands on some, Jacque turned her attention to him. Biting the corner of her lower lip anxiously, she took his hand. "Cecil, now that we're alone… I was wondering what you planned to do once we get out of here. I had some thoughts about what we might do. Together."

Forgetting the catalyst alloy, he looked down at her sadly. "Jacque, you don't understand. Once we're topside again, I have to finish what I started. Then, that's it for me."

"No, no, Cecil." She faced him square on now, bashfully looking down at her huge boots. "I know. Jafa figured it out." Her huge, black-brown eyes looked up, begging him. "That's why I want to stay with you. Make sure no one hurts you. I don't like the way Ezekiel and Khalil look at you. Like they want your blood for bloodstones. Alchemy, Cecil. Alchemists take vampire blood and create bloodstones. They're terrible things, sold for profit."

Amused a little at her care, Cecil graciously gave her a smile and pushed her thick braids back over her shoulder. "Don't worry about me, Jacque." He shrugged her hand off.

Tears instantly filled her eyes.

"Why not focus these attentions on Ezekiel?" He raised his brows, half-smiling. "He will be king, you know."

Jacque dropped her hands, her eyes going icy. "Of course. A king would be quite a catch." She turned to head back.

"What about the catalyst?" Cecil called after her.

"Ask Khalil," she retorted.

The nomad nodded when Cecil asked about the catalyst alloy. "I know exactly where to find some. But it's too risky for me to go out and get it," he said in a monotone. "Red has had his men scouring the streets for me. I've technically run off with government property, you see." He held up his mechanical arm. For the first time, I noticed a small inclusion in it where it looked like a gem had been plucked out. Or where one would go in.

"Tell me who or where, then," I offered, still too ill from the fever I'd caught from the caves to get up. "I'll bleed anyone to get what I need."

Khalil's eyes glittered. "Well, I suppose if that's how you want to play it, we could…" He eyed Cecil.

*No*, I thought. I was the only one allowed to use his blood in trade. And I needed him strong right now. I couldn't risk him losing more blood. Not while he was starving.

"Fine," he said, tossing his coat aside.

"Don't do it!" I exclaimed, pushing myself up out of the chair by the fire.

"I'll be fine, Ezekiel." He rolled up his sleeve and smiled weakly at me. "This is for you, after all."

I didn't want him to hurt himself for me. I fell back down, the fever making my head spin.

"Much obliged." Khalil all but hid the manic glee on his face as he cut Cecil, taking a few ounces of his blood into a bottle. "Relax, Ez," he said when he took in my pale face. "Rest up and have Jacque make you something hearty. You're going to need your strength." He saluted with the bottle to Cecil and slithered out the front door.

"I think he was a vampire hunter topside," I said weakly as Cecil plopped down on the floor by my feet. He faced the fire. "I found a hunting chest. An alchemist set. That pendant of his is timeplatium. Certain Syndicates use bloodstones and timeplatium—a catalyst—to buy humans more time. Life. I'm surprised you don't know that."

The vampire crossed his legs and leaned back to take in the heat. "I'm not so old I know ever secret of the world, your highness."

I nodded. The glimpses I'd seen of his life were short. In the silence that followed, I got another shot of his emotions: worry, fear. He was hungry again. But I caught something else, too, something I couldn't identify that had to do with me. It gave me a warmer feeling than the fire before us, but nothing else discernible.

"Be better by tomorrow," he ordered me, closing his eyes. "We have to go to The Red Mary and celebrate the second task. And pretend we don't know the final task."

I waited a moment. "Cecil," I whispered, following his lead and shutting my eyes to sleep. "When I get out of here, I am going to do terrible things. I have plans for revenge against everyone who had a hand in putting me down here."

He hummed in slight concern. I watched his chest rise and fall with the unforgotten habit of breathing.

"Do you want to keep me down here?" I asked.

"No," he replied. He opened his lavender eyes and looked up at me. "I have hope that you may change your mind."

I smirked. Stupid vampire.

The crowd screamed cat calls, war whoops, and stomped their feet in manic glee as the beer and rustwash flowed. The musicians on their one-man-bands tried to outplay each other, creating a phenomenal ruckus to celebrate the ending of the second challenge and those who had returned.

Hardly any of the contestants had come back with the coral, and the ones who did drank heavily. A few had died to undermen, and more had drowned and floated into the well of rank smells that I could not identify earlier. All tasks complete but the last. Those who were still alive drowned themselves in drink and company, knowing they died tomorrow in the thunderdome or lived to tell the tale. All men and women who had not fought were due to fight at some point in the next twenty-four hours or be assassinated by Redbeard's men for dodging. Rather than be known as a coward, they all came to drink and whore the last few hours away. Jacque had finished our engine, taking a break to join us. Tonight, she was dressed in red and black frills she'd dug out of her family's old home. I'd never seen her, let alone most other women, in a skirt before. I made no attempt to avert my eyes.

Her hair, still thick with oil and grime, had been piled on her head with some moldy ribbons. I had rarely seen her waist before, since she always hid it under heavy coats and overalls. The hard work had covered her bones in muscle, making her not as slender as the girls at the bar. But it also made her heart tougher than buffalo hide. The corset held her in place and let her luscious form round itself to its full potential. She had strong, defined shoulders. I looked at her neck from where I sat, wondering if Cecil had ever looked at it as well. I, too, felt the urge to bite her. To kiss her.

She danced with the frilly Mary girls, avoiding the grabs of slovenly drunken prisoners. Her eyes went to Cecil where he loomed in a dark corner. Her smiled dwindled and her eyes lost some of their smolder. I took a huge swig of the rustwash and ran to join her. At first, she looked disgruntled as I took her waist in my hand and pulled her against me. One last glance at Cecil being aloof and she gave in, letting me twirl and spin her around the floor. I was no dancer and tread on her feet multiple times before I let her lead.

"You're really very bad at this," she called over the music, white teeth smiling behind red lips.

"I think I still have a broken rib," I offered as an excuse.

She winced playfully, catching my fib. "He says you'll be king, you know." She allowed me to spin her out and back in. "He has a lot of faith in you."

Her face shone red with drink. I smelled the rustwash on her breath. Seeing a chance, I grabbed the back of her neck and pulled her into a kiss. She mumbled into my lips for a second before groaning and reciprocating. She pulled away and looked over my shoulder. I watched her face turn stony.

"Ah, spades," she said, sighing. She resigned herself to me. "What could it hurt?" She grabbed my head and slammed my face into hers, biting my lips. Locked together, she stumbled to the back rooms and threw open a door. Inside waited a trashy four-poster bed. She poured herself a shot and tossed it back.

"What…?" I started, but she cursed at me in French, holding up a finger. Everything inside me turned to ice and fire at once.

"What am I worth to you?" she asked, unlacing her top. "A way out? Do you think we'll get out in just a few days?"

I took a step back, but she seized me, flinging me around. I stumbled and fell onto the bed. She slammed the door, taking one more shot.

"You're sloshed, Jacque," I said, inching away.

"Don't simper at me, your highness," she slurred. "I know what I'm doing. I see the way he looks at you. He'll smell me on you."

"Cecil?" I asked, my breath hitching. "What do you mean?"

The way an underman looked at you before they leapt, ready to eat you… That was the look Jacque had in her eyes.

"Promise me one thing," she whispered, flinging her leg over my hips, shoving me down. My throat was too dry to answer. This was a nightmare and a dream come true all at once. "When we're out, we take back my home, the Deleon Estate, from the Syndicate."

"You're a Deleon?" I asked, looking up at her.

Not royalty, but a notable family from the topside. She shook her head, then nodded, half-shrugging. "It's a long story, Ez." She fell onto me again, biting my neck, pressing my wrists down into the moldy mattress.

Her hand went to the buckles on my belt, making quick work of them. I sank away from her touch. Yes, I'd dreamed about having her, but not like this.

"What are you doing?" I asked.

"This is how you value me," she growled, becoming more and more aggressive.

*No, it's not.*

I didn't stop her.

I woke up in the rank darkness to a soft, sad sound. Beside me, Jacque quietly cried into the mangey pillow and bed clothes. I should have stopped her, but I hadn't. I was a little shit like that. Not a drop of regret trickled down my insides. In fact, I felt as if I had won. I'd taken something I'd lusted after for years.

In my head, a bolt of Cecil's thoughts hit me hard. Khalil had the catalyst. Cecil didn't know how to mix it with the telemantium they couldn't get to. He was plotting when a fit of hunger stopped his mind. I sat up, starved as well. I saw the gyro-arachnid in his mind. It had fangs. Something innate inside me drew me back to him. I got up, pulling my boots on when it hit me.

"Shit," I mumbled. I had an idea how to get both geos in my blood at once. It wasn't going to be pleasant, though.

# 20 The Thunderdome

For the rencounter, all the machines, mining, and other work stopped some time ago, making a kind of weird silence in the tunnels. Now that the fights in the thunderdome were happening, the crowds congregated there. Even the ones who mined in secret to line their own pockets stopped digging. Every last tunnel lay so silent, I could hear the drops of water raining down from higher up. Then the ruckus started again. Cheers, shouts, clanging of metallic noise makers, and little fights between firms in the street broke the temporary peace.

Jacque gripped Cecil's arm the whole walk from the house. I kept glancing sideways at her, but she ignored me. I'd not seen the thunderdome and it drew my attention when we rounded the outskirts of San Sous-terre. Thousands of makeshift chairs surrounded the gaping mouth of the tall, cruel walls, yawning open for more blood. Spikes and spires made from wood, steel, metal, and all kinds of geos lined the inside of the sandy arena where guts, limbs, and grey matter smattered from row to row of seats. From where we stood, we could see it all. We had come out from the wooden forest of supports and stairs in the middle of the many levels of chairs and benches. In front of us, on a kind of sick dais made of bones from every kind of living thing in the dungeon, sat Redbeard, the Don, and their posse.

The Don proudly displayed his already bloodied face like warpaint. His smiling lips said he had not been hurt; he had finished off someone in a one-on-one just before the thunderdome. Someone trying to avoid death by the steam-powered creatures inside. He leaned far back into his throne-like chair, legs splayed out in total relaxation as he watched the bloodshed.

In the arena, a woman ran screaming for her life from the automatonic gyro-arachnid. She had a bad limp, but took two of the spider-machination's legs in the process. She had jabbed a long, jagged spear made of found metal into one of its swiveling eyes.

"Mercy!" she screamed, reaching one hand to the Don.

"Will he grant mercy?" Cecil asked, eyes fixed on the bloody display.

"Mercy just means a quick death," I answered.

By the looks of the remains in the arena, the gyro-arachnid did not kill you slowly. A severed limb suggested it simply grasped a person's arms and legs and pulled.

The Don stood up, pulling his singing blades from his hips. With ease, he leapt into the arena and sauntered towards the screaming woman. I saw now that part of her body had burned away. It had melted right off, one of her eyes glued shut by her own flesh.

With ease, the Don spun his blades like the eye of a hurricane with all of his might and launched one into the woman. She wept with no tears on her face. The blade nestled itself into her skull with a dull thunk and the metal vibrated, singing a soft farewell to her as the audience moaned in melancholy over missing the gyro-arachnid's big finish. With her final breath, she let out a weak cry that matched the singing metal. The tone pushed the Don back a few steps. He kicked her over to stop her from screaming like a banshee. Flicking the chains, he pulled the blade out of her corpse.

"We cannot all die an honorable death," the Don cried, raising his arms to his adoring audience. "Let's have another!"

The people screamed for blood. Like most folk, the citizens in The Château d'Oubli loved to see other people's blood. Meant theirs wasn't flowing.

"Do you have the catalyst alloy?" Cecil asked quietly so no one else heard.

I tapped a small, brass-clasped leather pouch on my laden belt.

"Khalil powdered it for me a few hours ago." I held up my arm where a leather bracer covered an open wound. A little clasp on the top could be flipped open to expose the lacerated flesh.

"And you're sure you know how to get at the telemantium?" His tone ground his patience. I hadn't told him, and I wasn't going to in case he panicked.

Suddenly, his worry struck me. Picking up his emotions always put me on edge; I never knew if they were mine or his. The suddenness always took me by surprise.

"What is it?" I asked.

He nodded up. Following his gaze, I saw Mateo looking at me.

"Time to go then," I said, sighing.

I raised my arms to the audience as I leapt into the gross sand of the arena, the mauled gyro-arachnid being herded back into the corral. They started to chant my name.

"Ezekiel for a new regime!" some said.

"Go, go, Ezekiel!" a little crowd of men and women wearing red, white, and blue cockades chanted.

I looked up and saw the Don watching me. I faced him, pulled my black hat low, and bowed with a sarcastic flourish of my hand.

"Hail, Caesar! We who are about to die salute you!" I shouted. The people guffawed, raising their rustwash to me. I turned to face the door where my own brand new gyro-arachnid waited to come out and dismember me.

"Don't do anything stupid," Cecil called. His fear was palpable in my head. I needed him to relax and stop mixing his fear with mine.

I pulled my fingerless gloves tighter. Then I ran my fingers along the brim of my hat, taking a breath. Crouching, I readied to jump onto the machine. I shook my hands in an attempt to dislodge the nerves in them.

The gate didn't creak open as I had suspected. It blew off its hinges, destroyed by the crazy thing as it charged out, monstrous fangs snapping. It lumbered toward me on jointed, un-oiled legs. I saw what had burned the lady. Some kind of purple acid dripped from its mechanical pincers, burning through the tough metal of its own face already.

Somewhere on it, its key spun, winding the gears, making a sickening ticking sound. Its belly was a fiery engine.

"Get on the gyro!" I heard Redbeard shout. "If you do not top it once, you will be disqualified!"

My feet tapped rapidly, like a cat about to pounce. My eyes bulged in their sockets. My chest constricted and I launched myself up. I caught a piece of the machine with my hand, thankful for my gloves: the heat made holding on painful. Then I swung my leg up and crawled up the monster like a spider. I got to the top and saddled myself on its neck.

The minute I got there, the machine bucked and several of its eight legs reached up to snag me, all tipped with points. The monster made one buck and I groaned in pain as my groin screamed at me. A scorpion-like tail shot out from its back end and made jabs at me while it bucked.

I stood up and lassoed a notch on the gyro. Pulling it tight, I leapt down, swinging around to the back where the tail connected. Its little spiky hands tried to stab me again, but I rolled off, swinging on my rope again back to its head. I looked down through its gears and cogs and saw through its skeletal structure to its pincers.

I released my lasso and jumped, trying to jump over the thing's head, but misjudged its reflexes. Like a true spider, it snapped at me as I flipped over its head and caught me in the acidic pincers. A scream of burning pain forced its way between my lips. There was nothing as terrifying as hot, sharp metal with acid on it biting into your hips and missing the roots of your manly member by mere centimeters. I had to act instantly or I would be two pieces of carnage just like the others. The bite came sooner than I had expected.

Mustering my strength, I slipped my hand between its top maw and my hips, digging out the catalyst. The arachnid waited a moment, preparing to shake its head like a coyote with a rabbit in its maw. Flipping open my vambrace, I smeared some of the grey, glassy powder into my wound. It ignited inside of me instantly. Lifting my hands, I shoved them apart, out to my side in a tearing motion. The pincers expanded with the motion of my hands and split the thing's head in two. I fell to the ground with a sad little thump.

In a confused rage, the key still twisting, the gyro-arachnid stumbled and tossed its destroyed head, flinging the acidic chemicals all over the thunderdome. A few in the audience got a face full and screamed. With the telemantium magic still in me, I reached up and grasped the key with my temporary telekinetic powers. I heard my skull crack from the use of the geo, but the key stopped, cutting off the steam engine. The thing fell, dead.

The Don stood up and began the applause. He smirked down at me, impressed. A few of his supporters around the arena scattered their applause, too, confused, no doubt. I saw them looking at each other, whispering. I looked back to Cecil and Jacque. He made eye contact, shaking his head and smirking in relief.

I had done it. I'd made him see me conquer. I'd feared he'd decide I wasn't worth all this and would rather piss off than have me defy him again and again.

"It is well played!" Redbeard shouted into his brass microphone. "Do not murmur so amongst yourselves. Geomancy is an understood part of the competition, if one so desires." His eyes drifted to me now. "If one has a knack for it and can bear it." He smiled, interested. "Very bold to gamble with one's own life. Let's hear it for the risk!"

The crowd screamed in pleasure and appreciation.

I took my cue, bowing once more to my own firms, and fell forward. The cheering had died down significantly. Most were probably disappointed. They had wanted some great spectacle, and instead I had given them geomancy. Pushing myself up, I gave the Don the bird and stumbled back to Jacque and Cecil. The vampire pulled me out of sight and clamped his mouth onto my arm. I didn't push him off as he sucked the poisonous blood out of me. Jacque turned pale and looked away.

Letting go and licking his lips, Cecil mumbled, "Well done. After that, most in here should be keen to support you." He flicked his head to the left, eyes on Jacque.

"On it," she confirmed, hopping out of the thunderdome to start gathering leads for some final transactions.

Cecil slung my arm around his shoulders and started to slink away through the streets of San Sous-terre to get me back to our headquarters. "You should have told me what you had planned," he growled. I saw his nostrils twitching as he smelled my blood.

With his feeding on me, our tether was renewed, and I knew his every thought. "You think Mateo will find me and challenge me?" I asked, sensing his fear.

"I think he will hunt you down. I think that's why he's here." He stopped a moment, his eyes going to the wound on my arm near his face. He pushed on. "That's my fault."

The scene from his capture at the Big House filled his mind and mine. I saw my uncle, the Duke of Dakota. He looked good for a man his age. I hadn't seen him in years. Cecil's theories bubbled up over the memory.

"Good question," I mused, hearing one thought in particular. "Why would Uncle Jethro send you down here…if he knew I was here and that you were looking for me?"

Fortunately for me, Cecil could not see my mind. I didn't care why Uncle Jethro had sent Cecil down here. All I cared about was that the vampire got me out and I could start my revenge.

Behind us, the thunderdome cheered, signaling another death. Our time was coming. While The Château d'Oubli was in the throes of the rencounter, we'd make our escape.

# 21 A Family Affair

The next day, after Cecil stitched me up and wrapped my wounds, Jafa came down from above to take us to our ship. Khalil, who had been hiding out in Jacque's house to avoid Redbeard, came with us.

"Why haven't the celebrations been announced yet?" Cecil asked nervously as we followed the old man up into the cliffs by the river behind the house.

I explained for Cecil. "Once the rencounter is over, Red will announce a final celebration to the survivors at The Red Mary. Usually gets pretty wild. Lasts a few days, with the last one being quiet and depressing."

"Before we go back to work, hey," Jacque said, sighing. She clenched her jaw in excitement. "Not this time." Her eyes went wide with the expectation of showing us the ship. "Just wait until you see her, Cecil."

I watched the back of her as she skipped ahead in her too-big overalls, taking his cold, dead hand in hers. Khalil nudged me and shook his head when I glared at him.

The five of us were panting by the time we reached the top of the cliffs. The river below had filled drastically from the rains topside. This drove out several tribes of undermen. We even spotted a few crawling over the walls on our walk. Jafa turned his light away to not attract them.

"I hope you have a plan," he said softly, setting his lantern down on one of many workbenches lining the steep drop. It was too dark to see out where we hoped the ship waited.

"You've been working up here the whole time?" I asked, looking around into the darkness. "How have you not been caught?"

The older man didn't grace me with eye contact as he replied, "You are not the sneakiest one in the underground. The rencounter keeps most occupied," he added honestly.

"Khalil?" Cecil asked as lanterns were lit all along the cliff face.

The nomad came forward, producing maps from his pied coat. He slapped them onto the table and started to spread them out. Jacque helped Jafa light some torches and Cecil and I looked over Khalil's shoulder.

"Where'd you get these?" Cecil asked, running his long finger over one of the maps.

Khalil ran his tongue over his front teeth in thought. "They take me out by ship," he started. "For my little tasks topside. Same way every time. This time, I'm not coming back."

At last, Cecil met my eyes and I caught his thoughts. He wasn't completely suspicious of Khalil. We had no reason to be. But the fact that his familial Syndicates worked so closely with topside royals and politcals gave him pause. Cecil and I had the same thought: once we were free, we had a few loose ends to deal with before they got away from us.

Khalil traced the river on the map. "This is pretty open. Red's airships follow it all the way out."

I frowned, touching the edge of the map where the river vanished. "Is it guarded? Why haven't more people escaped through there?"

The Egyptian looked up at me, questioning my intelligence. "The wall would be near impossible to scale without being seen by Red's guards. The river goes down into the unknown. You'd need an airship to get out the opening above the skydocks."

I nodded. "Understood. So, his hoard?"

"Moved into metal crates," Khalil said with a sigh. "It's all on the docks, though, like he's getting ready to transport it."

"Oh, hell," I breathed. "He has the same idea we do. He's getting out of here."

"Why?" Cecil asked.

I shrugged. "Doesn't matter. Do you think he hasn't announced the celebration yet because he's fixing to fly the coop?" I nudged Cecil when he didn't reply.

He bit down on his index finger, unsure. "Where is she?"

On the other side of the workbench, Jafa and Jacque smiled. "I thought you'd never ask." Jacque's voice rang with glee. She touched a lamp to a fuse-like rope that spit and hissed as it ignited. The flame ran down the rope, touching more spidering out from it. The web lit up the vast darkness before us. Floating just yards away was a crimson hull with a mainsail, a set of jibs, and a driver. Above them hovered a canvas and tar balloon that kept it afloat. The crimson and white clashed in clean, stark contrast. It was beautiful. The name *The Scarlet Liberty* was splashed across its stern in gold leaf.

"Well done, Jacque," Cecil said softly, beaming.

Jacque blushed deeply.

Cecil had to explain to me over and over again that we had to wait for the docks to empty before we made our move. After seeing *The Scarlet Liberty,* I'd wanted to leave right then. But yes, he was right, we'd be shot down before we ever saw a blue sky.

We waited a day or two more before heading to The Red Mary to see what the hold-up was. Work had not resumed, so the saloon was packed. I went with Cecil while Khalil, Jacque, and Jafa made last minute checks and packed our meager belongings aboard the ship.

The saloon went quiet when Cecil and I entered. I spotted Red in his usual seat at the bar. At least he hadn't ran yet. I had expected to see the Don with him, but he wasn't there.

"The hell's the hold up, Red?" I said, making my way in. "The people want a victory celebration."

Red took a long draw on a cigar. A golden emblem encircled the body of it. I recognized it as the royal seal.

"They will have one once the rencounter is over," Red mumbled with a dark grin. "One more participant needs to fight a one-on-one. We've been waiting for you."

I looked around and felt Cecil tense beside me. "I fought in the thunderdome," I argued. "That covers missing the one-on-one."

Red nodded, turning his lips down comically. "Except I am partial to favors and bribes." He pointed at me with two fingers, the smoking cigar clutched between them. He closed one eye, aiming at me. "You're worth a lot, it turns out."

I gulped and started to back away, my cowardly coyote taking over. I had no idea what might be coming. Four men charged us, grabbing Cecil by his arms. I thought he'd throw them off easily, but he struggled. His thoughts shot through my head: confusion, fear, and pain. Turning, I saw the men who had grappled him wore silver vambraces with crosses soldered to them. I snapped back to Red. He knew. How?

"Go on, Ezekiel," Red mumbled, hopping down from his throne. "Let's go outside. It's high noon and I have someone waiting for you." He approached me, gripping me by the back of the neck and steering me out into the street.

I realized with Cecil pinned down, I was weak again. I needed him more than I thought.

The crowd followed us to join an already clogged street. Below the clocktower, about eight yards away from me, stood the Don. Red shoved me out at arm's length, facing my uncle. He motioned his four goons closer, Cecil held tight between them.

"One last duel, I think," Red hissed in my ear, his stinking breath choking me. He shoved me forward and backed away into the audience.

The Don stood in the middle of the street, his hands on his hips. I surveyed his physique. Pure muscle, all lean and leather clad. "You can't give these people what you promised," he called to me, one hand on the chain that hung from his belt, ending in the singing blade.

"Can it, fancy pants," I shouted over him. The girls booed me. "Why don't you tell them why you're really here?"

He smirked and half-shrugged. "They don't care who you are down here. I'm giving you a fighting chance."

"For your conscience?" I shot back. "That won't change what you did to my father."

Mateo frowned slightly. "I didn't touch Markus."

"Save your lies," I hissed. I slid one foot back and touched the brim of my hat. I already knew how I'd defeat him. Just like my last fight. I saw the magic the singing metal would imbue me with if I could just get it. And live to activate it. "Come finish what you started eight years ago, Mateo!" I shouted.

Cecil's voice penetrated my mind in bits and pieces. He might be able to throw the men off if he tried hard enough. Then he could help me.

"I got this!" I shouted over my shoulder to him.

He calmed, letting me fight.

"Positions, then!" Redbeard shouted. "Mateo, we have faith in you. Don't let us down."

The Don leapt to the right, dodging my snake-like whip lash, and swung out with one singing blade. I bent backwards under it and it missed my head by a mere inch. As the Don leapt through the air, I flung my lasso to my left, catching his ankle. He fell as I pulled. I jumped back to tug him completely to the ground. He flailed and grunted, his wrist breaking his fall. He brought one of his blades down on my lasso, severing the rope.

We continued this dodging, feinting, and parrying for some time before I finally landed a whip strike to his face. He screeched as it cut across his eye, drawing blood. He stumbled backward, covering his ruined face, gripping his remaining axe hard. He glared at me through his bloodied face. I winced, a little more terrified than I thought I'd be.

"Well, now, look at you. How will you ever see what's coming with only one good eye? Ladies don't like a maimed man," I taunted. I lashed out at him with my whip to keep a safe distance.

He raised the arm that had been covering his mangled eye and the whip cut his wrist, wrapping around tightly. He twisted his wrist and grabbed the whip. I only realized my mistake when he yanked me hard toward him. I put my heels down, stopping myself just a few feet short of him. But he had long legs. He kicked out with his black boots, hitting me square in the forehead. A white light blinded me and my ears buzzed. I fell straight back, flat on the ground. I should have been more afraid of his strength.

"Get up!" I heard Cecil scream as the Don brought his whirling blade down into my hip. I couldn't even scream. My eyes widened and I puked from the pain instead. He hadn't brought it down with all of his might. He didn't want to kill me yet. It broke through my healing wound and the shock paralyzed me. I looked down and saw the singing metal in my hip bone. Blood pulsed out of me. My firms cried out as well.

"Get up!" Cecil shrieked again. His vampiric thoughts pummeled my brain. He wanted to drink dry the men who held him. He wanted to rip the Don's head from his shoulders.

I smiled now. I could hardly concentrate through the pulsing headache, but I had to wait just one second more. The singing metal was what we called marrow metal: it had to enter deep to be used for geomancy. That was probably why no one ever really used it. But he'd hit bone.

The Don stood over me, looking down. I had to render him immobile or dead if I wanted this victory. I needed to win.

"I didn't kill Markus," he said softly, meeting my eyes. He put his huge foot onto my stomach, holding me down. "I take no pleasure in killing you, Ezekiel. But it must be done."

I beckoned him closer to me. He leaned down. I gripped his leather coat and pulled myself up a little higher. Closer to his ear. Singing metal was a sore whore.

I shrieked at the top of my lungs, the metal's magic in me. Everyone panicked, covering their ears and scattering in madness. Banshee metal they also called it. The power of maddening voices. The Don's ears bled instantly and he fell over, writhing in pain. I had only experienced the metal once at the hands of a torturer in The Château d'Oubli. Marrow metal was not spared on torture victims.

I pushed Mateo all the way over as he clutched at his head, suffering from the voices in it. I sat up, gave a thumbs-up to my firm, and pulled the blade out.

"Thank you, my people," I coughed, spitting out the last of my vomit. "Would anyone mind fetching me a medic?"

They cheered loudly once they recovered. So loudly. Cecil ran to me, tossing the blade aside and putting his hand over my new wound. He shook his head at me, wanting to chastise and preach, but he held it in.

"You have to stop doing that," he mumbled.

I smiled, nearly fainting once again into his arms, happy with my little victory.

"The fight isn't over!" Red shouted. "One must die."

"You're right." I pushed off Cecil a little to grab my revolver. I struggled to pull the hammer back.

His grip on me turned to a warning. "Don't do this, Ezekiel. You'll regret it. Don't start your reign with blood."

I shoved him off me, using both hands to grip my gun now, determined to pull the hammer back. Mateo rolled over onto his side, preparing to stand up now that the effects had dissipated. "One day, Cecil," I said, defeated. I was too weak to aim, let alone pull the trigger, "we'll compare body counts. I'm no saint." I flicked my head away from San Sous-terre. "Take him to the brig, then," I ordered.

His eyes tracked me for just a moment before following my orders. He used all his strength to grapple the Don and march him out of town.

# 22
# The Scarlet Liberty

The next day marched by like clockwork. Every soul in The Château d'Oubli got sloshed out of mind and body to celebrate that, for once, someone not sponsored by Redbeard had won. This would be a turning point for the underground world. I had proved that someone could beat him. I knew they'd be looking for me at The Red Mary, so I sent word that I'd be making an entrance, and everyone should be on the lookout for my arrival. That would give us more than enough time to get out before suspicion set in.

I'd slept away the rest of the day before, waking only to be force-fed hearty stew with mystery meat and water by Cecil, who insisted I needed my strength. He'd once again bound my wounds and wouldn't let me walk more than a few steps to save my energy. Early the day of the celebration, we heaved our packs onto our backs and slinked down to the mine tracks that would take us to the perimeter. Red may have been unseated as master of The Château d'Oubli, but no one yet knew where his hoard was.

"The magnetic pulls on the bottom of her will drain the engines," Jacque explained as the fortified walls of the hideout loomed before us. "We can fly over the hoard—all in metal, bullet proof containers—activate the pulls and secure the crates of shinies under us. We don't have enough power to keep the engines running and hold on to the hoard for very long, so we'll have to go down and manually tie down the loot once we're in the clear. We've got cargo nets. We'll be home free in just a matter of moments, hey."

*The Scarlet Liberty* floated expectantly off the side of the cliffs. Jafa had made a rope bridge from the ground to her deck. We went across one at a time as it swung dramatically with the weight of us.

"The Don?" I asked Cecil as we all stowed our packs below deck.

He nodded upwards. Once back on deck, I spotted the semiconscious Mateo laying against the main mast, hands shackled before him. I didn't say anything, heading to the rope bridge. I went back across to untie it from the hitching post back on the cliff. Cecil said to untie it from the ship, but I didn't want to leave such a good resource behind. I untied it, then gripped it hard, putting one foot on a rung. Holding my breath, I dropped off the cliff and swung dangerously far out on the bridge turned ladder. Heart thudding in my throat, I climbed up.

Jafa flipped the levers, silently manning the engines, boiler, and other such necessities with Jacque. Khalil took the large helm in his automatonic arm. Behind him, Cecil held a compass and the maps Khalil had made. The beautiful red ship shuddered as the engines revved on and she lurched. I flew forward several steps and gripped the rail, watching the ground below start to move. Her engines were so loud in the uncommon silence that my heart raced, knowing we may have just signaled to the entire Château that something was not right. Ten minutes later of slugging forward, from where I looked over above, I saw dozens of long, rectangular boxes behind Red's wall come into view. *The Scarlet Liberty* shuddered as her magnets turned on.

Jafa called commands to Khalil and Jacque, lowering the ship enough to make the crates shudder. "Hold on!" the older man shouted as we entered the magnetic range. Red's hoard snapped up, smacking against the bottom side of *The Scarlet Liberty* so hard she tilted from side to side.

"Even it out!" Jacque shouted to Khalil to get him to crank the helm a little.

I got too nervous from the sound and the movement. "Navigator!" I called to Khalil at the helm. "Take us out of here!"

The whole airship lurched as the boxes soared up and magnetized to the bottom. It bobbed as it fell a few feet with each new load. The engines kicked in another notch, raising it back up.

"Follow the river," Cecil shouted over the roar of the engines. "Take the first right. It's a sharp one."

Jafa pulled his goggles down and pulled a lever that released pendulum-like, oscillating propellers on the sides that steadied the ship. *The Scarlet Liberty* jerked and bucked, flying forward on all cylinders. Below, we heard a few musket shots go off, but they did nothing. Shouting and orders followed. They knew we were gone, and they knew we had the hoard.

"I hope you have a plan," I shouted to Cecil over the rushing air. My adrenaline coursed like a fiery river. "The whole of the American Empire will hear about this in tomorrow's newspaper. We won't be very conspicuous."

Cecil blanched. "It's time for *you* to get creative, your highness!"

I gnashed my teeth. Khalil's knuckles paled on the helm. Jacque dripped with sweat, heaving coal into the massive furnaces. I turned to face The Château d'Oubli as we flew farther away down the tunnels. I prepared to say a goodbye to it, maybe get emotional. Then two white hands reached over the railing. Arms flexed, bony elbows popping up into view, pulling up a white, soaking body. A spear sat in one pale hand and an evil glint in one good eye; the other eye was shut from a bloody slashing wound. The underman from the coral tunnel.

Behind the scarred one came a whole tribe of undermen. I had forgotten to roll up the rope ladder.

"We've got company!" I shouted.

"Keep them away from the prisoner!" Khalil shouted as the leading underman lunged with a skull-tingling screech toward the helpless Don.

I ran first at the leader, whom I had wounded previously. I slashed out with my long knife but missed as he dodged and leapt up into the rigging to perch. With a screech, he signaled the others to charge me. I planted my feet and pulled out the blade I had taken from the Don and then a small pistol. I had no grace at all, but I could move faster than soggy undermen. I dodged, shot one, and brought my arm around, cutting half the head off another.

"Keep them away from the machinery!" Jacque squealed as two ran to the engine and began to hammer on it. With a new lasso, I caught them and pulled them back. Firing once more behind me to keep the others at bay, I dragged the other two to the edge. With a screaming heave, I rolled them over the side. But something caught my eye: a whole other airship appeared out of the darkness behind us.

"Cecil!" I cried. "Redbeard! He's following us."

I turned and screamed as the lead underman appeared beside me. With his strong arms, he shoved me hard. I fell backwards, my backside hitting the railing. I tipped. I'm pretty sure my stomach came out my mouth in terror as my arms flailed, nothing to grab. I screamed into the darkness and caught sight of the Don fending off the last underman despite his bound hands.

"Cecil!" I screamed this time, panic taking my voice twelve octaves up. I spiraled over the rail, about to plummet to my doom.

Cecil roared and leapt towards me, but two undermen stayed his progress with their attacks.

My head spun as I went boots over head into the air. The last thing I saw was the Don, suddenly free of his shackles, charging towards Cecil and raising his singing blade.

# 23 The Escape

The bottom of *The Scarlet Liberty* zoomed further away. I plunged downwards into the eternal blackness of the dungeon. I looked to my left and saw a light. Daylight? Was I already dead? I imagined hitting the ground and how badly it would hurt for just a second. My skull would burst and my brains would smatter everywhere. I had accomplished nothing in my life, and something like guilt made me hate myself in my final moments. To my right, Redbeard's ship gained on us.

A huge bat shot towards me like a rocket on the fourth of July. Two claw-like hands reached out for me. Without thinking, I desperately reached up and caught the monstrous arms of Cecil in his vampiric form. He shot up like a bat out of hell at a speed that made my eyes tear up. I could feel his muscles pumping with every beat of his wings.

"I've got you, your highness," he said sarcastically. "How many times do I need to save your ass?"

"I would have thought of something," I snapped. We both knew that wasn't true in the least.

Cecil dove like a hunting falcon. He soared around the airship and dropped me on the deck with the singing blade. He rounded the ship again, taking two undermen with him and throwing them through the balloons of two of Redbeard's ships. Cries from the men rang in the dark, stony air as the ship's hydrogen burst into molten flames. The ships crashed below.

I gripped the blade, rolling to my feet to face the leading underman. His long white hair whipped around his face, and he opened his gaping maw to scream a war cry at me.

"Come down and fight me, then!" I challenged him. I had leftover cockiness from the fight before still boiling under my skin.

The underman leapt down and charged at me on three limbs, his spear raised in the other. Behind me, Redbeard's artillery fired a barrage at us. Behind the underman, the Don watched me, one blade in hand. I spun the blade I had, crouching to prepare to engage with the underman. But then the Don ran to catch up with him, his own blade singing in a whirlwind.

"Hey!" he shouted at the charging underman. The shout made the creature turn and thrust his spear out in defense.

This underman had marvelous aim, like a military man. He hit the Don in his left thigh. Blood spattered out and he went down. I took the chance to sling the blade at the underman, hitting him square in his back. He shrieked and turned to face me again. With a great leap, he tackled me and sunk his teeth deep into my shoulder. Sick of being bitten at this point, I clawed at his head, pulling at his brittle hair so fiercely some of it came out.

"They're gaining on us!" Khalil shouted. "I can only keep so many off us!"

"Light ahead!" Jacque replied. "Hold fast!"

Khalil scanned the tunnels for Cecil. He'd be weak in the sunlight. We all would be, though. Most of us hadn't seen sunlight in more than eight years. Except maybe Khalil.

I kicked the underman off me and reached for my revolver.

"Don't shoot him," the Don panted. With one mighty, muscled arm, he ripped the spear from his thigh. The underman licked my blood off his lips excitedly and didn't see the Don approach him.

"Take my kill, will you?" I snapped, clapping my hand to my shoulder. I clicked the hammer back.

Before I could fire, the Don shoved the underman over the railing.

"What the hell?" I shouted. "Just let me shoot him."

He checked over the side and watched the now severely wounded underman run along the riverbank, raising its fist at us. The immediate threat gone, the Don watched me. Not attacking, not angry, not plotting. I didn't like the look in his eye, but I ignored him for now. He couldn't do anything this high up with an angry fleet behind us.

"It's the dawn!" Jacque shouted as she opened the dampener to shoot us forward. The narrow exit looked hardly big enough, but *The Scarlet Liberty* made it out with only a few bumps. We burst out into a flurry of white and cold. The dry, thin air immediately choked me.

A large, black flying shape dodged through the exit, squeezing through at the same time as the back rudders: Cecil. The exit too small, he bounced off the rocky opening, trying to avoid fire from Red, and careened into the rigging. His massive batwings got caught in the ropes, tying him like a pig over a fire. We broke from beneath the surface and the sun hit him. I heard him scream from below even amongst the shots from Redbeard.

"Take us into the clouds!" I commanded.

My hat and bandana had flown off sometime during the fight and I tried desperately to re-cover the rotlead band around my neck. I waited for the searing, rotten smell of the rotlead to sizzle and melt through my flesh like we had been told for years. It was what kept even the daring among us from escaping into the sunlight above.

Nothing happened.

I whirled around to look at Jacque. Her brown eyes were huge and her mouth open as she watched my collar fizzle away. She reached up, tearing the bandana away from her own neck. I almost shouted for her to stop, but was too late. She touched the band gently and parts of it drifted into the rabid wind. It did disintegrate in the sun, but that was it.

"It's turning to ash," she called to me.

Yes, the rotlead disintegrated in the sunlight. Just floating away like a dandelion carrying a wish. In a matter of moments, the entire disgusting band had vanished in a waft of smelly ash. It had all been a lie. A lie that kept us invisibly tethered to an underground nightmare. I looked back at Jacque, but she was already concentrating on getting us higher. She had been vulnerable, rotlead exposed, but had taken us out anyway. She'd thought she was about to die, but she'd pressed on. Damn, I loved her.

"Up it is." Jafa tightened his goggles and pulled the helm back towards him.

We had come out right into the sun and the huge peaks of the Rocky Mountains. My eyes instantly streamed in the freezing air of the mountain altitude. The sun blazed a white light, piercing my eyes like a dagger. It hurt to inhale the cold, clean air.

The jolting from the ascension knocked me over and my head spun. All my wounds pounded in agony and my ears filled with the rushing sound of my blood. The clatter of Redbeard and the attack faded underneath us as the special engines and propellers shot us up into the clouds, over the mountain. I glanced back but didn't see his ship leave the same opening. He'd either crashed trying to chase us or had given up. A sound of thunder and a cloud of orange told me the former had occurred. The thin, dry air wasn't enough and dizziness swirled my head.

"Breathe," I heard a deep voice say as a mask slipped over my head and latched snuggly over my face. The Don dragged me to the foremast and propped me up on it.

"Get Cecil before the sun hits him again," I panted, clinging to the brass oxygen tank. "He won't break the ropes for fear of hurting the ship."

The Don looked up, spotting the smoldering vampire. Then he ascended the rigging gracefully. My vision got less fuzzy as I breathed through the mask, taking in sweet oxygen.

Remembering the hoard, I ran to the edge, looking for a way down to tie it up.

"You can't go down there," Khalil shouted. "Not at this height."

Just as I was about to throw myself over anyway, the ship shook, the magnets gave out, and the crates crashed to the snowy peaks below. My plans for revenge fell with them. With sickening thuds, they exploded into puffs of snow and slid over the mountainside. Some didn't break, but every last metal crate vanished. My heart sank. Lost for what to do now that the means of my next move had plummeted hundreds of feet below, I went back to the crew.

"Well done, everyone," I found myself saying, unable to keep the disappointment out of my voice. A strong, mysterious gratitude for being alive held me in check.

Jacque had on tinted goggles, but she smiled at me, looking like a joyful ladybug. "Pretty good, hey? Not bad for a rusty old man, a nomad, and engineer, and a uh…" She smiled at me again. "A rat of a leader."

Her face fell as she caught sight of something over my shoulder. "Cecil!" she gasped through her mask.

I turned and ran with her and Khalil to where the Don descended with a bleeding, charred Cecil.

"I'm fine," he said softly, bracing himself on the railing, under the shade of the main sail. "Nothing a long day's rest can't fix. Might I suggest we find a place to tie up for the day?"

"Not yet," Khalil slipped around Cecil and grabbed the Don in his metal arm's tight grip, twisting his captive's arm behind his back. "We have a prisoner who needs seeing to."

"Wait," Cecil and I said at the same time. He looked at me, curious at the reason for my interjection. I stammered, though. What should I say? Mateo knew me, he'd saved me, and he'd saved Cecil. I didn't understand. I'd lost my loot and needed another in.

We met each other's eyes, no words coming to mind. There were no secrets amongst us. Even Jacque didn't seem surprised, almost like she knew already. A strange kind of jealousy lighted in my chest at everyone knowing my vampire's secret. I had to get the situation under control. Back to the task at hand.

"Khalil, get him out of here," I ordered. "Take him below deck and make sure he can't escape."

"He saved Cecil," Jacque said softly.

"Don't trust anyone too fast, Jacque. Trust is the thirst for blood." I chanced a look down at the Don. "Trust is the betrayal of family and years of darkness and torture."

He didn't argue. With a strange glare on his face, he let Khalil lead him away. His lips pinched together and his eyes turned to fire, but he didn't speak.

Khalil and I spent a moment figuring out where we'd exited The Château d'Oubli.

"Has to be Nouvelle Montagne," Khalil said, mispronouncing the name.

"Nouvelle Montagne," I corrected, using the French pronunciation. "We're in Kansouri. It's the only mountain range in the territory."

My eyes surveyed the horizon slowly. I hoped to see something I recognized, but also dreaded it. Jafa was still silent beside me, now at the helm so Khalil could help with the maps. Jacque hunted down wrappings for Cecil, to help protect him from the sun.

The sun beckoned me. I walked to the rail and looked over into the new nothingness, eyes burning like hell. Cecil followed at my side, wrapped tightly in his old duster and a hood over his face. A dirty rag of a scarf covered his chin to the bridge of his alabaster nose, where his red sunglasses perched.

"What is that?" I spoke so softly that my voice barely made it out of my throat. Was I afraid to wake up from a good dream? I couldn't stop marveling at the sky. The thick, white clouds. The air was almost too much.

"The sun?" Cecil asked, looking at me as though I were a stupid baby just learning to speak. "It's a giant ball of gas, constantly exploding—"

"No," I interrupted, not even showing my anger at his condescension. "I don't know if it's sunrise or sunset. I can't—" My voice broke and I stopped to clear my throat and try again. "I can't tell."

The vampire winced into the rays and pulled his wrappings over his nose more closely, his hands safe in gloves. I could still smell his burning flesh. "It's an empty sky, and the rays are weak, not hot after a day's work. So it's sunrise. Dawn, as Jacque said."

"It's not empty," I said softly. I put my hat (which I had found once we leveled out) on his head to shield his face more. "The sky is not empty. The sunrise is filling it all up."

"Mmm." He sighed. "One tiny sun for this entire sky. And yet it's not empty, as you said. It is full. That one star," he reached out to the sun with his gloved finger as if to touch it, "fills miles of the sky with color."

"I didn't expect to hear a vampire speak so fondly of the sun."

"And I didn't expect you to lock up the Don after he saved me. And helped us escape."

The sky lost its charm. I glared ahead of me, not giving Cecil the satisfaction of seeing me angry. He'd ruined the moment. "Do not judge my actions."

He nodded and turned to me. I faced him. He bowed. "Yes, highness," he said softly.

We were dropping below the clouds now to see the land below and get our bearings more firmly. Khalil came above deck now with one of those maps he had lifted.

"Ezekiel," Cecil said softly. "The Don needs dealing with."

"We kill him," I said simply. "Right now, if we can. Toss him overboard. Then we go on as planned."

He turned me to face him. His eyes shone with disbelief.

"What else can we do?" I asked harshly. "He'll ruin my plans. We can't let him go. He deserves this after what he did. He can deny it all he wants."

"What if he's not lying?" Cecil pressed.

"Why do you care?" I snapped, raising my hand to shove him should he come closer.

He turned away to face out over the railing, lost for a way to convince me to let my uncle live. He knew as well as me that he was a loose end that could not be let go. "I must admit," he said softly, "I thought finding the prince of MidWest would be simpler—also more complicated, since everyone thinks you're dead. But I thought putting you back in the palace would be easier."

I scoffed. "My plan is to do what these topsiders do. Become rich, take a title, engross myself in their materialism and ways and get close to them. Infiltrate them as one of their own. Find every person responsible for putting me in that damned place, who made me choose between life and a cup of water, and make them suffer as I have. Then destroy them from the inside out. All of them."

A moment of silence passed before he asked, "Even your mother?"

I heard mockery in his tone. I refused to face him to answer. He couldn't read my mind. "All of them," I lied, my voice quivering.

"I've failed, then."

Shocked, I turned to face him. "How?"

"I made a monster out of a man."

Now I smirked. "All you did was ease my way. Try to remember who the monster is here, vampire."

Inside me, the two coyotes fought over me, as if I were prey to be devoured. One wanted to believe my mother had nothing to do with my eight years of suffering; the other hid in the shadows, urging me to eradicate every last soul who might be connected to my imprisonment. That coyote was rabid, infecting me with its anger without warning. I wish Cecil could have been in my head like I was in his. He'd understand then. But I needed to seem strong to him, dauntless.

I turned to leave, but he seized my wrist, turning my arm so the soft flesh hovered just under his nose. He inhaled deeply. He was starved after his misadventure in the rigging. Healing took a lot of strength. His lips twitched and his teeth parted slightly. I wanted to pull my arm away, but the tether stayed me. His iron will in this moment of weakness impressed me.

I checked over my shoulder and saw the other three busy with the maps, paying us no mind.

"Fine," I hissed quietly.

This time he bit down gently, his teeth slowly popping into my wrist, pinching and puncturing my sensitive skin. I moaned loudly, pressing my lips closed. The feeling came again. The rushing and the panting. My arm ached as he sucked the life out of me. I involuntarily shivered when I felt his cold tongue caress my sensitive flesh as he drank. Our tether snapped together in a fiery forge of blood against flesh. His thoughts and emotions cascaded onto me like a maelstrom. Attached, a feeling of sudden panic hit me.

Cecil ripped his bloody lips off me. He'd caught sight of something over my shoulder.

"Pirates!" he shouted.

# PART II

# PIRATES

# 24 Pirate Attack

"They will outrun us," Jafa called from the helm. "See their solar sail? We are not fast enough."

"I thought you said the pirates would leave us alone," I shot to Khalil. "That we are empty enough."

Khalil ran to the railing and pulled out a pocket telescope. "The only way they know we have value is if they recognized Red's mark on those crates."

"It fell," I said, desperate for a solution.

"Well, pirates will be pirates." Khalil squinted. "It appears to be Japonais pirates." He trailed off. "Salazar." He dropped the glass from his eye. "What bad luck."

"Give me that," I snatched away the glass and looked for myself. Next to me, Cecil looked with his vampiric eyes. "Forty guns. Spades, it looks like a man o' war." I looked over at Cecil. "What do we do? I don't know squat about warships or navigation or anything."

Cecil brushed passed me but quickly whispered, "You'd better think of something, *your highness*."

My eyes followed him and saw that the other three looked to me as well. I wanted to shout, "What do you want me to do?" but I dared not let those weak words past my lips. I met Jacque's eyes, but she couldn't see mine through my tinted goggles. She waited for me to take command. The pirate galley rumbled behind me.

"You know them?" I asked Khalil.

The nomad's face paled in the daylight. "I've spent a considerable amount of *time* on them, yes." He glanced back at the ship that gained on us. "They might take us alive. They might shoot us down."

If we got caught, we could bargain for our lives with the location of Red's fallen hoard. But I'd rather not get caught…

"We out maneuver them," I started. I planted my wide-brimmed hat more firmly onto my head. "Jafa, take us into the clouds. Jacque, get those boilers hot, and Khalil, go to the rudder board. We'll need careful hands."

"What are you thinking?" Cecil asked. "I don't fancy being abducted by pirates."

"I'm trying," I grunted. "Jafa, strong on the main helm. Don't let anything slip an inch. Jacque, get those engines as full and steamed up as you can. When I give the word, open the hatch and let it fly. Khalil, take those rudders and swing them right. Then, Jafa will let the helm go, turning the mainsail horizontal."

"Is your head full of snakes?" Khalil's eyes widened. "We'll pivot hard into the mist and clouds. What if we hit something?"

I smiled to hide my nerves, running my hand over the brim of my hat. "Tally-ho!"

They ran like navy rats across the deck to their stations. Something about life-or-death situations always makes a team out of people. The stupid ones argue and are the first to die. But the wise realize that for the moment, doing as one man says may keep a ship aloft a little longer.

"Cecil, come," I commanded, but he had followed beside me to the forecastle railing before I'd commanded him. "Look back and tell me if you see them."

He turned and squinted ever so slightly. "It's a forty-gun ship. The flotation devices must be massive. I see someone!" I turned to look, but couldn't see them. "They are trying to stay in the clouds, too. Doesn't look like they know we've seen them. I believe that's the captain. Black greatcoat with blue trim, and his hat is magnificent. Wonderful feathering."

I groaned and rolled my eyes.

He looked up at me.

"Crew? Weapons?" I asked.

He reeled backwards suddenly. "Chain shot!"

"Now!" I screamed to my frightened team.

Jafa leapt back from the helm, Khalil cranked the rudders from the control board, and Jacque threw open the boilers, leaping back in a shout as the hot power burst out. We all jerked to one side and then were thrown to the floor when *The Scarlet Liberty* bucked and flew to the right. My head swam as we spun around, piercing a dark cloud.

"Spades, they are close!" Khalil shouted over the roar of the wind and the engines.

The ship creaked and groaned. I even saw the masts and the towering propellers bend a little in the stress. Made my stomach clench. My knuckles turned white as I clutched the railing. We all held something for dear life as we careened through a barrage of fire, bullets, and shouts from the pirates. Jafa maneuvered the ship as best he could, throwing us all over the deck.

I scrambled up with Cecil's help and ran to the rail with the telescope to look over. We leveled out and the pirates turned to watch us vanish into the clouds, which turned thunderous. The air got thin again; I heard Khalil and Jacque behind me gasping for air as they looked for the masks we had used before. I clenched, nervous and breathing shallowly. I smiled at the sight that greeted me through the glass.

"Well done, boys," I said. The others met me at the rail, looking down into the clouds. Thunder cracked across the sky below us and flashes of cannon fire lit up the white clouds. "We may yet taste freedom."

We were silent as the shots slowed. They'd lost us.

"Turn the engines off," Cecil suggested. "We'll float and wait for them to pass."

This made me nervous, but I didn't argue.

At my side, Jacque whispered, "Red didn't make it out. Will the topsiders hear of an escape?"

Khalil answered for me. "The Château d'Oubli is a horror story for topsiders. They hear of it, but many think it's code for an execution or a quiet exile. That kind of thing. Political agendas and all that."

"I recall," Cecil agreed. "We may be safe from the wide world knowing we've escaped, but perhaps not so much the royals. Especially when the Don doesn't return."

All sound around us quieted. Lights on our pursuer's ships went out, and no more screams and shouts of orders and final breaths came up from where we'd led the pirates right into a brewing storm. In the distance, explosions sounded and the smell of burning fuel, wood, and dirty rope eventually met us.

"Take us down, Jafa," I said. "Slowly."

The older man looked at me, shocked. He panted harder than the rest of us and clutched his chest. "I... I..." He couldn't get words out.

"Grandpère?" Jacque gasped, running to his side. Her face paled. "What's happening?"

"Be quiet!" Khalil hissed. "I can still hear the flutter of their sails."

"Jafa?" she cried as he went down, sweat pouring from his white hair.

We broke through the clouds when he released the helm to be greeted by a front-mounted ballista on the deck of a grand ship. We were able to see the smiling faces of the pirates as they took in our shock with glee. They launched their harpoon into our hull, knocking us all off our feet again as they pulled up starboard side and boarded us with shouts and raised fists.

"Don't fight!" Cecil yelled as I took out both the Don's singing blades and began to twirl them.

We had instinctively formed a back-to-back circle with each other around Jafa and Jacque. *The Scarlet Liberty* leaned heavily to her starboard side as the weight of the ballista harpoon dragged her down. Pirates swung onto the deck from grappling hooks and others leapt across with great wings attached to their backs by leather apparatuses. In a shorter time than it took me to grasp and get the blades spinning, we were surrounded by probably twenty pirates.

"Check the hold and the other bits of this sad shanty ship," a deep, feminine voice barked out to the men. White cowhide boots ran all the way up a firm, strong set of thighs attached to a tall woman. Her breeches, coat, and tricorn hat glared white even in the grey light. Only the trims of her coat and feathers in her hat were various shades of black and grey. She wore men's clothes better than any man I had ever seen. She also stood taller than any man. She planted her boots on the railing, one hand steadying her from the pull and tug of the ships. She glared at Cecil.

"You the captain of this vessel?" she asked in a thick, Allemande accent. She laughed before he could answer, clutching her chest with the effort. "Of course not. I am now. Kapitän!"

"We have friends," I started.

She leapt down and seized my face in her gloved hands. Cecil stayed my blades. "You mean those smoldering Château d'Oubli rats on the peaks below?" She smirked. Her magnificent combination of red and gold hair whipped in the wind.

"I thought you said the captain was wearing black," I hissed to Cecil.

She smiled, smoothing her breeches. "I am not the captain," she said, "of that ship," pointing to the man of war. "I am captain of *this* ship now."

"She's ours!" Jacque shouted in reply, cradling Jafa's now unconscious body. "We made her. You can't take her."

"And she's ravishing," a voice said from behind the crew of pirates. "For a cobbled together monster from below. Her parts will do nicely for outfitting *The Kimiko Fire*."

The pirates all kneeled at the sound of the strong, deep voice. Some even removed their hats.

"Hell's bells," Khalil cursed softly.

The man Cecil had described earlier appeared in all his finery. He stood shorter than the woman in white by a head and shoulders, and stayed atop the railing where he could see us all. He was dressed in the western and Europian styles, but his fine black hair, elegant features, and the beautiful swords at his sides came from Japon.

"Rats from The Château d'Oubli?" he asked the woman in white. "Not our usual aeronautical liberation of valuable assets."

She reached over to me and ripped my mask, goggles, and hat off in one strong swipe.

"Jawohl, kapitän," she replied in her native tongue. "Pasty, fresh ones." She eyed me like a hawk hungry for a dive. "I think this one is the captain."

"No, he is." I pointed to Cecil.

"Enough!" the Japonais captain shouted. His eyes landed on Khalil. A kind of hunter-like glint spread a grin over his face, as if he'd finally caught his long-pursued prey. "Khalil Rashad," he said, savoring the name like a delicious flavor. "I thought I'd never see you again in this lifetime."

"Satoshi," Khalil replied darkly.

The pirate captain's eyes went to Khalil's metallic arm. "I see the Château has equipped you with more ways to steal the lives of innocents. How fortuitous this is. This pleases me." He scanned the rest of us. "Bring them all aboard. And have that one shackled below." He pointed to me. "I don't like the look in his eye."

I spun the blades and threw one towards the captain. It whirled at him, but missed as he bent to the side to dodge it. It buried itself in the railing. A very sloppy throw. The woman in white pulled out a long-barreled revolver and pointed it at Cecil.

"Drop the other one," she quipped to me, pulling the hammer back.

I scoffed. "Shoot him."

Cecil snapped to me, his thoughts piercing my mind. He believed they *would* shoot him.

"Are you crazy? Just drop it!" Jacque pleaded. "Jafa?" She looked down at her grandfather. He hadn't moved. His face had started to turn white.

I met Khalil's eyes. We had the same thought: no way in hell were we going to be prisoners again. I lunged at the woman with one hand out in front of me to push her out of the way. Khalil followed me and covered me from another pirate as I ran across the deck. I prepared to jump and fling the last blade when the revolver went off, Khalil shouted, and the bullet ricocheted off his arm. I leapt away and clashed singing steel to singing steel as the pirate captain defended himself with his odachi. I pressed down on him, being at least six inches taller.

"Stop!" the woman in white screamed at me.

I looked back to see my whole team being held down—even Cecil —by the pirate crew, Jacque with the long barrel under her chin.

"Please stop," Jacque cried, her eyes already red with tears.

I might have considered it until the pirate captain pushed me back and seized my throat with shocking strength and dexterity. Probably something that came with clean air and a proper diet. "You've already lost this one, cowboy." He turned to his crew. "Lock them all away. Throw the body over." He indicated Jafa. Even I could tell he was gone. His old heart couldn't take the escape.

Jacque screamed and cried to hold her grandfather one last time, but we were all bound, gagged, and dragged on board the man of war the pirate had called *The Kimiko Fire*. Cecil glared at me with his dark eyes, but stopped when the sun hit him as they walked us across the plank to the other ship. He moaned against the gag, but tried to not show his pain. My wounds freshly opened as I struggled and felt the wet blood all down my pants.

"You don't know what you're doing," I shouted to the captain, fighting against my captors. "You don't know who I am!"

Satoshi Salazar, the captain, rounded on me. "All I know is you're traveling with Khalil Rashad." He pointed his curved sword at the nomad. "The man who stole eternity from me."

# Time Thief

They shackled us, hands over head, in the brig. On the way down, they led us past storerooms of strange and foreign instruments: violins, harpsichords, harps, all manner of brass, and some things that didn't even look like instruments. Those rooms were clean, and some even had red carpet. But gunpowder and grime covered the brig. It must have been used for those forty guns before they'd converted it into a cell. Obviously done by inexperienced hands, screws and shackles hung about like laundry on a line. But they were strong and did the trick. They weren't traditional or even widely used cuffs and chains. I didn't know how to pick any of them, and by the look on his face, neither did Khalil. It wouldn't have mattered. Blood loss had made me weak. Cecil, also still weak, watched me like a loyal guard dog, measuring my breaths and my pulse with his keen eyes.

"I thought you could spring us, if it wouldn't be too much trouble," I spoke into the muggy air.

Khalil shook his head and smirked. "Is this a bad time to tell you I have double-crossed this man more than once on my trips topside?"

Jacque sobbed a little at this, her heart still broken over her grandfather.

"I'm not surprised," Cecil mused.

"Thrice," the Japonais pirate said from the other side of the bars. "But the last time was the worst."

The pirate leaned against the bars, smiling, and pulled his long black hair over one shoulder to smooth it. "I see the Château has not been kind to you, Khalil. This brings me joy. You know I hate to play the bad man, but you always bring it out in me." His eyes flitted to the metal arm and back.

"I see that woman hasn't grown tired of you and killed you off," the nomad shot back, testing his metallic arm's strength against the shackles. They held.

"Still a time thief, then?" the pirate asked. He nodded towards Cecil. "Must be, or you wouldn't have this one in tow."

Khalil glared at the pirate, keeping his words to himself now.

"Enough of this," I snapped. I felt the blood drain from my face and out my wound. "What do you want, pirate?"

"Captain Salazar," Khalil and the pirate said together.

The pirate smiled. "I'm so glad you remember our little game."

Khalil pursed his lips together and clenched his mechanical arm. "If I wasn't chained, I would rip your heart out."

"Fine words from a traitor, whispered through bilge bars. They're just your currency, Khalil." The captain looked at me now. "You're right. I don't know who you are, and frankly, I don't care. However, anyone can be useful to me. If you're willing. I am a sporting man when I can be. I'm not unreasonable."

My heart raced at the opportunity to find a way out of the brig and off the pirate's ship. "Tell me what you have in mind." We'd come so far. I couldn't be stopped now by a mere pirate in the Kansouri skies.

His dark eyes danced to Cecil, taking in his whole form. "You know about alchemy?" he started.

Swallowing tensely, I nodded and half-shrugged. I knew things could be alchemized. I'd stolen geos and chemicals for alchemy for other people back in The Château d'Oubli, but had never done it myself. There was a time I'd planned to. But something about Cecil had changed my mind.

Captain Salazar pulled a keg of gunpowder over and sat on it, careful to push his coat out of the way first. He crossed his legs and closed his eyes as though meditating. He breathed in the black air and held it before a long exhale.

His placid behavior confused me. I'd thought being captured by pirates would be a short affair, ending swiftly with us all walking the plank and shattering on the rocks below. But Captain Salazar was hardly hostile.

He said, "This Egyptian joined our crew, not telling us he worked for his Syndicate. The story of how he came to be amongst us is a good one to be told around vardo fires with full tankards. But in short, I saved him and joined us for a few adventures."

"Your honor will kill you, Satoshi" the woman in white said, appearing behind him.

Salazar opened his eyes. "I hear it, Khalil. I hear the ticking."

Cecil looked at the chain around Khalil's neck. "The medallion?"

"What is that?" I asked.

"That is a chronos pendent, the weapon of a time thief," Captain Salazar supplied. "They let him out of The Château d'Oubli, he gathers others' time, and brings it back to those willing to pay for it. Time is such a powerful currency. Anyone will pay anything for it."

"They let you out of that place on a regular basis and you came back?" I tried to keep the disbelief out of my voice but failed.

"No, no, my simple prison rat," Salazar corrected me. "A time thief is always carefully watched. I doubt your friend here ever had a chance to escape. What he does is too valuable. There are factions within the politicals who want more people to do what he does. But it's difficult. Dangerous. The ingredients for passing someone's time to another are hard to come by." He gestured to Cecil.

The vampire's eyes snapped between all of us. One second later, understanding dawned. "My blood?" he asked.

The pirate stood up now and took out his odachi. He slipped it through the bars and laid it on Khalil's chest. A few chains clinked in tension, but we could do nothing with our arms bound so. "It makes villains of us all," Salazar whispered.

With quick movements, he flicked the tip of the sword, not drawing any blood, and caught the loose pendant in his graceful grasp. "One day, Khalil discovered a nest of vampires, his family being hunters. Very uncommon for the Syndicate. Most are just spies. Couriers. But he'd hit the motherload. Promising me eternity, with the use of alchemized vampire blood—bloodstones—and timesteel, I would live forever. Free to roam the skies. Eternity, unshackled by man's laws or the promise of death. Together." Salazar's face darkened and the lady in white stiffened. "But, as is the way of liars and rats, he spoke of the nest to the patriarch of their Syndicate. This patriarch swooped in, taking the nest, and had his own son arrested and sent below. But only after Isolde and I had been given time."

Carefully, he unlaced the top of his shirt and pulled it and his coat aside. Over his heart, attached to his flesh, ticked a device not unlike the medallion. "A catalyst device that uses the bloodstones to give us life. Without it, the stones make one a monster. But with it: eternity. That pendent he carries is a smaller version, temporary."

Behind him, the lady in white, Isolde, pulled her coat down to reveal matching, ticking technology. Her blue eyes swam in sorrow.

"Eternity isn't all it's cracked up to be," Cecil said darkly.

"Probably not," Salazar said with a deep breath, pulling himself out of his reverie. "I'd like the chance to try it out for myself, vampire. I was promised freedom forever." His eyes went back to Khalil. "Once he came out of that underground world, he stole the last of our stones, ripped the ones from our chests, and sold them to the patriarch to give to his employers. Tell me, Khalil, does the patriarch of a small MidWest Syndicate value you now? Will he take you back after you defected? Or were your double dealings with the royals too much to forgive?"

Khalil's eyes shone with hatred. "I cannot change what I've done."

"And I cannot kill you," Salazar lamented.

"Why not?" I asked. "If he's the one you're after, take him and let us go."

"Ezekiel!" Jacque cried from behind me. "You can't sacrifice him like that."

"It's complicated," Salazar replied. "And his death is not worth my conscience. You see, I don't like to be a bad man. So, here is my proposition, dungeon rat. I'm sorry." He smiled. "Here is my proposition, Ezekiel. I'm a reasonable man. I like freedom, and I see you are desperate for it. You duel Khalil, kill him, let me take this vampire, and you and the lady go free."

Jacque made a desperate noise behind me.

I didn't mean to look weak, but I looked to Cecil for guidance. He looked just as lost and desperate as I felt. That didn't help. "You will be sure to kill us if I refuse?" I asked.

"Oh, yes. I have no qualms about that. Khalil will be more difficult to get rid of, but I'm sure someday I'll find a way." He sheathed his longsword.

I reached out to Cecil's mind, but our weakened bodies made the tether faint. He had no help to give. I was on my own. I couldn't risk losing Cecil. I needed him. He'd come this far with me, and the part of me tied to him felt I owed him the chance to complete his mission. This new loyalty added a frustrating component to my calculations. I didn't trust Khalil, but I needed him, too. His connections to the Syndicates and the royals would come in handy as I put my long plan into action.

"Captain," I said steadily, still forming a new plan in my mind, "as you can see, I am in no condition to fight. This brings me no pleasure, as I'm often eager for a chance at violence. I know how to deal with violent men. But I'd lose against Khalil in my state."

The pirate narrowed his eyes at me, listening to my every word. He heard the ulterior motive in my voice. "Go on, Ezekiel."

"Spare us," I asked, keeping the dignity in my voice. "I can see you are perhaps not an evil man. I don't think you will kill us out of spite."

"What is it you want?" the lady in white shot to me. Her icy eyes penetrated me hard. Where Salazar seemed open to discussion, she was closed off. Cautious.

Salazar inclined his head, agreeing with her. "I have very little time left in this world," he said, tapping the machine on his chest.

"Why not get it removed?" Cecil asked.

Isolde took an aggressive step towards us. "It cannot come off. It is forever."

I glanced quickly at Khalil, then to Cecil, then back to Salazar. "We can get you more bloodstones. As you said, it's dangerous work. Spare your crew and let..." I was about to say "let us." I changed tactics. "Let *me* get them for you."

Salazar smiled at me. "I like you, Ezekiel. I see ambition in you. Something akin to a leader lurks under your rather slimy exterior. I like to see where dangerous deals go. I like to take risks. Makes me feel alive and gives me a sense of freedom." He stood up, smoothing his coat and sheathing his sword. He eyed Jacque, taking in the oil under her nails and the tool belt on her hips.

"Engineer?" he asked.

She nodded. "I-I built the ship," she offered weakly. "Me and Jafa."

The pirate rubbed his chin, the gears in his skull churning. "She has some unique features I am very interested in. Those oscillating propellers are intriguing. A trial run," he said after another short moment. "I will keep you all alive. This lady engineer seems to be worth the most among all of you. She's too valuable to kill, anyway. She'll do well for the aeronautical liberation of valuable assets."

Jacque gave a cooing sound of relief.

"I could kill you and take your vampire, but his blood would only get us so far. I am not like the Syndicate and their hunters who would imprison a monster like a vampire, feeding it and harvesting the blood over and over."

Beside me, Cecil exhaled in scared horror.

"You see?" Captain Salazar smiled at me. "I am not a bad man. And I'm curious about you. So, Ezekiel, you have saved yourself and your friends for a time. By the power vested in me by the skies and all the gems I have not yet set my fingers to, welcome to the crew, boys. Lady." He winked at Jacque.

Behind him, Isolde's face was lined with livid anger, eyes burning into Khalil. Salazar turned to leave and stopped.

"Oh, and one more thing." He faced us. "We found a prisoner aboard your ship. One Don Mateo, the bastard Don of San Muerte." He feigned curiosity, tapping his chin. "How the hell did he end up in the brig of a patchwork ship bursting out of the side of Nouvelle Montagne?"

"*Why* the hell, more like," the lady in white added. She almost smirked.

"What'd you do to him, captain?" I shot. "He was my prisoner."

"And you are mine," Salazar quipped. "I suppose for now, we have to just wait and see." He narrowed his eyes at me, curious. "Are you capable of waiting? Of harnessing that desire for violence you said you have?"

# 26 The Refinery

It is not with a heavy heart that I tell you about the months spent aboard Captain Salazar's airship. The Japonais pirate had a spell-like way with people and soon settled into us all. Once Cecil understood that the captain would not be draining his eternal-life-giving blood, he warmed up to the idea of doing his time aboard *The Kimiko Fire*. I wanted to run away on occasion, but I never got far. Jacque was not so much taken with the captain as what he allowed her to do. For the first several days, Salazar locked us in the brig when they raided a ship or refinery. Cecil, Jacque, and I had one cell, Khalil another, and that's when I finally laid eyes on Mateo again. He sat shackled and gagged in a third cell. I didn't speak to him. Sooner than the rest of us, Jacque was released and allowed above deck, no doubt doing clever things with the machinations of the ship. Salazar was right; she was a genius engineer and had a way of taming the machines.

One day, while I was being forced to braid rope, trying to keep up with Cecil's deft fingers and Jacque's quick movements, Salazar broke from the circle of his crew and approached us.

"Lady Jacquline," he said to Jacque, "were those oscillating propellers on that shanty ship entirely your idea? Can you replicate them on your own?"

Jacque smiled shyly and nodded. "My grandfather, Jafa, helped me make them. We needed them to navigate the tight tunnels of The Château d'Oubli. They take a lot of power, though." She looked hopeful. "Why?"

Salazar offered her his hand, helping her up. She tossed the bundles of unbraided rope aside and followed him to the edge of the ship. Curious, and a little jealous that she got out of rope duty, I followed her. Cecil stayed under the shadow of the dirigible, wrapped in his duster, hat, and red glasses to stay out of the sun.

When I reached Jacque and Salazar, they were discussing how best to attach such propellers to the side of *The Kimiko Fire*.

"But," Jacque was adding, her eyes brighter than they'd been since I'd known her, "you'd need to run rigging all along the side. Then it takes two, or for a ship this size, three at the helms. You'd have to run new rigging underneath the deck and out the sides. Three times with the secondary helms." She pressed her lips out and rested a hand on her hips. "That's a lot of materials. Not cheap ones, either. They need to have flexibility."

Salazar glanced over at his tall, Allemande first mate. "I think we could handle that. If you'd be willing to pilot with us."

Jacque gasped, mouth open and eyes wide. "Really? I've been an engineer all my life, but I never dreamed— She's such a large vessel. Oh, Captain, thank you!"

To my shock, she leapt onto him, hugging him. I realized for her, being a prisoner aboard the pirate vessel wasn't as antagonizing. Cecil and I wanted off. I had plans to pursue. But I'd made a deal.

Salazar pulled her off and shook her hand. "We're going to need materials, then. Isolde!" he called to his lady in white. "Set a course to Nouvelle Espagne."

"South?" I asked. "What's there that's not nearer Kansouri?"

The captain gestured for me to follow him back to his navigation table, pointing at the little filled-in area in SouthWest. "Aerosteel. Mined in their dry climate, but then refined into a wonderful, flexible steel. Perfect for our ship." He turned to the rest of the crew. "Set sail!" he commanded.

"Four thousand acres of badlands and you find the refinery," Salazar praised Isolde. "Your eyes are not the only thing I love about you."

Isolde stepped away from Salazar, but I caught her blush without smiling before doing so. "Remember, men," she barked to the crew, ready to disembark, "no killing, no prisoners. Only take the materials." She glared at me when she reminded us that murder was not the way of the crew of *The Kimiko Fire.*

"Don't make me regret letting you come on this little jaunt," Salazar said to me and Cecil. Khalil remained chained below with the Don.

"We won't," Cecil promised. He rolled his shoulders, eager to get out and fly. The days spent hiding from sun and hunkering down had worn on him. I knew he craved the hunt. Our tether had weakened since he'd not fed on me. Which meant he hadn't fed recently. He had to be starving. And I missed our bond.

Armed with chemical guns that shot knockout gas, goggles, masks, and repelling gear, we hung over the edge of *The Kimiko Fire.* Jacque manned the helm to position us just above a smokeless chimney of the refinery. She'd guided the ship in, but shut the engines off about a mile out, letting us drift in soundlessly over the mark. I looked to Salazar for his signal to drop. He and Isolde locked eyes. He stretched his neck out and kissed her deeply before turning to the rest of us. Swinging his hand silently over his head, he signaled us to drop.

I released the clamp and fell several feet before reengaging it to slow down. Cecil dove past me, a dark bat shape in the night. He met me on the lip of the chimney when I landed. Isolde, Salazar, and a few crewmen landed next to us. The captain ran to the edge of the giant stack and looked over into the yawning opening.

"That's the loading dock," he whispered into his mask. "Isolde and I will rappel down and get the door open." He looked at her.

Isolde pulled a white leather case from her coat where lock picks and other tools of her trade waited.

"Good," Salazar replied. "Ezekiel, don't get caught and don't kill anyone." He signaled one of his men to go with us and the other went with him and Isolde over the side. "Show me you can be on a mission and that I can trust you," he whispered.

I joined Cecil where he already looked down the chimney stack with his vampiric vision. His huge wings arched over his head. "It's pretty quiet," he whispered.

"Good," the crewman muttered. "The captain does foolish things for his first mate, but we tolerate him."

"This is for her?" I asked, fixing my gear to the huge grate covering the top of the stack.

The crewman nodded. "Everything is. They think they'll die at any moment. They hunt down these things called magicsche musik. Something to do with the Allemande holiday on which they met. He needs those oscillating propellers to navigate the mountains and docks where the instrument may be stowed." He shrugged. "Our captain is eccentric. But he's good to us."

"So you do ridiculous missions for him?" I asked. *What an aspiration,* I thought. How could I get people to follow me? It might be easier if I weren't alone. I was afraid once Cecil finally believed I sought bloody, murderous vengeance, he'd leave me. "Come on," I said, tipping into the grate.

Cecil slipped down after me, landing before me and beckoning us to a hiding place. Inside the refinery, huge wheels slowly churned belts and chains and the blazing furnaces warmed the cavernous insides. Other huge machinations waited dim and cold for the morning shift. Piles of refined aerosteel lined the catwalks and pathways. Pyramids of ingots waiting to be used sat under thick tarps.

I stood up to make my way to a trailer full of refined aerosteel when Cecil grabbed me back down, clamping his hand over my mouth. I glared up at him. He pointed with a quick flick of his brow to the left. A single worker in thick overalls, boots, and a mask hanging off the side of his face lumbered lazily down the aisle. It took the worker forever to move down the catwalk to where he started a forge. A cauldron of heated metals and fires slowly glowed to life below us. The man quickly ran to a vent and tossed it open wide. With that, the forges rumbled to life and more machines growled around us.

Satisfied, Cecil released me and he and the crewman ran to the trailer. The crewman went inside the auto cab and started to coax the engine to life. Cecil motioned for me to stand guard while he went to the docking bay doors. The single worker would wonder why the doors had opened, but hopefully he'd wonder long enough for us to get out before raising an alarm.

I lost sight of the man as he trundled up some metal stairs only a couple yards below me. Annoyed, I climbed down a ladder to look for him. I just needed to get him into my sights. The heat made sweat build up under my hat and in my mask. I went down one more flight of steps before dropping down right in front of the worker.

"Hey?" he stammered, seeing my gear, gun, and unofficial dress for such a job. He looked up just as Cecil got the door open. *The Kimiko Fire*'s sails and balloon cut a hard silhouette against the purpling sky. "Pirates!" the man shouted, more as a question to himself before repeating the word with more fervor.

To silence him, I pulled my chem gun off my belt and shot him with a tiny canister. The smoke choked him, cutting off his words. He lunged at me, gripping my neck, and we tumbled over one another. Eventually, he passed out and I shoved him off me. In my embarrassment, I shoved him hard and he rolled, tipping over the edge of the catwalk. I gasped, shouting to reach out and grab him. I touched his shoulder before he fell, smacking loudly with a crunch into the open vent. I stared in shock. Not so much out of what I'd done—I'd killed before, for far less—but out of fear of him being seen by another worker. I waited a minute, the forge below dimming the longer I watched. No one came.

Grunting with a hard decision, I scurried back up the ladder to where Salazar and Isolde directed the loading of the aerosteel. I ran to join them, glad we would make it out with at least a bit of what we wanted.

Salazar's brow furrowed as he calculated. "How many?" he shouted up to Jacque where she manned the crane that pulled the stolen loot up onto *The Kimiko Fire.*

"Can you get one more trailer?" she called back down.

The captain looked back and saw one more trailer, only half full, with a few ingots on it. "A few," he shouted back up before charging into the dimming refinery. Cecil, Isolde, the crew, and I loaded up the last of the steel onto the crane and Jacque pulled it up. The crewmen ascended the ladder while Salazar started the engine of the last trailer. Cecil stopped, his nose twitching as he sniffed.

"What is it?" I asked.

"Fire," he said, going pale.

"No shit." I laughed, preparing to climb up. Then I stopped. The entire refinery rumbled.

Isolde froze for only a second before dashing back down the dock to the trailer. "Get out!" she shouted to Salazar. "Run!"

I froze as she galloped back in, tearing him from the auto cab. She shoved him, then ran to the edge of the catwalk to look over the edge. She turned and dashed. "It's going to blow!" she screamed.

Understanding, Jacque disappeared to the helm and the ship dipped to allow us to jump from the dock. If we missed, we'd plunge several hundred feet to the sandy badlands below. Cecil grabbed me, prepared to fly me away. Just as the railing of the ship fell to our eye level, the refinery rocked with the first explosion. A hot mushroom of flame, gas, and debris shot out of the dock bay doors. Isolde screamed, vanishing into the flaming cloud. Salazar fell forward from the blast, rolling dangerously close to the edge.

"Isolde!" he shouted back.

Cecil used his wings to jump us both onto the ship. He dropped me, then went back for Salazar and Isolde. His fear struck my brain as a second explosion rocked the ship again. I heard the chimney crack. It was going to fall and crush the dock. I got up and gripped the rail just as Cecil, two bodies in his arms, launched onto the deck.

"Hold on," Jacque shouted, spinning the helm to get us away from what would be a final, grandiose wave of fire as the refinery incinerated itself from the inside out.

The sunrise started to peek over the horizon when the ship leveled out and the crew calmed down.

"Get the loot below," Salazar barked before rounding on me. "What happened?"

Stammering, I quickly confessed to what I thought had caused the blockage of the forge and consequential explosion.

"You killed the man?" Salazar growled. "Destroying this city's refinery in the process, putting hundreds out of work and devastating them."

"What? No, I—"

I felt his rage before he moved. He charged at me, hand outstretched. Cecil shouted at him to not lay a hand on me, but he was trapped by the rays of the sun, cowering by a lifeboat. Salazar was deaf to his threat, drawing his long, curved blade. He held me to the deck with it pressed hard against my gasping chest.

"Get him," he snapped to his men. The crew flew forward, hauling me to my feet and holding me tight. They waited for his next command. "The cargo net," he said just as shortly.

Understanding, the men dragged me kicking and screaming across the deck to a hanging cargo net made of thick rope. They shoved my face into the net and pulled my hands above my head, lashing them there. That was when I understood.

"It was an accident," I shouted. "I didn't mean to kill him." Through the net, I saw Isolde on the other side, lying unconscious. Her white clothes were blasted with black ash and singed on the edges.

Salazar appeared right against the left side of my head. "It was," he hissed. "And accidents have consequences. Men, do we kill?" he shouted, ripping my shirt from my back.

They replied with a strong, chorused, "No."

"Do we lie about our actions?" he asked again, to which the same reply came. "Take responsibility for your actions, Ezekiel. What you do affects more than just you. Even if you think you had no choice, you always do. You are at fault, no matter who you blame for why you made that choice. Some choices are not easy to make because you think it makes you look weak. Or because it means giving up." He turned his eyes to Cecil, hand outstretched towards his crew. Someone handed him a whip made of thin ropes with metal nuts tied along each strand. Salazar gripped it and stepped up behind me.

I braced when I heard him raise his arm. The first strike sent me wild with pain. The little pieces of metal clattered hard against my skull and shoulders. The second hit struck my lower back, one of the ropes wrapping around to leave a welt on my stomach. The third, fourth, and fifth strikes blurred together. That was when I felt the rope sticking to my blood. To my left, Cecil crouched, moaning softly. His thoughts finally pierced my mind. Starving, the smell of my blood drove him wild. My own pain mixed with his fight spun my brain.

*I can't hold on,* he thought, holding back the memories of how savory he found my blood. Some of the best he'd ever tasted, according to his inner voice. He started to apologize in his head, sorry he was about to kill me. Anguish took him then. He didn't want to take my life.

"Stop!" I shouted, choking back the pain. "For him, Captain. Don't…" I gasped for air. "Don't force him to endure this torture."

Another blow did not fall. The captain panted behind me. How many lashes had I received? I heard the rope whip hit the deck. "Get him down," Salazar ordered.

I fell when the crew released me, then crawled backwards away from Cecil to put some distance between the smell of my freshly spilled blood and him. To my horror, Jacque had thrown herself onto him, holding him down. They both looked at me with varying degrees of concern. I heard Cecil's thoughts saying he wanted to see to my wounds, but he didn't trust himself to come near me.

"I'm fine," I told him to calm him.

He shoved Jacque off and disappeared below deck. Jacque came to me then, helping me up, and took me to be cleaned and bandaged. That one lesson was all it took to force me to realize I had to adapt if I wanted to make it through my stint with Salazar's crew and on to revenge.

"Spades," Jacque hissed, fingers fumbling with a cleaning solution below deck. "I can't believe he did that."

I felt her hands shake as she gently wiped away my blood. "It was an accident," I repeated softly. "What does he think a flogging will show me?"

Jacque didn't answer, her mind on my flayed skin. I winced and hissed as she did her best to lay my flesh flat and bind my wounds. I didn't have an answer, either. I just knew that unnecessary casualties were not an option with this pirate. I'd have to be more careful, watch my every step.

# 27 The Prize

Salazar went back to locking us up at night to sleep after my careless mishap. Every once in a while, the Don vanished from his cell, returning hours later flanked by guards. Jacque and even Khalil were allowed out before Cecil and I were. I tried to understand Salazar's reasoning behind it, but the darkness and isolation ground my gears. Cecil didn't speak much in the days we spent locked away, holding in his desire to feed on me. My flogging healed without infection with administrations from a mystery tincture Jacque applied to my back every night, along with fresh bandages.

Moving in to the second week of my imprisonment, I woke to find Cecil leaning against the wall, cheeks sunken, eyes half open and fixed on my pale, bare forearm. He wouldn't die if he didn't feed, but I didn't know what might happen. Seeing him weak, something pulled in me. I sat up, ready to burst through the bars if we didn't get released soon. I moved across the cell and sat next to him.

"You look like death," I said genially.

He grimaced in good spirits. "I cannot stand looking worse for wear. It's not fashionable to be so dead-looking."

I rolled back my sleeve and held my arm up under his chin. "For your vanity."

He looked sidelong at me, but his violet eyes ignited.

"Yes, I'm sure," I said, resigning myself to the now-familiar pain and agony that came with being bitten by a vampire.

Fast as lightning, he had his fangs in my neck, shoving my arm out of the way. I gasped and tried to pull away, but he gripped my head and neck with his hands. I calmed down when I realized his teeth tore at my flesh when I struggled. He pulled me closer, his hand sliding down to my side. Just before the weakness shot to my head, he stopped and pulled back. Our minds instantly melded together, the sensation of his relief filling me. He gently touched my cheek and whispered a thanks, sitting back to let the blood satisfy him. This little interaction always left me dizzy. I breathed for a minute until the world stopped spinning.

In the cell beside us, Khalil watched with interest. "Do you think he'll ever let us out?" he asked. "We cannot uphold our end of the deal while locked away."

I assumed Salazar was waiting for the right moment to send me after some bloodstones. Until he felt I wouldn't take the haul and run. I looked up through the grate above me. I could see the canvas-and-tar balloon and one of the long yardarms of the mainsail. Salazar sat atop it, one leg dangling down into the long drop. He held something in his hands, and I couldn't make out what it was until a sweet, sad melody sang out from the strings. A violin. He played it softly, somehow making the instrument whisper. He moved passionately with the sound until Isolde appeared, walking easily over the yardarm. She sat down with her back against his. I couldn't hear their words, but saw them talking.

The conversation must have turned sweet as soon both idly swung their respective dangling legs. Isolde leaned her head back and Salazar met her, craning his neck. They kissed. Isolde laid her head back after they broke apart and Salazar began to play his melancholy tune again. The scene gave me an emotion I was not familiar with. This musical ritual repeated more than once. I spotted them three more nights before they came below deck.

One morning, the bunghole above opened and Salazar's flashing black and silver boots appeared. A cold, sharp, salty gust of wind followed him. He trotted down the steep stairs easily and stopped, facing our cells. Not a second later, Isolde's long, white-leather-clad thighs followed him down. She stood behind him, a slight scarring on her neck visible from the incident. She rested her hand on the butt of her blackpowder gun and glared at me.

"Gentlemen," Salazar said, clasping his hands behind his back. "We approach our destination, the Isle of Skye. Our lady Jacque has outfitted *The Kimiko Fire* just in time for our biggest haul yet."

Khalil flipped his pendent through his metal fingers. "Come to finally let us out, Captain?" he asked darkly.

"Against good council, yes," he said, and Isolde's nose twitched into a deeper glower.

I stood up, too excited to be out of the cell and darkness to care, and gripped the bars.

Salazar glared. "Excited are you, Ezekiel? More killing to do, perhaps? Still thirsty for blood?"

"Let's try to be positive about the blood," Cecil said. He only held his face straight for a second before he cracked a grin at his own stupid pun. I hadn't missed the blood puns. "But really, Captain, he cannot prove himself while locked away down here."

"You're right. So." He opened our cells, then flicked his finger for us to follow him.

Khalil and Isolde followed Salazar up. I grabbed the rope railing on the stairs and looked back into the darkness. Mateo's black-brown eyes caught mine. His huge shoulders were tight from being bound and he looked pale. I watched as his chest rose and fell with each ragged breath. It wasn't unlike looking at a caged panther. Something inside me wanted to let him out.

"Ezekiel!" Cecil shouted from above. Before he could command me, I leapt up to join them.

We came around the Isle of Skye. A light, cold mist made me shiver right away. Clouds and fog obscured some of our vision, but I could make out the many tiny, elevated skyports along its mountains and cliff faces. Jacque manned the primary helm with two other crewmen behind her. Salazar signaled me over to the forecastle and handed me a telescope.

"The green one," he said, pointing to a skydock covered in little personal vessels. Snaking up from there, a system of bridges linked to a more sturdy, richer looking dock. A large, green pleasure boat hovered there. Dignitaries, silken-clad lords and ladies, and others of that caste milled about the deck of the large vessel, sipping champagne.

Scanning it, I saw it had a hull that would function as cargo space. "It's huge," I breathed. "Do we know where to go?"

"Not too big for us," Isolde smirked, lightly elbowing Salazar. "This is it, isn't it?"

"Aye, it is," the captain mused, a grin pulling his lips up. "The *magicsche musik* is most likely below."

We were here for something Salazar hunted for Isolde. According to the crewman during the refinery mission, it had something to do with a holiday from her homeland.

"Just like the day we met," Isolde said, smiling down at Salazar.

"Finally," he replied, a private joke passing between them. "Get the gliders!" he called back. "We go in quietly."

The gliders were retractable wings—not unlike Cecil's—that strapped to our backs. Armed with goggles and chem guns, Salazar, Khalil, Isolde, and I leapt over the side. Cecil soared around on his own. The gliders were guided by leaning right and left. I followed Salazar to latch onto one floating rock, held in place by stringy moss and veins. From there, we leapt to the system of rope bridges and scaffolds until we had circled around the vessel. They were preparing to disembark and take longships to Skye. Once most were gone, the vessel released the gang plank from the skydock and hovered several yards out, anchoring offshore in the air.

Salazar signaled me and Cecil to follow him quietly onboard. Isolde split from us, going into the bridge of the ship. These larger vessels had a bridge inside where a whole crew would pilot the thing, working together for the kind of smooth sailing these types expected.

"Once she has the engines shut off, the ship will drift," Salazar whispered.

"Just shut them off with geomancy," I hissed back, taking a tiny spike of firequartz out of my belt.

Salazar raised his brow at me. "You use geomancy?" Judgment dripped from his tone.

Matching his tone with my own smirk, I slashed my arm open, placing the tiny quartz inside. I quickly tied a bandage around my arm, holding it in. The fire filled my veins quickly. My arm burned from the inside, letting me feel all the fire around us and pinpoint its location. I instantly felt sick, but I found the engines. Letting the stone lead me to get them in sight, I reached my infected arm out towards them and gathered the tongues of flame under my control. The more I grasped, the more the burn heated my blood. Once I had most of the coals in my hand, I snuffed them out. With it went most of the agony of using the geo. The moment the engines shut off, the vessel jerked and drifted far away into the mist.

"Well," Salazar mused, slapping my shoulder. "If you want to destroy yourself that way, be my guest. Appreciate it." He leapt out of cover, blowing a whistle to signal the rest of his crew. He drew his odachi and gun.

"Ladies and gentlemen," Salazar snarled in his fiercest pirate way from the top deck, "we're taking over the vessel."

A fat man, perhaps the captain, swung the helm, but the ship didn't reply. With the anchor having broken from the stress, the vessel began to peel away in a strong, swinging motion.

Once the crew came aboard, they ran through the routine: take the captain and pack the remaining travelers into the brig. Salazar tried to bribe a few crewmen into telling them where the valuables were.

"You cannot offer us enough to betray our queen and country!" one brave crewman shouted.

"Brave men die in war," Salazar said proudly. "This is not war. I want just one thing this vessel carries. Something I have tracked for a long time." His eyes swept over his crew. "A very long time."

"We have nothing of value you could not find somewhere else," their captain pled. "This is a cruise ship. Pleasure! Most of the valuables are on shore with the patrons."

"Captain!" Isolde shouted from below the huge ship. "Over two hundred rooms in this blasted ship and we've found it in the cargo."

Captain Salazar motioned for Cecil and the lady to follow him. "Ezekiel, watch him." He pointed to Khalil. "And grab whatever you can from the first few rooms. The men deserve some loot after this." He motioned to the rest of the ship's crew to do their appointed tasks.

Khalil ran below deck into the long hall of lavish rooms for guests. I'd not been on board a boat like this since I was perhaps five years old. Mother never was one for taking me on her travels. And father stayed at the palace. Khalil quickly made his way through the drawers, skipping over some chests all together.

"How do you know which ones have good loot?" I asked the nomad.

"Years of practice," he panted, tipping over an old sea chest.

Something inside the chest made a strange sound when it clinked against the pommel of a ceremonial gunblade. It rang in my ears like marrowsilver.

"Hells bells," I groaned, turning to see what it was. Khalil hadn't noticed anything. He frowned at me, then followed my eyes down.

"By Anubis," he gasped softly. He bent down and pushed the gunblade aside to pick up a necklace.

The chain was simple silver, as was the backing that held the stone. The stone, however, caught my eye. It was a dark sapphire blue, but had darker and lighter veins throughout it that snapped and crackled under the surface, a reaction brought on by the silver it was encased in. I could see the stone's inner core moving. It made me flinch, but I wasn't sure why.

"Bloodstone," Khalil whispered, still in awe. "They put it in silver to get that glittering effect," he explained, holding it up to his eye. "Even after alchemy, the vampire blood reacts to it." He looked up at me. "Are you keeping Cecil to harvest him later?"

Shockingly, I was repulsed by his question. "I could never do that to him," I replied quickly.

The nomad looked at me incredulously. "Don't turn noble now, Ezekiel. It's not like you. No one likes a kind and merciful king. Rule by blood and fear, and the empire will be yours." He winked at me.

He pocketed the bloodstone, taking away the indescribable fear with it. Then he pushed past me to finish rifling through the rooms.

Kind and merciful? I would never be that kind of king. That wasn't who I was.

Right?

Back aboard *The Kimiko Fire*, and once we'd left the stranded ship, the whole crew gathered around Salazar's find. It was something huge, hidden under silken sheets. "So?" I said, unwrapping my wound. It stung, and the quartz inside had not dissipated yet. "Where's the prize?"

Salazar nodded to me. "Brave, but geomancy is dangerous."

I nodded, feeling a hot gurgling in my stomach. Then I puked so profusely that I began to lose consciousness. I fell forward, my hands landing in my sick. I couldn't breathe.

The captain knelt next to me and pulled me up. "Yes, that's it. You'll feel better once all the poison is out of you."

Cecil appeared, pulling me out of sight of the crew while Salazar and Isolde spoke quickly to each other in some language I didn't know. Cecil raised my arm to his lips, unwrapping it the rest of the way. I was about to ask him what he was doing, but he gently placed his lips over my wound. He sucked a few times and I felt the quartz slip out from my flesh. He spit over the side, the orange stone going over.

"I'm sure the captain appreciates your efforts." He smiled at me and re-wrapped my wound.

"I don't think the bloodstone job is even on his mind anymore," I replied despondently, nodding to where Isolde and Salazar stood.

Isolde kissed him excitedly, then pulled the silken sheets away and showed us the strangest instrument I had ever seen in my life. Large like a piano, but no keys. In fact, it was all strings. Necks covered in frets like a guitar and lute stuck out in at least five different places. A bit in the middle looked like a dulcimer, and holes in various places showed it had a hollow inside like a stringed instrument. On the side a large crank waited to be spun. Salazar wound it up and then let go. Little wooden jointed arms began to pluck the strings. The sound of an entire band of players plucking harp strings and a slow guitar rift rippled out. Then it picked up, plucking faster into a minor jig, more pieces of it moving, played by the cog-and-gear fingers dancing up and down the frets. The crew smiled and cheered when the melody picked up and they began a cacophony of ungraceful dances, enchanted by the machine. I smirked and shook my head. Grown men, spinning, leaping, clapping, and laughing—quickly drunk on rich food and port taken from the pleasure ship. Salazar and Isolde disappeared.

Across the deck, I spotted Jacque sitting on a tethered pile of cargo, tapping her foot and watching the crew enjoy themselves. When she caught me watching her, her faced changed to a guarded, dark, blank canvas. I'd thought about rushing over the deck, taking her in my arms, and dancing with the others. But that one look warned me to not try my luck.

The rest of the crew drowned in celebration and glee over the long-sought after instrument. I'd never seen anyone living such a life and not want more. But the pirates lived moment to moment, no plans, or plots. I understood why Salazar might seek an eternity of this. I slunk below deck to brood.

# 28 The Choice

Eastern Europa flitted in and out of my vision through the clouds. The heart of steam-powered inventions lay just miles away. Europa had started the steam revolution in Angleterre when Eastern Europa opened a supernatural gate in the late 1700s. Tech and inventions exploded once geomancy and other magics started to walk the night.

Somewhere down below, Isolde had taken a landing party and was trading with a local dock. I absentmindedly picked at the scar left on my abdomen from my flogging several weeks ago. Normally, Cecil glared at me to stop since he could smell the fresh scent of my blood. But he hung upside down below deck during the day to preserve the blood he did take from me.

"Your highness," Khalil said jovially, joining me at the rail. "I thought I'd never get you alone." He looked around for Cecil. "Where is our resident blood bank?"

I pointed below. "Hanging upside down below deck. 'Ezekiel, my heart doesn't pump,'" I said, imitating Cecil's posh accent. "'If you want my brain functioning, I've got to get it there somehow.' I think he's lying."

"He doesn't let you think for yourself, does he?" Khalil mused. He reached underneath his shirt and pulled out the long silver chain with the blue bloodstone on the end. It hissed and whispered to me. "I think it's time we parted ways with our dear captain," he said steadily. "We've waisted enough time aboard this ship. Don't you think, Ezekiel?"

My alertness went up. He'd asked my opinion, but I knew he didn't mean it. He'd been too interested in Cecil for me to let my guard down around him. I couldn't decide if I cared about whether or not Cecil lived or died, but our tether made me think I did. I didn't like the threat in Khalil's voice.

"What do you want from me, Khalil?" I asked. "We got you out. That's all you wanted. Why don't you leave?"

The nomad pressed his palms hard into the railing of the airship. "I can't. We promised Salazar we'd get those stones. That's what we should do. We're close enough here off this shore."

"To where?" I asked.

He smiled, his eyes unfocused, remembering something. "Augustine Island, in the province of Dacresylvania, the heart of the history of the vampire. Used to be a very dangerous place, where one of the first pits to Hell was dug up. But in the last hundred years, it's become little more than a city of ghosts. But there might be one vampire left. An old one."

In wonder, I looked over at him. "An old vampire?"

He nodded. "One ready to die. Their blood would be strong. There will be enough of him to satiate Salazar and take some of our own."

"From one vampire?" I asked, a little in disbelief.

Khalil tilted his head and shook it. "It will be powerful, but where there is one, there will be more. They don't often sleep alone."

Cecil was alone when he found me miles below. Thinking of him, our minds touched again. He stood below, no longer hanging, his vampire eyes able to see the Don in the darkness. I'd almost forgotten about the Don. He needed to be dealt with. I couldn't let him go. He'd go back to the Duke and tell him what we'd done and that we were on our way. The world was a big place, but MidWest would light like a prairie fire if word of my survival came out.

I shoved off from the railing, not hearing Khalil continue to talk about the magic of bloodstones, and pushed past Jacque, who had just come towards us.

"Where's Cecil?" she asked, following me.

I didn't reply, sliding down to the lower deck. Cecil turned to face me when I did. Jacque tiptoed down behind me, quickly followed by Khalil.

"I was just thinking about what we should do," Cecil said softly, moving out of the way of the sun coming through the open bunghole.

"I know," I replied, tapping my temple.

"Do you have any ideas?"

"I have one," Khalil mumbled. His metal arm clicked as he closed each individual finger.

I shook my head, walking to Mateo's cell. Salazar had foregone the chains around his arms and now Mateo sat in the cell with a single shackle around his ankle.

"I was beginning to think you'd leave me with these pirates to be killed," Mateo said through the bars. His tone was cautious but not yet broken. Something of his fire had smoldered away, but an eagerness for discussion brought some life back to his knotted muscle.

I crossed my arms and leaned against the bars between us. "I hadn't decided yet," I said flatly. "My natural thought progression was to throw you overboard. I'm used to taking a beating, not giving them out. Knowing I can decide if the man who killed my father should live or die has gone to my head, shall we say." Cecil's reaction lit up in my head like a torch in darkness. "But some would convince me otherwise."

"He doesn't need to die, Ezekiel," Cecil said earnestly. "Don't start your reign with his death."

Mateo stood up, his big hands empty at his sides. "I told you, I didn't kill Markus. He was my brother."

I narrowed my eyes at him. "Mother told me. Just before Uncle Jethro sent me away on that damned train."

Cecil stirred. "You remember?"

I scoffed, nodding furiously. "I was ten, not stupid. Ten, Mateo!" I shouted into the bars. He flinched.

Jacque gasped, covering her mouth.

"I was a mere decade old when I was sent down to that place they call The Château d'Oubli. A child. Do you know how many children there were down there?"

His black-brown eyes showed emotion and it took me off guard. "Jethro said they'd killed you," he replied.

"If only!" I laughed callously.

"I was fifteen," Jacque whispered, "when they took our house, our land, and put me, my father, and grandfather on that train." Her hand lightly touched my shoulder. It took every muscle in my body to not lean into her touch.

Mateo shifted, easing himself against the wall, matching my stance. "Did you think you could escape The Château and just walk back into Palais Kansouri?" He shook his head, almost mocking us. "It has turned it into a fortress. The people haven't notice, but over the last decade, it's been fortified by our AeroForce, the Gaia Militia, and even started research into sub-nautical warfare. There is an elite few who even use geomancy. Camille calls them her mancers, led by one Grande Mancer."

"So?" I snapped, shrugging with one shoulder. "Every kingdom in the west has a military. Why don't you go back to telling me about how you *didn't* kill my father?"

My uncle averted his eyes, scanning his cell for how to start. "A patriarch from a Syndicate took Markus's life when I couldn't."

I turned slightly to Khalil, brow raised.

He shrugged, shaking his head. "There are Syndicates all over MidWest. Some larger cities have two or three. Usually we're too busy fighting with each other over turf and more golden crimes."

"Golden?" Jacque asked.

"As I said before," Khalil elaborated, "we're not murderers. We usually deal in land, finances, secrets, and rumors. Moving of wares." His eyes almost flitted to Cecil. "Very few Syndicates are assassins. Those are hard to find. But I suppose not impossible."

Mateo agreed with a small grunt. "We'd worked with this patriarch before. As payment for his service, Camille gave him the Deleon estate in the northwestern part of Kansouri."

Jacque gasped again, straightening up. "We were removed for a member of the Syndicate?" Her voice growled for the first time. "A king killer! Father always said something was going on beneath the surface. I never knew it was the royal family who took it."

I stammered, turning to her. Should I apologize? Beg for forgiveness?

"It's not your fault," she supplied, almost rolling her eyes at me. "Sounds like the Duke of Dakota has been plotting something for a long time."

Mateo frowned doubtfully. "I don't think it was him alone."

I waved my hand impatiently for him to go on.

He struggled to speak, but finally sighed. "I think, with all the business abroad, it's Camille."

I scoffed and immediately ignored him. No way in hell would I give a moment of thought to my mother being the one who'd ordered my death and the death of her husband. After all, Mateo told me back in the prison that he'd do anything for Jethro. Maybe even lie to me now.

Cecil's thoughts floated over to me. *His scent has changed,* he thought. I knew, through our tethered minds, that he meant this in reference to Khalil. I turned to the nomad.

"You sure you don't know this patriarch?" The accusation laced my question to Khalil.

"Yes," he snapped. "Ezekiel, I told you, I'm on your side. I want out of this situation just as much as you. I want my freedom. I want to leave this part of my life behind like a bad dream."

I pushed my hat back, gripping my long hair. I couldn't trust anyone. I was just as trapped as the day I'd entered The Château. Cecil came up behind me so close, I could feel the cold emanating off him. He lightly touched my side to get me to stop pacing. *Focus on the Don,* he thought. *This is our chance to get information. He's right: we can't just walk into the palace.*

I took a calming breath. "Fine, Uncle," I said shortly. "Tell me how it happened. As I said, I'm not used to having a man's life in my hands. You wouldn't want me to make the wrong choice and let Khalil rip your guts out with his little experimental gift, would you?"

"Experimenting on the prisoners was Camille's idea," Mateo started again.

I shook my head, a sick feeling filling me. "My mother would never. She wasn't like that. She left France because of the Revolution. It sickened her. She was a kind, gentle woman. She loved me like father never did. Jethro, however, was a warlord, wasn't he? Fighting battles in Afrique and other such places."

Mateo's face took on the same confused grimace I often wore. "She didn't love you."

A cold stone dropped in my gut. I moved just one finger to feel Cecil still behind me; he might need to hold me back from charging the Don's cell.

Mateo went on, "She came to MidWest with the expectation of marrying Jethro. Word hadn't reached France yet that the oldest son of the previous king had abdicated the throne to his younger brother. She left her fiancé in France for Jethro, only to be greeted by Markus. She saw it as a cruel joke."

Jacque made a small noise. "Arranged marriages breed contempt," she mumbled.

The Don inclined his head in agreement. "Camille never loved Markus, only wanting to go home to France once she realized." He locked eyes with me. "She committed adultery more than once, nephew."

That was the last straw. My blood boiled. Every fiber of my being launched myself at Mateo. A cold, stony hand gripped my upper arm, yanking me back. I fell into Cecil from the force of his pull and he wrapped his arms around mine, holding me back. Everyone else jumped at my sudden attack.

"*Your* mother was a whore!" I spat. "Grandfather didn't know when to stop. He should have when that Espagnole tart flaunted herself in front of him. Almost destroyed our young country with a single tryst!"

Mateo laughed gently through his nose. "She was. But can we blame a woman forced into marriage with a man she doesn't know? For the sole purpose of creating an heir?" His eyes drifted to Jacque, then back to me.

"Don't look at her," I growled through barred teeth. Cecil's hands left bruises on my arms. I felt my blood vessels break under his grasp. I made a pained sound and he let go. To keep him steady, I didn't return to my tirade. "Are you saying she had father killed?" I asked. "Or are you covering for Uncle Jethro?" I smirked now. "Don't be too loyal to him, Uncle Mateo. He hasn't exactly come looking for you."

The Don averted his eyes again. The dim light hit his chest, showing he breathed more heavily. "I was supposed to kill Markus. Jethro asked me to. But I swear, it was on her orders."

"Lies," I growled again.

"But I couldn't. Camille wanted me to pay for my cowardice, but Jethro protected me. I've tried to prove my strength ever since. Done whatever I can."

Every plan I had started to crumble away before me. Of course, he could be lying. Cecil didn't think he was and that carried over to me. Almost like I could tell Mateo wasn't lying. But I couldn't believe that my mother, my soft-spoken, beautiful mother, had plotted to kill father…and me. Or if she had, was there a chance my return would mean anything to her? Could she have been forced to give the orders?

"Jethro had to be manipulating her," I reasoned out loud. "It was him the whole time. It *had* to be. He regretted his choice to abdicate and used my mother as the scape goat, letting her take the blame." It made sense. "Then, when he's king, he grants her mercy publicly, taking her as his queen."

I could see it playing out in my mind. Jethro declaring before the court that, though Camille had plotted to kill Markus and I, he'd show her grace, granting clemency and taking her as his wife for the good of the country, to keep the ties to France. He'd be a savior; a kind and merciful king. It made my stomach roil.

A long, thought-filled silence loaded the brig.

Jacque spoke first. "I'll stay with you, Ezekiel," she said flatly. I wish she had said it differently. "There's no reason we cannot stick with your plan, hey? Integrate. I know a little about royal behavior and circles. I…" She choked on her words. "I can be your trophy woman. No one will know who I am. It will be simple. I know how to stand like a royal, what to say. I know what the tiny fork is used for at expensive dinners with ambassadors. I'll be useful to you in public."

Vengeance secreted in her tone now. "Help me in return, hey? Once you're all sitting proper, get me my home back."

I mulled over her suggestion when Salazar dropped down with a thud among us. "Plotting, are we?" he said easily. Isolde fell in behind him. "Decided it's time to disembark and part ways, *your highness*?" he emphasized, looking directly at me. He crossed his arms and fell against the wooden supports. He smiled, shaking his head. "The dead prince. On my ship. It's a miracle, Isolde."

"You can't ransom me to the royal family," I said too quickly, realizing that I basically gave him permission to kill me if he wanted.

"So I heard," he said, still casual as ever. I waited for him to go on as his eyes traveled up and down my scrawny person. "To think I flogged you on my decks like a common criminal," he went on. "Why didn't you tell me who you were?"

"Would it have stopped you?" I asked, genuinely curious.

"No," he replied quickly, smiling almost condescendingly. "Onboard a pirate ship there is one law. Not one law for the ruling class and another for the ruled. You should take that lesson with you, your highness. But perhaps you were frightened we'd hold you for ransom as you suggested."

"The fewer people know, the better," Cecil said warningly.

"Couldn't agree more," Salazar said, pushing himself up. "This doesn't release you from our agreement, your highness. I'll not turn away my immortality for any resurrected prince."

"Khalil says we're not far from where we can retrieve some bloodstones for you, as per our agreement," I supplied, getting back to the task at hand. "But there's a loose end needs tying up." I half-heartedly indicated the Don.

Salazar smoothed the plume in his hat, narrowing his eyes in thought. "Sometimes accidents happen."

We all turned to him, shocked. "I thought you didn't believe in killing," I said darkly.

The captain nodded, clicking his tongue. "I don't believe in killing innocents, or people I cannot deem worthy of death." He pointed at Mateo. "I'm not sure about this one. We all know about the Espagnol bastard and his gladiators. His arenas of death and mayhem. What I don't know is what he'd do to live."

"You'd give me a fighting chance?" Mateo asked.

"Not in the way you think," Salazar said. "I am no judge or jury." He shivered exaggeratedly, disgusted at the thought of political law. "I will give you the opportunity to finish what you started." He indicated me. "And to prove you won't take it and show how much your life means to you. As a man who has fought for his life every day of it, I admire those who would do the same. You would also prove to our prince here that you won't kill him." He shrugged simply. "I leave it to him."

Salazar turned to me, hands clasped in front of himself. "What say you these days, Ezekiel? Do you have it in you to spare a man?"

I staggered back, looking between all of them. "I'm not taking him with me."

"And I won't keep him," Salazar quipped. "If you don't take him with you, he's free to go and I don't really want that either, now that we all know who you are. What if he sent the military after me for harboring a pretender to the Duke's crown?"

"Let him come with us to get the bloodstones?" Khalil asked.

The captain inclined his head. "There's a lot down there that could end up taking him out *for* you."

"Damn pirates," Mateo growled. "I won't let a monster like a vampire kill me."

"I don't want to be constantly watching my back for supernatural monsters *and* him," I interjected.

"It will be two against one, Ezekiel," Khalil offered. "He can't take us both. You beat him one-on-one, remember?" He winked at the Don, reminding him of his ear-piercing beating.

"I could go," Cecil interjected, coming to stand close beside me.

Khalil shook his head. "We need to take crosses, silver, and go when the sun is out. You won't be able to get near us, let alone help."

Defeated, I heard Cecil audibly swallow. *I can't let you go alone,* he thought. I shot my eyes through the bars to Mateo. Once we'd gotten to talking, he'd been honest, open. Almost like he was looking for a way to freedom—same as me.

And perhaps it was time I did go alone, without Cecil. After all, if all went well and I did end up on my father's throne, I wouldn't have Cecil with me forever. Wasn't that the point of him springing me from below? I'd have to get used to him being gone. The thought put a lump in my gut.

"I'll be fine," I promised Cecil. To Khalil I said, "Have my back or else."

The nomad smirked, nodding an affirmation. "As promised, once we're done with all this, I'll do what I can to help you ascend that throne."

# BLOODSTONES

The country of industry was a smog-covered monster of stone with a million streets I could not hope to maneuver in my lifetime. Romania had eaten up most of that side of the Black Sea. Literally. Werewolves, ghoul gates, vampires, shifters, blemmyes, and half-humans converged there. The air in Romania didn't blow but hung frigid, frozen from the presence of so many supernatural beings. As we approached the towering castles, turrets, and spiking citadels, I ran my hand through the air and looked at the ice particles clinging to my black gloves. I looked over at Cecil. The ice gathered on his long lashes, staying still on his white skin. Ice didn't melt on him.

"So this is it?" I asked him. "The place the first Hell gate was discovered."

Cecil moved closer to me. "Perhaps. There were monsters and magic in the world before Romania dug too deep. They say vampires were created by dragons. Who knows where these curses and magic came from?" He didn't look at me, he gazed hard into the city we could not see yet. "This side of Europa is called the Graveyard by most others. For obvious reasons." I saw him run his tongue over his fangs behind his closed lips. "Killed itself with industry, and then when science and technology failed, they turned to magic."

"Geomancy?" I asked.

"Geomancy is bad, but this was worse," he whispered. "We should not stay here long. The air here is too supernatural for you mortals."

Just then, the first of Romania's million towering cities loomed into view. Planks and braces covered the stone structure, waiting to create more city higher and higher into the air. I thought at first it must have just been one tall stone city, but then I realized that the rubble below was not rubble at all. What I had taken for broken rocks below us were sprawling structures, reaching out like a black oil spill for miles and miles. They had expanded out and then up. On the wind—quite suddenly in an updraft once we went below the clouds—came the black, rank smell of death and rot. Even I put my hand over my mouth and gagged.

"Not pretty, is it?" Salazar said behind us. "It's amazing what happened here. A whole country working towards one goal: utter destruction. Like the Tower of Babel before them."

"Where do I start?" I asked through my glove.

He looked at me. "I have a map," he said flatly, all emotion gone from him. "You, the Don, and Khalil are to retrieve that which was promised when I first spared your life."

I narrowed my eyes. "I don't know how to get the blood."

Cecil arched his brow at me.

"You were easy," I replied.

He blanched, clicking his tongue in disappointment.

"How do we incapacitate this vampire?" I asked Salazar.

The captain nodded towards Khalil. "He knows. And you're a good enough killer to know. Use the silver. Use the solar adamant. But don't forget to come back with vampire blood. Don't let Khalil whisper sweet promises into your ear. If you don't come back…" He sighed, dropping his head. "I'm so sorry, Cecil."

"What—?" Cecil began, but Isolde nodded, and a herd of crewman descended on him. He backed away for just a moment, ready to leap away, then stopped and let them take him. They wrapped silver chains around him and pulled him below.

"What are you doing?" I cried. I tried to run after him, but Isolde's giant body stopped me. "That will hurt him."

"I know," Salazar admitted with a grimace. "It gives me no pleasure, I promise you that. He will be held, surrounded by solar adamant, and bound in silver until you return. And," he flicked his head back, "I will take Jacque with us. She's a great navigator and has made my ship better than I ever thought it could be. Don't leave her behind."

I clenched my fists, glaring at the pirate. "This was unnecessary."

"Was it?" he quipped. "Forgive me if I don't trust a little boy on a quest for vengeance and his evil companion."

"Me?" Khalil said in fake shock. "I only do as I'm told."

"Then do it now," Salazar warned him. "Ezekiel, take the lead. Come back with the blood and I'll let you go free. I'll even take you to Kansouri and give you a nice haul to start your new life. As payment for the time spent as part of the crew."

I opened my mouth to argue, but realized it was futile. The longer I spent up here, the more Cecil suffered in his silver chains. "Fine," I snapped. I was done being bullied, someone else forcing me to do their bidding. It was time for me to take control of my destiny.

We jumped over the side with the gliders to make it down into the guts of the city. Red leather wings expanded over us from the sides. They were quiet and stealthy, but I hardly trusted their rickety design.

"Make a noise and you could be barraged with hungry supernaturals," Salazar had warned us. He'd given us a map of the city, for all the good that did, with a blue circle around a house on watery Augustine Island. The city had expanded too far, built out into the sea like Venice of old, and then the parts holding it to the shore had collapsed, isolating the island city. A small comfort. The blemmyes, werewolves, and most ghoul gates kept to the mainland. Out on the island there were water creatures and vampires. Maybe other immortal dead. At least these were more familiar.

We had been instructed to travel light and disturb nothing, but Mateo had his singing blades at his side and Khalil had taken a large gunblade, which was slung across his back. I'd brought my lasso and pistols. Inside my leather vest I had tucked little things from The

Château d'Oubli: solar adamant for the vampires, silver dust, and rubylead for emergencies.

We pulled our goggles down and silently leapt over the edge without ceremony. My gut wrenched as gravity caught up with me. Not only the free fall made my stomach turn tricks. I didn't trust the Don yet. And Khalil had my nerves fried from wondering if he would really turn on us after all we'd been through. I dove into a thousands-of-years old nest of supernatural monsters to find the perfect killer with these two men. According to the map and the detailed drawing next to it, we had to find an ancient-looking container inside this old structure. I didn't want to bother whatever lived inside the hiding place. I had enough to worry about when it came to my companions.

Mateo and Khalil landed like panthers on a turret roof and hooked in before sliding off. I landed hard, tumbled, broke the wings of the pack, and plummeted twenty feet into the murky water where Khalil had to fish me out.

With Khalil in the lead, we began the awful, dark, and smelly trek through Augustine Island's murky streets. I expected them to be full to bursting with the villainous monsters we had all been imagining for the last twenty-four hours, but no sign of life stirred. Well…no sign of something moving, anyway.

"Daytime," Khalil said in his infinite knowledge. "They are asleep."

Mateo and I both looked up. "Not much sun to hide from," he observed. "How long until sunset?"

Khalil took out his cursed timepiece and examined the face. "A few hours. We really do need to be out of here by then because they will smell fresh meat instantly."

"I imagine we are the first new visitors in some time," I put in. I pulled my hat down harder onto my head, tightened my belt, and took the lead.

If you have ever been to Venice before it sank or on a large ship with tiny hallways, then you can imagine Augustine Island. The Romanian architecture made it more horrible, though. I can't explain how packed the city was. Strange things seemed to be growing out of every surface and crack like a cancer: electronics I could not fathom with sleek, perfect surfaces that I didn't know how to operate; something old from before the continents broke up that resembled an idol or some deity loomed out of corners; wind-up automatons; one crate had wafting black-with-purple mist from arcane magic hanging around it.

"Wait," Khalil breathed, pushing us all against a wall to hide in the shadows. Down the alley, a man in a plague doctor's mask, all dressed in white with black, slick gloves dug through the trash. He seemed to only be partially aware of his surroundings. His bare feet trod over broken glass and more than once he ran into a wall. When he finally vanished around a bend, Khalil said, "Zombie."

After an hour, we had lost our sense of smell and direction. Khalil sighed. "Don, take the grapple and see if you can find…" He studied the map. "This tower." He pointed to one of a million illustrated towers on the cramped map. "What draws it apart is the dragon insignia that should be visible somewhere on it. A crest under the window."

Mateo eyed the Egyptian, but took the rope and grapple anyway. A tinge of jealousy hit me when I watched him scale the rope, hand over hand, easily, his muscles defined impressively.

As I watched him vanish over the parapets, a sudden iron grip had me by the throat and pushed me against the wall. Kicking my feet out from under me, I gasped, choking. Khalil had me pinned with his automatonic arm. It clicked madly as it crushed my throat just a little more.

"Snakes!" I cursed, taken by surprise.

"Stop struggling!" he hissed through gritted teeth. His other hand went down the front of his shirt and pulled out the silver chain. Where once the blue bloodstone had been now hung a tiny vial. Blue powder and several tiny, needle-like spikes of blue nestled inside.

"Get off me!" I managed to cough through my strangled throat. "What's wrong with you?" But the effort to speak just made me gag. I coughed and my head exploded in pressure and pain.

His other hand appeared before my eyes, holding a pinch of the blue powder.

"No, no, please!" My strangled cry didn't get far. I didn't know what bloodstones would do to me, but I was not ready to find out. I reached out to Cecil's mind and touched it. He was in pain, too. If only he could hear my pleas.

"Hold still," Khalil commanded. He thrust two of his fingers past my lips and down my throat. The powdery substance flew down my lungs as I coughed. "Not enough," he said, sighing and dispensing more from the vial. He repeated the force-feeding until I felt it hit my gut. Cecil's mind was instantly cut from mine in a violent inner slash as the other vampire's alchemized blood roiled inside me. The sudden absence of him made me feel empty. Alone. I hadn't realized until that moment that his eternal presence had elevated the loneliness inside me. All the old feelings of being a prison rat came back on the waves of the other vampire's blue blood. I wanted to scream for Cecil.

I looked up, begging for help, but Mateo had moved too far ahead to hear me gasping. Would he have helped me anyway? I looked at the glassy needles in Khalil's hand now. At first glance, they appeared opaque, but under the surface swirled something like thick, sapphire veins. The stones inside me finally reached my heart. Once I tipped over the side of the magic from the stone, it felt like plunging my head into fiery, smoldering lava.

When Khalil saw me pass the threshold, he took one of the tiny needles and pressed its sharp edge into my left eye. A gooey, hot lava ran down my face in the form of tears. I couldn't scream, his grip too strong and the stones taking me over. The stone hypnotized me just enough to hold me still. A cold spread through the left side of my face, down my neck. It hit my heart as well, slowing my life-giving beat. I cried and panted, dying for air, and my heart almost stopped. I tried to call for Mateo, but no words came.

The next thing I knew, the entire world detonated into an oily, sapphire fire. My pulse stopped. A new kind of life filled me like a hot gas. A lust and craving for something I couldn't name rose up in me. Like when you haven't touched water in two days and you hear a toxic river: your mouth waters, you want it, but to drink it will kill you. The craving gave me strength and I felt the draw to another source. I blinked and looked to find what pulled me. When I did, my vision blurred, then came into fiery focus again, wavering like oiled glass.

The entire world was on fire in blue. Khalil blazed brightly with life and flowing blood.

"Ezekiel," I heard Khalil say as though he shouted right next to my ear. I faced him and he took a step back. "Hell's bells," he cursed. "You must have the vampire vision now. Your eyes are blue. Can you see the other vampire? You have to find it now. Before the Don comes back from his snipe hunt. Track it, Ezekiel. Find the vampire."

Utter abhorrence overtook me. I hated the Don. I hated him so much I wanted to bite his neck and rip his veins out with my teeth. I heard myself snarl. Khalil put one hand on his silver-bullet-filled gun and held one hand up to me like a ringmaster to a lion.

"Calm down, Ezekiel. I knew this would be hard, but it was the only way. Don't make me waste what precious little I have." He focused back on me. "Ezekiel," he commanded, and I felt myself come to attention, like when Cecil ordered me around. He held up his hand where the last of what he had shoved in my eyeball laid in his palm like blazing blue light. "Find the vampire." He stopped and looked over my shoulder. "We have to move before the monsters come out. Hurry!"

I felt extraordinary. Invincible. I dashed down the street, not caring if any ghouls heard me snarling or if the zombie came back to me. I knew exactly where to go, like I had been raised on these streets. They were familiar. A master waited not far. A head vampire. Someone the blood in me was forced to respect and serve.

I wove through the streets and then the underground tunnels like a rat myself, fully recognizing the places I passed. In no time at all, we were at a gate to a castle. I scanned the front and the huge portcullis. We'd have to climb it. I could see past the walls to the inside of the castle. Sort of. There were shapes behind the walls on the third floor. I saw a red, glowing light like the blue one in Khalil's hand. It called out to me, drawing me further in. I tried to wake up my brain and ask Khalil why he had done this.

The vision started to evaporate, and I looked for Cecil in my head. "Where am I?" I gasped and spun around. The rabid coyote in my head howled, excited for the new hunger bursting up in me. All the bloodlust came gushing back.

I almost got a few more words out when Khalil grappled with me again, slipping the last of the blue needle gems into my eye and forcing the rest down my throat. I cried out and rubbed at my eyes. The pain almost brought me back, but the stone took over too quickly.

"Go get them," he ordered. "Trust the stones. You are one of them."

# 30

# A Long Overdue Death

With the geomancy working in my veins, all other shadows feared me. A monstrous wolf a few blocks away that had decided to track me changed its mind. I felt other sets of eyes turn away. I'd had no idea we had been tracked by creatures we could not see. The bloodstones made them double back, leaving me alone. I had a clear, uninhibited path to the castle gates. I practically vaulted over the portcullis, using my lasso, and landed with a grace I still envy to this day. The fresh supply of gems lubricated my senses and the daredevil nature inside me.

Through the walls and floors, I saw a throne room of sorts. Not as large as the one in my family's castle, but I could see from the central seat, tall-backed and bejeweled, that it was indeed a room for a king. I leapt up the spiraling red velvet stairs and cantered down the halls lined with spears, smeared with old, decaying blood. The rank air should have made me gag, but I hardly noticed; in fact, I almost enjoyed it.

I stopped outside the thick metal doors. Gears and cogs ran up and down it in an intrinsic lock that I could have never hacked. The key, thick, black, and greased, hung loose in the lock. I took the key in both hands and cranked it like a slave in The Château d'Oubli.

The key clicked and the entire surface of the doors moved as the first gear spun, releasing a chain that activated the others, unlocking the bolts inside the giant door. Made of iron and froststeel, it creaked and cracked from nonuse. If anything inside lurked, it knew I was coming now.

Deciding that whoever waited inside knew I was coming, I took a stance—legs wide, hat pushed down— and hurled the doors open with one hand. I grunted from the effort, even with the mysterious gems inside me. Slowly, I looked up, expecting to be attacked, waiting to see a fearful face. The stones were on the throne at the end of the narrow room. No, not the stones. But yes, at the same time. It sat on the throne. An old vampire with black hair longer than the royal cape flowing behind him already had his eyes locked on me. Red eyes melting into me like fire, he didn't blink. His pale skin was covered in dust. His fingernails grew long and hooked over the arms of the throne.

I couldn't see the floor. Bodies, bones, and discarded clothing of ages past littered it. As I took them in, I noticed they piled higher the closer they got to the enthroned vampire. That was when I noticed it: his throne was made up of brass piping, glass tubing, and intricate valves. They looped up behind him, disappearing into a complex machine with a huge, empty crystal tank. I recognized some of the machinery as alchemy tools. This ancient creature had been augmented to the alchemy machine, fed all those bodies to keep him alive while his body turned to stone from the inside out. A horrific eternity.

A sound like softly breaking glass cracked and popped as his jaw slowly opened in jerky motions. He spoke in what I assumed to be Romanian but stopped. "Marius?" His voice cracked. Then, in English, he asked, "Is that you, Marius, my wandering, Welsh flower? Come to feed me one…last…time?" he whispered. With a scratching sound followed by a great crack, he lifted his head. His solid, stony blood shattered with every move. The light in his red eyes dimmed. "No. Not him," his deep, monstrous voice said sadly. "Hot, flowing, red river in this one. Bloodstones in this one," he said.

"I came for bloodstones," I snarled. My tainted blood pulsed hot inside my neck. I narrowed my eyes. "Where are they? Inside you?"

The years pressed down on the vampire as he slumped into the chair, shards of glassy stone scraping together in his veins. He inhaled deeply, savoring the scent of my blood. Then he let the air out as though a heavy weight had just been lifted from his chest. His glassy, never-blinking eyes roamed over me.

"Was it your will to have bloodstones put into your clean, fresh blood mortal?" He moved his hand to point one long, bone-thin finger at me. It took an age for him to move, and every gesture cracked his solidified veins more and more. "Did you sacrifice that much of yourself to obtain more?" He inhaled again. "I smell another on you. His little pet, you are."

His voice was so deep and soft. If it weren't for the echo of the chamber, I might not have heard him. He spoke slowly, as though he had eternity to get his words past his shriveled lips. He tasted every syllable on his tongue before they passed from his mouth. Every sound languished in age and dust.

I didn't have the mind to reply, so he nodded slowly. "I have seen it before. My blood is the envy of all mancers, as was the blood of the vampire I took this grand facade from." Slowly, like an aged turtle, he waved his hand to present the throne room. "I was a mancer once. Judging from the scent of gems in your blood, you are no stranger to geomancy…or vampires?" A smile pulled his ancient lips like a clockwork automaton: twitchy and slow, and it didn't look right on his face. "It will kill you." He motioned to himself languidly, emphasizing his argument. "Or force you to find other ways to survive."

"I didn't do this," I managed to say. My hand hovered over my six shooter. It didn't bother him at all. When I looked down, I saw my veins, blue and bright, through my pale flesh.

"True," the old vampire sighed. "You would have killed me already and taken my calcified blood if you were here of your own will." He clenched his fist and I heard something inside him break louder than before, similar to crushing glass in gloved hands. "The earth and her magical, poisonous gifts are not a dead thing like me that you can take and enslave. It was not something I could control, it turns out." His eyes roamed to the window, where the sun would soon be peeking into the room on its way down. He reenacted his long, deep sigh. "Do not be entrapped by power, mortal." He met my gaze, simpering sadly at me. "But I see that you are already infected. You carry a great prison on your back, never free. There is more poison in your blood than you know."

"The stones," I said in reference to the ones I wanted to steal.

But he shook his head. Some dust fell from his scalp. "You are infected with the blood of a vampire. But that is not the illness I speak of. He was consumed by the same poison in you: revenge." He slowly licked his white lips. "Revenge ruins good blood. Makes it sour."

Something inside me clicked on like a drill from The Château d'Oubli: sudden, loud, and frightening. "You can read my mind? You going to eat me, too?"

That dark smile broke the vampire's face again. "No. You simply wear your revenge like a badge of honor. It is your armor. Revenge is already eating you alive. It blights your essence like the geos you put into your blood. That will kill you, too."

"Yeah," I mumbled. The wildness from the blood rose up in me again. I wanted to hunt. To attack.

His shoulders heaved in a shrug that took all his strength. Above his head on the throne, the first orange rays of sunlight dipped down through the open door as it set. "At last." He heaved a sigh.

I gripped a silver blade in my hand, thinking he might attack me to close the doors.

"I cannot stop you, though I wish I could." The vampire sighed. His gaze went to the open door behind me. "Never stop fighting for your life, mortal." He shook his head, almost laughing. "I wish you had come at a different time. Harken to the sun and see its setting." His eyes watered, gazing out over the horizon. "See it come. How bright." His eyes winced in sad disappointment. "So red. I wish…it were…a yellow sun."

Sanity began to creep its way back into my head as the stones started to dissolve in my blood. I wondered how I had the blade in my hand. I tried to keep the surprise and fear out of my face. "What are you doing?"

"My death is long overdue," he said slowly.

I swallowed and it stung. "But you said to fight. To never give up." Tears stung my eyes, and I shook my head, trying to arrange my thoughts. Emotion forced its way out of me, and I couldn't tell why. "What have you done to deserve death?"

He unclasped his cape and let it fall to the arms of the grand throne. "I have done enough to make others seek revenge on me. When you follow that trail, you dig two graves, as you say in the west: one for yourself and one for the man you desire to kill."

The sun dipped into the room through the doors I'd left open and hit his old, pale skin like a beam through a spyglass. His flesh burst and crackled instantly, catching his hair and his dusty clothes on fire.

"No!" I shouted.

"Bring a pine box, mortal," he said calmly through the flames that devoured his face. "The sun is setting even on you."

The scorched scent hit my nostrils deep and made me gag. Burning flesh was one thing, but old, moldy, rotted, dusty vampire flesh being burned was another. The flames ran over his body like fire over gunpowder. Engulfed in the flames, he turned to cinders in almost ten seconds flat. I blinked. In his place, in the perfect shape of his likeness, sat a statue entirely made out of bright, glowing red stone. Then, just as suddenly, I was myself again. The last of the bloodstones boiled away in my veins. It hurt for only a second.

Waking up from the bloodstones was like waking from a lucid dream. It took me a moment to realize I was indeed standing in a castle in Romania. The adrenaline from the bloodstones left me exhausted and the urge to lie down right there almost pushed me to the stony earth. Before me on the throne sat every spidery, glass vein of the vampire that had just burned away. His veins crisscrossed and webbed over one another in the shape of his body.

I stumbled around the castle and finally found my way out, all the while curious as to how I had gotten there. Where were Khalil and Mateo? Some of it I remembered. I opened my mouth to shout, but stopped. Something like the smell of wet dog filled my nostrils. Above me, two werewolves glared down, ready to pounce. I glanced back at the dead vampire. I reached to my side, but realized even with the guns and silver blade, they'd overpower me. I could try to run, but I was not supernatural-pissed-off-monster fast. I needed to match their abilities.

I turned and dashed back into the throne room to grab some of the bloodstones. Breaking off one of the glass fingers and squeezing the bloodstone, I cut into my palm. The unparalleled power that came with the bloodstones erased the tiredness, cold, and fear. I felt it right away. This stone was stronger, and just having it touch my blood was enough. I literally gasped, alarming the wolves as they landed behind me from their perch. They stopped long enough for me to break the stone off inside me. Just a small piece, like a splinter of glass. I felt a little prick before my mind went berserk. I jumped at the wolves, and all went black as I roared.

"Ave Maria," Mateo swore softly.

I spun around to face the duo, who suddenly appeared. Mateo stepped back, taking out his singing blade and warding it towards me, Khalil behind him. Covered in carnage, I still had the head of the wolf in my hand. Fur, entrails, bits of muscle, and blood were all over my clothes, hair, and teeth. I spat.

"I'm fine," I said, hating how weak and awkward I felt. Inside I was terrified, not fine. The blackness, the losing track of time, the taste of death. Bloodstones would have been a fine trip if I knew what I had done, but I didn't. I liked control, and right now, I could not control myself.

The final wave of the bloodstones slowly gathered, creating a storm in me. I had one last bout of uncontrolled rage coming. My coyote howled in greedy anticipation.

Overhead, the ship glided into view, engines humming at half power to avoid rustling up the dead. Ropes and ladders dropped down for us through the smog. Khalil snatched the head from me and tossed it aside. He ascended quickly, a large, leather pack slung over his shoulder. Inside, I could smell the same bloodstones that were in me. Mateo came to me and ripped the silver blade out of my hands. The sinking sun struck his dark eyes, letting me see every subtle color in them: black, brown, gold, and amber tones...and something I couldn't read. Concern? Fear? I glared at him, the world engulfed in red fire as the wave rose. Underneath the red ocean of vampiric hunger, I screamed for them to not let me aboard. Not yet, not while the wild coyote ravaged my desires. But I only screamed in my head. No words left my lips. They didn't hear me. The bloodstones forced me up the ladder.

A landing party waited for me when I got up over the ship's railing. Relief trickled through me when I saw Salazar's odachi still, thankfully, in its sheath. But they were all there, all watching me. Cecil's eyes caught mine. I could tell from the way his face pinched that he knew our tether had been severed.

*He thinks he's the only one who can own me?* the blood in me raged. *Thinks you are his pet.*

Jacque stood at his side, clinging to him. My coyote didn't like that.

"She should be mine," I growled. "I loved her first."

"Ezekiel?" Cecil asked, slowly raising his hand out towards me to ward me off.

This time, I felt myself run—leap, rather—before the blackness and time loss kicked in. I heard her scream. I tore her clothes. I stabbed someone who tried to grapple me. Jacque screamed and cried, begging me to stop. I wanted to.

"Ezekiel, no!" Mateo shouted. I felt him thrust his arms around me and try to pull me away. "Stop!"

I took my six-shooter out and put one in him at point blank range. He fell backwards right away. The loud shot pulled me back to reality. I gasped for air and came to just to be clubbed over the head by Isolde and the butt of her shotgun. I fell over like a sandbag and lay there, no feeling in my arms. I looked up into the rigging and watched the steam sail up and into the clouds. Cold filled my veins.

Rolling my head to the side, I saw Isolde lift Jacque up, cradling her and holding her tightly to her chest. She spat at me, shouting in angry Allemande, and retreated below deck. Cecil rushed to shield me from the raging crew and their drawn weapons. The shouting rang from every direction, muffled and in parts. I was so tired. So cold. And hungry.

"Mateo?" Salazar shouted from somewhere to my left, pressing his hand to the Don's chest. Blood leaked between his fingers. Salazar shouted for his men to move. My mouth watered at the sight of his bright red blood as the last wave ebbed away.

"Cecil, take this monster below and chain him there," Salazar shouted.

Without another look, Cecil dragged me down the stairs and into the brig away from the confused and frightened onlookers. He leaned me against the wall and then knelt before me. My heart didn't beat. I had basically become a corpse.

Our eyes met and I felt mine heat and moisten. I remembered how emotion used to make me angry, but not this time. So close to death, I realized this might have been the last thing I ever said. My heart hurt.

"I don't..." I coughed. Words hurt my throat. I had to try. "I don't know how to be anything but what I am." I almost passed out, but managed to take a breath and recover. "I tried, Cecil."

"Stop that," he cut in. He shifted to squat in front of me and took my cold hand in his. "These stones made you into a monster today, but that's not who you are."

I shivered and my lips turned blue. The bloodstones were too strong for me. "I want revenge, Cecil." I had to stop and recover again. The world began to shift to grey. After seeing it on fire, everything looked extra colorless as my heart fluttered. "I don't know what else to do. I have been a prisoner. I *am* a prisoner." I looked at the red stain on my palm where the splinter was still lodged in my flesh.

Cecil gripped my hand and clamped his lips tightly onto my palm. He sucked hard and I felt the piece slide out of my flesh. He gagged on it, spit it out, and threw it out a gunport. Then he put his hand on my chest to feel my heart beat again. "You are strong," he said, relieved. "I don't believe you will always be driven by revenge. I see you changing every day."

The cold ebbed from my limbs and I felt parts of me throbbing. The last several hours were a blur, but they were coming back to me. With each beat of my heart, the overwhelming emotion from the bloodstone started to wane. The feelings of rage and hunger was replaced with genuine remorse. For just one moment, I saw myself as others had: like eating rotten bread, the kind with the white and green mold all over it, with no water to wash it down. It stayed behind on my teeth and in my throat.

"I want out," I choked suddenly. "Did I hurt Jacque?" With the magic and power of the bloodstone gone, fear and remorse filled me. "I love her, Cecil. But she doesn't want me."

The vampire grimaced. This monstrous, disgusting human weeping like a jilted maid must have been horrifying. I could tell he didn't want to be near me, but his graciousness held him there. He sat down next to me again and put his arm around my back. The pressure and presence of another person astounded me, lifting my spirit.

"You stabbed me," he said off-handedly. "Fortunately for you, I can take a beating. From here on out, we trust no one else and focus on the task at hand."

I nodded in agreement. "It was Khalil. He poisoned me, forced me." I frowned. "Where is he?"

"Ran," Cecil mumbled. "While you distracted us, he took a sloop from the side. He left the bloodstones, though. I think he is hoping Captain Salazar doesn't come after him again."

I glared ahead into the darkness. The pirate might be satiated, but I wasn't. Yes, I had to focus on getting back to Kansouri and figuring out how to re-enter the royal circle, but revenge was a hard thing to set aside. Maybe I could squeeze revenge on Khalil into my full schedule. The old vampire said I would kill myself if I carried on with the vengeance. Could I just stop?

I breathed, but I felt dead inside. I finally knew the monster inside me, and it was high time that monster died. No one could kill it but me. I had to try, though. A long overdue death.

# ONE BY ONE

I woke in the brig that had now become so familiar to me. I slipped my arms into Cecil's over-fashionable greatcoat, which he'd given me in lieu of a blanket. Since the bloodstones, no one but Cecil had been down to see me. I'd shouted at first that it wasn't my fault. Khalil had tricked me. After a few days, I decided that sounded like excuses. As the one who had taken in the bloodstones, I knew they opened a gate to a beast that was already inside me; they didn't change me, they just let me be what I'd always been underneath. That creature that salivated over revenge and violence had been released. I knew it was there now and knew what it wanted.

Leaning my head back, I closed Cecil's coat over my bare shins. My old pants had very little wear left, and the soles of my boots were coming off. The cold air made me shiver as I pulled my knees to my chest. Cecil's thoughts came in a steady stream to me, since he'd fed recently. The renewed tether brought me great relief, easing my loneliness again. The time with the stones inside me—cutting him off from me—filled me with an unfamiliar dread. The weaker our tether became, the more I wanted him to bite me again. As I drifted in and out of consciousness, a conversation he engaged in became more vivid. When Jacque floated before my eyes, I tried to listen harder, pulling at the tether.

I regretted attacking her. I knew what the beast wanted. I'd shot

Mateo and stabbed Cecil to try to hurt her. She'd come to me once, but hadn't so much as laid a finger on me since. She despised me.

"You can leave," Cecil whispered somewhere above me. His muffled voice drifted in and out of focus. "No one expects you to stay. We all understand. Satoshi will arrange for a crew to take you wherever you want to go."

Jacque's face contorted in controlled anger. "Leave?" she asked softly. Almost gently. "Am I some wilting flower who can be tossed out now?"

Cecil ran his hand through his hair. I almost felt it on my own scalp. "No one sees you that way. I just mean you don't have to stay after what he tried to do. We would understand."

Jacque nodded. "I appreciate the concern. I am..." She fought for a word to describe just how she felt. She couldn't find one. "I am hurt, but not weak." Her voice trembled. "I am scared. But I have nowhere to go if he doesn't help me take my home back. Once I have my family's land, I can collapse in on myself and weep. But not now."

I wanted to take her in my arms and comfort her. But those arms were the ones she feared. Her strength in this moment made me love her more. Heat radiated off her; I could see it through Cecil's eyes. Her heart beat irregularly, skipping and fluttering.

"You are willing to stay?" Cecil asked, his voice full of surprise. "To follow him?"

Her next deep breath came steady and strong. "Yes," she said. "I cannot forget what he tried to do, and will never forgive him. But I cannot faint now. I'll get over it. I know I will." She pressed her hands to her stomach, taking a deep breath.

Then, she reached her hand out to take Cecil's. He hesitated, pulling back, but then let her. He did not move to be closer to her.

She licked her lips. "Do you see me as broken?" she whispered.

"No," he replied quickly.

"Then why won't you hold me?" She came close to him, gently rubbing the tip of her nose against his alabaster neck.

Cecil didn't move. Like a statue he stood, his eyes fixed on their hands. *I can't*, he thought. I abstractly came to his mind. "He loves you."

With a shout of disdainful laughter, she pushed away. "Like a wolf loves a rabbit. The fairytales say love can change a..." Her voice hitched as her dark eyes moved up to his one last time. "Love can change a beast."

Now Cecil scoffed softly. "The fairytales were wrong. Only a beast can love another beast," he said.

Jacque frowned, crushed, giving up. "I will stay," she said flatly, spinning away and ascending the stairs to the upper deck. "I told him I'd help him navigate the politicals and royals. I keep my word. Once he's satisfied, I'll leave."

I was drifting off under Cecil's coat when the rough march of three men coming down into the brig stirred me awake. Salazar, Cecil, and Mateo slid and jumped down the wooden steps to stand just outside the bars, looking in. I couldn't muster the dignity to stop hiding in the corner. I'd been beaten down into submission too many times before.

The Don didn't cross his arms or puff out his chest. His huge, muscled arms hung at his sides under his black, fur-lined duster. The wrappings of a large bandage over his chest were visible under his shirt. His eyes were guarded. Salazar smiled pleasantly at me and leaned up against the bars.

"These cells have not gotten this much use in almost a decade," he mused, running his lithe fingers over the bars.

"Much obliged," I said stiffly, touching the brim of my hat.

Salazar nodded, facing me. "Do I get to tell my great-great-grandchildren that this is where the High King of MidWest spent his days just before one of the greatest royal coups in history?"

I shifted. "We got you your stones, Captain. You said you'd let us go."

The pirate nodded before clicking his tongue in thought. "I need you to make me a promise, your highness," he said more seriously. "I have this feeling letting you out into the world is the wrong thing to do. I could stop you now. Save MidWest, perhaps."

"Save it *from* me?" I asked.

He nodded gravely. "I'd feel just awful if in a year's time a bloodthirsty rogue like you was on the High Throne. So, I want you to promise me something."

I looked to Cecil. His face was passive but alert. Mateo's visage was much the same. They were waiting to see what I'd say.

"All right," I offered the captain. "And if I say no to whatever you propose?"

He smiled and laughed a little. "Promise me that you will not slaughter on your way up. That you will not water the fields of your vengeance with the blood of innocents. If you do, I will come for you."

As I waited, wondering if I'd agree, I heard the ticking of the catalyst machine under his shirt. He'd be around a lot longer than me.

I stood up, tossing aside Cecil's coat. "I promise. If you swear to come if I need your help. I'll need all the friends I can get. Someone in your area of expertise could be useful. Never know when I might need someone who specializes in the aeronautical liberation of valuable assets." I shot my hand through the bars. "What do you say, Captain?"

The pirate smiled crookedly and gripped my hand. He shook it hard. "Agreed, your highness." With a final shake, he left back up the ladder.

Cecil and Mateo stayed behind.

"We've come up with a story for the Don," Cecil said to me.

"What are you talking about?" I asked with a little more aggression than I should have. "Even Salazar was all for killing him the other day." I pointed harshly at the Don. "We can't keep an eye on him all the time, and we sure as hell can't let him go. He'll run back to Uncle Jethro."

Mateo's jaw clenched hard, flexing the muscles on his face. "I won't go back, Ezekiel," he said. "Jethro sent me down to find you once your vampire was taken care of. He didn't know if you were alive or not. I can't come back without proof of your death."

"Great," I said snidely. "So, if we keep you, I have to worry about when you're going to slice my head off with those spinning blades of yours."

My uncle shook his head. "As you said, Jethro hasn't come looking for me. You don't believe Camille is behind the whole thing. We both want answers."

"Cecil?" I shot, angry and at a loss for what to say.

My vampire inclined his head to me. "I have one job: to get you on the throne. I like your idea of panache and grandeur. It will allow us to find answers before we reveal you to them. And we'll look good doing it."

"And him?" I gestured to the Don.

"You'll be an acquaintance of his," Cecil started to recite, walking towards me. He had an energy in his step now that he'd made it over the hard part of convincing me, and his hands moved in flighty motions. "You two met the last time he was on this side of the pond and have been in light correspondence. Simple as that. This explains Mateo not coming back to the palace right away and gives you an in with a cohort."

"Will it be simple?" I asked my uncle.

Mateo sighed slowly, eyeing me behind the bars. "Nothing I say to you will satisfy you. I didn't want to kill you then, and I don't want to kill you now. We've both been used."

I hummed in thought. He was right. My hate was based on eight years of slavery in an underground prison. And he was family, something I hadn't had in a long time. Blood—as I knew from the tether with Cecil—was a strong bond.

*You can do this,* Cecil thought. His purple eyes bored into me.

I reached down, grabbed Cecil's coat, and whirled it around, slipping my arms into it. "All right, then. Where do we start?"

After passing on to Salazar that we'd had a discussion, Cecil and I took the next week to prepare my plan. My revenge still in place, I just needed to set it in motion. After the discovery of the bloodstone, I didn't want to wait. I needed to feel in command again, like I hadn't lost the use of every piece of me.

I slammed a map down on the table the crew had brought up for me. "The Colorado Territory," I started. Cecil stood at my elbow,

Salazar on my other side, and Jacque a good distance away, but her eyes on the plans. "In the Rockies there is a mining town with a single bourbon baron, right? Owns the whole town, basically."

"Yes," Salazar said with a smile. "I used to do trade with him. Before all this." He gestured to his crew. "His mill is not your typical mill, though." He smiled. "Makes the best beers, ciders, bourbons, and meads I've ever had the pleasure to liberate." When Captain Salazar traded with someone, it usually came in the one-way variety.

"How much would he sell for?" I began. "How much is our cut?"

Salazar gave me crooked grin again. "I have your hoard, actually."

"Red's treasure?" I exclaimed.

He nodded, the feathers on his hat dancing. "Picked it up right after we got you settled. It's in one of our vaults in the Spine near there. It breaks my heart to give it up, but..." He tapped his chest where his catalyst machine ticked away. "I owe you. It's rightfully yours. Well, by pirate law."

A wave of relief washed over me. "Perfect."

Jacque spoke up. "People will wonder why he has no family if we come in like a royal or nobleman."

"Struck gold," the Don suggested. "Somewhere outside the west. Bought up a mill here to set up a new life. The mystery will be more than they can bear."

"Nouveau riche," Jacque said in understanding, tapping her chin in thought. "They'd want to be your friend, get to know you. Like an investment."

"Yeah," I replied stiffly. Thinking about mingling, attending parties, shaking hands, and hobnobbing—everything that had to do with interacting with these wealthy plotters and murderers who'd killed my father and ruined my life made my body shake. I had thought that backstabbing, buying rumors, and all other dirty tricks were a thing of the past. That was something they did in The Château d'Oubli. To escape and have no change? What was the point?

There was only one person I could trust.

"Come on, Cecil," I ordered. "Let's get the loot and get ourselves a home base."

# 32 The Mill

"Captain," Isolde called. "The ship is ready and the company is embarking."

One of the many loot vaults of the sky pirates nestled in the Rockies of the Colorado Territory, deep in the crags of the snowy peaks. I didn't go through the great vault door under the mountain. I couldn't make myself go underground again. As I watched Salazar and Isolde take some of their crew in to load *The Scarlet Liberty* for us, Cecil stayed with me outside. After taking our ship, they'd stored her here, too. Jacque nearly cried upon seeing her again.

"Can't make yourself go inside another network of tunnels?" Cecil asked. His fingers picked at the long-frayed lace of his sleeves. "I can't blame you. Though I cannot wait to buy some new clothes. I don't believe I've ever gone so long in the same coat."

I knew he was making light of the situation for me. While I had mostly followed his lead, it was time for me to step up, and he was quickly reading how terrified I was. The coyotes did battle in me, fighting for dominance. My time with Salazar had shown me that forcing my way by blood and violence might not be the strong choice I thought it was. If nothing else got in the way, angering my rabid coyote, my meek beast might take over. I could do this without anger poisoning me.

Making that decision, my chest felt lighter and breathing made me feel good.

The small, three-masted ship with a fresh scarlet hull appeared in the darkness under the mountain. It sailed out with swooping, elegant ease. They'd made her better than she'd been before. Jacque stood at the helm, unable to hide her grin at being behind the helm of her ship again.

Salazar kicked down a ladder for me to ascend. I scrambled up, clinging to the ropes in the rough wind. Cecil came up behind me to ensure I didn't fall. We landed on the deck to find Mateo coming up from the bunghole.

"It's all secured," he called to Jacque.

"Very good," she shouted back over the rumbling of the older engines. To Cecil, she smiled and said, "Didn't she polish up real nice?"

I ran my hand over her new scarlet paint. "We'll make her even better. The ship of a wealthy young man with no regard for money. We can't get everything at one shipwright or they'll track us." I finally smiled, too. "She'll be unrecognizable when we're done with her."

Salazar finally met my gaze. "Stay the course, Ezekiel. If you should need me, there is a woman in the Colorado territory who will pass your messages on to me. I am at your service."

"How will I find her?" I asked.

Salazar smiled impishly. "She will be the only samurai in the Territory. Her name is Kimiko Salazar."

Confused and a little curious, I nodded, thanking him.

"I hope your time with us has been, at the very least, enlightening." Salazar bowed low to me and nodded his head. "Your majesty," he added softly.

Cecil clasped my shoulder with his pale hand. "Off we go. To conquer and to take."

*The Scarlet Liberty* jerked away from Salazar's mighty vessel and we drifted into the cold air of the Rockies. I turned back to watch as Salazar became a smaller figure on the deck of his ship, the lady in white by his side. I had forgotten how large and beautiful *The Kimiko Fire* looked from a distance. I turned back and met Mateo's dark eyes suddenly. I actually opened my thin, pale lips to say something, but the words stopped in my throat. I didn't owe him any words. Not yet.

"Personal upgrades first?" Cecil asked, turning his red sunglasses towards me, grinning widely.

I shook my head. "Home first."

He stammered, looking down at his worn garments.

Leaping to the prow of the ship, I pushed my wide-brimmed hat down over my head harder against the wind and looked out to our destination. I hadn't thought what would happen if the current baron of the Rocky Mountain estate didn't buy my offer. I couldn't imagine someone denying the offer of crates of loot until I saw the estate break through the clouds several hours later. Western castles had never been much to brag about. Anything on the east coast had long lost its glory, often old and run down. Anything farther west quickly devolved into blocky manors and lacked any imagination. Salazar had picked me a good one. Borrowing from the Italian renaissance, the square roofs of the palace glinted golden and the white arches rose elegant and smooth. The sprawling grounds were manicured and green. A waterfall gushed behind the estate, watering the vineyard and giving the whole place a look of constant motion. The general layout inspired me; I saw where I'd put the sky docks, knew where a two-story greenhouse could go—this place would be the talk of all the surrounding territories. It was a priceless spot of land.

"He'll never sell," I said, sighing.

"Never underestimate the bloody good powers of persuasion from a vampire," Cecil whispered to me, a small smile like his old self appearing. "We have our tricks. Coupled with our hoard, it might just work." He gestured to me with one long, white finger. "I need your blood."

"Now?" I asked, unconsciously holding my wrist to my chest as if that would protect me from his vampiric bite.

He nodded, eyes widening. "I can only hypnotize moments after feeding." He held his hand out.

Pouting in resignation, I held my arm out to him. He yanked me closer and bit down. The tingling of my blood rushing back down my veins and out into his mouth made my arm shake. He pulled away, licking his lips.

"Always delightful," he muttered, patting my shoulder as he pushed past me to the ladder.

I decided to bring Mateo, Jacque, and Cecil with me. Mateo took a large leather satchel below our tiny deck and scooped up a variety of our jewels: gold, diamonds, rubies, and of course various special shinies like moonstone and glittermetal. He didn't say a word as I ordered him to follow me down.

We got as close to the front gate as we could and were fortunate in our timing. Guards would never let our ragged fellowship in. But to our luck, the baron of what I found out later was called Noir Pierre was out with his little nephew and a hunting hound. Cecil marched out in front of us in the best coat he could steal from Salazar, and flourished his exuberantly plumed tricorn hat in a bow to make a dancer jealous.

"Good day, my lord baron of this fine Colorado Territory," he sang in his heavy English accent.

The lord on the horse painted the image of everything an old man of his standing should be. His brows were furrowed, and he held his reins perfectly in the western style, his heels down and his nose up. I noted all of this to apply to myself later. I still walked with my shoulders drawn up to my ears to guard against attacks. My hands were balled with anxiety, and I constantly gnashed my teeth. I tried to relax into a pose similar to his. Dropping my shoulders exposed my neck, and I almost ducked down to hide from the strange feeling. I had a long way to go.

"What are you doing here, ruffians?" He spat a large wad of tobacco to his left. "I want none of your religion or politics. And I won't buy whatever you're selling."

The young nephew strained to get a better look at the Don and the bag left open by design. The gems inside caught the setting sun perfectly. The child licked his lips as though desiring to eat up the jewels.

"Look, Uncle, shinies!" he exclaimed. "Geos, even!"

"Arthur, do not use that country speech in my presence!" the noble man chastised. But he did glance at the Don's burden. "What do you want? Selling gems? Fanciful trinkets?"

Cecil smiled through his dark glasses. "We are here to purchase your estate and title," he said with a gentle laugh as though it should have been obvious.

"My summer home?" the lord said with a gasp. "This is my favorite among my estates." He scanned the mountaintops, but then his eyes lighted on the bag. "Let me see what you have to offer. I would be remiss if I didn't at least listen. The tribes have been awful loud lately."

Cecil took the large satchel and opened it for the lord to gaze upon. He lifted out some glittering rubylead and tossed it to the baron. The older man examined it with an expert eye. I hadn't realized before that perhaps some men were so wealthy, they could be bothered to give up one estate.

"You will be most glad to take this, won't you?" Cecil smiled. He did that malicious grin where all his fangs showed and lifted his dark glasses off his eyes. He winced into the grey sunlight, but had to make eye contact to use his hypnosis. My blood in him helped protect him from the sun, which currently hid behind a veil of clouds and did not ignite him like gunpowder. I saw the light begin to shift as he worked his magic; the blessed clouds were about to release the sun. "Two crates full await you in the ship."

"Show me," the baron quipped so quickly, I'm not even sure Cecil had the time to hypnotize him.

I turned back to the ship and signaled Mateo to drop the back door airships had for easy loading. Inside, the crates glittered with Red's stolen treasure.

"Mon dieu," the baron said, a chuckle in his throat. He turned to Cecil. "Who are you?"

Cecil inclined his head in a deep bow, then pointed to me. "A humble servant of…this grande marquis."

"A grande marquis?" the baron asked, looking me up and down. "Est-ce vrai?" He narrowed his eyes at the Don. "And the Don of San Muerte? A friend of yours?"

"Of a fashion," I replied. "We've just returned from an adventure you would not believe. Apologies for our garb."

"Oh?" the old baron raised his scraggily brows at me.

I nodded, plastering a coy smile on my pale face as best I could. "I'm something of a professional adventurer." Cecil's mind touched mine, encouraging me. Better to start my reputation now. "Oh, where haven't I been?" I said, sighing and putting on a show of thinking. Even this small interaction was exhausting.

The little boy, Arthur, craned to look around his uncle at me. "Have you met any pirates? There are pirates around here. They steal our bourbon."

Without having to lie, I replied. "Yes, I've met pirates. Hundreds of them, up in the sky."

"Seen a wendigo?" he tried again.

Cecil took this one for me. "One doesn't go looking for a wendigo, son. The wendigo finds you. And if you're not careful, he'll chase you over the snowing prairies until your feet burn away. Or worse."

Arthur gasped, clinging to his grandfather.

"What an extraordinary life," the baron mused, his eyes still glued to the crates of shinies. "I see I am getting the better end of the deal, anyway. Be careful of the natives. They like to practice their mancer-tech just beyond the vineyard." He pulled the bag from Cecil's hands and tried to hide it under his horse's blanket. "Arthur, we must go. Fetch your mother and don't say a word of this to your father." To Cecil he said, "Bring the ship around to the river and you can unload the cargo."

"Sir!" Cecil called after him. "The keys?" He held up his pale hand, ready to catch them.

"Oh..." The old baron fumbled at his belt and waited a moment before tossing them to Cecil. "The deed will be on the table in the great hall. Please don't come until after sundown. Must get the family, you know."

Cecil smiled handsomely and bowed again. "I wouldn't dream of moving before sundown, sir. Thank you." He flourished his plumed hat once again.

I put myself to work quite quickly that evening. The lord had told the servants about selling the land, and most of them, as I would have done, left for other employment. Some brave ones stuck around to see what this new country marquis would do. Cecil pilfered some of the baron's clothes from a bedroom before I addressed the farmers, miners, and workers who'd remained. I stood in the great hall, clad in the highest pants I had ever worn tucked into the shiniest boots I had ever put on my feet. He put a greatcoat on me that weighed more than I did. I drew myself up with my entourage behind me, also bedazzled in the best finery we had ever pillaged. Jacque wore a green silk dress with beautiful colonial sleeves and golden trim. Her lips were wet and red.

"I suppose you are my people now," I said to my little audience. "I am Le Grande Marquis D'Noirpierre, as these lands have dictated I be named."

"Pretentious," Cecil mumbled with a jovial grin. "I love it."

"Not the time or place, sunflower," I hissed. To my people I said, "I intend to be a fair and just lord, and I expect good work. You will be paid double what your last lord gave you, and you shall have every Sunday off." I cleared my throat and took a breath.

"These are my comrades," I went on. "Obey them as you would me. Don Mateo is my guest. Cecil is my voice and eyes. Treat him as you would treat me."

When it came to Jacque's turn, I didn't know how to introduce her. Did I say she was a long-lost Deleon? A beautiful, strong woman from a family who had been wronged and chained away like a sick animal? I realized I stared at her as these thoughts passed through my mind like a pony express rider. *She is a lady, so treat her like one.* No, that wasn't enough.

"I am his wife." She stood beside me, stiff with anxiety. I didn't have to be a vampire to taste her anger and discomfort. She showed no affection and did nothing to complete the image: no taking of my hand or loving glance. "We are pleased to see so many of you have stayed," she said sweetly.

After this, we spoke a little more, answered a few questions from the workers, but dodged all the most telling ones. The night passed as a blur until I could get Jacque alone. We had had a long day, and I was exhausted, so I dismissed everyone to their chosen chambers and instructed them all to meet in the morning.

I followed Jacque a few corridors into the west wing and finally stopped her beside a giant painted landscape opposite floor-to-ceiling windows showing us the glorious peaks.

"Do you mean it?" I gasped, running to catch her, my hat falling off in my haste. "I don't understand."

She fixed me with her black eyes. "I do. But make no mistake, Ezekiel. It is for the image. No one wants to be bedazzled by a rich lord with no wife or family line. Cecil told me it would be best."

"Cecil?" She always listened to Cecil. "But it can be for you, too. We can take back your home. We could start a new life together. You could be queen of MidWest."

She raised her gloved hand and I flinched. But she didn't strike me. "Never. I do not trust you. Make no mistake." Tears burned her eyes and anger smoldered there. "I do not, cannot, and never will love you." She trembled with rage. "Ever!"

She lifted her skirts and ran down the corridor away from me. I felt numb and confused.

"What can I do?" I called after her.

"Avenge my family," she replied before slamming the door closed. She locked it from the inside.

I stood alone in the long, winding, dark, cold hallway, not knowing where it led to. It reminded me of the time I hunted the undermen. Despite the grand velvet tapestries and the soft humming of heating pipes, it felt like The Château d'Oubli all over again. I was alone. Jacque thought of me as just Ezekiel, a rat from The Château d'Oubli looking to take advantage of her.

I began to walk the halls alone. It was quiet. At least in The Château d'Oubli, noise, light, and someone close by made you feel not so isolated. Here, I didn't know where to start or what to look for. The kitchen? The great hall? A place to sleep? I kicked off the tight boots and went on bare foot.

Unable to find a lamp or figure out how to turn on the gas lamps in the halls, I found my way in darkness to a library with a study off to the side. Overcome by the memories of the prison, I knelt by the grate and tossed in some old newspapers to make a fire. I tore through the drawers of side tables and the desk before finally locating matches. I'd never wanted to cry so much before. I lit the fire and sat in a large, wing-back chair, pulling my knees to my chest. Was it always going to be this lonely? This hard?

"What are you doing?"

I spun around in the chair to see Cecil in the doorway. He had on only dark pants and a loose, white shirt with the laces hanging open.

"I couldn't find the damned master bedroom," I mumbled, looking into the fire's licking tongues. "I'm tired. I want to sleep."

Without a sound, the vampire appeared beside the chair, taking my hand. "Come on, your highness," he said, rolling his eyes with a gentle smile.

He led me out of the study, one hand around my waist the other holding my forearm gently. "Thank you for your help today," he said. His fingers softly touched the bite marks on my wrist.

I nodded, exhausted. "I'm selfish. I let you suck my blood for my own gain."

Cecil found the master bedroom easily and guided me inside. He laid me down on the bed and covered me with the most elaborate bed clothes I remember ever feeling. They were heavy and pressed down on me with a kind of comfort. His thoughts blinked through my tired head. I didn't catch anything solid, just feelings. Something warm filled me as his fingers caressed the dirty tendrils of my hair. The emotion came from him.

"I'm sorry you have to wait out the night," I said, drifting into sleep now that I was comfortable and safe. I leaned into the warmness coming from him. "But it will be worth it. To you, anyway. You have to dress me for the part."

A small sound of delight came from his throat. "Gold trim, ruby-encrusted canes, rapiers made of glass, shoes with heels impossible to walk in! This is where I really get to shine, your highness. It's going to be wonderful."

"Much obliged," I mumbled. Safe with him beside me, I drifted off into the first deep sleep I'd had in over eight years.

# PART III

## LE GRANDE MARQUIS D'NOIRPIERRE

# 33 STAY THE COURSE

Cecil took over preparing the estate for our big reveal. For the next couple of weeks, I was a doll in his hand. He dressed me up, told me how to speak to nobles and how to smile charmingly. I was terrible at it, and the more he made me repeat phrases and postures, the more I added in sarcasm to every move and word. Oddly, that seemed to help.

He hired what he called "a man of etiquette" to teach me about the copious amounts of silverware at a dinner party, what the different hand and fan gestures of women meant, and what it meant when a man held his cane by the neck, not the top. A lady tutor was hired as well, since I needed a softer touch. The vampire buzzed around in pure joy. So much so, I didn't have it in me to stop him or tell him to calm down. I just did my best. But one day, I'd had enough of pinkies, bowing, "my lords," and left in the middle of a dance lesson. I needed to breathe.

I ended up in the mill's storehouse near the river that cascaded down from the mountains and went into the loft, looking out the double doors where the kegs would be lowered out after the winter. I could see Long's Peak from there. One side sloped, dangerously covered in ice that had no doubt been there for years. The other side jutted up, tall and sturdy. I imagined flying there and setting up camp in the keyhole between the two distinct sides. I had heard there were dragons in the Rocky Mountains, though. I could never hunt one of those.

"Ezekiel," said a deep, smooth voice.

I tried to hide my jump by scowling at the intruder. The Don, in his angled-jaw, glossy-haired glory stood there. I stumbled over nothing and caught myself on the bottom half of the Dutch door and bit my tongue. My blood tasted sour.

"What?" I finally managed.

He licked his lips and took a breath, but didn't say anything. I watched his hands; his fingers were spread, but his arms hung limp. "I've come to say something." He drew himself up. "You don't have to kill Jethro. You don't have to kill any of us."

I finally met his gaze. Hell's bells, he thought I was going to kill him? The thought hadn't occurred to me in some time, honestly. But now that he mentioned it…

"You helped them kill my father. You are half the reason I was in that stinking place for ten years of my life! I was a child, Mateo!" Emotion leaked out of me like an over-filled keg, seeping and threatening to explode.

He held his ground and his face turned serious. "I've stayed with you as a sign of trust, hoping you might change your mind. I cannot stand by and see my brother slaughtered."

"You know all about slaughter," I shot back. "The Butcher of San Muerte, famous for your torture engineering. Needless violence for executions. If you were not the son of the high king of MidWest, the Espagnol monarchy would have never tolerated you."

"I cannot excuse my past," he said simply, joining me by the open door overlooking my land. "I did what I did, just as you will. But you have time to stop before you spill the blood of your family."

He waited for me to reply. So, this was the moment he'd decide once and for all whether he could stop me?

That hadn't been what he'd come to say, though. He hadn't gotten to the point yet. "You won't stand by and let me kill Jethro," I said at last. I had decided to perhaps not kill everyone. But Jethro for sure. "Fine, Uncle. You want to know why I will stay the course?"

The edge in my tone made him face me.

"Jethro wronged us both," I started. "He hasn't come looking for you. The papers do not decry the death of the royal bastard. He sent you down there to either die, or kill me. He used you."

"Camille sent me," Mateo interrupted.

I raised my hand, pointing a single finger to shut him up. "You're famous in those penny dreadfuls. Those cheap paperbacks of the Espagnol Butcher made their way down into The Château d'Oubli. Good news for Red, of course. So let me tell you a story about me."

His eyes didn't waver.

I gave a crooked smile and nodded. "Once upon a time, there was a little prince who had done nothing wrong. His mother loved him—"

"Ezekiel, trust me, Camille—"

"Shut it!" I snapped, laying my hand on my revolver. "One day, the abdicated uncle—now a Duke—decides it might not be too bad to be High King of MidWest, oversee the wildest new country on the globe. He lusted after the French queen he'd given up. Who knows why the evil Duke did what he did? The king is killed by his half-brother and is told to slaughter his nephew as well, erasing the line of Markus Aureliam. Then, the queen finds out the bastard is coming for her son after her husband is killed."

He didn't interrupt me again, but I expected him to. He didn't argue or bring up excuses. What was he waiting for? What did he want? If I were him, I'd fight tooth and nail.

I went on, "To save her son, the woman gave him to a man who was to put him on a train. By the Duke's design, a man came to fetch the prince and put him on a train headed for The Château d'Oubli." I tapped my fingers together, recounting my trip into the prison. "Scared and alone, the man not going with him, the prince wept as the sunlight vanished for what he thought was the last time. The songs and stories of The Château d'Oubli played through him and the ride from hell became real. The boy was taken like all the other prisoners and made to work until his little body broke. He had to find a way to survive.

"One day, he overheard that a man they called Redbeard was planning on collapsing a mine with a man inside who owed him something shiny. The boy, still encrusted with goodness, ran to warn the man, saving his life. As payment, the man told the boy a secret about Redbeard." I smiled and shook my head. "I cannot recall what either rumor was, but that became my currency. I fished out secrets, rumors, sniffed out when someone was being stiffed on a trade. But the rats in The Château d'Oubli figured out I was good at it. Rather than kill me, they used me." I met my uncle's eyes. "Every day, a new torture. A new beating. All to get a secret out of me." I clicked my tongue and tilted my head. "Rats in the tunnels get pretty creative with their torture after so many years. The things that have been done to me in The Château d'Oubli are worse than anything you have done during one of your executions, Uncle. Some scars are on the inside."

As I spoke, his face changed with an agonizing mix of regret, horror, and guilt. "I did what I had to," he started, his voice croaking. "They knew I had failed in killing Markus, and I didn't have the stomach to kill you. I had to try to take back my pride. Show Jethro and Camille I was not weak." He swallowed audibly. "But *this* is far more difficult."

I frowned. "What is?"

He knelt onto both knees. "I kneel before my prince, my king, and beg you. Not for my life. I know I am guilty of the murder of King Markus and the exile and torture of his son. At the first test of loyalty, I have betrayed my family, my blood—all to prove my strength. I beg for your forgiveness. I beg you to dole out justice onto me. If not for your own satisfaction, then for your father's. I believed it was too late for me to make right what I did that day. Perhaps there is one way to redeem myself."

He bowed his head and waited in silence. My mouth hung open in shock. I shook my head, taking a few steps back. I had never, in my life, heard such an honest plea. I never thought someone would beg *me* for their life. I'd begged for death some days and my life on others. I knew what it was like to beg for mercy. I'd never been allowed to give it out.

Looking down at him now, I wondered if I would have to kneel before someone someday in recompense for what I wanted to do. Cecil told me to not drink from the cup of revenge. I had tried to change my mind on how to go about it. But Mateo deserved justice, too. Jacque needed her home back. For now, the plan stayed. But I could taste mercy just this once.

I reached my hand out, hovering it over his head like a priest about to give absolution. Could I ever kneel as he did? Could I ever sacrifice myself, or the revenge I wanted, like he did now?

"We are family," I said at last. I stopped talking, the emotion coming back. Snakes and spades, feelings were annoying. My voice deepened as I controlled it. "I never thought I was worth saving. But this stupid vampire has shown me that people should not be judged by their own understanding of self. He sees something in me I don't. I guess that's a good thing," I said, not believing my own words.

A strange feeling came over me. With this strong man kneeling before me, a man who could choke the life out of my frail body with one hand, I felt like a king. Something about people begging to you on their knees, I guess. But I didn't feel vindictive. I felt…merciful.

"Uncle," I said in a much stronger voice than I had ever used in my life. "For the crimes you have committed against the MidWestern crown and the personal injury you have done to me, I must judge you as the burden of my crown directs. Mateo." He looked up at me. I choked. "I forgive you."

His amber eyes shone with a kind of restrained gratitude.

"But I cannot forget what has happened to me. To forgive you means that I will not hate you and I will make an effort to trust you. But know that I will never forget."

He didn't speak. Now that I understood how my uncle saw himself, it was like talking to my reflection. Like I knelt before myself, begging this new king for forgiveness. I could see myself asking for forgiveness, but I could not see granting it.

"Get up," I said awkwardly, wanting to move on. He stumbled up onto his booted feet and resumed his strong, manly posture. "As recompense for your crimes, I have a mission for you." I stopped to think. Recompense? Had I used that large, formal word correctly? Better to stop now and act the king later. "I need you to go and find out about the Deleon land for me. Jacque's father was a baronet, and she is his heir. I'll admit I don't want to go myself. But I think your face won't be so strange there. At last, I'm hoping not."

He nodded. "I know the place. Only been there once while delivering some cargo from the palace."

"So it's a holding ground," I thought out loud, more to myself than to Mateo. "Go in quietly. Just because you might not be seen as an intruder doesn't mean I want you walking in the front door. Take Cecil so I know what's going on. If anything goes south, then shin out as fast as you can.

"Give it some time," I said, still thinking. "I'll have Cecil look for an opportunity. In the meantime." I sighed, leaning my elbows into the opening of the Dutch door. "Back to lessons, I suppose."

# ROUX DEMARQUE

"I cannot take your savagery much longer, my lord!" the old lady spat from her side of the little tea table. "Were you raised in a barn?" She kneaded her forehead with her fingers and took a deep breath to regain her lady-like composure. Her every mannerism triggered me by the end of the tea lesson. "Do you delight in vexing me?"

I smiled, showing my newly white teeth. "There is a certain charm to it, mademoiselle." I toasted her with a little brandy.

Her face fell in disappointment so much that I thought it would slide right off her skull. "My lord," she started, putting her hands together in a matronly fashion, but speaking from behind gritted teeth. "You have so much untapped charm. You are young, very handsome." She blushed. "Your humor is…trying, but I assume only to me. Please stop putting sugar in your scotch!" she shouted after a vein burst in her temple from watching me plunk six cubes into my teacup. "If you insist on drinking when you serve your guests tea, I suggest you grow a taste for it."

"You would not believe the kind of stuff I drank in my lifetime, mademoiselle." I plucked at my new, lacy cravat while swirling the sugary concoction in my teacup. "And I must add the sugar or the jig would be up. They would know I am serving them grass water while I am enjoying a finer drink." I took a sip most elegantly, trying to mimic Cecil. "Brandy, mademoiselle, not scotch. Perhaps you'd like to visit my mill before you go? A nice brandy would do you wonders." I smiled as charmingly as I could. "Maybe loosen a few things inside that tight head of yours."

She blushed again and smoothed her bodice.

*I'll be damned, that worked,* I thought. It was exhausting channeling Cecil, but it was the only way I could get to the right levels of charm and pomp-assery.

"Really, marquis, you are so vulgar." She called her steam-powered puppy over and petted him nervously.

"I didn't suggest anything, mademoiselle." I winked at her. "Your mind found its way there all on its own." I took another sip, watching her. Eye contact had proven to be important against all my tutors. The economics tutor found it intimidating, my social tutor found it mesmerizing, and this wonderful old dove found it enchanting.

She swallowed hard. "I suggest automatons," she said, sweat beading on her delicate lip. "A butler or a groundsman. You are wealthy, yet you have none. That is something people will look for." She nodded. "I know a cook looking for work, should you need more help for your grande soiree. You will want servants, one for each room of the house so any wandering guests may be attended to. That ought to do it. Is there anything else I can help you with today, marquis, before I go?"

I stood and helped her to her feet, taking the robot pooch in my other arm. I made sure to hold my hand with my palm parallel to the floor so hers could drape elegantly over mine. I held our hands at about shoulder height. "I have enjoyed our time together, mademoiselle. I thank you for your aid. A wild adventurer such as myself hardly remembers what to do amongst civil society."

"Oh, it's been divine." She smiled at me. "The places you have been and the things you must have seen. Any nobleman would trade his upbringing for such a life of adventure. Tell me, will you finish telling the story about the dragon in Europa before your party?"

I laughed, trying to mimic Cecil's high, lilting laugh. "Mademoiselle Vianne, anything for you."

We reached the great, grand doors to my home and I handed her back the dog. It had been a present from me to entice her, in addition to the astronomical sum I'd already paid her to keep quiet about the marquis who didn't know which side of a dinner plate the knife went on. "I am simply glad you will be coming. I cannot wait to show you what you've taught me. I may just make you proud."

She left in her gilded airship and I looked up at the sunset over the peaks.

With a savage cry, I slumped down into the chair. My back hurt from sitting up straight. My head hurt from remembering all the posh ways to say things. As I slouched, Cecil entered, frowning at me for my outburst. Glaring at him, I ripped the buttons from my waistcoat, spilling them over the shiny floor. With the tight embrace gone, I gasped and bent almost double in relief.

"Ezekiel!" Cecil gasped, diving to catch all the little white buttons. "That's hardly befitting a marquis, let alone a prince."

"I can't breathe in that thing," I growled, kicking off my high-heeled shoes as well. I spread my toes in their stark, white stockings and stretched my legs out.

"These are ivory, your highness," Cecil went on, searching with his violet eyes for the last button. "Do you have any idea how hard it was to get them imported? Not to mention illegal?"

"And yet here they are." I smirked, annoyed.

He stopped and surveyed me with that way that made me feel warmth from the inside. "You've come a long way," he offered, holding his long fingers out to me to take the buttons. "But you're still an underground savage."

I glared at the ivory in his palm. Somehow, taking them felt like surrender. Growling, I snatched them and shoved them in my hip pocket. "It's exhausting. Every word is planned out in my head before I say it. I rethink every inflection. Every smirk and wink must be timed." I glared at the teacup. "Do I sit before a duchess or after a Duke? Is the waltz four counts or a square—"

"Both," Cecil interrupted, rolling his eyes so hard the purple disappeared into the back of his head.

"—and what the hell does it matter if I use the same fork for a salad as the pie?" I finished loudly.

Cecil looked personally offended. "Manners maketh the man," he quoted. He reconsidered his next words when he saw my face fall. He knelt quickly, placing his hand on my knee. "Ezekiel, we can work on this. It doesn't matter near as much as you learning to be charming. They will forgive a brash man so long as you make them feel important." He shrugged. "Make it part of your charm. Let them know you are boorish and the few manners you do manage to retain will come across as…" He winced, looking for the right word. "Endearing." He reached up and smacked my cheek hard before turning on his heel to leave. "I've intercepted word that a host of ships are inbound to Deleon. Just the distraction we need, so Mateo and I will be back later. Keep wary, Ezekiel."

I watched him go, pulling up the collar to his greatcoat as he entered the setting sun. With our tether, I could see the missions I sent him on, like being there myself. But I still worried, cloistering myself away until he returned.

Endearing? Is that how he saw me? A stupid oaf in need of his ever-present support?

I took one of the buttons out and looked at it. The imperfections, the faint, grey veins, and the inclusions made it…endearing. Sighing, I gripped it hard. I'd never be a perfect marquis. But maybe I didn't have to be.

Alone in the great house, I listen for sounds of Jacque. She'd been tinkering with the fountain out front, making a few clockwork dancers and other things to keep her busy and out of my sight. I turned back inside, ready to track her down. My hunt was futile, of course. But later that day, Cecil's thoughts reached me: images of what they did rolled through my head like the film of a photographer.

Cecil and Meteo flew out towards the Deleon estate in the cover of darkness just to scope the place out. I wasn't sure how to get it back for Jacque, but force came to mind. Once I was king, I felt sure I could do anything, but I wanted to find a way before that. To show her I would keep my promise.

"Skydocks are lit," Mateo said to Cecil as he looked through a telescope. "Your information was accurate. Shipment of something is coming in. Or a royal vessel."

Cecil locked the helm of the small ship in place and joined him at the side. "Do my eyes deceive me, or is that a ship from the motherland?" He squinted, using his vampiric sight to look far into the dimly lit docks. "I see royal guard, but no markings on the ship."

"They don't want France to be spotted. Why?" Mateo asked, still scanning the area. "What's that?" He pointed to a lower dock under the huge airship where crates were being unloaded. "They're locked."

Cecil tapped his lower lip, thinking. "I could get close."

Mateo looked up at him, his brows knitting. "Ezekiel will kill me if I come back without you."

The vampire smiled, leaping up onto the railing and spreading his wings. "Then don't leave me." He leapt from the airship. A bat in the night, he swooped around the Deleon estate. The warm night air pushed his coat and hair back behind him as he flew. He skirted under the ship, looking for any sign to give away what the patriarch of the Syndicate was up to. He landed softly, clinging to the side of the hull of the French ship. The escort onboard wore black cloaks over obvious blue and silver tabards embroidered with the fleur de lis.

*Musketeers?* he thought. *The French royal aegis is guarding something aboard this ship.*

They were trying to hide themselves under those cloaks, but couldn't hide the velvet from flashing into view as they moved. Quick, hissed French came from a man in a tricorn hat.

Crawling along the bottom of the ship, Cecil popped up on the other side. His blood immediately boiled in his veins and his entire body erupted into revolting agony. He almost dropped from the underside of the skydock where he clung. Peeking through the slats, he saw the crates above him. Slowly, he stuck his long, thin finger through and touched the crate. He hissed as his flesh blistered.

*Silver,* he mused, knowing I was privy to his thoughts. *They're lined with silver.*

He crawled up and crouched in the shadows. One set of men unloaded the crates, putting them on wagons that trailed down the docks to inside the walls below. Above, on the upper dock where the gangplank linked it to the upper deck of the ship, a herd of the hidden musketeers escorted someone inside the manor.

Dodging around the crates to try to get a better look, Cecil stepped out of his hiding place. An invisible wall met him as he tried to jump up to the underside of the top dock. He hit it hard, falling back down onto the wooden slats. It was not unlike the times he'd tried to enter a church. He had to skirt around the edge and look for a way past the invisible barrier. One catwalk appeared open. He walked out onto it, intending to fly up when the same thing happened, but this time far more violently. He was thrown from the catwalk by a burst of energy and tumbled into the view of an automaton standing guard. The thing caught his shadowy movement and started to scream an alarm, pointing at him.

From where he lay on the ground, between two silver-lined crates, he looked up. Perched on one of the highest towers of the grand manor loomed an enormous iron cross. The arms of the symbol expanded out just beyond the walls to the edge of the docks. The Syndicate patriarch knew what he was doing.

With the alarm blaring, Cecil heard Mateo rev the engine of the sloop and spin the little ship towards the skydocks. *He shouldn't come back for me,* Cecil thought, enraging me. But I knew Mateo wouldn't leave without him.

A man in a long red leather duster rounded the silver crates. He wore a red hat in the shape of the Musketeers of France, one side pinned up with a black feather tucked in the flap. He wore two sets of belts diagonally across his chest, laden with little pockets and bottles. The bottles carried a variety of very fine geo dust in reds, oranges, and yellows.

"What is going on here?" the man quipped in a gentle French accent.

Mateo swung onto the dock just then and faced the man in red. To Cecil and Mateo's surprise, the man gave him a slight bow when he recognized him.

"Don," the man said. "No one from the palace mentioned you'd be among us tonight. I'd not heard you returned from the Château. A pleasure to finally meet you, as well." His sharp, orange eyes shot around the docks. "Unless someone else sent you?"

Cecil and Mateo stayed their hands. This last question piqued their interest.

"Were you expecting someone from the palace?" Cecil asked, standing up as the man in red silenced the screaming automaton.

"Pas exactiment," the man said, his eyes till trying to read the Don. "But you may tell the Duke that everything is on schedule and according to plan."

"And you are?" Mateo asked.

The man tilted his head but smiled politely. "Roux DeMarque. The Grande Mancer, appointed by her majesty Queen Camille. We've not corresponded before, but she and the Duke have mentioned you." He inclined his head again in a polite bow.

"Mancer?" Cecil mused, shocked and a little confused. He took in the geos on the belts once again.

Roux DeMarque nodded and ran his hand over his geos. "Fire and heat mancy are most compatible with me. As the Grande Mancer, I have been tasked with seeing to the shipment of the geos and the…*cargo* from France." DeMarque scanned their faces carefully.

I sensed from Cecil as I watched from a great distance that DeMarque had a hidden motive. Something he looked for in Mateo.

"Jethro does not know you're here?" DeMarque asked the Don, taking a step closer and lowering his voice.

Lying quickly, Mateo fibbed, "He does."

DeMarque's shoulders fell, and he stepped back, assuming an at ease pose, disposing of whatever anxious thought had risen in his mind. "Je comprends. I thought maybe you brought other news. Apologies."

Cecil took in the crates now. "All these are full of geos for geomancy?"

The Grande Mancer nodded. "As per the queen's instructions. You may tell her the plan will go on as expected. We have had a few bumps in the trail, but nothing she need worry about."

Mateo and Cecil shared a dark, meaningful glance.

"Queen Camille?" Cecil reiterated.

At this, Roux DeMarque narrowed his eyes and clasped his hands behind his back. "Indeed." His tone turned cautious again. "Everything is here. Down to the last of the bloodstones."

"And the cargo from France?" Cecil asked, pointing up.

The Grande Mancer nodded. "All well." He gave them a final, quizzical look and turned to walk away. He waved his hand and a few hired men appeared.

"You seem hesitant," Mateo noted.

DeMarque's face remained impassive. "It is not my place as Grande Mancer to agree or disagree with the queen. It is not up to the soldiers to question their orders. No matter how much I may disagree. I just do as I am told."

"That will be all," Cecil said stoutly. "As you were." He gripped Mateo by the arm and made their way back over to the ship. No one followed them.

"That was close," Mateo mused. "And I'm worried we don't have any good news."

Cecil half agreed with a grunt. "We know the Grande Mancer may be a crack we can exploit. I sense his allegiance to the queen might not be as strong as the soldierly bond he claimed. Something unsettles him. We need to move. We can't delay any longer."

"He could be useful," Mateo added, pulling the ropes from the docking cleats to disembark. "He holds a high position and seems hesitant." He glanced up again at the unmarked ship. "Maybe we could… persuad him to give us information."

Cecil took in Mateo's suggestion with only mild caution. "Perhaps. Talk of soldiers and mancers and such a large shipment of bloodstones make me wonder what the royal court has in mind. Almost like they're gathering weapons to launch an attack."

# 35

# Le Grande Marquis D'Noirpierre

The day of my masquerade soiree—my entrance into royal society—came at last. I'd decked out my castle-like home with every piece of finery I could lay my hands on, including a servant for every room and an automaton butler, as my tutor had suggested.

"This balloon thing is ridiculous," the gilded vampire said as he gazed upward at the glorious monstrosity that I had personally chosen as my mode of transportation for the evening.

"It's a tear-drop dirigible. That's what the saleswoman called it," I corrected. "And I am not the only one who likes things dripping in jewels and gems." I picked at his extravagant coat and examined his bejeweled heels. "I want to make a lasting impression tonight, and you make it very difficult. My dirigible is only half as glittery as you."

"As it should be," he said, smiling. He turned away but stopped. "Ezekiel," he hissed to make me turn and look.

Curious, I did. Standing by my newly repaired fountain was Jacque in blue satin, absolutely flecked in diamonds and sapphires. Her skin glowed like polished mahogany and her hair flowed in elaborate curls and waves on her head, accented with tiny white feathers and glittering stones. She approached us and made a perfect curtsy.

Cecil bowed, kissed her hand, and departed, saying he would make sure all the lights were lit and the automatons were scrubbed to a shine. Jacque watched him go, her hand hovering in the air where he had left it after his bow and kiss. Realizing I came as second choice, I offered her my hand. She took it but didn't look at me. Instead, she gazed up at the gaudy zeppelin. I noticed she had a significant amount of meat on her bones now that we'd left the dungeon. Her corset couldn't even contain her growing gut, and her arms were fuller and flushed with life. Even her chest had filled out and nicely spilled out the top. She sighed and fanned herself.

"Your balloon reminds me of the night sky, hey," she said softly. Her Château d'Oubli ways melted away faster and faster as she returned to the life she had been born into. "Silver metal work. Diamonds like stars. I see they used a Murdoch-Melville engine for the gas and steam. Those were not even patented yet when I went under. Very nice."

I almost combusted with the praise.

"You use hydro-gas?" she asked, still scanning the aircraft. "That's the one that uses steam to expand the gas, so you use as little as possible, but still get a good lift. They're very light, though, so be careful when it goes up. You don't want to get caught in the…" She trailed off, realizing I was gazing intently at her.

I took a chance. "It's nothing compared to you tonight."

"Are you comparing me to a balloon of hot air?" She almost smiled. "I saw the doctor today. Everything is going well."

"No, not the balloon. The night sky," I corrected. "The stars aren't nearly as bright as your eyes. And the moon not near as elegant."

She finally met my eyes. She searched me, looking deep to find a bit of me to love. Finding nothing, she turned back to the ship and watched its slow hover. The motion must have affected her because she started to sway a little. She took a step back and put her hand to her stomach.

"Excuse me," she said, sounding dizzy. "I feel…"

She jerked her hand away from me and made a mad lurch into the fountain, spewing her dinner into the clean water. Her face shone red with shame as she mopped her mouth with her gloves.

"Forgive me," she said. "I thought that would have stopped by now."

"Are you ill?" I asked, coming to her side. I took her hand and made her face me. Then I saw it.

Her hand clutched at her stomach. The corset she had on did not reach down over her lower half. I knew what a woman's frame looked like in a corset: weirdly flat and curved.

My favorite memory, the best thing to ever happen to me, came back. That night in The Château d'Oubli, when she'd come to me, and we'd made love.

"Yes," she hissed, breaking my trance. "Congratulations, your majesty. You have a child on the way. Your line will go on. And I am its harbinger. Your future is set in my flesh." She traced her stomach, eyes glassing over. "I've done more than I promised for you."

I could not stop the wild grin that flew over my face as I grabbed her beautiful, strong shoulders in joy. "Jacque!" I cried. "You're amazing!" I dove in to embrace her, to kiss her.

A crack crunched into my face not once, but twice: once into my teeth, and the second into my eye. I stumbled back, clutching my face. She'd punched good and hard with her tiny, strong fist.

"Hell's bells!" I groaned, glaring at her with my good eye.

"I didn't want this!" she snarled, pointing one elegantly bejeweled finger in my stinging face. "Remember that." She glared and nodded to herself. "Yes, this is the only way to make you see once and for all." She drew herself up. "I don't love you and I never, *ever* will."

Desperate, I took a step towards her. "Jacque, we're not the people who escaped The Château d'Oubli anymore. I'm not even the same man Salazar tied to the mast and gave a flogging to."

"You were that day you came back with the bloodstones!" she roared. She didn't tear up. Her face burned red. "You came at me. Under the spell of the geomancy or not, you *came* at me! Cecil tried to stop you. Mateo tried to stop you. You hurt me and almost took me against my will. You ripped my clothes off before the entire crew, Ezekiel. Your intent was clear. Those stones didn't transform you. They opened a gate on a monster already living inside."

I felt the blood drain from my face and my arms went numb as she pulled away from me, dashing inside the house. Leaving me alone and taking my child with her. I looked back at the sick in the fountain and then after her. Joy and fear mixed in my gut. Would she keep it? Would she run away and take my child with her?

Getting her home back suddenly became my first priority. I needed her to stay. I needed my child.

"Ezekiel!" Mateo shouted. "Your guests are arriving."

I had gone over and over in my head how to greet my people. I had worked on elegance, manners, dancing, walking, and Mateo had relayed to me the ways of the royal people. "Shallow social norms I try to never partake in," he had said. But of course, someone wanting to join the ranks of the nobles had to know these things. I had tried to create new habits for myself. I had also tried to get rid of old habits. Did I want the royal circle to see me as wealthy and pompous? A resource to be considered in their scheming? A charming scoundrel?

"Keep it mysterious and charming," Cecil said behind me. "Smile like you have a secret."

"I *do* have a secret, Cecil," I reminded him stiffly.

We stood on the landing between the balconies that flanked my ship. Below, the gardens glowed with romantic lighting, entertainers, and enough wine flowed to make Bacchus jealous.

"No, like you have *their* secrets. You know what they do at night after they draw their curtains closed." He gently put his hand on my shoulder and faced me with his piercing eyes. "You know what they drink when they lie and say they are away on business. You know that the lord of the neighboring duchy paid to have his wife poisoned."

I shivered as Cecil loomed only inches from my face.

I swallowed. "Got it."

I had Cecil go into the crowds first. He floated among them like a duchess plied with the best wine in town, greeting everyone with flamboyant gestures and tales of my supposed journey across the globe that had been slowly filtering out from us. Stories of a lifesaving, adventurous marquis. According to his tales, I was generous, kind, loving, something of a gallivanting lover, a rogue, and—most importantly to them—young, naïve, and very rich. I had friends in the inner royal circles of Afrique, where I had saved more than one tribal princess from loveless marriages and counseled many a now-wise prince. Some even pretended to recall rumors of my adventures to seem more important than those merely listening to the stories. Cecil was right: they lied to seem like they knew. How convenient and horrible at the same time. It helped that the Don of San Muerte in Espagne corroborated many of my stories. Of course, the people wanted to hear his as well. Why not rub elbows with the brother of the soon-to-be king?

I watched the masked guests like a child hidden behind a curtain. The orchestra started to play some lively music and off in one corner some guests took the marble dance floor outside underneath a high gazebo. I spotted government officials in their bowler hats making a ring near the banquet table, their cigars and brandy glasses clutched in sausage-like fingers. Some Japonais royals fanning themselves by the fountain, and others I did not quite recognize, all mixed on my land. There were also those from the nearby city who held no office mingling with the wealthy.

I blinked, breathing heavily. My palms moistened.

"Cecil!" I hissed when he glided close by.

He slipped behind the curtain without hesitation. "What game are we playing, hiding here?" he asked, a little giddy from all the socializing.

I didn't know what to do. Nerves grated at my insides. "Help me," I finally spat.

He sighed. "You've got this. Your little cunning brain can handle appearing on the balcony. Greet them and then slip into the crowd. Someone has to keep this party lively." He pushed his red glasses up his thin white nose.

*Do this for me,* I wanted to say. *Let me disappear into the night instead of you.* I scanned the crowd again. "They're not here."

Cecil looked over his shoulder. "Who?"

"I invited the Duke and Mother. I figured she might not come, but he's not here. Shouldn't he be?"

Cecil clasped my shoulders, squeezing my arms. "I'll ask around.

Meantime, get going. Mateo has started to lead the people outside for the fireworks." He leaned into my face again and said solemnly, "You know all their darkest secrets."

I walked alone outside and into my balloon that hovered a good distance away from the crowd, hidden in the green. Everything I'd learned leaked out of my head. I boarded my glittering vessel and tried to imagine what my life would have been like had I never been imprisoned as I drifted up and over my towering estate.

Nothing came to me. Instead, I was back in The Château d'Oubli, scared, hiding, in pain. I knew who that man was. But what made Le Grande Marquis D'Noirpierre? Was he educated and well-traveled? Was he forgiving or vindictive? I wanted revenge. He didn't.

He could be anyone I wanted him to be. My mind went blank, and I gripped the cleats along the railing.

"Ladies and gentlemen," Cecil crowed from the balcony below me. "It is my greatest honor to finally introduce you to the man of the legends you have heard. The lord of grace, the king of justice, the father of adventure!"

The fireworks exploded and my bejeweled dirigible slipped over the parapets into view. Everyone gasped once they beheld it. Colored lamps hung from the balloon, and garlands of flowers showered down petals on their awestruck faces. My manservant tossed the silver ladder down. I met the eyes of a few gaping faces, threw the ends of my long coat out behind me, and put a leg up on the rail, ready to climb down. To my delight, some girls giggled and covered their mouths. A few young peacocks below exchanged jealous looks.

"I give you Le Grande Marquis D'Noirpierre! A prodigal son returning to his empire of birth," Cecil finished. He was loving this a little too much.

The fountain turned on, colored lights reinstalled and water reflecting the fireworks and all their sparkle. I leapt over the edge and caught myself on the ladder to many gasps and applause. I tried to execute Cecil's instructions. I flourished the plumed hat and smiled darkly, but let it spread to my eyes, making them glitter.

I leapt down jauntily, and Cecil and I exchanged bows. After the ship finished sailing over the towers and domes into darkness, the people exploded into applause. I took a glass from a nearby automaton and raised it before me. I almost choked on my own saliva as I opened my mouth to speak.

"My most gracious friends," I started. I stopped at hearing my own voice. It rang strong and merry. "I am humbled by your warm greeting. It is I who owe you my gratitude. I am far too wild and uncivilized to be blessed with society such as yours."

A few laughs and "awws" followed this.

"No, it's true." I smiled down at them. "I have not been on the shores of the American Empire since I was a small boy. I have been raised amongst primitive people. I fear I have no manners. You will have to forgive my barbaric ways." My head rushed and the world tipped around me. I did take in two girls who cooed and pressed their hands against their chests at my humble words. "My invitations were too short notice, and yet here you are, gracing me with your kindness and acceptance. You are a giving people to put up with me. Brave as well. You don't know who I am, yet you drink voraciously and consume of my storehouses."

A few exchanged confused frowns at this.

I smiled down at them. "Perhaps you are as savage as I am?"

They giggled and raised their glasses up to me.

Cecil practically glowed next to me, his pale skin reflecting the moonlight.

"You've brought trade back to the valley!" an older man in a gilded hat said, raising a glass to me. "The Colorado Territory needed a good trade. Even the natives are trading with their mancer-tech. You brought us back to life, marquis!"

I forced myself to make eye contact and smile at him. "But I see we are not blessed with the royal Duke Jethro, however. Perhaps he has heard of our barbaric ways and wisely chose to stay away?" I took a drink. "Or perhaps he cannot handle a real soiree?"

They all laughed, and some drank to my health for calling out the Duke.

"He celebrates this evening at midnight," one fat lady said with a laugh, winking at me. "But I'd rather dine with a rich marquis than see another heir come out to society!"

Everyone cheered at that and raised their glasses. They mumbled something about "to the prince" and took respectful drinks.

"What?" I couldn't stop myself. I whipped around to look at Cecil, who had turned even paler now. I glared down into the crowd and found Mateo. His face now matched his white garments. We all seemed fitfully surprised and shocked. But Le Grande Marquis D'Noirpierre couldn't be. Glancing at my pocket watch, I saw it was just past eight. We had to hurry. We'd planned a long, rumpus night with events well into the break of dawn. But this was more important.

"What!" I shouted louder this time. "Avoiding me?" I forced a pompous laugh. "And I so wanted to entice him to come. I know we had plans and you were looking forward to the circus I brought into town. But I have a much better proposal. What say you, good people? Shall we take my ship and give the Duke a visit from the Rockies he won't soon forget? Join me on an impromptu adventure?"

Thank God everyone had been drinking. They all laughed and cheered, thinking it would be a rodeo to fly to Palais Kansouri in this crazy Marquis's airship. Their spirits were high and very agreeable to my suggestion. I called for *The Scarlet Liberty* to be brought down from the skydocks. We boarded as many of my guests on it as would fit. It was tight, but I had spared no expense in cabin and deck room expansions. I laughed with them for a few more minutes, then had the crew go full speed, making the fires work, to Palais Kansouri and this mysterious heir. It was at least a three-hour flight, and I had to keep the people busy the entire time.

Cecil, not needing to use his vampiric powers to sense my rage, stood apart from me. The words in his head spun in madness I could not keep up with. All I felt was confusion and…betrayal? He wouldn't look at me, choosing instead to glare into the night ahead of us. I got the feeling he wondered if I had lied to him all those months ago. I'd proven myself, hadn't I? Did his desperation to save his soul make his trust in me so fragile?

I checked over Cecil's shoulder at Mateo, his face warped in confusion. I wanted to threaten him, to warn him not to lie to me, and demand he tell me what this was about. But that would destroy the trust we had built. I knew the news shocked him as well, but part of me wanted to ignore it and try to force the information out of him.

Either we'd find out Uncle Jethro was lying now, or my entire life was about to come crashing down one last time.

# 36 THE OTHER

With a little help from an enchanting instrument onboard my ship—a gift from Captain Salazar—and more heavy wine, the people stayed jovial to the point of perfect agreeability after the three-hour flight to the high castle at Kansouri. Many gathered around me to hear my stories in my own words. Fortunately, I had had a lot of practice lying and making myself out to be the biggest and blackest bull in the pasture. I stole stories Salazar had told me and used them as my own. Men were jealous of my adventures and bravery, and women pined for me, desiring to be the subject of my passion and kindness. Many jealous eyes flashed Jacque threatening looks as she stayed by my side, eyes empty, one hand on her belly.

"How have you been through so many trials and traveled so far and yet find the strength for this kind of joy?" one pretty girl asked me, her face flushed and her eyes weepy with desire. "The death of your family to plague, the capture and torture by pirates— I'd have given in long ago."

I smiled kindly at her. "The trick, and admittedly the hard part, is this: always have one or two good friends. When you are weak, they will be strong for you. Never deny yourself the chance to love, and always go to sleep with a purpose for the next sunrise. And sleep with your boots on." I winked at her.

They all laughed, and one young son of some lord asked, "Why sleep with your shoes on? Won't your feet get cramped?"

"It's better than waking up the next morning with a rattler in them." I laughed and toasted the lordly boy.

"My lord." Cecil pushed his way through my adoring audience. "Palais Kansouri." He pointed ahead to another, far grander celebration.

A typical Kansouri midsummer night surrounded us as the prairie castle jutted up to greet us: warm air, insects singing in the long grass and the trees, more stars than space in the sky, but still the bonfires blossomed around the castle like sunflowers. And the Duke's fireworks were far larger than mine. A fleet of dirigibles and other types of airships surrounded the hilltop castle like honeybees around a freshly blossomed apple tree. We hovered and dropped our own anchor, fastened by the groundsmen before we disembarked.

"Remember, my friends," I said to my giddy entourage, "be polite! We are crashing a coming out party, after all."

I had the stairs dropped for the drinking hordes and we made our way down the path and across the drawbridge like a pack of rams, all braying and pushing to be in front. I'd had no intention of entering my old home this way. I hesitated as the gate opened to admit us after Mateo took the lead.

"My lord Don!" A man in royal garb, holding a scroll and a staff, ran to greet us. "Shall I announce you, sir?" the herald asked Mateo.

The Don shook his head and motioned for me to enter first. Cecil sensed my hesitation and appeared at my side. We all three walked in together, Jacque in tow.

The palace looked almost just as I remembered it. Huge, spacious, white, clean, and full of antiques and unique things from around the world—my father had been a collector and a lover of all cultures. It made me glad to see his things were not touched. To our surprise, no one greeted us in the entryway. The music lilted in from outside in the back courtyard. A well-polished automaton informed us that the party had moved outside to welcome the prince. It seemed my uncle and I thought alike when it came to grand entrances.

But the people were not gaping at a mysterious prince. A demonstration took place in a tiny arena that had been set up like a bull pen. Inside the arena were two men. They were both dressed in the same uniforms, but in different colors: a wide-brimmed hat with one side tacked up, a feather jutting out, soft, leather dusters with so much length in them the wearers could have used them as tents, and belts of geos crisscrossed their chests. The two men stood at attention while one in red, whom I recognized through Cecil's and my tether to be a man named Roux DeMarque, marched back and forth, giving some kind of speech. But I looked past them and up to a dais where I saw, war metals gleaming on his chest, Jethro, the Duke of Dakota. He looked exactly the same as the last time I'd seen him, except his black head now sparkled with grey streaks.

"As promised," Jethro said to his court around him once Roux DeMarque finished. "The mancers are our top performers and have passed all the tests we set before them. We like to think of them as our special forces, like the motherland's Musketeers, if you will. But we've taken it a step further. Using compatible geos, we reduce the risk of death by use dramatically."

One lord looked doubtful. "But there is still a risk. This is hardly the revolution for battles we were hoping for. We must be stronger than our enemies, not hurting our fighters."

Jethro held a hand out towards Roux DeMarque.

The Grande Mancer replied, "It's not perfect. But by screening our recruits, we can find what they are most compatible with. This reduces the illness of using geos *and* makes it stronger. It is true, it is not for everyone. But we have to get out ahead on this research before other countries with far superior mines do. And..." The mancer cleared his throat and steeled his gaze. "It's a better option than augmentation."

Jethro sighed and rubbed his temples. "What DeMarque means is that it will couple well with augmentation."

"Are you still augmenting, Jethro?" a fellow royal asked, arching a brow. "We decided as a court that augmentation was for war only." His eyes flashed to the Grande Mancer, who averted his fiery amber eyes.

"And will you submit to the queen's augmentation?" the lord asked DeMarque. "If it comes to that?"

The Grande Mancer held his pose but didn't reply, hesitating.

"I see." The lord sat back in his chair, rubbing his mutton chops. "So, what you spoke of, Jethro, *is* coming to pass?" He looked crushed.

Jethro smiled and shook his head. "Tonight is not about the mancers or foreign affairs, but you must see a little something more." He gestured to the mancers. One of the other mancers, a tall Haitian with long, beaded hair held up in a ponytail on top of his head, stepped forward. His eyes were green.

"Emeraldsmoke," Jacque whispered. "It makes one able to—"

With a flick of his hand, the Haitian flung a tiny blue stone out to the other side of the arena. Just as it exploded into a plume of dark blue smoke, he smashed another at his feet and fell into the smoke. He appeared on the other end of the arena, stepping out of that smoky doorway he had created.

"Well spotted," Cecil praised Jacque.

She blinked quickly, hiding her blush. "His eyes give it away. Must be compatible with him."

"That's a very dangerous use of the stone" the doubtful lord said, clutching his heart. "Men have come out in half or not at all."

Jethro smiled and sighed. "Knowledge is for the wise. Let *us* handle it." Some people laughed. "I don't want to show you my entire bag of tricks, councilor. I just want you to know we have them. As the ambassador to the motherland, I felt it was wise to share with you what we have here in the empire."

The man looked uneasy now, stroking his mutton chops again. "We are not at war, Jethro," he said cautiously. Almost like a warning.

"Angleterre is still smarting from the sound beating we gave them one hundred years ago," Jethro said coyly. "France did not willingly come to our aid."

"America est Française!" a man with a heavy southern accent added. "C'est vrai!"

Jethro's smile broadened as he ignored his fellow leaders. "Shall we get to the main event? I don't want to dampen the true meaning of tonight." He checked his pocket watch.

With a wave of his hand, the two mancers flicked open another bottle from their belts. They rubbed the stone between their hands until fire erupted, lighting up the arena where they had been showing their skills. Standing like torches, they heralded in what we'd been waiting for: the mysterious prince.

Walking out from the crowd came a tall, strong, younger version of me. Maybe fifteen years old. He looked far healthier, no dark circles under his eyes, no strain in his gate. No frightened slump to his shoulders. And his teeth were white, made more so by the sun-touched look of his skin. His hair hung glossy and thick, not thin and oily like mine. I didn't think he looked entirely like me. But a healthy diet and sun might have made those changes. He had my nose and eyes, but not the square jaw I did. Something about him reminded me of my mother, but the rest of the features matched Jethro more, including his dazzling green eyes. He looked like a king. Even in my finery, he cut more of a princely picture than I did. He carried himself like Jethro, waved like him, smiled like him.

"I am honored to present you, my good American people, to High Prince Ezekiel Aurelium, son of high Queen Camille. Lost some years ago, he was discovered in France among our family there who did not know the young man they'd taken in. He returns to us now, ready to take the empty position of prince and soon, take up the mantle of High King."

"That's Ezekiel?" someone whispered.

"Indeed," Jethro replied. "We made plans to send Ezekiel away for protection when my dear brother was murdered. But the boy disappeared amidst the disaster. We feared the worst." He beamed down at the younger boy, gripping his shoulder hard. "Camille came across him in the French royal court where he'd been found and raised by a nobleman there. Recognizing her son, we made plans to bring him home." Jethro teared up in earnest as he looked on the boy. "I am pleased to have him here again."

Was Jethro lying? Was this prince a pretender? Another plan of Jethro's to ensure the throne?

Cecil swallowed loudly. "He looks a little like you."

"He does," Mateo whispered. "What is happening?"

I didn't think we looked too much alike, but the look on Cecil's and Mateo's faces said differently. "Who is he?" I asked.

I suddenly felt a chill slide its cold finger across the back of my neck. I turned to see Cecil nearly glaring at me. His violet eyes were fierce, angry, and questioning. I shrugged it off, but felt his gaze as I pushed my way through the crowd to the dais. Mateo melted behind us. If Jethro saw him, the jig might be up. We shoved our way to the front and faced Jethro. My heart slammed against my ears.

"Oh, Duke!" the rich lady from before exclaimed when she saw me. "Duke! This young marquis has a bold tongue and a lashing for you, no doubt, for not showing your face at his gathering this night."

Raising my head so the brim of my flouncy hat no longer concealed my eyes, I looked up at Jethro. The young boy sat next to him now. The closer I got, the less like me he looked. No, this was not me. Not even a good impersonation. But they had not said it was. Jethro's dark eyes looked at me with little care.

"La!" I found myself exclaiming. "Who would leave Palais Kansouri on this of all nights to see the reclaimed property of a marquis who knows more about the skinning of a gazelle than the finer points of social interaction?"

"I've heard about Le Grande Marquis D'Noirpeirre," Jethro said, almost bored. "I've heard more about you than I have heard congratulations on the recovery of my nephew." He showed nothing on his face. His eyes roamed over my glitz and glamour and a small glint of approval sparked in his eye when he caught sight of the Afrique war medal on my chest. I had found it amongst the previous owner's things.

"Tell me about that," I said, trying to keep my voice light. "Who is this strapping lad here? Surely not the *dead* prince, the late son of Markus Aruelium?"

Jethro gingerly fixed his over-waxed mustache. "You have been gone a while by your own admittance, marquis. Everyone knew the royal family was put asunder. It was no secret. But with tensions with France, it was time to find a proper heir. Ah, my queen." He stopped and turned to greet a woman.

I swallowed, mouth dry.

A tall, chestnut-haired woman with a swan's neck and the eyes of a goddess appeared from behind the thrones. She wore a silver dress, full and frilly. She ran her fingers through the boy's hair, smiling down at him like a proud mother should. Jealousy ignited in me. When she looked up to see the men Jethro spoke with, even I saw her turn to stone.

Our eyes met behind my mask. My heart slammed just once, hard and desperately, against my chest. Cecil reached behind me and gripped the back of my coat, warning me to remain calm. Queen Camille, my mother, did not look away from me. I couldn't breathe.

Jethro went on proudly, taking the queen's hand. "It was Camille's training techniques and desire to include geomancy and augmentation in our military that kept enemies at bay. But we cannot defend our borders from an attack if we do not clean up inside the empire first."

"Are you expecting the motherland to attack?" I said stiffly. Had things changed so much in my eight years of imprisonment?

Camille jerked her hand away from Jethro and retreated. I almost called out to her, but Cecil moved his hand to my lower back, commanding me wordlessly to stay.

"No," Jethro answered. The flesh under his eye tightened like he smiled, but his lips didn't move to indicate it. He smiled behind his eyes.

Just then, the other prince turned to Jethro, away from a small herd of reporters with little books hanging from their necks who had been monopolizing him. The boy's eyes were wide and nervous. "They are asking me questions," he stuttered in a clean, French accent.

"Etienne, please," Jethro mumbled to the other prince, thinking none overheard him. He eyed me and said even more softly, "I told you not to let yourself go. We've been over this. All of it. Just hold on a few more hours."

"Abroad, were you, *Ezekiel*?" I said to the other prince. "Just waiting for the right moment to reappear on our shores?"

The other Ezekiel's, who Jethro had called Etienne, eyes went positively monstrous in fear at being addressed directly. "Um, I, well there was—"

Jethro glared at me. I shut up, biting back the questions I wanted to demand of this new prince. I couldn't interrogate him with Jethro standing there, looking right at me. Even behind my mask, I cowered, hoping he didn't recognize me.

"Calm down, boy," Jethro said with a laugh, patting the other prince's back. "So, Marquis, tell me about Afrique. I see your medal there. What battle was that you fought in?"

"My dear Duke." I had to excuse myself. It was clear Jethro would not let this welp speak for himself, and I had other ways of finding out who he was and what Jethro was up to. Ways that didn't require me to suppress my panic. "I would love to continue our military chat some other time. But my estate is in general disarray, so mark your calendar for a bit later, yes? I'll send you a note."

I made a sweeping bow and practically ran out. Some of my own party called after me to come back and regale them with more of my stories. "He was so delightful," some were saying, wondering why I was leaving. I took a small dingy from my ship and flew it home, leaving *The Scarlet Liberty* for the guests I had abandoned. It took longer to return to my own estate, but my mind reeled the whole time. He wasn't me, but everyone thought he was. And worst of all: Cecil thought now that I lied to him about who I was. Would he turn on me and suck me dry without a second thought, knowing there was some other prince he could put on the throne?

My story was about to come to an end.

# 37 CONFRONTATION

"Who are you?" the vampire screamed, his right hand pinning me to the wall by the neck, holding me a good foot off the ground. His wings arched over his head and his teeth were all fangs.

"Stop, please," I gagged through his crushing fingers. "Cecil, I don't understand!"

"Are you who you said you were?" His eyes flashed and he licked his lips. "Are you the Prince of MidWest, or is he? Or did you lie to me to get out of that hellhole? Do not lie to me now!" He roared the last sentence, shaking me like a cat.

"Cecil, put him down!" Mateo raged from behind.

"Silence!" the vampire shrieked, his fangs popping out.

Mateo hovered his hand over his singing blade, ready to strike a monster he could not hope to overtake.

"Ezekiel is Markus' son. This *is* Ezekiel," Mateo tried again, this time with a bit of warning in his voice.

"Did you lie to me?" Cecil asked again, his teeth clenched, his eyes boring into mine.

I tried to speak, but the sides of my throat closed up in his grip. I couldn't breathe and my head throbbed, my eyes popping from the pressure. I had to speak, though, or he'd choke the life out of me. I tried again, but to no avail.

"He can't speak!" Jacque cried from the doorway of the study. "Cecil, please, let him down."

After glaring into my eyes and commanding me, "Do. Not. Run," he let go and I fell to my knees at his feet, coughing and nearly puking. I tried to back away, but the wall held me close to the monster as he faded back to his genteel look.

"I warn you, prison rat," he said far more calmly than he had been just seconds ago, "do not lie to me, for more than *your* life depends on your answer. Are you the prince and heir to the MidWestern throne?"

I found my voice, but just barely. It hurt to speak, but I had to. "Yes!" I coughed. "You're in my head. Can't you see?"

His eyes were still black. "I can't see your memories, fool. Just distant feelings so I know when my blood bag is in danger."

Why did his words hurt? I trembled like a coward.

Cecil backed away and Mateo hurried to me, pulling me up. "It's true and you know it," I said. "I was there."

If I had lied, Cecil's redemption would be in danger. I understood his rage. Had he gone to The Château d'Oubli for nothing? Had he wasted time with a liar?

*Was there more than one?* His thoughts slammed into my head, questioning. *Have I gone down the wrong path? Started something I needn't have?*

I saw it from his point of view now. He'd risked a lot going underground, getting caught, divulging his vampirism and his task to many people, essentially risking his very soul that he was trying to save. And all the time there was another prince, tucked away safely somewhere he could have fetched.

"I was an only child," I argued, begging him to listen to me. "I don't know who he is or what Jethro is trying to pull. Jethro called him Etienne when he thought I couldn't hear him."

"We can solve this mystery," Mateo said to Cecil, something of anger in his tone. "The nomads, the one's at the Deleon estate. They know all the royal secrets and have been involved with the royal family longer than most of the servants. I bet my blades that ship from France we saw brought that little weasel here that night."

I chanced taking my eyes off Cecil and glanced at Mateo, "You've never seen him?"

He shook his head. "Chances are, he's a plant. There are stories everyday of missing heirs suddenly showing up for nefarious reasons in many countries. Sometimes they are paid actors or imposters. We just need to think of a reason someone would have to put forward a false prince. And who."

Cecil sighed heavily and waved for Jacque to call for tea. She scurried out of the room with a quick breath of relief. "Now is as good a time as any to make contact with the inhabitants of her home. You did promise, *your highness*." He turned to look me up and down in the firelight. "I suppose any other common dungeon rat would not have gone on this long pretending to be the prince."

I nodded hopefully.

He cleared his throat and held his head up high, smoothing out his coat and the lace at his throat. "Then our next step is to the Deleon estate."

I lay awake in my bed, the grand hearth burning to smolders before me, when Cecil came in. I sat up, taken aback by his boldness. A tiny tinge of fear prickled my skin when he slowly made his way to my bed with not so much as a sound.

"Lie back down," he ordered, sliding onto the bed. He wore only black pants and a loose-fitting shirt, opening deeply to his chest.

The fear grew. Had he come to kill me, away from the witnessing eyes of everyone else? Did he still not believe I was who I said?

"How else can I—" I started, intending to ask him how I could prove I was the prince of MidWest.

He cut me off, pressing his finger to my lips. Then, he laid his hand against my cheek. He looked into my eyes before gently taking a strand of my forelock between his finger and thumb and moving it out of my eyes.

"Calm down. Your fear stinks," he mumbled. His hands dropped to the bedclothes. He slowly peeled them back, exposing my arms. Taking one gently, he pushed my sleeve up to my elbow and dipped his head to my skin. He inhaled long and slow. Opening his eyes, he inspected the scars on my arms where he constantly bit me.

I suppose if he did kill me, the empire wouldn't really lose anything. "It's okay," I whispered, lured in by his slow, gentle movements.

His mouth popped open and he bit down into me. My heart did the panicked flutter and dance it always did, making my chest cramp. He held me tightly as I squirmed. It would never feel normal; the tingling panic would never go away.

As he drank, he opened his eyes and looked into mine for the first time while drinking away my life. It made me freeze. My hand started to shake as he took long, hard swallows. My body turned cold. He was taking too much, and I knew it. Sweat beaded on my brow. I knew my face screamed of dread. I thought maybe if I showed him I trusted him to stop, his suspicion and anger would dissipate.

I lost all feeling in my fingers where his hand gripped me. The dark corners of my room turned even darker.

"What are you doing?" My feeble voice cracked.

Just when I thought my heart would beat its last, he let go of me. My blood colored his fangs red in the firelight. He hadn't spilled a single drop down his now rosy chin. Exhausted, I sank into the pillows. I could not move, let alone feel my limbs. He leaned down over my neck, the tip of his petal-soft nose touching my skin and throbbing vein. He ran his long fingers through my hair and sighed, forlorn.

Our tether stronger than ever, I saw into his mind nearly perfectly. Like we shared a single brain. He thought back to the day we first made our tether.

*Vampires tell tales of the tether differently,* he'd said to me. *Having a mortal pet can be a weakness. We are warned away in our covens from keeping our victims alive… I've known vampires that have fallen in love with their tethers, making foolish choices to save them. It's a complicated place between the unnatural, ravenous love vampires are capable of, and mortal friendship. Something new, strange, and even perverse. This will not happen to me, understand?*

But had it?

"Cecil?" I whispered, unsure if I understood. Had our tether made my supposed betrayal worse? Maybe even hurt him? With that realization, I wanted to snap at him. Tell him how easily him suspecting I lied wounded me, too.

He pushed up off the bed. "Rest," he ordered before disappearing out the door.

I focused on breathing, knowing I would not soon recover from such a feeding. My head ached. I'd have to wait until my footman came in the next morning before I could get hot sustenance into my belly.

Just as I drifted into unsatisfying sleep, the door opened again.

"Cecil, please," I moaned. "I can't."

"He's not here?" a soft, sweet voice asked.

I cranked my head over to see Jacque peeking inside my bedroom. Desperate to share her company, I forced myself up into a sitting position. "Jacque," I wheezed, "come in."

"So he was here, hey?" she mused, coming in. She lifted the hem of her silken sapphire robe and came to the side of my bed. "Hell's bells," she said softly, catching my face in the light. She reached up for the bell pull by my bed and tugged on it. "You need something hot inside you."

Her kindness shocked me. She'd taken little interest in me. I knew her eyes looked only on Cecil. But I'd revel in this one moment.

"Thank you," I said, sighing as she walked up the velvet steps to join me on the massive bed.

She reached behind me and plumped up the pillows so I could sit up. "You let him feed too much," she mumbled.

I nodded. "I think he was trying to prove a point."

My footman, Josiah, appeared in the door, hastily dressed, his hair a mess.

"Hot stew, Josiah," Jacque commanded, taking the cloth from the basin and wringing it out. "Beef, if you can. And a slice of that cake from Lady Vianne." She pressed her lips hard to the side, frowning, then added, "Two slices of the cake."

He bowed and vanished into the dark hallway.

I glanced up at her. "Two?"

"Both for me." She raised her brows, face turning to stone again. "Your son is a glutton," she snapped, dabbing at my head with the cold cloth. "I eat and eat, but he is never satisfied."

"Son?" I asked, my spirits rising. "Are you sure?"

She nodded. "I saw the physician today. Or, yesterday. Whichever. I told you." She blinked and shook her head. "I can't recall. This boy inside me makes me so weak and tired. He fights constantly with himself." She scoffed lightly and smiled. "Just like his father."

I caught the disdain in her voice. "Jacque," I started, loving her fingers on my brow. "I will get you your home back. You will be safe again."

"Of course I will," she snapped. She dipped the rag in again. This time, she took an ointment out from the vanity in my room and put it on the rag before returning to me. "I'm not a fighter, Ezekiel. I am a survivor, though."

Something in her tone put me on edge. "Are you going to keep him?" I asked.

She froze, meeting my eyes, hers wide with horror. "Of course I am. I came to you willingly that night. He is *my* son as well."

She had done it again. Something else lurked just under her words.

"You're going to take him away from me." I couldn't stop the choked-up sadness in my voice.

This took her off guard. "You don't want him."

I shoved myself up. "Of course I do!"

"Oh," she said, laughing darkly. "How silly of me. He's your heir. The next high prince of MidWest. The high king must have an heir. Silly me."

She dipped the rag again and wrung it out with her lithe fingers. Even in my bloodless state, I noticed her soft, round breasts growing in size. They pressed hard against the blue silk of her robe. I wanted to kiss her, touch her. But I dared not risk it now.

She reached up and untied the strings of my shirt, exposing my chest. She scooted closer and pressed the cloth to my skin. One of her nails grazed my pale flesh as she dabbed at me. The ointment warmed the surface of my skin. She continued her administrations, much to my agony.

"That's not it," I said, the scent of the oils making me lightheaded. "Jacque, I've loved you for years."

"Lusted after, is more like it," she snapped.

Guilt rose up. "Maybe at first. I was a different man then. I didn't know how to love."

"And now you do?" Her black-brown eyes met mine.

I stammered to find an answer.

"Let me be free, too, Ezekiel," she whispered, pressing her hand against my chest. "Please. Before anything else. Give me my home. *Let me go.*"

She saw herself as a prisoner still. I enjoyed the new life, the wealth, the revenge. She still felt trapped. Looking down at her round stomach where my son waited, I realized just how trapped she must be. She wanted to leave. She wanted to take him. Have someone to love.

I swallowed. "Will you love him?" I almost begged. "Take care of him? Tell him who he is should he ever want to…know me?" Tears pricked into my eyes. I didn't want her to take him away. I wanted her to stay.

Jacque took a measured breath and dabbed at my neck now. "Of course I will love him. Not everyone is as nasty as you, hey?"

I took the assault soundlessly.

She met my sad, weepy eyes and something in her melted. "You really do care about him, don't you?" One hand went to pet her stomach. I witnessed the realization and shock slacken her face. "I never would have thought…"

How much of a monster did she think I was?

Nodding, she said, "Of course I love him. And one day, I will tell him. But by then, you will have a wife, one who strengthens your country's bonds to another. She will bear you many children and you will forget about me and Ezra."

"Ezra?" I gasped. It was a play on my name. It gave me hope.

"You don't like it?" she asked.

I shook my head and took her chin in my hand, a tear finally dripping down my cheek. "I love it."

A small, warm smile pulled at the corner of her lips. "Good. I wouldn't change it even if you didn't like it." She dropped the cloth into the basin and stood up. "Stew should be here soon. Eat, sleep, and have that cake sent to my room, hey?"

# DJANGO

I waited three days to leave an impression on my lands and the city folk who worked with my mill before I departed for Deleon. I hosted an impromptu ale festival and had the people begging me to invite them to my next shindig. Some of the wealthiest landowners dropped by uninvited one afternoon and I got good at dressing up in a matter of minutes. I presented myself as a jovial adventurer and they loved it because I was generous with what I had. I even played host to a rather unfaithful gaggle of women and their daughters the night before we left, all of whom had hopes of turning my head from my wife.

With the days growing cooler, Mateo, Cecil, and I sailed in a more modest version of my now-famous airship to the northeast of MidWest: to the Deleon estate. The first thing we saw, jutting out from the hills and the forests of the northeast, were the tallest gallows I had ever seen. Visible from five miles away, doubling as a beacon, they rose up on Deleon Hill. Above these loomed the enormous metal cross, its arms outstretched, embracing the house in safety.

The Deleon estate was entirely made of white marble and silver. The pillars, the floors, all shone white and gleamed. The sealing of cracks in the foundation, and anything that had been repaired, had been done so with silver. We had to halt and skirt around being invited inside the manor so Cecil could cross the threshold of the protected estate. He audibly groaned as we were let into the spacious entryway. It was open to the air, the windows glassless, and the front gate was made of silver bars. A statue made of marble depicted an Afrique warlord posed in the center of the entryway, his muscles tense, a spear poised for throwing at an approaching leopard.

"Le Grande Marquis D'Noirpeirre!" a tall black-haired man exclaimed, coming at me with his hands outstretched. "And the Don of San Muerte. Imagine my surprise when DeMarque mentioned having seen you in town." Each one of the man's nails were painted a different color to match the mottled theme of his garments. I had thought he'd wear gold, but every single piece of jewelry on his person was made of silver.

I clasped my hands behind my back and made a bow in reply, not touching his hands. So DeMarque had lied about where he'd seen the Don, opting to say he met him in town rather than sneaking onto the skydocks? Interesting...

"You know me?" I asked with as little emotion as I could muster.

"By the gods, what has happened to your neck?" His brown eyes calculated me in an instant, roving over my garb and stance.

I quickly straightened and tried to hold myself taller. Cecil's handprints still shone on my neck in light purple bruises.

"A drunken brawl." I laughed, hiding my grimace behind a laced kerchief. "My parties are something to behold, monsieur, as you've heard. I'm a man of passion. I cannot help it if I offend someone who wishes to choke the life out of me."

"But you overcame the tussle?" His amber eyes twinkled just like Khalil's. I wondered if this patriarch had any connection to my personal traitor.

"As you see." I smiled humbly and motioned over my person.

"Oh, how rude of me!" the patriarch burst. "I am Patriarch Django. To what do I owe the honor of a visit from the marquis and his men?" His eyes drifted to Cecil, taking in his tinted glasses and long coat.

He motioned us in and I fell in step beside him, letting him lead us into the house. "What else do you know about me?" I asked, trying to sound amused. "Is my estate in the Rockies already crawling with Syndicate spies?"

Thank God he laughed. "Merci for the compliment, Marquis, but my spying days are long over. Gin?"

In the inner rooms of the house, the influence of Afrique and the American south were more obvious. Voodoo trinkets and paintings of southern life peppered the walls. Wild animal skins and hunting trophies from the Serengeti interrupted these with bold colors and strange patterns. The curtains were drawn closed in here, and a solar adamant bangle on the patriarch's wrist began to glow brighter. Cecil kept a cautious distance, already having been touched by the daylight even in his broad-brimmed hat and long coat. Django poured us gin into silver goblets.

"Monsieur?" He held one to Cecil.

"I am the pilot," Cecil said soberly, his lips—for perhaps the first time—not smiling. "I need my wits about me."

Nodding, Django turned back to us.

A Few voices carried in from the outer halls. I turned, not expecting anyone else in the house and spied a woman out in a garden. She bathed completely naked in the sunlight. Her dark skin glowed warm as she ran her hand up and down a slender arm. My mouth hung open and I snapped it shut when Django laughed.

"My wife," he said proudly.

I stammered. "I'm sorry, I didn't know you had family."

"Many live with me," he said relaxing. "My family. Some Syndicate family, some blood.

"So, Marquis," he said when the woman vanished around the garden wall, "to what do I owe the honor of your presence? Your reputation has preceded you on wings of boisterous praise. Though I must say, I am hurt I have not received an invitation to these magnificent soirees."

Snakes and spades, I should have thought of that. It must have come across as suspect that a nouveau riche had not invited a nearby influence like a Syndicate patriarch. I had to play it off, like a game of Black Assassin. I had to be faster, smarter, and think as if my life depended on it.

"To be honest, patriarch, I was not sure what you would think of a young, nouveau riche marquis inviting you to his shindig. Would it seem...?" I pretended to think, tapping my chin. "Desperate? Reaching?" All those years of keeping secrets and feigning ignorance pulled hard for me in that moment.

The patriarch smiled, legs crossed, watching me as I lied.

"But I am nouveau riche, as you say," he said, flinging his hands up to draw attention to the decor that obviously didn't belong to him. "This has not always been my home. My children were born on the street before I joined the Syndicate. I shock you?" he asked when my gin stopped halfway to my mouth.

I took a swig of it. "I did not expect such candor—"

"Stop, boy." His amber eyes turned to ice. "Khalil told me about you. And you. And *you,*" he said to Mateo and Cecil in turn. His fingers traced the silver necklace around his throat and rested on the glowing adamant. "I know DeMarque lied about where he met you, Don, but it matters little as he's scheduled for augmentation soon. That should squash any thoughts he has of defecting."

"Khalil?" I choked, the gin burning my throat as I coughed.

"Khalil is my son."

"Oh, shit."

I hadn't felt this trapped since Redbeard and his men first assaulted me in The Château d'Oubli. Khalil had, of course betrayed us. "Have you seen him recently?" I asked.

Django's lip twitched in what I could only assume was distaste. "My son thought he could cross everyone and get away with it. Maybe in the Châteaux. But not up here. Topsiders need friends. He doesn't understand that."

I gathered my wits. "Care to elaborate?" I felt myself slipping back into the prison rat. Panicking, deciding which violent act would take me out of here.

The patriarch glanced at Mateo. "You went into The Château d'Oubli months ago. Been missing a while, which made DeMarque's report suspicious. Have you been riding with this gang ever since?"

The Don's amber eyes glittered. "I know your tricks, Patriarch. I won't say anything."

Django raised his brows, knitting his fingers. "So you have. Why?" His eyes went to Cecil. "This is him, isn't it?"

My entire body tensed. He said it like a predator eyeing prey he could not help but hunt. If only a weak, frail human like myself could be of any help protecting Cecil. "What do you mean?" I asked.

"Khalil is a sadly useless boy," Django said, pouring himself more gin. "I sent him to The Château d'Oubli to keep an eye on the high prince many years ago. He never wanted the Syndicate life, so I had to use him where I could. I waste nothing. Not an opportunity, not a man, not a stone. He came out every now and then when they saw fit to release him back to me for a job."

"The time stealing," I mumbled.

The patriarch's kohl-lined eyes squinted at me. He smiled like he'd just found a missing key. "I thought perhaps he could stay above ground. They wanted to experiment on him with Jethro's new mancer-tech, and I saw no reason why not."

I shivered.

"But he begged for another job," he went on. "We received word from our employer in the palace that a vampire had appeared." He ran his hand over his solar adamant bracelet. "And that he said he was here to find the dead son of Markus Aurelium." His eyes drifted to Cecil now. "He was supposed to stop him from rescuing the prince, for of course I knew where little Ezekiel had been sent all those years ago." Now his eyes fell on me. "Do you remember me, boy? The night Jethro had you arrested?"

I shrank away from his maniacal tone and bloodthirsty eyes. The memory suddenly came back. I remembered his hand on my shoulder, smelling of basil and smoke. He dragged me over the tracks to a dirty, mysterious train. I cried. He smacked me. A wave of empathy washed over me from Cecil as he tasted the memory through our tether, my fear piercing him as well.

Django nodded. "I see you do. I thought you were him. You've grown so much, I hardly recognized you. But with your undead friend and uncle in tow, I knew it had to be you." He tilted his head, smiling. "So, prince, what do you really want from me?"

A tiny twinge of relief came over me. At least he'd opened up for negotiations. "I need information," I started, but he cut me off.

"About the Duke and the new prince?"

Damn Syndicate. Was there anything he didn't know? "You live up to your reputation, Patriarch," I chanced to say, almost stuttering. "How is it that you know so much about the royal family?"

"He's worked for Jethro for decades," Mateo cut in, giving me time to breathe. "Like the time he tried to have me killed for not finishing the job."

The patriarch took a drink, keeping his eyes on me. "The past is the past, isn't it, little Ezekiel? Am I to think you have forgotten who killed your father? And are just here to buy information from me?"

Gathering my courage, I leaned forward onto my knees and touched the tips of my fingers together. "Patriarch, I have lived eight years of my life under every boot in The Château d'Oubli. I've been beaten, tortured in ways you cannot imagine, and turned into a feral monster of the underground. I don't care what you did or when. I want information about Uncle Jethro and that little princeling he claims is the prince of MidWest."

The line came from me so earnestly and dangerously, Django didn't move to refill his gin. His voice dropped low and he spoke slowly now. He wagged a gilded finger. "He's not supposed to be *you*. That was High Prince Etienne. Etienne is the heir apparent and sole son of her majesty Queen Camille and Lord Jethro, the Duke of Dakota."

"Etienne?" I whispered, fear and anxiety gripping me. "Heir?" I blinked stupidly like I had done when operating a drill for the first time. I thought back to the night we saw the prince. Jethro told the people he was me, Camille's son. "Jethro's son? My mother?" I snapped my head to Mateo, who looked just as perplexed as me.

"Mmm, yes." Django's lips curled and his eyes narrowed. He enjoyed this. "Your half-brother."

"Explain!" I shouted, the fear and uncertainty taking me over again.

Django's lips curled even harder, deforming his handsome Egyptian face. "When a woman is married but sees another man who can be more easily controlled…" He spread his fingers. "She takes him, removing the other."

Fire flared up in me. This was not the first time someone had accused my mother of being the vile, villainous one. "You lie," I growled.

Django threw one leg over the arm of the chair and lounged, sipping his gin. "She is more close-lipped than I. I assume she hated High King Markus. She couldn't manipulate him like she could Jethro. Jethro regretted abdicating and she used that against him. When she was heavy with Etienne, she had Markus killed." He pointed to himself. "You were sent away, alive, just in case. She visited France often where Etienne was raised by a political ally. Now that he's back, I assume the real meat of her plan is coming to fruition." He signaled to his servant to bring in meat cuts and a tray of fruit.

*No,* I thought bitterly. *It wasn't her. It was Jethro. Django said it himself: he regretted abdicating. Jethro used her.*

"Who gave you the order?" I growled.

I had a memory of her chasing me down in the train station, screaming my name. Someone had grabbed her, pulling her back as I crossed the tracks. A crowd had gathered to see the hysterical French queen. Yes, they lied. Jethro might have used my mother, but she was not to blame.

Django told it like a simple story. No emotion. Not a care in his tone. "Jethro gave every order," he finally answered. "But he belonged to Camille."

"How do you know?" I snapped.

Django narrowed his eyes, contemplating. "You think she's innocent?"

"Why are you telling us this?" Cecil asked from his shadowy corner when I didn't speak. I realized my mouth hung open, so I closed it. "Information is not free. What do you want?"

Django smiled and pushed himself up from his chair. "I am so glad *you* asked, my dear child of the night."

The emphasis on the word made me tense up. The Egyptian's attention shifted to Cecil completely, ignoring me.

"Here is the thing." He approached Cecil, who took one cautious step back from the silver and solar adamant that lit up his darkness. "The Syndicate traditionally deals in rare items. The rarest of items."

"Time?" Cecil offered, his face not playful anymore. "Khalil showed us."

Django shook his head. "Not just time, though that and assassinations are our big sellers. Well, that and love automatons." He took a moment to laugh. He reached inside his mottled coat and produced a brightly shining purple gem. "Guess how old I am, vampire."

I gasped and stood up. "Bloodstones."

"Khalil was harvesting them for me, sweet prince. I was rather cross with him for using you to fetch them, but then the nomad heart is one even I cannot control." He faced Cecil again. "I am ninety-eight years old. Some think vampires are the hunters and we the mortals are prey. But our Syndicate is not so weak. Give me your blood. I'll let you, dear prince, walk out of here alive. And." His eyes roved over Cecil like he might eat him up. "I suppose not alive, either." He laughed.

"Spades," I hissed. "Those stones are damned. You don't know what they do to people."

"I know exactly!" he screeched back, snapping around as if to bite me. He turned back to Cecil. "I am asking nicely, your highness. I don't have to. I have hunted the likes of him for longer than you've been alive. Give me your blood. I'll sweeten the deal: I won't mention to the queen or Jethro that you're here. Or that Jethro's bastard brother has turned sides and is helping Ezekiel come for him."

"And you?" Cecil asked. I saw him swallow hard. "What will happen when Jethro finds out what you've done?"

Django held the purple gem to his mouth and licked it long and slowly. "What will he be able to do?" His eyes flashed. "I worked for his father and grandfather. I am more permanent in the royal family than he ever will be."

Cecil clenched his fists and I noticed him blinking more than usual.

"You can't!" I held my hand out to stop Cecil from coming forward. "I know you'll recover, but think of the power you are handing over to this rat."

But Django and Cecil never broke eye contact. The patriarch hissed like a python, his neck muscles tense, ready to strike.

"Fine," Cecil whispered.

"No!" I shouted, trying to insert myself between Cecil and Django.

"Khalil has been trying to get his black paws on your blood since The Château d'Oubli."

"Oh, so brave," Django mocked, simpering. "Little tether protecting its monster."

A small flicker crossed Cecil's eyes, but he wouldn't turn to look at me. "I'll go willingly," he said. "If you swear to let us walk and not alert the palace."

Django smiled. "I am paid to be honest."

Cecil made me leave with Mateo. Django said he'd send for us when "the vampire is properly drained." We went to the city and rented one of the nicest rooms I could find in a hotel above a lavish saloon. Posters plastered the saloon walls about an Independence Day Carnival coming up. I ripped one off the wall in frustration as we laid low. I paced only a little, but my footfalls were heavy. Mateo didn't interrupt me as I schemed and worried.

"It's just a little different now, is all," I said through gritted teeth. I shook. The vibration started at the base of my skull and shook down my shoulders to my fists. "It's my throne. I have not suffered these eight years and been treated like an ass by Jethro to not sit where my father intended. I'll do what everyone down in that prison did when someone gets in the way."

I drew my revolver and fired it into the water basin, shattering it and causing water to cascade down. Someone downstairs screamed and I heard the piano man stop playing. Mateo leapt up and took the gun from my hands, but I didn't stop raging.

"A small wrench in the works, but no more!" I screamed with all my might, losing all my air. I sat down.

"Does this change your plans?" Mateo asked, softly.

"Oh, no. It's going as planned," I snapped. "There will just be one more casualty."

I leapt up, swallowing, and marched to the door. I made sure my strides were loud and long as I retreated, trying to leave fire in my wake.

"One more?" Mateo cut off my retreat. "Who else are you planning to kill?"

My rabid coyote howled away again in me. Jacque didn't love me, never would. Jethro had found a way to replace me, using my mother. Khalil had betrayed me to the Syndicate. Etienne, though I knew little about him, needed to be taken out of the way. Spades to being noble. And damn setting aside revenge.

I let my eyes grow stone cold, narrowing them to venomous slits, not amused at him stopping me. "All of them."

# FAMILY PLANS

It only takes about a minute to drain a body of blood. Not all of it, obviously, because there is still some lingering in the tubes, but you get what I mean. Django sent a messenger for us only moments after the Don's and my little interaction. I had been in the saloon's lean-to, admiring the gallows I could barely see over the treetops, when the messenger came to me like a Pony Express rider.

"All's well," he had said as if I'd just brought in a dirigible for a tune-up.

It turned out that in the space of the hour and a half it had taken for us to get to the saloon, argue, and travel back, Django had drained, fed, and re-drained Cecil fifteen times. I try not to be an emotional man anymore, but I could not fathom the horror of what I heard relayed to me so casually when I re-entered Jacque's estate.

They brought Cecil to me and dropped him at my feet like a malfunctioning automaton. His limbs made a smacking sound against the marble, and I heard his wrist break as it got caught under his weight. Mateo lifted Cecil in lieu of me so I didn't have to bend over in front of the evil patriarch.

"We're all settled, then." Django smiled vilely. "A little alchemy, a little time, and my most profitable market will be open. Can I interest you, your highness?"

"No," I growled, taking in Cecil's unconscious form.

Mateo draped Cecil's limp arm around his sturdy shoulders.

"The deal is done then?" I asked.

Django let his wicked little grin widen into something only demonic toads could achieve. "Indeed. We are, as the country folk say, squared away. Enjoy your hostile takeover, and I hope to see you with that golden crown on your head." He toasted us with gin and drank to my health. "Until our next business venture."

I measured my steps back to my little airship, knowing Django watched me go. I wouldn't run. I wouldn't stutter-step and let him know he'd gotten to me. I used my eyes to glance sideways at the Don carrying Cecil. Cecil's head lolled to the side, his lids half-open behind his red sunglasses. I reached out to touch his mind and found the tether weak, but intact. He'd only ever fed on me, creating that tether. Since I could still hear him, I realized that meant the ones he'd fed on were…dead. He told me that day in the Château that he'd taken an oath to not kill another soul. He'd broken that oath for me.

"Fifteen times," Mateo muttered as we laid Cecil on the only bed in the one-cabin airship. "That mad man killed fifteen of his house for his prize." He studied the blood stains around Cecil's mouth. "I supposed he takes pleasure in feeding…" He wasn't asking and he didn't even sound accusatory.

"He needs blood." I threw my coat off and started to roll up my sleeve. I didn't like knowing he'd fed off others. "He's weak." His guilt at having killed again rose up in me as I exposed my skin.

Mateo moved to stop me. "Does it have to be you?" he asked.

I nodded wordlessly and held my wrist under Cecil's nose, to his lips. He didn't stir. Grasping my knife from my belt, I cut my wrist just enough and slowly lowered the gleaming blood to Cecil's mouth. His pale nostrils twitched, but that was all. Even when a small drop fell on his lips, he didn't so much as lick it away. His sorrow filled me and I couldn't stand it. He'd broken his oath to not kill again, and it was all for me.

"Cecil?" I gasped, shaking his shoulder.

With determination, I pressed my wrist to Cecil's lips and flexed my fingers, squeezing my arm with my other hand, making the blood flow. Like a sleeping baby, Cecil's breath caught and I saw his lips begin to suck and his throat swallowing. He gagged once, then clutched my wrist. Just a few seconds later his eyes opened and he let go.

"You didn't have to." He sighed, lying down limply.

"Yeah, I did." I sighed as well. With him conscious, the darker thoughts from before started to dissipate like breath on glass. But I couldn't let them go. "We're going home. I have a new obstacle to take out."

When we landed, I spotted Jacque outside in the orchard behind the mill. Zillions of brass knick-knacks, tools, materials for balloons, and furnaces lay around her booted feet. Her stomach stuck out from her too-large overalls.

She didn't look up as I approached. Grease covered her hands and a black smudge right under her nose showed me where she had scratched herself in thought earlier. I tried my luck and walked up behind her, putting a hand on her waist. She took a step away to reach for a screwdriver and began twisting it into a small engine. I gently pulled her hair back over her right shoulder and kissed her neck. She stopped.

"What is it you want, Ezekiel?" The acid in her voice would have melted all the metal on her workbench. "I thought we had this discussion."

"What do you want me to say, Jacque?"

"If you have to ask, you won't say it right even if I tell you." She side-stepped and picked up a bag of gears, looking through it.

"I like seeing you work again. It's like the old you."

She picked one out and threw the bag down with malice. "I am so glad. I am here to please you. I'd hate to upset you. Let me be a dutiful wife." She reached up to her hair, untied a small silver nut from a braid, and spun it onto a screw.

I studied the messy curls of her black hair and the other odd adornments she'd tied into it. The bright colors of her earrings and matching necklace accented her dark features. She had taken off the rings and a thick blackness had built up under her nails. I had tried to explain to her that I loved her and that I would never hurt her. Explaining didn't seem to matter to her. But I had news.

"We've met Django, the Syndicate patriarch who was given your estate."

She kept working but chanced a glance up at me.

I told her about Etienne and the patriarch's part in the whole affair.

"He was raised in France?" she asked, genuinely interested in the turn of events. "She hid him away." She straightened and patted her stomach. "I'd like to think it was for protection, but…"

"What?" I asked, taking a seat on the work bench, letting my legs dangle.

She scratched at her brow, leaving another dark oil stain. "If I were Camille…" She trailed off again. "No, never mind."

"Tell me," I pressed.

She finally looked me in the eye. "If I had a son by a man I did…" She choked. "Did not love, I'd go with the man I did love. If the man I did love gave me a child, I'd protect that child with all I had in me. Send him away to be safe, hope he could come back, fulfill his destiny."

That stung. My face burned. I reminded myself she'd said she would not abandon our son. Our Ezra. I had to believe it. I took her hand in mine and kissed her dirty knuckles. Once again, the blame on my mother. I could not believe it. I would not.

"I suppose you want him dead?" she asked, watching her hand in mine. "Etienne, I mean. He's in your way."

I thought I did. "He's just another detail in the plan," I said instead. "But I wanted to tell you about your home. I wanted to show you that I am doing as you asked. I want you to be happy and have *your* revenge. I will get your estate back for you."

She finally pulled away, retrieving some paints, and went to work on a porcelain face. "I've quite disappeared from your story," she said. She didn't say it jealously or angrily. A kind of peace laced her tone. Like she'd accepted her role. "Whenever you see me, you look at me as though just remembering I am there. I have nothing to do with you anymore. Why did you take me with you from The Château d'Oubli?"

"You were an engineer," I said honestly. Not the time to lie. "And I loved you." Curious, I added, "Why did you come? You didn't need me like I needed you."

Her hand slipped on the face, making the smile she painted into a manic downturned mouth, prepared to wale in agony. "Spades." She wiped it quickly. "I wanted to leave. You were an easy ride. And if you must know, I thought once I had my title, my land, Cecil would see me as someone worthy of his affection."

My heart fell. "You love him." It came out more accusatory than I had intended.

"It doesn't matter," she shot back. "He won't have me with you around."

Jealousy tore my heart. "Have you slept with him?"

Her black eyes shot imploding stars at me, scorching my pride. "You suggesting *me* being unfaithful is just fine, Ezekiel." Her thick, red lips turned to angry thin lines. "But how dare you believe *Cecil* would ever betray *you*. He knows your feelings for me and would never let me near him like that. I may love him, but he only has eyes for you. He honors you by not giving in to me. He's more good than you will ever be."

This set off my rabid coyote. I wanted to hurt something. I was preparing a retort when she gasped sharply, clutching her lower stomach.

"Your bastard is just as angry and hateful as you." She stopped, horrified at her words, and covered her mouth. Tears spilled from her eyes. She hugged her stomach. "The doctors say the pregnancy makes me short tempered. I swear to God, Ezekiel Aurelium, when this is over—you on the throne and this child is born—I am leaving. Do you understand?"

All the rising hate left me, my good, fearful coyote coming back. The emptiness inside me got slowly replaced by a trickle of fear, loneliness, and hurt.

What about my son? Did she intend to take him with her? Would she be cruel to him? She'd said only days ago that she'd love him. Had something changed?

I swallowed. "I will see to it that your estate is prepared for you in time."

I went to check on Cecil in his chambers the next night, the thick curtains drawn shut. I'd fed him once more before we closed off his rooms for him to recover. He lay in the bed, the curtains on the posts drawn against the already closed windows, just in case.

"I wanted to talk to you," Cecil said softly, his strength still returning.

"Wait. Let me speak first." I wanted to kneel by his bed, but I didn't want to seem emotional despite what I had to say. "Thank you for what you did. I didn't know he would be so cruel." I took a steady breath. "Cecil, I couldn't do any of this without you. Thank you for saving me. And for sacrificing yourself for me."

I hoped he'd smile and say something wonderful in return about how I was turning into the man he hoped I would be, and that he was proud of how far I had come. But his face rested in a grim mask.

He took a breath. "Ezekiel, I did it hoping you might give this revenge scheme up. I hoped that after we found out who Etienne was, you might choose another path that has been provided to you."

"What new path? Nothing has changed, Cecil." If I didn't have my revenge, what did I have?

His face fell even more and he shook his head. "I was afraid that's what you thought. Etienne is a legitimate heir. Let him be high king. Take your wife, your riches, this mill, and become a new man. Leave MidWest to its new king. You have a chance for peace, love, and a full life."

"Do you remember the first time you saw me?" I asked. He frowned. Our combined memories in my head painted the perfect picture. "I was trapped under that truck. I had killed five men because I had been given the chance to finally make others feel like I had."

I watched understanding dawn on his face. "Yes, I remember," he whispered.

I went on. "And you told me to be ruthless. Encouraged me to fight to get my way. You let me harm myself with geomancy to win and escape. I've come this far. I'm so close!"

"I was wrong, Ezekiel," he pleaded. "I didn't know about Etienne. I didn't know you would have a chance for a life better than the throne. Nothing that starts with revenge ends well. You need to let it go."

I sneered. "There is no better life than a king's life. No, I won't stop. I will do what I set out to accomplish. And I will bring vengeance on all those who had a hand in putting me in that prison for eight years! I'm sorry, Cecil. Still, thank you for aiding me as you did. Get strong. We have a lot to do."

Not in the mood for anymore talk, I went to my study. The flyer I had taken from the hotel sat where I had crumpled it the day before. I scanned the advertisement for the Independence Day Carnival. This would be a good place to take my next step. Etienne's silhouette shone in the center, declaring that his coronation would take place during the festivities. I needed extra help. Someone sneaky…but trustworthy. Etienne may be a legitimate heir, but there was a mystery about him. He'd been raised in France, in secret. What if Jethro had groomed him to be a little royal puppet? Do his bidding? The councilor at the event where Jethro had revealed Etienne had mentioned plans, war. I couldn't let Etienne on the throne without knowing what he'd been brought up to do.

I sat down at my desk in the huge library I had not even begun to explore, penning a letter to my pirate friend. A soft voice spoke behind me, the sound accompanied by the clicking of a mechanical arm.

"I have a proposition for you, your highness," Khalil purred from the shadows.

I leapt up, overturning my chair, aiming my revolver at him in one smooth motion, and cocking the hammer back. "Thought you'd jumped ship, you two-tailed goat. Told Django about us, did you? Oh, yeah, and did you just forget to mention he was your father?"

Khalil smiled and shrugged. "I like to have my bases covered, as you westerners say."

"Bases covered or betrayals in line?" I said, just as cocky. "You better keep track of who you stab in the back before the circle comes complete."

He pulled the time pendant off his neck with his mancer-tech arm, now encrusted with solar adamant and inlaid with a layer of silver. "I can offer you hundreds of years of life if you let me help you attack the Deleon estate."

"I was going to anyway," I snapped, not lowering my gun. "What's in it for you?"

"Just let me come with you to do it," he said steadily. "I can get you in, make it easier."

"How?"

Khalil stepped out of the shadows next to the balcony window he'd come in through. He helped himself to the port on top of a credenza on the other side of the room.

"I can get in. My father and I had a kind of…falling out." He smiled darkly. "But I can still get into the manor, remove the patriarch, and supply you with anything that has been stationed on the estate."

"Like what?" I asked. "What's being kept there rather than at the palace?"

He smiled. "You know. The Grande Mancer, Roux DeMarque, and the other mancer are being kept there. Not to mention mancer-tech. It's also a port for the secret materials and dignitaries coming in and out of MidWest. A very busy place. With me in the patriarchal seat, you'd have eyes and ears on everything coming and going from Palais Kansouri. Take over the estate, and you have the artillery to attack Jethro."

I scoffed and shook my head. "Roux DeMarque seems like an opportunity, true. Even Django seems uneasy about DeMarque. But he reports to Jethro."

Khalil pulled a mysterious smile. "Only just. His communication goes through the patriarch. I'm sure Django didn't mention it. Replace my dear father with me, and all you need is a little extra shove, since DeMarque is commander in chief to the militia. And…" He took a long sip of the port, considering his next words. "I happen to know DeMarque is what they call 'a moral man.' He is a good mancer—in fact, that's what's kept him in his place, despite his misgivings about what Palais Kansouri is planning. That bit of information is free.

Consider it a royal sample. Now, how could you convince a man like DeMarque to really switch sides?"

I didn't have the stomach for his games. "How?"

The Egyptian pulled out a lens from his pied pocket. "Ephemeral quartz, tumbled to a clear shine."

"Hypnosis?" I asked. Interested now, I liked that Khalil had the same ideas I did. I still stung from his betrayal in Romania, but I needed someone on my track, even just for a moment. I still needed to get the estate back to Jacque. But if it worked like he said, I could remove him far more easily than Django. My Château d'Oubli ways were right behind me, fighting to resurface and make me do something violent.

Khalil nodded. "Coated in spectral for far sight. Neither need a catalyst, but are part of the geos that can be enhanced by internal use. So, take some of the powder, and the glasses I have made from these coated lenses will be strong enough for you to use if you can get your eyes on them." He nodded again. "Focus on DeMarque. Ezekiel, trust me. I benefit from this, too, I wouldn't lie."

I saw the shadow pass over Khalil's eyes. Something told me not to get mixed up in the nomad's Syndicate, but the idea of using geomancy to overtake a couple mancers and get the secret comings and goings of the royals appealed to me. I should have listened to my misgivings, but I'm not the sharpest spade. If Cecil thought I was getting too out of control, then I would.

"Fine," I quipped. "But not right away. I have a little family business to take care of before I finish off someone else's. Where can I contact you? I want you to lay low until *I* give the word, understood?

Khalil's brow twitched into a smirk. "I have a room at l'Hôtel Emeraude in town. Across from the bank. I'm staying under the name Enoch."

"Fine," I repeated. "And get out of my house. Use the door next time, coward."

# Independence Day

The American Empire had won its independence from Europa eighty years ago. On this Independence Day, they planned to present Prince Etienne officially to the rest of the Empire as High Prince Ezekiel. I wrote a letter for Salazar and went into town to find the mysterious samurai he had mentioned. Asking for Kimiko Salazar got me a few curious glances, but led me to a saloon down the street from the courthouse.

Pushing open the flapping doors, I spotted her right away. She sat alone, fingering a shot glass full of something clear. She wore the typical rough-rider gear of chaps and a wide-brimmed hat, but carried a katana gunblade at her side. I approached her cautiously.

"Ezekiel?" she asked, not looking at me. Her head was down so I couldn't see her face reflected in the mirror behind the bar. She held her hand out, curling her fingers rapidly to indicate I should hand her something.

Understanding, I pulled the letter out of my pocket and placed it in her palm. I opened my mouth to ask a question, but she hissed at me.

"Go on, don't linger," she whispered. "Come back in twenty-four hours."

I broke from her quickly, keeping my own head down as I left just in case. I had a reputation to protect now.

Curious, I came back the next day but she wasn't there. When I asked the bar tender if he'd seen the mysterious samurai, he nodded and silently handed me a letter sealed over in blue wax. Salazar was coming.

"What are you planning to do to the prince?" Cecil asked while I dressed in my best carnival garments on the day of the presentation.

"To capture him and save him all in one day, thereby earning his trust and friendship." I smiled at him over my shoulder as he did not reflect in the mirror. This put him a little at ease.

"Salazar has agreed to swoop in, raid the carnival, kidnap the returned prince, and demand a ransom from his adoring public and mother. I will fight the daring pirates and rescue the heir to the empire's throne, all without giving in to the blackmail of vicious pirates. He will thank me, and I hope, in the throes of gratitude, invite me to dine or some other nonsense that will get me closer to him. I need to get to him in a safe place where he can divulge to me the best way to make him suffer. Grateful people are usually very open about how to hurt them."

Cecil sighed and turned away. "If you must, I suppose."

Our tether showed me his real thoughts: he hoped getting to know Etienne would make me see the error of my vengeful ways. Perhaps I'd realize he was a good little boy and I'd let him take my throne.

"There's more at stake than that, Cecil," I said after taking in his thoughts. "With the mancers, and the secret ships coming and going from the Deleon estate… I cannot help but think Jethro has some other scheme. War, even."

Our eyes met across the room. "Jethro wouldn't put the country at risk like that. Would he?"

I shrugged. "I need to find out before I give up everything I've planned."

Was I really concerned about the safety of the country? I wasn't sure. It was a fascinating sensation.

As Kansouri was at the center of the American Empire, the carnival took place in its streets. Travelers, churchmen, the monster hunting Wardens of the Creed, performers, traders—folks of every caste came to celebrate. Huge squares were blocked off for performances of all kinds, and military displays boomed in the prairies. The sky clouded with smoke from a million dirigibles, all anchored helter-skelter at varying heights on skydocks lit with blue, white, and red over the big top where the rodeo commenced. Cecil booked us a room at a gilded hotel, but we didn't spend much time in it or enjoy its nightly accommodations.

"Ah, Marquis!" squealed a gaggle of girls and beautiful fops in glittering rodeo attire. "We were hoping you would turn up." The fops had been lassoing the women and kissing them before we pushed our way through the crowd.

One girl made a mad dash at Mateo and threw her arms around his neck. I saw him grimace a little at the stench on her breath that gave her the courage. He let her hang on him.

"Come to the right place, have I?" I joked, forcing a smile to the glittering patrons. "What is this for, then?" I pointed to the leather tassels and spurs.

"Rodeo!" the boys chimed together. "The first show is at noon in the big top. You must see it. It's so much better during carnival than any other time of year."

"How many people see it?" I asked, putting my scheme into motion.

One of the boys shrugged. "Everyone! Especially the first show. That's where the bets are placed and everyone can size up the competition. It's basically a free-for-all. Say you'll come!"

I traded my plume hat for one of their glittering pinched-front hats with a laugh. "I'll be there. You can count on it." I added in a false whisper to one of the swooning girls, "Tell me which to gamble on, will you, sweetheart? I'm no good at such things."

She giggled obnoxiously and smeared my cheek with her too-red lips. "Of course, Marquis!"

As the ridiculous gang had said, the big top was packed like an old tin of sardines: standing-room filled, children perched on adults' shoulders, lovers on each other's laps. In the center, a pre-show of barrel riders, trick shooters, and—to my surprise—the talented mancer Roux DeMarque performed. Only now, he performed simple manipulation of fire and steam that still delighted the onlookers. I spotted the royal entourage just to the right of DeMarque. Jethro was adorned in his military medals as always, his ruby ring with our family crest on it glinting in the dim light. Etienne looked every bit like western royalty.

"Lucky charm, monsieur?" a Japonois vendor asked me, shoving a jade pendent into my face. He met my gaze and winked at me.

"Captain." I grinned. "I think the big top is looking like the perfect stage for our pantomime. What do you think?"

Behind him, Isolde stood hooded in rags to peddle tea. She met my gaze, unamused.

Salazar straightened up, his eyes roaming over the big top. "I think it will be fantastic."

"Remember your promise," Isolde hissed at me. "You do not harm him."

"Of course," I mumbled.

We waited a few more minutes until the sawdust cleared and a horn blared. The sides of the arena were opened by rickety automatons who were blasted into spare parts by the impact of the doors. Twenty-seven huge bulls ran out, all with a strong, most likely doomed rider on their backs. Behind these, glamorized cowboys on giant warhorses with lassos rushed in. I thought the spectacle ridiculous, but the people loved it. I had never been to carnival as a child, so this was my first rodeo. It reminded me of the thunderdome. I didn't understand what went on, and Cecil looked just as displeased as I did.

"Americans." He sighed in confused annoyance.

Mateo watched, and finally, after about twenty minutes of mindless noise, he exclaimed mightily.

"Now is good?" I asked.

"Yes, now is perfect." He went back to cheering on a particular rider.

I turned and signaled Salazar. In a flash, he disappeared. From all corners of the big top, smoke bombs exploded, sizzling and casting tiny bolts of lightning in their wake. The crowd coughed and teared up. I covered my mouth and pulled on some goggles alongside Mateo. Above us, the engine of the familiar pirate ship roared and a dozen swords slashed open the top of the tent. Ropes dangled down and a plethora of pirates dove into the sawdust, stopping the rodeo. The bulls cried and quickly passed out, their lungs heaving in more of the stuff than most. The cowboys coughed and reeled as the pirates kicked them over.

"Jethro, you maggoty bilge rat!" Salazar called from the center. To my surprise, he already had Etienne lassoed and in his grasp. The prince's head hung limp in the masked pirate's clutches. "The future of your kingdom and your villainy lies in my hands."

I could hear him smiling behind his cover as he swung haphazardly on the dangling rope ladder.

"What quarrel do I have with you, pirate?" Jethro shot back in his most diplomatic-I've-done-nothing-wrong voice. "Or is it my kingdom you hate?" He raised his hand to signal his guards.

"Nothing so sinister," Salazar said honestly. "I just want ransom money."

"You can have anything!" Jethro cried back. "Right now, I'll have my men get you whatever you want."

Like Cecil often did, Salazar put on a good show.

"Haha!" he cried, leaping higher up onto the ladder, ascending out of the big top. "It's not so easy, Duke. There is a way in which these things are done. Don't be a savage, let me have my adventure. Wait for my letter!"

What had once been a deafening audience now stood a mute, coughing, weeping, confused horde. I strained to watch the royal seating and waited until Jethro ran out.

I nodded to Cecil and Mateo through my mask and goggles. "Let's go save a prince, lads."

As planned, we ditched our masks and ran from the big top. I shouted to anyone listening in the streets that I'd bring the sleazy pirates to justice. The three of us made a show of running between the crowd, through the streets, to a parked autogyro.

"Thief!" the lady shouted as we kicked the little aeroship into life.

"Mademoiselle Vianne!" I cried, dramatically brandishing my hat.

"Marquis?" the owner of the machine gasped.

"I must commandeer your aeroship to save the prince. I will bring it back in one piece."

She smiled and clapped her hands. "So that's what happened. Oh, my. Go, go!"

A slew of onlookers cheered as we sped after Salazar's ship.

"This is going well," Cecil chanced to say. He turned up the collar of his long coat against the grey sun.

"Don't jinx it," Mateo whispered, crossing himself in his Espagnol church tradition. "Sorry," he added to Cecil.

"Here we go!" I shouted in glee as we broke over the railing. I screwed up my face to look fierce and offended at the injustice of kidnapping the prince. We leapt over the side of *The Kimiko Fire* in perfect synchronization, drawing swords, revolvers, and blades in unison. "Unhand the prince, pirate scum!" I declared.

Salazar turned around, his eyes tearing up with the effort to not laugh out loud. "A noble gesture, Marquis," he hissed back, falling into his role just fine.

His men appeared, holding Etienne up between them, his head lolling to the sides as he tried to focus on what took place around him.

"Is he conscious enough to see this?" I asked, halting the moment.

Salazar nodded. He took Etienne's hand in his and brandished a knife. "A finger with the royal ring on it should suffice in getting the Duke's attention for a ransom." He cackled maniacally and set the knife to Etienne's finger.

Etienne struggled, but only just as the chemicals still permeated his system. "You will never get a penny from my father," he said in his French accent. "Capture me like a coward, fight me like a man!"

"Oh-ho!" Salazar laughed, impressed. "We have a real man on our hands here, lads!" He reached up and pinched Etienne's cheek most humiliatingly. The crew laughed raucously.

"Unhand me and I dare you to try that again!" Etienne shot back, trying to get his feet under him. "I am the prince of MidWest. I fear no vulgar pirate!"

I had to admit, his bravery inspired me. Alone, a thousand feet in the air with the threat of pirates all around, he had the guts to challenge them. I think I'd have pissed myself and made a bargain.

Salazar shrugged. "No matter. Isolde, bring me a box for the royal finger."

He pressed the knife to Etienne's finger again and the boy cried out.

"Fight me, pirate!" I shouted, firing a shot into the rigging. I leapt at Salazar.

Isolde made a commotion within the crew, jostling Etienne so he couldn't quite make out our fight. Salazar came at me with a cry like a fisher cat and the rest of his crew attacked Cecil and Mateo. What I had hoped to be a friendly banter kind of fight turned into a too-real workout. Eventually, Etienne freed himself and engaged in battle with Isolde, shaking the chemicals from his brain. The boy moved fast. He took up a cutlass and began to drive her back. Isolde let out a gasp as the curved blade just missed her shoulder. Distracted by the danger Isolde was in, Salazar landed a rapier thrust to my side. I gasped and stumbled back, gaping at my wound. Blood already covered my hand. The pirate stutter-stepped back, his head firing back and forth between me and Isolde.

Cecil's mind cut through my skull like a knife. He smelled my blood and his mouth watered. He dove through, knocking Isolde away from Etienne. I disarmed Salazar and Cecil backed Isolde into a corner, freeing up Etienne.

"H-hand over the prince, p-pirate," I stuttered when we finally gained control, hand pressed to my wound. I glared at Salazar.

Having had his fun, Salazar raised his hands. An awkward moment of me not seizing Etienne and diving over the edge in a daring escape passed without me noticing. Cecil did it for me while the Don warded off the onslaught of more pirates. He dragged me away, too.

We dangerously dove into Mademoiselle Vianne's stolen autogyro and spiraled down safely back to the grounds outside the loudest part of the carnival. I used every inch of my willpower to pull myself back to the moment. I trained my gaze onto Etienne's face, hand over my wound. I told myself not to be angry at Salazar. It made for a good prop in my daring rescue. I leaned onto Cecil.

"How can I thank you?" Etienne nearly sobbed. He stood a little taller than me, far more muscular, and was tanned with soft hair so the sight of him almost blubbering made me cringe. He took my blood-soaked hand and shook it in both of his.

"It was nothing," I said, trying to turn up the charm. I focused on his face and imagined myself cutting his head off and then seating myself on my throne. His blood would make a steady dripping from my hand as I rested it languidly over the marble floors. I got morbid when weak. "A mere marquis doing what I can, when I can, for my country. Besides, it was your bravery in the face of danger that gave me courage against an entire fleet of brigands."

Etienne smiled shyly, fingering the cuffs of his shirt. "It was all a front. Father says I am not allowed to show fear. As king, you know. But I shook inside." His face brightened suddenly. "Come to the palace! You must meet my father and mother. They will want to thank you properly."

The smile slid from my face.

Cecil put his hand on my shoulder and grinned broadly and far more dazzlingly. "When shall we call on you, your highness?"

Etienne's face lit up. "So you will? I've heard so much about you, but alas, I have not been able to attend your gatherings."

"Shindigs," I corrected with a wave of my hand. "I call them shindigs. Mere trifles to show off, I assure you."

"You're so modest," the other prince praised me softly.

I heard Cecil snort behind me.

"Tomorrow, then?" I said through gritted teeth. "I fear I must get home and get stitched up. We will be in town for a few days."

Behind me, Mateo said, "Let's go before you pass out."

I clasped Etienne's shoulder and smiled. "No rest for the wicked. Tomorrow, then."

# Patricide

"We are here to listen to him," Cecil reminded me when we docked at Palais Kansouri. "Remember that." He let me lead across the precarious rope bridge between the docks and the castle. The wind shoved the bridge so it swung, making me watch my step. "We could still turn back," he added when a set of guards arrived to take us in.

"It's too late now," I said.

He arched his black brow. "Too late as in we are already at his doorstep, or too late as in you have made your mind up to kill him?"

"Can it. It's rude to discuss someone's murder on their threshold."

Cecil kept his lips shut as a man greeted us once we were on land and led us into the more common area of Palais Kansouri. Libraries and mysterious rooms filled with planetariums and maps of the globe separated the little gathering areas. Finally, we arrived in a small, more private parlor set aside for guests. It opened up onto the expansive grounds, looking out over a great lake filled with water features. A vast veranda sprawled outside the open glass doors. The interior was occupied by the prince and his tiny entourage. Cecil's words still rang in my ears: let Etienne be king, give him my country. He had said once before that his task was to save me. Maybe that meant not setting my royal ass on the throne. I couldn't remember the exact wording. Did the technicalities matter? But I couldn't stop thinking how Jethro had lied to the people, calling him by my name. Shouldn't I find out why?

"I'm so pleased to see you!" Etienne proclaimed exuberantly. He stood apart from his young, gilded company, choosing to watch them play at archery outside rather than partaking in the sport. "I wish father could be here, but he had business to attend to in NorthEast with the church."

"Father?" I parroted, tensing up. I glanced at Cecil. To Etienne I said, "You mentioned a father when I rescued you yesterday. Of whom do you speak?"

The boy's brightness didn't diminish. "Jethro, the Duke of Dakota, is my father. But he won't be king." He smiled at me, completely taken by me for saving him the other day. "I have no secrets from you, Marquis. I feel you will be a strong ally."

So, his parentage wasn't a secret. At least, not behind closed doors. Would they tell the Empire? Or would they keep it a secret as they took over the five kingdoms?

I wanted to strangle him on the spot, but I suppressed my urge. I thought I had conquered that part of me that came up from The Château d'Oubli. I had wanted Jethro to be here. But I had wanted him there as my uncle, not as Etienne's father.

"You will have to tell me how you grew up," I said, coming back to the present. "I suppose we shall make do with just ourselves, then," I offered as jovially as I could. "No adults need keep us young lords in check." I pulled a bottle of my mill's moonshine out from my inner pocket. With this cue, he laughed heartily. The ones outside came in, eyes on the bottle.

Etienne spared no expense for his hospitality. He had a small feast of stag prepared in my honor that he had hunted himself in the few hills that dotted Kansouri. One of the young Dukes lamented that we did not feast on bison. One was named Desmond and was a Duke from Angleterre who had grown up with Etienne near Paris, but had a thick Anglais accent. The other was an overweight, sullen boy named Sir Percival from SouthWest. He was not knighted, but his father was, and he'd taken the title for himself.

"Family bears the rank and title of the man of the house," Percival argued snobbishly when it came up. "Besides, one day, I will be a lord anyway. So what's it matter?"

I set the mood by regaling them with a carefully curated set of stories from my time with Captain Salazar, forgoing the fact that he was the one who'd kidnapped Etienne just the day before. Rather than hear about me, they asked about the immortal pirate lovers. By the end of the adventure, the younger Duke had collapsed onto the palm of his hand and gazed longingly out the window.

"Oh, to be so in love." He sighed. "Willing to die and yet craving eternity with your fated love."

"How goes the courtship with Lady Elisa, Desmond?" Etienne asked with a tone that said this was a teasing game they had played many times.

"She's fat," Desmond replied, sulking now. "And stupid as a plow. She didn't believe me when I said moths were not, in fact, butterflies." He crossed his arms. "What about you? Has your mother found a lady to burden you with yet?"

Etienne blushed and looked down at his plate, pressing his lips together. He pushed around some vegetables before saying to me, "Marquis, you have a wife."

I'm sure he meant it as a question, but also didn't want to sound ignorant in front of his friends. "I do. Jacquline, but she insists we call her Jacque." I held my tongue for a moment, but decided there was no harm in dropping this kind of information to the young boys. "She is pregnant. With a son."

At this, the three young men toasted me and drank deeply.

"I am curious, Etienne," I said once they had replenished their moonshine. "You called the Duke your father. But you were raised in France? Help me understand what this all means."

By now, we had finished eating and went out to take turns firing Anglais long bows at the targets outside. Cecil remained inside, away from the sun.

I let the boys play while I observed. I'd never once in my life touched something as primitive as a bow, and I wanted to maintain my aura of confidence and adventure. Nothing would snuff it quite as fast as hitting myself in the face with the menacing bow string.

"Mother is French," Etienne offered as an explanation. "She said it was best I was raised in France so I understand when I am king."

I swirled my glass, frowning. "For what? You will be high king of MidWest, not France."

"I will be both," he said simply, closing one eye to aim the huge bow.

I choked on my shine. "What?"

Etienne stopped aiming and let the bow slacken. "Oh, merde! Very few know." He smiled at me. "But what's the harm? You saved my life. I'm going to be emperor of France once I'm High King."

Desmond and Percival grunted in delight and took aim with their bows. "Bring some much-needed civilization to MidWest," Desmond chortled.

"And promote me to your royal court," Percival put in.

My blood slowed to a cold crawl in my veins.

"Don't look so shocked, Marquis," Etienne offered. I hadn't noticed my face turn to cautious horror. "You are on the right side. You've done my mother, father, and me a service I cannot repay. Mother has said that once I am high king, as the American Empire is a leading power after beating Angleterre quite soundly and seceding from the king, we can take back what is ours."

I swallowed hard. "Why not marry a French princess? Many provinces in France have very strong royals, much like we do. There are many kings with daughters who'd love a western king."

"Mother says beating a country into submission is the only way. Besides." He aimed with one eye open at the target. "It's not France we'll be attacking. It's America."

The arrow flew fast, whistling past me. It hit the dead center of the target. I stumbled backwards as if it had hit me. "But why? How?" I asked.

"America is a free country. Despite your ties to France, she is not your master," Etienne said, picking another arrow. "America needs to be tamed. And we'll do it with your geomancy and augmentation. Mancer-tech. With the help of the Grande Mancer, we will train more. Once he proves he is loyal to France."

"Roux DeMarque," I chanced.

Etienne nodded. "Father had him picked out as the strongest mancer, but he had to be—as Mother says—beaten into submission." He aimed and hit another perfect bullseye. "He will be augmented, as will his new army. A mancer-tech army. There is not one like it in the world. An entirely new army with the power of the earth in our hands, all under the French flag. You will be singing *La Marseillaise* before you know it."

I couldn't speak. Suddenly, my personal revenge felt small and insignificant. "The queen has said all this?" I asked to clarify.

Etienne nodded, aiming again. "They are father's ideas. Or so she says. But she loves me and wants what's best for me."

"I see," I whispered, checking the setting sun. A jealously I had never felt before boiled. "And *you* want this?"

The arrow flew, hitting the mark for the third time. Etienne smiled. Something in his grin made me shiver. Like when you think you see the shape of a predator in the dark. "Mother has prepared me all my life to stride confidently into the setting of the American Empire."

Distracted, I passed the last hour in a haze, eager to leave. I couldn't believe my mother would plot something so dark against my country. Against me. I needed to know if it was true. Or was Jethro using her?

I threw my greatcoat and wide-brimmed hat so hard they nearly flew into the fire of my study. Cecil seized them, pulling the luscious fabric out of harm's way, scorning me with his eyes.

"I cannot sit back and let him take my throne," I snapped. "He will lead my empire into ruin. He will kill my people and make himself the next Emperor Napoleon. I was never wrong to seek revenge."

"I never said you were," Cecil started, following my pacing. "Will you stop!"

His command jolted my legs. We had promised to not command one another. He broke that promise as my body buckled.

I threw my fist into his face, cracking my knuckles against his alabaster visage. "Gah!" I clutched my hand.

"Do you feel better?" He lightly brushed his hair over his shoulders and snapped his broken nose back into place with a loud crack.

Sighing in a way that told me he pitied me, he sat next to me on the ground where I had collapsed near the fire. "Hitting those who are loyal to you is not very kind," he said in his old pompous manner. "I know you know that. Ezekiel." He changed his tone, lowering it and adding a note of pleading. "Do this for the empire now, not yourself. There has to be another way that doesn't start your reign with the blood of your family."

I growled, shaking my head. "This just makes it easier."

He shook his head, knowing I wouldn't listen right then. Shadows appeared in the door. Mateo and Jacque. I turned my face away, not wanting her to see me in this defeated, angry state. Cecil tried to catch my eye one last time, but gave up when I didn't allow him to look into my soul.

"What's happened?" Jacque asked.

They entered the room fully. Mud caked the Don's boots and he panted to catch his breath. "I've got news," he said. His deep voice dropped a few octaves and turned gravelly.

We all waited for him to go on.

"The patriarch at Deleon has been killed," he said carefully. "Django is dead. Khalil has planted himself as the leader of this chapter of the Syndicate and moved into the estate."

"What?" I stuttered. We'd had a plan, one he'd concocted himself. He had moved without telling me. This could be one of his classic backstabs, or could be him signaling me to come. I'd not told anyone about Khalil's and my little meeting that night.

Jacque moved in the shadows beyond the firelight. "You promised me."

I looked up. Her eyes fell onto me with pleading and accusations. "I have a plan," I said defensively. "But—"

Her brows twitched down into knitted disappointment. "If not now, then when?" she whispered. She cradled her huge stomach in both palms. "You *promised* me."

Glaring into the fire, I reached my hand out to it. The flames reached back to me, attracted to the rubylead in the ring on my finger.

"Then we get rid of him. Now. Jethro is using Deleon as a hub for his more covert shipments. I'm sure that's where Etienne came into the country. If we can get a hold on it, then we get a little foothold into disrupting their scheme."

I tried to look beyond my personal revenge. What would I do once I had Jethro and Etienne out of the way? I'd have to make my return public, just like they had. With Mateo at my side, it would be simpler. And if I could get my mother to support me, perhaps the transition would be smoother. Then what? Be high king? Use my power to dole out suffering on anyone who'd had even the smallest hand in my torture?

"Uncle," I said to Mateo. "Do you think my mother would want to attack the empire from France?"

Jacque made a small noise and raised her hand to her mouth in shock.

Mateo shifted, his black duster dripping muddy water onto the fine, wood floor. "I can't say. I hardly know the woman. But she is ruthless. I wouldn't be surprised."

I had to know for sure. There had to be a way to get close to her.

"But that's another thing I wanted to tell you," my uncle went on. "She's there. At Deleon."

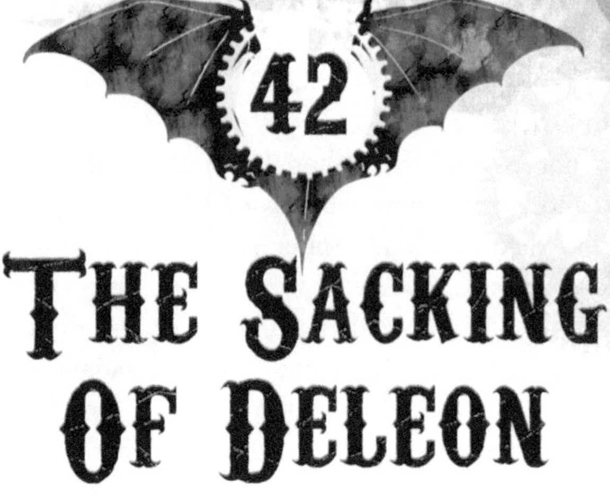

# 42 The Sacking of Deleon

Unsure if Khalil had preemptively struck or if he'd honor our agreement, I set about making the lenses that would tilt minds in my favor. I'd have to look my victim straight in the eye and speak. For good measure, I asked Mateo to lead the way since anyone in command would recognize him as a member of the royal family and hopefully heed his words.

I started to set up my alchemy station when Jacque entered, mask on and goggles over her face.

"Don't breathe this in!" I shouted, running to her.

With a sigh and a grunt, she shoved past to the gas burner and turned it up. "That puny flame won't get anything to reflux," she shouted over the churning of the mill. "I've worked with this geo lots of times before. You have to manhandle it, show it who's boss. But *you* have to do it." She waved her hand for me to come over, handing me a keg of the ephemeral flakes.

"What do you mean?" I asked.

"It's magic, hey? It will be stronger for you if you make the lenses." Her hand gripped my belt and she pulled me into her spot by the cauldron.

My face reddened at her touch. I tried to look into her face, but behind the mask and goggles, she looked like a badly constructed automaton.

"Thank you," I managed.

I dumped a keg of flaked ephemeral into a bronze cauldron over a gas burner. Gold and mythril cauldrons were better suited to the spiritual realm, and were things the religious Creed used when hunting the supernatural. At her instructions, I added glycerin and set the ephemeral to reflux in the copper tank.

"The moon!" Jacque cried.

I ran and opened the Dutch door for the light of the full moon to hit when it reached its peak. When the moonlight hit the simmering liquid, it began to thicken. I dashed to the other side of the workbench and started the glass fire to blow the material into lenses. The empty frames sat waiting for their all-seeing spectacles. For ephemeral to work, I had to see the one I wanted to influence. Normally, one only coats lenses in ephemeral. In this case, I coated them in a fine, iridescent oily substance made from spectral glass, which allowed the user to see long distances. It would get the hypnosis started, but they had to look into my eyes.

"Why not just have Cecil do it?" she asked, motioning for me to turn up the already high flame.

I did without question. "He has to feed to do that, and I need my wits about me. Can't risk being weak from blood loss. And I want the Grande Mancer to think it was his idea. Cecil says people go blank with vampire hypnotism. I need the mancer to know he made a choice so it makes logical sense in his mind later when we're gone and any hypnosis wears off."

Jacque hummed. I heard a smile behind her mask. "Clever, I suppose. I never would have thought you'd think that carefully."

"I've never had occasion," I offered.

A fire inside me burned, my lust for blood strong, and the hope I had that it could finally be satiated for a time gave me more energy than a good night's sleep ever had. And I'd finally experienced a good night's sleep in a giant red velvet bed with a heater in a house where no one wanted to kill me. I had slept with my boots off. Spades, I had slept naked in silk sheets.

I poured the mixture into the glass fire and carefully blew them into round, perfect, ripple-less lenses. While they were still hot, I placed them into the little copper pot of simmering spectral glass, giving it that iridescent sheen Jacque liked. I pulled them out and blew on them, making the spectral crackle and harden faster. I had an ephemeral mixture in my solder oven to enhance the psychic effects. There was a side effect to using geomancy outside the body (not in one's blood). It made it weaker, and in some cases, never worked at all. Well, I didn't settle for weak.

I tried not to tremble as I took up a needle-like shard of ephemeral and pushed it slowly into the corners of my eyeballs.

Jacque gasped and stutter-stepped towards me, hand outstretched. "You could go blind!" she cried.

I topped it off with a sprinkling of the spectral glass ground up into dust. My eyes watered and bled, but I kept them closed, soaking up the effects. I'd have to look the Grande Mancer right in the eye to overcome his hesitations and influence him to my will. By the sounds of it, it wouldn't be hard to turn his mind. I'd lead with Mateo and walk right in if we could. Khalil had crossed me for the last time, and I needed him out of the way and away from my family. The time had come to hit the Deleon estate and take it back. For Jacque.

She sighed when I opened my eyes. "You could have just put it in a vein."

No. For her, I wouldn't risk it not working.

The night we sailed to Deleon, the sky raged with thunderstorms. More lightning and thunder than rain cracked the sky and rumbled in the clouds as I led our assault to Khalil.

"Give the order for the men to signal back in five minutes," I told Cecil. "Mateo, with me."

We climbed up the crow's nest and he handed me my goggles. Behind us flew my smaller ship. I had finally decided to take out the disgusting jewel-drenched zeppelin again. It might lend us some much-needed pomp.

"The small ship will signal the rest of the fleet," I said, pulling the glasses over my eyes.

"We have no fleet," Mateo reminded me. "Those men back there are miners and millers."

"They are our second guise." I screwed up my face and blinked, trying to see through my magical lenses. "But Khalil doesn't know that. Just keep them back in the storm clouds so they cannot see they are cargo ships."

I signaled my navigator to take us to the skydocks and tie down. The confused dock workers of Deleon rushed to grab the ropes we tossed and tie us down with the help of a little tug ship bumping up closer to the dock. I flicked my head for Mateo to disembark first.

Mateo whispered through his gritted teeth to Cecil, "If something goes wrong, just get him out."

I hoped it didn't come to that. The three of us and a few of my men marched down into the wide-open hangar of the Deleon manor. We made it halfway across when a figure in red appeared in the grand entryway. I recognized Roux DeMarque.

"Don?" DeMarque asked stiffly. "We were not aware of your coming to Deleon."

I stepped to the side and glared into DeMarque's eyes through my lenses. My eyeballs watered as the geomancy flared up inside me. The veins alongside my eyes throbbed. I felt the geos cutting me on the inside.

"DeMarque," I said as boldly as I could, "I am a friend and ally of the Don of San Muerte. We are here to remove the murderous Syndicate and purge this place of its influence. Where is the patriarch?"

The Grande Mancer's lips parted and his eyes narrowed as he looked into my eyes behind the iridescent lenses. "Are you—" he started, but then blinked rapidly. He looked away, hand to his temple.

"DeMarque, look at me!" I shouted. My hands shook. The mancer glanced back up, clearly against his will. "Khalil killed his father behind the Duke's back. He is not meant to be here."

Under the brim of his red hat, DeMarque's face fought for control. "Django is dead?" he asked. His head snapped to an empty stall in the hangar where I guessed Django's personal airship must have been. It was empty. "That's not right," he mumbled.

"Look at me," I said again. He did. Glaring at him, blood dribbling from my eye sockets, I said, "Tell me where the patriarch is. Take your men and…" I swallowed, feeling the coyote rise. "Remove his family by any means necessary."

"Ezekiel," Cecil hissed beside me.

"We cannot spare anyone right now," I growled back.

Even DeMarque's eyes shone with a little trepidation. "Sir?" he looked to Mateo. He fought to keep his lips closed.

"Tell me what you're thinking," I ordered him.

To my surprise, no doubt aided by the geomancy, he said, "I've been watching the Duke these last months. I don't trust him. He claims to want to protect MidWest, but I fear he's building a war. I am no one, but if I have the status to stop him, I will. I was just a soldier, but saw the opportunity. Even if I had to volunteer to sacrifice my body to the mancer-tech…I would, to save MidWest and France from war."

Taken by surprise, I glanced quickly at Cecil and Mateo. Was this what had given him pause when Cecil and Mateo confronted him on the docks? Perhaps I hadn't needed the lenses after all.

"DeMarque," I commanded again. "I'm here to stop Jethro."

His orange eyes dropped some of their guard now.

"Your loyalty to your kingdom is noble," I said. "Help me remove the Syndicate."

DeMarque half-smirked in acknowledgment. "Yes, sir."

"Now," I said, the rabid coyote howling inside me again. "Remove them. By any means necessary."

The Grande Mancer nodded, gave a strange kind of salute to me, and turned on his booted heel. He snapped his fingers to the few men who accompanied him. "The patriarch is on the third floor," he called back to me. "Assemble the militia," he barked to his men.

With nothing more to stop us, I ran inside. To my right was the room where I'd drunk with Django. Through a forest of southern decor and more stuffed lions, I found the staircase. Cecil and Mateo stayed right at my side. We ran up a flight of stairs as wide as a hallway when I spotted him in the window of what had been his father's study. To my surprise, his form rippled. His glowing outline twitched and ticked. The effects seemed to be pulsating out from his chronos pendant.

Using less caution than I probably should have, I took the glasses off (the ripple effect around Khalil vanishing) and fastened them to my belt. I had Mateo and Cecil wait on the landing to approach him alone, showing Khalil how unafraid I was. To my surprise, Khalil come down from the room above to greet me. He smiled. For once, his hair was glossy and shiny and his skin glowed warm and dark. I had never seen him clean.

"I just couldn't wait," he said jovially to me, bowing. "I've never been one to work around another's schedule. But I'm so glad to see you here."

I straightened my back and faced the nomad square on. Below us, the lower mancers entered from the back of the entryway, a slight hurry in their step.

"What did you tell the estate?" I asked.

"That father left for the homeland and won't be back until—oh, no, it seems he was taken ill while traveling." He feigned surprise so horribly it belonged in a farce. "I suppose he won't make it back for some time." He smiled like an angler fish.

"We had a deal," I said suddenly. "This estate belongs to the Deleons and Jacque. I want you and your family to leave. Take only what you can carry and get out."

Khalil's face wrinkled into a mocking laugh. "Or you and your useless vampire will eat me up?"

I drew my revolver and pulled back the hammer. His eyes darted to the left where two great red doors stood locked.

"Is that where the bloodstones are?" I asked simply. "Khalil, I'm disappointed in you. You know me. I never lie about what I'm going to do."

"She's here!" he said quickly, raising his flesh and metal hand. Along the forearm, I noted glittering stones. He was armed with geomancy as well. The silver etching sparkled in the firelight.

"Who?" I snapped.

"Your mother," Khalil whispered, relaxing a little. He pointed to the red doors at the end of a hall. "It's she who wants the bloodstones. We have a shipment of timesteel coming in a fortnight as well."

"Lies," I mumbled, but something in me paused. Why could I not believe everything I'd heard about my mother? Why did I deny that she'd condemned me to my fate? Perhaps it was time I revealed myself to her and found out for myself. "Where is she?"

Khalil locked eyes with me. "The west wing."

I flicked my head to the left and Mateo charged up to retrieve his sister-in-law.

Below us, screams broke out and the electric sound of static geos and the whooshing of ice and fire consumed the terror. Cecil's sorrowful moans ricocheted around in my skull. *Don't do this,* he begged. *You don't have to slaughter them all.*

*I don't know how else to do this!* I screamed back.

Khalil's amber eyes went wide and he moved to run to the railing. I held my revolver up again.

"Why?" the nomad shouted over a barrage of gunfire below.

Just then, DeMarque appeared at the top of the stairs. Heat rippled and hovered over his shoulders as a fire smoldered out on his flesh. "We have them all," he reported to me. He glanced to Khalil. "We could lock them away. We don't have to kill them all."

I had done well by taking the mancers under my control. Made it so much easier.

"Why, Ezekiel?" Khalil screamed again. "They didn't do anything."

"Loyalty is a commodity, Khalil," I shot back. "What do you think they'd do to you once they found out you killed Django? For the murder of Patriarch Django, I am here for your capture…" I made sure Khalil looked into my eyes, "…and execution."

"Sir?" DeMarque asked cautiously.

Several bodies moved at once. Khalil cursed me and flexed the fingers of his mancer-tech weapon. Something in my chest jolted as he pulled me towards him. A blue, clear stone in his arm lit up when he did this. As I flew forward, snagged by his telekinetic powers, DeMarque got shoved back down the stairs, head over heels. Cecil leapt between Khalil and me. Khalil's silver-encrusted hand gripped the vampire's neck. I fell over, the telekinetic magic dropping me. The first thing I saw from the ground were Cecil's kicking feet. In my head, I heard him moan in agony from the silver.

"Without Cecil, you are weak, Ezekiel." Khalil guffawed at me. His eyes went wild as he squeezed hard. Something inside Cecil's neck broke and his legs went limp.

Our tether showed that something had been separated in his body. Not killing him, but incapacitating him. Like removing the head from a zombie. He still felt pain and his agony hit me.

If I hadn't been completely serious about snuffing Khalil, I was now. No one hurt Cecil and got away with it.

Khalil went on, "You can't do anything without—"

I scrambled up to my knees and fired my revolver.

The bullet hit the corner of Khalil's right eye, bursting it and ripping through the side of his head. He fell over, dropping Cecil. Gripping his bloodied eye with his flesh hand, he shoved through the pain and seized me with his telekinesis again. I struggled, but the magic flipped me over onto my belly. Khalil stepped over Cecil, whose flesh sizzled from the silver.

Khalil stomped his foot between my shoulder blades, shoving my face into the ground. He dropped his flesh hand, exposing the wound I'd given him. His eyeball hung just on the edge of his fractured skull.

"Damn it, Ezekiel," he roared. "Now I'll have to augment a new eye."

He flexed the arm and reached down to pin my neck against the floor. I gasped, kicking at any part of him I could find. He'd let go of his kinetic powers, so I used one hand to dig into the pouch on my belt.

"You understand why I had to kill Father, don't you?" Khalil asked. "Like you, I just wanted what was mine. We are very much the same, Ez. He was making deals with you. That was my plan." He smiled. "You aren't so different topside as below. It was easy to get you spun into madness with those stones in Romania. You haven't changed at all." He laughed.

"This place belongs to Jacque," I grunted.

He laughed bitterly and shook his head. "Leave me be, Ez. Besides, I'll be a great one to know once you're back on the throne."

Above us, two sets of footfalls came rushing down the stairs.

"Shit," Khalil mumbled. "Well, damn." He reached to his belt to unholster a chemgun.

With a shout, I stabbed a small shard of icesteel into my palm and grabbed his metal arm. The frost, strong and thick, spread from my hand over him, trapping him where he gripped me. Bloodying my nose on the ground, I twisted to see who came down the stairs. Mateo had just lost his grip on a beautiful woman in a grey, silk dress. She whipped his singing blade from his belt, spun it madly, and let it fly towards Khalil. The Egyptian couldn't dodge it, taking the deadly metal deep in his shoulder.

With a savage cry, I kicked him hard, releasing the ice. He fell backwards, screaming at all the torture we'd bestowed on him. Cecil appeared at my side, hauling me up. I could still smell his burning flesh. All the geos inside me fought for dominance, turning my gut.

DeMarque ran back up the stairs, panting, shaking a ball of fire out in his hand. "We will put him in the holding cell in the keep," he said as two of his mancers, one in green and another in yellow, took Khalil into their grips.

"Wait!" I commanded the mancers. I smiled. "Take him to the gallows." I wiped a slippery, thicker than water tear from my eye.

"Ezekiel?" Cecil said softly to me. "Just lock him away."

I didn't pull away yet. "This is for Jacque. I promised her."

"Is it?" he snapped, this time squeezing my wrist. "This isn't the man you have to be, Ezekiel. You're not a prisoner anymore. You don't have to show your power to get people to follow you."

"I never have had power." I turned to face him, feet planted. "I don't know who I am, Cecil. Am I the marquis? Am I a rat from The Château d'Oubli? Am I king? I already have lost myself. Who am I?!" I screamed, jerking my arm away.

My mother's soft, grey eyes landed on me as Mateo grappled her again. She didn't fight him. She looked at me with recognition. Her face begged to know why, how, what was I doing here? Mesmerized by her open face, I couldn't speak. Too many words piled up in my gullet, choking me. Then, she nodded to Khalil. Somehow, I knew she meant to tell me I had said the right thing. I should get rid of him once and for all. At least someone was in agreement with me.

I strode up to Khalil, no fear at all, and ripped the chronos pendant off his neck. "The patriarch of a Syndicate?" I sneered. "You're not a king."

"And neither are you," he spat, tears streaking down his broken face.

I dropped the pendant, smashing it under my heel right before his eyes. Surprised, I looked at the pieces on the floor. I hadn't thought it would break.

"That won't save anyone I've taken time from," he said.

I shrugged. "I'm not here to save anyone. I'm here to take this estate back. And for you, of course."

Khalil swallowed. A thrill went through me at the sight of his fear. "What do you want, Ezekiel? I thought we were done. I got what I wanted, you got what you wanted. We were never friends, but we weren't enemies."

"Never enemies?" I asked. I glanced quickly to see my mother watching me. With her eyes on me, looking to see who I was, a boldness I'd never felt swelled in me. "You used me to get the bloodstones. You wanted Cecil. You knew I was coming for Deleon and yet you set yourself up here as a patriarch." I signaled the mancer. "Take him and hang him." I snapped my fingers and the mancers picked him up and marched him up the steps towards the towering gallows. "When he's dead, take the arm."

"Ezekiel!" Cecil shouted, rushing to me. I pulled away.

"Don't do this!" Khalil shouted from down the stairs. "Mercy!"

"No one likes a kind and merciful king," I reminded him.

DeMarque looked at me one last time. I froze, feeling Cecil's and my mother's eyes on me. I looked to Mateo instead. His dark eyes did not judge, condemn, or ask me to show mercy. He waited as if he trusted me.

My flogging aboard *The Kimiko Fire* came back to my mind so sharply, I thought I felt the welts on my back split open. No unnecessary casualties. I'd promised Salazar. Finally, the lesson Salazar had tried to teach me took root. Did Khalil need to die? Did I need his blood on my hands? The rabid coyote snarled softly, making way for the meeker one.

Taking a shuddering breath, I said to DeMarque, "Take the arm.

Get him medical help. Lock him up somewhere secure we can trust." I flicked my hand, signaling him to go. "I will…spare him."

DeMarque nodded and trotted down the stairs after his fellow mancers, following Khalil's cries for the mercy he didn't know I had given him.

I couldn't look at Cecil. I felt his emotions overwhelming me, suffocating me. They made me want to cry, knowing he was pleased with me. I had the chance to reap my revenge and had not taken it. His thoughts, coupled with the drastic revelation of my mercy, made my legs shake.

I rubbed my eyes, blood swelling from the corners again, but this time mingled with tears. I couldn't stand anymore. Weak from the geomancy, I let out a shuddering sigh and fell onto my ass. My mother struggled against Mateo's grasp, but didn't speak.

"Take her to the ship," I ordered.

"To the manor?" Cecil asked as Mateo obeyed my orders.

I nodded. My eyes seared in pain and I rubbed at them. Cecil caught my hand and pulled it away.

"Let's get home and wash your eyes out," he mumbled, helping me to my feet. In his head, his real opinions made their way to me. He didn't think I should bring my mother in as a prisoner. He wished I hadn't attacked Khalil's family.

My knees went weak at the last thought I caught: *Is this mercy enough? Is he right to rule?* Even now he doubted me, questioning my actions. But I had done the right thing, hand't I? It hadn't been easy, the opposing desires nearly tearing me in two. Would no one stand by me?

# 43 MOTHER

I think I have more instances in my life than the average person where I look back at a situation and think, "I should have known." If I'd remained the man I'd started as when you first saw Cecil and me meet, I would tell you I had known, but I'd chosen to ignore it because I didn't care. But somewhere between the dark and clanking halls of that place and where I was now, I became different. I saw things differently. Something that meant everything suddenly meant nothing. But there were still things I longed for that I didn't have, a touch of love being one of them. I had found someone to stand by me in Cecil, but his recent thoughts weakened the bond I'd thought we had. The way my mother watched me take command began to slowly replace the sadness I felt at knowing no matter what I did, I had let Cecil down.

When we landed back in the Rockies, Cecil split me from Camille and had her sequestered away from me. Drained and ill from the sacking of the Deleon estate, I didn't fight too much. He promised she'd be comfortable and I could see her once I was better. The geo sickness took me down hard and Cecil put me in my room for two days. Alone. My footman, Josiah, brought me food and water and eventually my strength came back. On the second night, my door opened slowly.

Jacque stood in the doorway to see if I slept. The moon glittered in her eyes, but I didn't move, hoping she would come to my bed. One hand supported her stomach and the other stuck out to avoid furniture. She felt her way to my huge four poster bed. A tender, warm, shaking hand found my face and she caressed me so lightly shivers ran down my spine. I couldn't feign sleep any longer and gently took her hand in mine.

"Jacque?" I chanced. She lowered herself slowly onto my bed and faced me.

She didn't speak, though I wanted her to with all my being. She touched my face again, and her palm was hot as a coal. With her thumb, she slowly stroked my face. She leaned her forehead against mine and I could finally feel her breath on my face. Her nose touched mine. My breath quickened so suddenly it nearly caught in my throat. Her hand flew to my jaw line and with the other she grasped my hair. She pulled me into her, kissing me tightly just once. Her lips were hot and moist, clinging to mine as if for life. Her hand gripped my shaggy hair and she broke the kiss, flinging her arms around my neck and resting her head on my chest.

She breathed heavily. Taking a chance, I touched her face. There were tears there. I forced my mouth closed, not asking her the reason for them. Talk would only drive her away. So I cradled her, soaking up and lavishing in her presence. Her weight on me. Her heartbeat against mine was precious. Tears came to my own eyes, and I wrapped my arms around her tighter. I never wanted to let her go. This was all I'd wanted. The sun, the wind, every hope and dream, every wish and need—she was all of it. In that moment, I could not have cared less about Jethro, Etienne, Kansouri or the entire American Empire and its five kingdoms.

If I could be sure my future looked like this, it would be worth it. I shifted us, my back against the headboard. She slid up between my knees, her back leaning into me. Her head rested on my shoulder. I covered us with the bed clothes. Taking a chance, I kissed her head. She pulled my arms closer around her and placed my hand on her stomach, clasping them. I could feel from her weight that she didn't smile, but also that she needed this intimacy. Did she feel as alone as I did? As desperate for love and affection?

"Why did you bring her back here?" she whispered.

Under my hand, the baby inside her kicked. Feeling it, my heart leapt. I pressed into her skin, searching for the little foot.

"I want to ask her myself—" I started, but Jacque cut me off.

"Why she sent you away?"

I cleared my throat. "No. If she is guilty of all the things they are saying. I can't believe it. I won't."

"Why not?" She turned her head to watch the moon outside my window.

I ran my finger over her stomach. "Because a mother is supposed to love her son."

She pushed up off me and slid to the edge of the bed, all affection gone. Had it been a ploy? "If you will not trust Mateo, trust me, hey." She glared at me, the firelight igniting only half of her face. "She doesn't love you and wants you dead."

Her bare feet hissed over the floor. She pulled the door open.

"No one does," I replied flatly. She waited in the doorway, her back to me. "No one loves me."

"You make it very hard," she offered, her voice quivering. "But someone does love you. And he won't leave your side. Don't take advantage of that."

The next night, I washed myself, brushed my hair, and ate to regain my strength before having Cecil take me to the rooms where my mother was held.

"Have you not heard a word Mateo has said?" Cecil implored as we made our way through the manor. "She's the one person we know had a hand in Markus's death and had you locked away."

"You wanted me to be a better person, to believe others can be good. I choose to believe her and hear the story from her own mouth."

Our tether was weak so I couldn't access his more detailed thoughts. I sensed the primal urge: he wanted to feed and make me weak so I wouldn't go see her. I wouldn't let him, even though he was weak from healing from the damage Khalil had done to him.

I paused outside the study door where she stood, Mateo waiting for me. "She knew me," I said softly so that anyone on the other side of the door could not hear us. "Even before that night with Khalil. She knew me at the rodeo. If she wanted me dead, I would be. She hasn't said anything to Jethro or sent a bounty hunter after me. She must have wanted to see me." I glared at Cecil. "This won't ruin your redemption, vampire," I added. "You're still getting the job done."

"That's not what worries me," Cecil argued gently. "You're volatile. Eager for affection. I worry she will reel you in without you knowing. She will hurt you."

Shaking my head, I waved my hand. "Thanks for the vote of confidence, Cecil. Now go away."

He didn't wait to be told again.

"I'll be out here if you need me," Mateo offered.

I glanced up and down the hall, then pushed open the door. The queen stood with her back facing me, her grey dress shining like a ghost in the moonlight coming from the window. There were a few lit candles and the hearth blazed; she did not stand near it. I closed the doors behind me.

I cleared my throat, palms sweaty. "Camille?"

She stiffened, fists clenched around a long silver chain that disappeared down the front of her dress. She'd been twirling it around her fingers, deep in thought. She dropped it. "I have…dreamed of this night." Her voice came husky and low, accented lightly with her French home. Just like I remembered it, thick with emotion. "I fear I dream now."

"I wish everything else had been a dream." I couldn't move.

She elegantly turned to face me, her eyes glittering with tears. "If you are my son, do not burden me with your pain. I cannot bear it."

I looked into her face. She looked just the same as the last time I'd seen her. Not a single new line etched her face. Her grey eyes shone like diamonds at night. Her chestnut hair was piled up on her head and had a few loose strands elegantly cascading over her shoulders.

"What do you know of my pain?" I asked, my voice catching dangerously in my throat. I could tell her everything. Every beating I'd taken, every dark alley I'd gotten dragged down, every foul thing that had ever happened to me. But would it matter to her?

After a moment, she opened her arms to me and let out a sob. "What happened to you?" She gasped, weeping. "Ezekiel?"

I tried to stay my ground. All I'd ever dreamed of was getting back to her, hoping someone would come down and say she'd sent them to find me. Instead, I'd gotten a vampire who sucked my blood and wanted me for his own redemption.

"Was it you?" I asked, muscles aching with holding me to the spot. "Did you send me to The Château d'Oubli?"

Her hand flew to her mouth. "The Château d'Oubli?" She turned away, her shoulders shaking with a sob. "Eight years?" She took a deep breath, eyes to the heavens. "They took you from me. I tried to find you."

"You did?" My breath shuddered. *I knew I had been right.*

She faced me again, one hand beckoning me—begging me—to come to her.

Eight years left me in that instant and I flew to her, collapsing in her arms as a child would. Her hands were stronger than I had imagined as they squeezed my shoulders, pulling me to her. I wanted to stay there, sob, and cleanse away all my sins and sorrows.

She wailed now, embracing me with a force like I had never known. Weak from the joy of the reunion, she fell, taking me with her. She pressed her lips to my hair, kissing me. We sat together until her breath calmed.

"What has Mateo told you?" she asked, pressing her cheek to my head. "Did he tell you what Jethro did?"

I thought a moment. "Sort of." I pulled away and stood up, wiping the emotion from my cheek. "He had father killed and sent me away, all to gain the throne he abdicated. He lusted after you, too. Please tell me you don't love him."

She blinked, releasing the tears in her eyes, struggling for words. Her face twisted as she fought to hide her emotions. "No. I never could love Jethro. It was for the empire that I was to take him as a new husband. I made him swear to not be king again, but to keep the ties that bind us to my home. America is weak. I could not risk it."

I believed her. I wanted to love her.

"And Etienne?"

"Yes." She grasped my coat, keeping me steady and not letting me run from her when she saw the shock in my eyes. "He is Jethro's son." Her eyes snapped with lightning suddenly. "When Markus learned of my infidelity, he flew into a rage. I was wrong. I admit that, my love." She stood and placed her long-nailed hand on my cheek and traced my neck down to my collar. "But I only ever wanted *you* to be king. But Markus left me no choice. He wanted Etienne gone. Dead. He couldn't stand to have a permanent reminder of my weakness in his palace. He never believed that I didn't love Jethro." Her head dropped in shame. "A woman doesn't have to love a man to make love to him. She simply realizes that something bigger matters." She took a steady breath. "I have suffered too, my son. We have been in agony, you and I."

Something like geo-sickness filled my gut. The night Jacque came to me down in the prison had permeated my dreams. Now it would haunt my nightmares. I had my answer. Had she manipulated me?

"What is it, my son?" Camille asked. She lifted her skirts and moved closer to me. "Ezekiel?"

I snapped my head up when she said my name.

"I may have suffered," she whispered, closing the distance between us, "but not as you have." Her elegant hand petted the side of my head again. She pulled me down to her height, resting her forehead against mine. "I wish I could take all that pain away from you. But we have each other again. Tell me what troubles you."

"Everything," I croaked. "I escaped with revenge on my mind. I wanted to kill everyone who put me in The Château d'Oubli. Except you."

She sniffled and sighed.

"Tell me you didn't hate me," I begged. "Tell me Jethro put me there."

"Yes, yes." She nodded quickly. "True. All true." She looked up into my eyes, waiting for me to go on.

I sighed sadly. "I brought a woman up with me. Jacquline Deleon."

Camille pulled back a fraction. "And?" Her voice turned deep, flat.

Why did it feel wrong to tell her? "She has my child," I said finally.

The queen pushed away, still holding me with her hands, though.

"I see," she mused. She smiled, eyes watering. "How wonderful. Now your line is secure."

Yes, that was true. "But I feel like she used me. To be free of The Château d'Oubli."

"She doesn't love you?"

I shook my head. "She loves Cecil. Always has."

"Cecil Corbeau?" she clarified. "The vampire?"

I nodded cautiously.

The lightning snapped behind her eyes again, but with a blink, it vanished. "No matter. You will be king, a great king. *My* king." She embraced me again. "Why do you doubt that?"

So many reasons. "I am not the boy who was sent away from you. I… I've wanted so many dead. I've killed even more. I've done awful things."

"A king may be forgiven, for he must do what is necessary," she whispered, kissing my forehead. "Surround yourself with those you love and trust, and together we will return you to your rightful throne." Her stormy eyes bored into me. "Trust me. I'm your mother and I love you."

Mothers have a way of making you say too much. "I am having second thoughts," I said quietly. "I wanted revenge. I've been driven by it so long. I've never had a choice in what I do with my life, just how I ride the bull it dealt me. But I have one now. I could stay here. I have a wife, a child on the way, and now you. Etienne could be king. I could slip away."

Her eyes flicked back and forth between mine as though reading a manual at top speed. I saw her try to form words, but she couldn't decide what to say. She seemed disappointed. Angry.

"The only one who needs to be served justice is Jethro," I said, hoping to prompt her to respond. "Right?" I honestly didn't know and wanted her to tell me what to do.

She held her breath a moment before sighing, "Yes. That is an idea." She took two steps away from me and studied the fire. "But you would make a much better king."

"And Etienne?"

She smiled like a thousand comforting lullabies. "He will understand once he knows who you are. He is not ready to take the throne. But you, one who has escaped The Château d'Oubli, made a life for himself, taken back what is his—*you* are ready to be king. You will be fierce. A force to be reckoned with."

The intensity in her eyes scorched my soul. At last, I had someone who believed in me.

# 44
# Ezra

With Deleon liberated, I moved the militia there to my estate, along with DeMarque and his mancers. I emptied the place as best I could and prepared it for Jacque. At last, I could check something off my list of things I had promised.

"Let me come with you," Camille said to me. I visited her every day in the chambers we'd locked her in. "I need to leave this place. Your vampire and uncle give me the cruelest looks. And I want to meet the future queen." She smiled at me, her grey eyes bright in the dull morning sun.

I scoffed gruffly. "She won't be queen. She wants to leave once I am back home in Palais Kansouri. She's taking Ezra with her."

Camille's pale brow twitched, and her lips tightened. "Is that so?" she said flatly. "You really only need your child. Ezra, is it?"

It hurt to hear her speak so callously of Jacque. "I think I love her. Have for years. I was hoping if I kept my promise—gave her back her home—she'd change her mind."

"Stop groveling, my child." My mother's face fell into a sympathetic simper for me. "That will never happen." She petted me gently. "You have a chance with your little Ezra. Take him and let her go."

"I could never separate them," I said, repulsed at the idea. Perhaps once I could. I'd gotten so soft since leaving the prison.

Camille tapped her fingers together impatiently. "Very well. Let me come help you move her in. I'll get her settled while you see to it all her little trinkets and machinations are brought over."

Glad to have put the other conversation behind us, I agreed and called for my household to pack up and move Jacque's things to the Deleon estate.

My men did well fixing up the manor and grounds. As we docked and unloaded the few boxes and crates of Jacque's things, Camille swooped in and steered Jacque away from me. I watched them go, wondering if I should let Camille be alone with Jacque. I didn't want her trying to pry Ezra from her.

"The music box fountain?" Josiah asked as four men grunted, lifting a huge wooden crate on beams threaded through metal rings.

"Uh," I stuttered. "Downstairs is an open parlor. Put it there."

I followed them down shortly after, realizing neither Mateo nor Cecil were near me to have a word with. Alone, I eventually made it down to that open parlor. I watched the hired engineers set up the fountain and connect it to make sure the gears and springs worked. The dancers clicked as the water flowed, pushing them through elegant movements. They stopped it and made some adjustments.

Looking around, I imagined Jacque working here. She'd make some wind-up solar system for Ezra to play with. Would she be alone? Or would she find a man she loved and bring him in to be Ezra's father? The thought made me choke. I hoped he'd have her skin, soft and dark. Her eyes, too, large and curious. He'd be smart like her, building things and planning the trajectory of a rocket from the prairie out back. I didn't want him to have anything of mine. Not my hate, my violence, my rage. Maybe I could watch him from afar, see him grow up. Then one day, I'd come back and Jacque would let me give him his birthright.

"I want to see your work." Camille cut into my beautiful daydream. She sailed down the stairs and approached me and the fountain. "Jacque told me about the fountain."

She made it down before Jacque, who stumbled down the stairs slowly, gripping the rail and the underside of her stomach. Taking the opportunity, I ran to her, taking her waist and hand to steady her. She sighed heavily and whispered, "Thank you." Louder she said, "Your mother and I have been having tea. Talking for some time."

One of the engineers reached down and wound one of the pedestals closest to us in the fountain: a ballerina with a parrot on her outstretched hand. It began to spin and move with perfectly smooth motions.

"Have you seen those music boxes with the disks in them?" Jacque asked my mother. I noticed an edge in her voice. "These use the same technology. I can put in different disks depending on how I want them to dance."

My mother smiled and clapped her hands in praise. "You are a genius."

Jacque shook her head. "Trifles, really. Compared to what I *can* do."

Camille held her head a little higher. "In The Château d'Oubli, you mean?"

I stepped in. "Jacque is a wonderful engineer, Mother. We couldn't have gotten anything done without her mind behind the drills and building plans. She's also a fabulous pilot."

I didn't know if she was tired or pleased, but Jacque squeezed my arm a little after I said this. "Can we speak, Ezekiel? Alone?" she cooed softly.

"And the mill?" Camille asked, shutting her down. "Have you done work on that as well?"

Jacque did not smile as she answered. "I have a lot of time to kill, hey? Your son is a busy man. He's out often with his men."

"Ah, yes." Camille clasped her hands and her face darkened in concern. "My darling, you trust Mateo?"

"I do now," I said. "He has saved my life more times than I deserve."

"And the monster?" she quipped.

"He is no monster," Jacque cut in, her face flushing.

"Oh?" Camille's eyes gleamed with a hint of malice. "And who is my son's servant to you, my lady?"

"He's not my servant." I didn't know how to put this fire out. "Cecil saved my life."

"We trust *him*," Jacque said shortly. She glared in that way that made her adorable. Something about my mother got under her skin.

I led the women back inside the parlor and called for tea. "I trust him, Mother, and I beg that that be good enough for you."

Camille frowned and pressed her lips together hard. She sighed in frustration.

"What is it?" I asked, choosing to sit with Jacque on a loveseat across from her. "You seem agitated."

The queen turned her face to look out the parlor doors, hands clasped with one resting on the arm of the chair. "I was hoping you and I would see eye to eye. That you might understand what I am trying to do."

Beside me, Jacque groaned and shifted on her seat. "And what are you trying to do?" she asked. Her hand gripped mine so hard, I thought my finger bones cracked. She was hot, her palm sweaty.

Finally, Camille eyed me. "Ezekiel," she said, sighing, "this is not the time or place. I am overly done with being your prisoner."

"Mother, I—" I started, but she held her hand up.

"I want to give you a chance," she went on. "I've seen that traitor DeMarque. I knew from the start his heart was not in it. I suppose we could not break him after all. But." She sighed again. "He showed resilience to the geomancy. He's too American. Too patriotic. I thought he'd make a good augmented pet, but now…" She waved her hand. "I don't want to—"

Jacque made a high-pitched gasp and grabbed me. She threw her head back. "I knew it," she growled. "I should have called the doctor this morning. Snakes, I *knew* it!"

"Jacque?" I cried. "What's wrong?"

Camille swooped past me. "Don't be daft, love. It's the baby!" My mother called to a maid in the corner. "Is there a house doctor?"

"Oui, majesté," the maid called, running out to get help.

"But…already?" I felt the blood drain from my face. "It's not time."

"How long?" my mother asked, moving next to Jacque, who was still moaning in pain.

"Um... I don't know." I racked my brain.

"Eight months!" Jacque screamed. She shrieked and coughed, puking all over me. "It's fine. He can't wait."

"Call a manservant to get a ship," my mother instructed.

"Why?" I asked, lifting Jacque in my arms and heading to the stairs to her room.

"Just do it!" Camille roared. "Here." She directed me away from the stairs to a small room on this floor instead.

Grateful for the idea, I swerved into the smaller guest room and lurched forward, practically throwing Jacque onto the bed. "I'm sorry," I panted.

"Ez," Jacque groaned. "It's happening fast. He's too eager. Ez, please." She gripped the front of my coat. "L-listen to me..."

"What?" I gasped, holding her face. She was acting so calm, but it had no effect on me.

Jacque panted quickly, breathing through a sudden pain. Once it passed, she opened her black-brown eyes to me. "Don't...trust...her. I tried to tell you, but I couldn't." She winced again, counting softly. "One minute apart. He's coming."

She leaned back and pulled her skirt up. In a matter of seconds, her undergarments flew at me and she kicked her shoes off. She knew what she was doing. Baffled, I stood there, her trousers in my hand.

Camille barked to me, "Get hot water!"

She dug in her corset and pulled out a vial at the end of a long silver chain. It was only half full of some herb immersed in a kind of distilled oil of a clear variety. "This will soothe her."

"No," Jacque panted, pushing it away. "No, no, no!"

"Will it help?" I asked.

Camille nodded. "It's just a tincture of chamomile and other soothing herbs. For the muscles and pains."

Jacque, sweating and in pain, begged me with her eyes. "Please, no," she whispered. "I can't do this myself. I need you to help me."

Taking my chance, I kissed her forehead. "It will be all right."

Camille tipped the remains of the vial into Jacque's panting mouth. My love gagged and dry heaved, trying to throw up. I took her hand, her shaking and sweat almost making her fingers slip between mine. I grasped her harder with both hands and kissed them fiercely.

"Jacque, please." I wanted to hide from all the eyes around me.

The summoned doctor burst into the room, his female automaton nurse rushing to us and slipping a portable table and leg rests under Jacque.

"No, get out!" Camille roared, suddenly.

I turned to see Cecil appear behind the nurse automaton. His eyes flashed to Jacque, fire burning behind his violet gaze. "What happened to her? She's so weak."

"The baby is nearly here," the doctor exclaimed, cutting off Camille's protests. "Nurse, the sustain chamber!"

The automaton pulled up a little wagon and uncovered a glass incubator attached to brass mechanicals, gauges, and the like. She flipped a switch and it turned on, a little yellow light softly glowing and pulsating above it.

"My lady, can you hear me?" the doctor said loudly and slowly.

Jacque merely moaned now, but her face twisted in pain and anguish. "She's trying to kill him," she screamed. "Please, save him!"

"I need you to push just once more. Your son is on his way," the doctor said sternly.

I didn't realize how much I shook until Cecil's steady hand rested on my shoulder. I leaned into him. "Help me," I managed to say. "What can I do?"

Cecil gently pulled me back, making me face him. "Ezekiel." He touched my face gently. "I would never lie to you. But I wish I could." He steadied himself, taking my other shoulder firmly. "I have seen so much death. The worst of deaths. When an animal is dying, it knows. There is a look about them that I cannot describe."

I did not deserve his kindness. In the last few months, he had forgotten what a monster I had been. I had seen death. I had caused death. I knew that look. The one that says, "Well, shit…" as your guts are in your hands or as you see the grey haze sneak into your peripheral vision. The one that says your heart has only ten beats left. I knew what he meant all at once.

"Marquis!" the doctor exclaimed before quickly shouting to his robot, "The chamber!"

In the doctor's hand rested a bloody, slimy, pile of limbs with bits hanging off. The robot rushed the chamber to meet him, wrapping the bloody hunk in a huge, thick blanket. The doctor stuck a tiny syringe into what I guessed was one of the arms and held it up, frowning. "His blood is… There's some kind of toxin." Gently, the doctor closed the lid and turned one of the gauges up higher. He held a kind of stethoscope up to the chamber and listened, counting on his watch. He smiled.

"Your son will live. But I must get him to the clinic in the city. He is too weak."

"What's wrong with him?" I cried in shock.

"Nothing frightening," the doctor said quickly. "He has a toxin in his blood that must be removed immediately. Please, monsieur, I must move quickly."

"I'll go," Camille said, beaming and shoving past me so hard I fell back into Cecil.

My mind snapped between tiny Ezra being taken away and Jacque, shaking and convulsing on the bed.

I let them go, of course. The doctor assured me my son would be all right and that he'd send a message for me the minute he became stable and settled.

"Don't touch her," my mother warned, pulling me back a little.

I leaned over Jacque on the bed, tears dripping down my nose onto her face. She had that look. I should have known. She would never come to me now. I'd never have that chance. She had been so strong just moments ago. Her sweaty face flushed pale and her eyes rolled back into her head as her muscles spasmed. She choked and her hands twisted back.

"What's wrong with her?" I cried.

Cecil stood still as stone.

She gasped, her back arching hard. Then she collapsed, eyes closed. I gently took her face in my hands. I kissed her forehead and begged her to open her eyes. I felt her breath ease. Her fingers relaxed and I took her hand.

"Jacque, please," I said again. I didn't know what went through her mind, but my life flashed before my eyes. Everything I had ever done, ever dreamed of, faded to meaninglessness. Stupid. Nothing mattered but her. How could I save her? I wanted nothing more than to give her the chance to live the life she'd imagined.

"Forgive me. Jacque, please."

I fell on her, grasping every part of her I could. This was it, her death rattle just a breath away. Someone patted my hair and stroked it. I looked up, thinking for some weird reason it had been Cecil. It was Jacque. But she didn't look at me.

"Father," she said softly, turning to face someone on her left who was not there. "I am so glad you are here, Father. I've got our home back. See?" Her eyes unfocused and jittered in her head before she looked back at someone only she could see. Froth rose up in her mouth, gagging her.

"What?" I said between sobs. She smiled and almost giggled, but was too weak.

"I haven't seen you in years, Father. Thank you for coming." She reached one hand, almost to me, but beyond me. To Cecil. "Father, this is my husband, Cecil. He saved me from The Château d'Oubli and brought me back up to see you." Now she did giggle. "I have a son, but it's not his. I don't know where the baby came from…" She frowned for a moment. "Cecil, love, say hello to my father."

I couldn't breathe. I choked and backed away, stumbling. Cecil caught me but said nothing.

Jacque remained looking at Cecil, smiling. Her face froze. Her hand dropped. In an instant, she began to pale. Her eyes never turned to me.

"I'm so sorry, Ezekiel," Cecil whispered.

The moon had long since risen and I hadn't moved. Jacque's hand had turned stiff and cold like clay in my fingers. My voice cracked when I finally spoke.

"I had just decided to accept that we'd never be together," I whispered hoarsely. "That I'd let her go. That I'd let everything go. Ever since escaping The Château d'Oubli, I have feared what I would do to reap my revenge, knowing my sins would overtake me. Well, they've come sevenfold, and I don't think there's any harm in rounding up a few more." I stood up. "Have her buried in the cemetery with her family."

"What are you doing, Ezekiel?" Cecil called after me. He could overtake me, force me down. But he didn't.

"You've done your part, Cecil," I called back. I signaled my footman to follow me. I needed Khalil's arm. "I'll handle it from here."

Hope had sprung up in me over the last three days and had been snuffed out in as many hours.

# 45 THE QUEEN'S FLIGHT

I'd never envied Khalil's torture at the hands of the experimental machinations of The Château d'Oubli, but I'd often wondered how he'd survived it.

"I will not," Mateo roared at me for the tenth time in the expansive workhouse under my mill. My alchemy tools, geomancy hoard, and other such things filled the dark corners. "There are other ways to go about finishing what you started. I'm not amputating your arm."

His new-found nobility annoyed me. I sat up on the table made of butcher block and threw my legs over the edge. "Any one of the men who work my land will do it," I snarled.

"Have Cecil do it," he shot back.

"No," I quipped. "He wanted to feed but I couldn't allow him. I can't lose all this blood in one day."

"I'm not severing your arm," he repeated. "Do you even know how to attach it?" He glared at the vile thing on top of a work bench beside me.

I shrugged. "I do have to call my doctor for that bit."

Mateo looked around. "Where is he?"

I swung my feet, looking down at the concrete ground. "On his way." I paused a moment. "Is Jacque buried?"

My uncle stopped his mad pacing. "She will be in a few hours. They fixed her up yesterday. Did you see her?"

No. And I wouldn't. Once a mortician got to a corpse, they dolled them up so much they didn't look like the person they'd been before. My eyes prickled with emotion the more I thought about it. I growled and punched the wooden table.

"Do this for me," I hissed. "I need this."

Above us, someone called my name. I hopped down and ran to the prison-like door that cut off the end of the dirty stairs. I flung it open and called up. Two sets of footfalls cascaded down the wooden stairs. Shocked, I stepped back to see the flaming coat of DeMarque and my doctor. He looked grey.

"What's going on?" I asked.

"The child!" the doctor spat at the same time DeMarque informed me that Camille had fled the manor.

"She went to my estate?" I asked, confirming what DeMarque had said.

The mancer nodded. "She was there with a child. I caught sight of her as she fled on a small ship."

"She had Ezra!" the doctor gasped. "Took him from me!"

I signaled DeMarque to go on.

"She took an airship, with the child, and left west towards Kansouri," he informed me.

Rage boiled up in me. I'd not even seen my son yet. "Why'd she take him? What's she doing?" I rounded on the three of them, but of course they had no reply. I'd thought she was on my side. I'd thought she wanted me.

Then it hit me. Of course, she had seemed like she was on my side. She'd manipulated me. Jacque, up until her dying breath, had tried to tell me. I had been so buys trying to love Jacque that I didn't listen to her.

"Doctor," I growled, "I need your assistance. DeMarque, prepare a fast ship and yourself. I'll need your magic."

I'll spare you the details of my operation. The arm, it turned out, was made of a catalyst metal. The familiar sensation overtook me once the good doctor grafted it as well as he could to my body. I, of course, passed out for hours after it was done and woke to prosthetic flesh under miles of bandages holding the thing to my torso. Moving the fingers took a few tries, but miraculously, I could. Everything hurt, but it'd be worth it.

"Your ship is ready," DeMarque called to me from outside my room.

I slung a greatcoat over my shoulders and tightened my belt laden with geos. I swore this would be the last time I used the earth magic. I took rubylead, banshee's silver, and sapphire for telekinesis. I fit my hypnotic goggles over my head as well, just in case.

Cecil, Mateo, DeMarque, and I sailed the airship as fast as we could over the Colorado Territory to Kansouri. I stayed at the rail, looking over, hoping I wasn't too late. I didn't know what Camille had in mind for my son, and I didn't want to find out too late.

Mateo ran to the railing with me, quickly pressing a telescope to his eye.

"What is it?" I asked.

"The lights," he said quickly. He motioned for DeMarque to make the ship come about with a wide swing of his hand. "The hangar is open. Something is preparing to launch out of the skydocks." He handed me the telescope.

Closing one eye, I looked through. He was right: a small sloop with a quiet, steam-powered engine hovered in a docking bay, the sails unfurling and the balloon filling to max capacity with hydrogen.

"Hurry!" I shouted to DeMarque. "They're running." I turned to Cecil and my uncle beside me. "Why are they running?"

I had a guess, now that I knew my mother. Run, take Ezra. Go to France and come back once I had crawled out of hiding and put myself on the throne. The political climate would be torrential, and the people might revolt. Even if it didn't work out how Camille imagined, France could still attack.

Gripping my hat and pulling it down harder onto my head, I prepared to make my first move as prince of MidWest: save my son and country.

"DeMarque!" I called. "Let us disembark. Follow after."

He nodded. Cecil leapt off, his wings tearing his coat as they unfurled. Mateo and I followed, swinging off the railing. A few dock workers and guards turned, screaming as the winged monster pounced at them. Cecil didn't harm them, simply winding them with hard thrusts to the ground. Mateo led me around the catwalks of the skydocks and many guards let him pass. It wasn't until spotting Cecil that one fired at me, raising an alarm. The bullet ricocheted off my metal arm. Seeing one fire at me, Cecil sprung at him, clawed hands burying deep and bloody into his chest.

We dashed, not quite out of breath, and entered the hangar with the prepping ship. I skidded to a halt. Jethro stood on the bridge, flipping open the hatches and gauges to let the engine flare into life.

"Stop him!" I screamed.

Mateo spun one of his chained blades and launched it directly into the controls, inches from Jethro's fingers. Jethro stopped, looking up and meeting his brother's eyes for the first time in months.

"Mateo?" Jethro gasped. He took two quick steps towards his brother before stopping. "Where have you been?" Jethro ran to the ladder but didn't descend. "I had men looking for you everywhere. I was worried. What happened in The Château d'Oubli? Are you hurt?" Finally, his eyes landed on me. "Marquis?" he asked slowly, but his voice faded away. His eyes brightened in recognition. "Ezekiel?" he said. He gripped the handles of the ladder like he might leap down but thought better of it. "You're here. You're alive."

He seemed sincere. Too sincere.

"Save it, Jethro," I snapped, aiming my revolver at him. "I don't want to do it like this. Where's Ezra?"

"Ezra?" Jethro asked, mouth agape.

"My son, uncle!" I spat. "Where is my son?"

Jethro paled and spun around to stop someone from running up behind him.

"Marquis, don't shoot!" Etienne said, pushing past Jethro, coming up from below deck. He held his hands up. "We're leaving," he said quickly. "Mother said the empire is yours."

I chanced a glanced at Jethro. His face contorted in turmoil. Slowly, he stepped in front of Etienne. "Shoot me, Ezekiel. Everything is my fault. Markus. You."

"Father, no!" Etienne begged. He glared at me. "Why are you doing this?"

I cocked the gun. All the mercy I had cultivated fought to stop me. Nothing mattered but Ezra now. Jethro closed his eyes so as to not look down the barrel of my gun. I couldn't squeeze the damn trigger. Everything I'd been waiting for presented itself willingly in this moment. But I didn't want this now. I wanted Ezra.

"Ezekiel!" Camille shouted, running up from the back of the ship. I didn't fire. "Etienne is your brother. Don't do this."

The other prince's grey eyes went wide. "Mother?" he whispered. Lips parting, realization dawned as he met my eyes. "The dead prince," he whispered. "If it's true," he shouted to the rest of us, placing himself in front of Jethro, "then I'm...supposed to replace you?" He met everyone's eyes, trying to understand. "Mother?" He turned to her.

Jethro took Etienne's arm and pulled him away from Camille. "We don't have to do this anymore." He glanced at me quickly. "Ezekiel, let us flee. You can have the empire. We'll disappear."

"No!" Etienne barked. "I've waited so long, father. Don't run now."

Camille's eyes roved to Mateo and his blade hanging by its chain, then to Cecil's bloody claws. Finally, they landed on me and took in the metallic fingers sticking out of the end of my greatcoat.

"Mother," I snapped. "Where's Ezra?"

The queen sighed despondently. "None of the men in my life have been strong. Every last one of you is a disappointment." She turned back to the ship.

"Don't move or I shoot him," I ordered her, flicking my aim between Jethro and Etienne.

"You won't," she said, almost sounding bored. When she turned back, she clutched five vials between her fingers. She rounded on me, liquid fury in her eyes. "Why couldn't you stay dead?"

My heart stopped. I tried to stammer. She held geos in her hand.

"If it was so hard and tortuous, why didn't you die? Why won't you ever die!" she screamed.

"Mother—" I started.

She laughed. "Mother, Mother, Mother. You sound like a simpering fool! Jethro, start the engine."

I couldn't leap up fast enough. Turning to Cecil, he understood before I could say anything. With a great flap of his wings, he shot himself up onto the catwalk towards the three of them. He tackled Jethro, who fell into Etienne. The trio tumbled backwards across the dock, giving me time to get up.

"Don't kill them!" I shouted to Cecil. Jethro's panicked look of relief and sincerity at seeing me haunted my mind.

Cecil stood up and a shot rang out. He spun, a silver bullet hitting his left shoulder. A strangled animal cry rang out from him as he crumpled on the dock. He folded in on himself in pain, gripping his shoulder. His bloody claws dug at the bullet. I couldn't get too close to him or the silver in my arm would harm him more.

Camille holstered her gun and ran out of sight. I grabbed the ladder and scrambled up as fast as I could. Jethro was just pushing himself up off the deck when I came over the top. Etienne stood right before me, so I grabbed him, shoving my own gun into the side of his head.

"Mother?" I called, sweeping the deck for her. Etienne struggled, but was no match for my metallic arm.

"Please," he begged. "I swear I didn't know what she'd done."

"Ezekiel," Jethro begged as well, "don't hurt him. It was me. I did this to you."

Even as he said it, I realized he'd lied. Cecil was right. Jacque was right. Why do we not listen to those who love us? Heed their words? I'd figured out the real villain before I'd even made it topside, but I'd refused to believe it.

I called out, "I'll let you all leave if you just give me Ezra." I found the engine as I looked for Camille. The engines on the little airships usually sat on deck, out in the open. This one was no different. I'd put the sapphire into my arm and rip the thing off with telekinetic magic. "You have Etienne," I continued. "What do you need Ezra for?"

Another shot rang out. Blood blew into my eye, stinging it. Etienne's panting stopped. He turned heavy in my arms. Gasping, I dropped him, stepping away from his now lifeless body.

"Camille, why?" Jethro choked from behind me. "My boy!"

I spun to the right and saw my mother coming out from behind the engine, her gun smoking. "You're right, my son. I don't need both. But I do need to start over, no thanks to you." Her eyes pouted as she looked at Etienne's limp body. "You'll never find Ezra." She smiled, blowing the smoke away from the barrel of her gun.

I stutter-stepped away from Etienne's body. "You shot him?" I gasped. That was when I realized there were no lengths she wouldn't go to in order to escape. And she was going to take Ezra, make him her own. *Holy shit.*

"Don't move, bastard!" she screamed when Mateo began to spin his singing blade.

Below, Cecil dug the bullet out of his shoulder. He glared at it before tossing it aside. A cross was engraved on the body of the bullet.

"You shot your son," I reiterated, still in shock.

Camille grimaced and shrugged, pointing the gun at me now. "It's all very Greek. Or Arthurian." She smiled and shook her head. "I didn't love Markus. It was an arranged marriage from France. I hate America. It's disgusting here. I have no allegiance to it, and it is getting more apparent that I will never gain the power over it I wanted. I was trapped most of my life. I made plans every day to run away, but then one day…" She gestured to me. "The heir to one of the boldest countries appeared inside me. Maybe this one can be mine, I thought. Maybe he will help me to freedom." She shook her head, pressing her lips together bitterly. "You were a tether. A ball and chain. But I saw myself in you just enough to pull your little head out of the basin of water that night."

A memory flashed before my eyes. I was maybe three. Mother had been angry. I remembered the water, but not how I'd gotten there.

She went on, "My only thought of solace was how I might one day rule this young empire. Train you up in my ways. But you had too much of Markus in you." She laughed sadly, hysteria taking over her senses. "You think you suffered? Try a lifetime of being with a man you hated. Simpering to his whims and orders. A child I did not love. Taken night after night, suffering an empire I found repulsive. No hope for a future. Useless."

Little did she know, I did understand. I had wanted her to love me, to let me tell her how much I understood.

"I thought about you a lot," I managed to say, but a sniffle gave away my steely demeanor. "You were what kept me sane. I hated Jethro all that time, but it was you."

I remember the moment I decided to shoot. It seemed to drag on for an eternity. I must have been moving slow, unwilling to pull the trigger because Cecil stopped me.

"Ezekiel, wait!" he screamed, commanding me once again.

Camille saw Cecil's command over me and how I jerked against his order. Acting quickly, she dumped one of the vials into her hand and squeezed something into her palm. Blood trickled out from between her fingers.

# 46

# Legacy

Jethro reached for his gun, but Mateo had already ascended the ladder and stopped him with a swift kick. Jethro had to leap and grab hold of the ladder before he, too, tumbled to his death down below. Camille took a sapphire from her vials and stabbed both her wrists with it. With a scream, she used the telekinetic powers to blast open the wall to the hangar, letting in the morning sun from directly above. She flung her arms in an arch, making a perfect half circle around the wounded Cecil, caging him in to where he stood just enough sun light to make him hiss and back away from the sunlight. We had come late in the night with no intention of staying till sunrise. Now, Cecil could be exposed to the sun.

With Cecil weakened, our tether vanished. I spun to face my mother, gun poised. She fired without hesitation, unlike me. The bullet ripped through my arm, flinging me back a pace. I dropped my revolver and clutched my wound.

"Geomancy?" I said through gritted teeth.

She flexed her bloodied arms and hands, throwing a silver bomb towards Cecil. The vial exploded from a mixture of other chemicals, sending the silver dust into the air. Bits of it landed on him, making him cough and recoil again. "Using earth magic is harmful, but I hear you have no qualms over using it, either." She smiled. "We take no issue with hurting ourselves to get what we want, my son. Seems to be a family trait. Our legacy is merciless killers, my darling, willing to kill ourselves and anyone else for what we want. You are a bad man, like your mother before you."

I straightened, my arm throbbing. "Geomancy is dangerous. It will kill you."

Camille smirked. "I have time. Lots of time. May as well spend those days in power."

Something in her tone sent a warning shiver down my spine and out my toes. She showed no fear. She had trapped my vampire. She sighed, looking over her shoulder at Etienne's bloodied body.

"I had hoped to start over with him. Men are so easy to control, you know. Disappointing, but easy." She reached down and ran her finger delicately down Jethro's jawline.

Jethro didn't move, eyes empty and red, locked on Etienne's lifeless body.

She went on, "He was wise enough to hitch his wagon to the strongest horse."

"She used you," I shouted to Jethro.

"You are the one who ended up in The Château d'Oubli," Jethro said. "She may have used me, but I avoided that fate. And the fate of my brother." He turned to Camille, begging for his life. "Let me go with you?"

Camille smiled at her weak-willed servant. "Where will I get a boy of royal blood to start over with? Oh!" She giggled. "Your son should do just fine. I've already arranged it. He will be the prince of MidWest. He's tiny, ill. But he will grow. Once I return from France with a new heir to the throne in a few months' time, no one will be the wiser. I've already sent word to my contact that I am with child. I will reveal Ezra as my own." She smiled sickeningly sweetly down at me. "Thank you for that, my son. The Empire will always know you as the prince who died. Forever the prince. Never the king."

I ran at them, but Mateo caught me and pulled me back, brandishing his blade at the pair of them. "Villains," he spat. "Sneaking around like cowards in the shadows."

"Sneaking? Coward?" Camille pursed her lips and slid her arm around Jethro's waist like a serpent. "Tell them what happens now, darling."

Jethro peeled his white glove off and cast it at my feet. "We'll fight like men, then. You win, your mother kills you with mercy. I win, we kill you slowly, letting you watch us take your empire over. First, we announce how the Grande Marquis D'Noirpierre killed his long-time friend, the Don of San Muerte, and the young prince. Then we advertise your capture. I find you, bring you in. Save the queen. We marry and present Ezra as our son." His voice shook and he looked down at his dead boy. "Either way, you are the villain here to your people. Camille says it's too easy, really."

I shook with rage. I glanced around to see if DeMarque had found us. I couldn't hear his boots on the docks yet. He might have gotten stopped by the guards.

"Ezekiel, let me fight him," Mateo cut in.

"Or let me eat the cowards!" Cecil screamed from his sun prison.

"You," Camille said to him, "need to remain silent." She blasted another hole in the docks, shooting sun towards Cecil so he had to back even further away. She winced, shaking her geo-infected hand.

I should have let him feed. It might have given him enough strength to push through the sun towards us.

I looked back at Jethro. His flesh had turned grey and his eyes had lost all their shine. He was an empty man. Cecil's words rang in my ears; if all I had to do was duel him as he wanted, I didn't have to kill everyone. I might not even have to kill him.

"Fine!" I shouted, wanting it all to stop. "I'll duel you, Jethro. One on one. Just like in The Château d'Oubli."

I dropped my holsters and belt to the ground. One of the lenses of my special goggles popped out when they hit the wooden floor. I drew my sword instead, a simple odachi given to me by Salazar. Jethro smirked and took out his rapier. We started by walking a small circle. I tested him by jabbing at his legs. He parried the blow far more easily than I would have imagined a rapier could do against my blade.

The instant I went to make another move, he flourished his cape to distract me from his dodge, and I saw my mother move out of the corner of my eyes. Cecil shouted Mateo's name. I turned to follow her with my eyes. Mateo fell to his knees, hands at his neck, blood gushing between his fingers. Behind him, Camille stood, holding what I thought had been a hair comb but was revealed to be a sharp dagger.

Her hair fell around her face, and she sighed. "Now things are a little more even."

"Camille, why?" Jethro stuttered. "You said…"

I left Jethro and ran to Mateo's side to catch him before he fell off the skydocks.

"Uncle," I started to say. I wanted to say so many things to him: he'd shown me any kind of man could change, how to ask for forgiveness and prove he was a better man. But proper villains never give you a moment's peace.

"Finish him off, Jethro, or I will!" Camille snarled, wiping her blade on her skirts. "Don't move!" She threw silver dust at Cecil as he stood up.

"Camille, wait!" Jethro shouted.

She shrieked at him to shut up, brandishing her knife. I didn't move.

"Stand down!" DeMarque's voice finally rang out from the forest of beams and ladders behind us. The light from the orb of fire in his hand lit up the hangar in an angry, red light.

"My own mancer," Camille mused. "Damn, Ezekiel, what a terrible time to start to be impressed by you."

DeMarque started to reply, but Jethro went for his dropped gun. When he did, the Grande Mancer hurled the fire ball. Jethro dodged out of the way, but the dry sails caught fire. Camille swore and ducked into the smoke.

I stayed, holding Mateo's fallen body, scanning for her. Something cold and thin slid between my ribs, stabbing into me from behind and out my front and back into Mateo. He choked on his blood as the pain hit him.

"That's for my son," the queen hissed behind me. "For the one I wanted that you made me kill."

Cecil roared from his prison, his face blackening from the burning silver. He smelled my blood. His panic, though weak, matched my own, amplifying my fear.

I gasped as the puncture in my lung took my breath. I cradled Mateo in my arms, my blood now on his face as well. I had to speak now. God knows how I found the strength to speak. Or why Camille and Jethro let me. Maybe the shock at how fast things were unraveling froze us all. I had dreamed about this moment for years, and it was coming to a close, not ending the way I had imagined, though. They had dreamed about killing me for a few days at this point, and they were getting their happily ever after.

I turned my angry red eyes on Jethro, who stood waiting for me to die. "Mateo was stronger than you. He was braver."

Jethro sighed, trying to justify his actions. "He was a fool. But." He swallowed. "Perhaps after all is said and done, he was the good brother. Even better than your father."

"I'll never know." I stood up, laying him gently down. My blood all over the floor, I could hardly stand. Far behind me, DeMarque waited for orders, another orb of fire in his hands. Camille was outnumbered. But I needed to know where Ezra was.

"Where is my son, Mother?" I said again, holding my wound. I couldn't get a proper breath.

She glared at DeMarque and ran across the gangplank to her ship. Jethro followed her at a quick pace. DeMarque arched his arm, ready to throw his flame.

"Sir?" he called to me, wanting to act. "She's getting away."

Despondently, I watched the pair of them release the docking lines. I could give DeMarque the order to throw the deadly fire. But it'd hit the balloon, igniting everything, taking away the last hope I had of finding Ezra. Cecil called my name, but I didn't hear him.

Watching Camille flee, the lines falling one by one, I realized Ezra wasn't on the ship. With the threat, she would have said something to stop me. My eyes drifted back to the castle. I couldn't reach it, the fire cutting off the hangar from the palace. Someone who could walk through fire needed to go.

"Do it," I mumbled to DeMarque.

With a grunt, the mancer heaved the flaming sphere towards the ship. Hot blood seeped from his pores with the effort of holding it so long.

Camille screamed as the fireball rocked the ship, hitting the small mainsail. The fire crawled up the mast to the hydrogen.

"Get off!" Jethro roared, abandoning the ship. I watched with no pleasure as he fled the deck. "Camille!"

But my mother didn't budge. In a mad rush, she spun the windlass to release the final tether that held the ship. But too late. I watched, dead eyed, as the flames licked the bottom of the balloon. I'd given her every chance to stop. To reconcile her choices. To return Ezra to me. She'd refused. Rejected salvation.

Jethro cried out as the balloon went up in flames. Shattering the skydocks above and setting fire to the interior of the hangar, the boat pitched and slowly sank down onto a dock. I ducked and DeMarque leapt down to shield me with his wide, red duster from the flames. The rest of the docks tilted. Once the initial blast settled, DeMarque stood up so I could see. Camille was gone and Jethro wailed, on his hands and knees, over the edge, looking down. She must have fallen.

Without another thought, he stood up to follow her.

"Jethro, don't!" I called weakly. "You don't have to follow her anymore. Jethro. No!"

But he couldn't be swayed. Wordlessly, he stepped off the dock and vanished into the plumes of smoke and fire, taking his weakness to his death. Finally, a huge beam from above collapsed, throwing me and DeMarque apart. Fiery ash filled the air and I almost passed out in a fit of coughing.

# 47 The Better Man

The fire blazed around us.

"I can't put it out," DeMarque called over to me. We were separated by several docks and the inferno. He clutched his arm, his orange eyes streaming blood.

I understood. "Get the ship," I called. "Find Ezra. Stop the fire from getting to the castle. Go!"

The Grande Mancer hesitated just a moment, then dashed away into the smoke.

I staggered over to Cecil, dropping the bloodied rapier as I limped. The hole in my lungs made it hard to draw breath. They were fast filling with blood anyway. I coughed, spitting my blood on the ground before Cecil.

"That was a strong spell." I laughed weakly, collapsing and leaning against a tank of hydrogen as near him as I could get. "Jethro might not be the only one not coming back from it." I began to shiver. "It gets so cold in MidWest during these months. I used to love it. My birthday was a few weeks ago. All Hallow's Eve and such, all happening at once. One time, there was a real vampire attack…" I gasped for air, but not enough came. Were my lungs collapsing? The sound I made trying to breathe made Cecil stumbled towards me.

"Ezekiel," Cecil whispered, coming to the edge of his sunny bars.

"Leave here. Get help. DeMarque is out there. He will see you back to your estate alive. You've done it."

He gave the most forced smile I had ever seen. I didn't know vampires could weep. The tears sizzled on his flesh. "It's all how you've dreamed. Now go and do something... Something good. Please. For me."

Something above cracked and a whoosh of hot hair pushed my hat off my head. I met his eyes. They were the violent burning color of his kind. His face started to peel. The sun rose, shrinking his prison. The silver dust covered him, making him like oil in a fire. I saw smoke rising from his shoulders, from his head, underneath his long, beautiful hair. He never blinked, but his tears fell. His alabaster nostrils twitched, catching the scent of my blood.

I could save him.

"I'll get you out," I stammered. I managed to push myself up. Once on my feet, I reached out to him and took his forearm in my hand.

He shrieked like a burned cat and shrunk away. "The arm, the silver. I can't get near you." Red sweat beaded on his pale brow.

I stumbled and fell again. "I can't touch you..." I put my hand, not the metal one, near him. His skin crackled the closer I got. "I can't save you?"

I staggered up onto my knees, tore my coat off and ripped my shirt open. With grunts and gasps, I clawed at my shoulder where the metal turned to flesh. I would get him out. But the pain, the weakness... I didn't have enough strength and had too much poison to get near him. I had used all my strength for revenge and didn't have enough to save him. He was all I had left, the only man who had ever stood by me. The only one.

"You can't do it, Ezekiel." Cecil smiled. He reached through the sun, burning the whole way, and pulled my hand from the metal arm, stopping me. He pulled back, smothering a flame on the back of his hand. "You need to get away from the ship," he said. "The docks are going to collapse, and when the fire hits this thing." He gestured to the balloon. "There's no way you will survive."

I wouldn't leave him. I slumped down. Looking up and watching a flake of ash drift out into the sun, I asked him, "What was the first thing you remember from your childhood?"

He glared at me, still wanting me to leave. Giving in for a moment, he answered, "My mother, of course."

"And from your vampiric birth?"

He smiled gently, violet eyes drifting out to the sun. "The one who made me. Jonathan. He was an old creature."

I tilted my head. "Did they have steam power when you were made into a vampire?"

Cecil laughed so hard he coughed. "I told you, I am not that old. I was mortal when the American Empire broke from Europa."

"What was that like?" I asked.

He sighed but smiled so wide his teeth shone. "I don't know. I was in Saoudite at the time."

"Right." I nodded, smiling too. "And now you want to go. To die and free your soul. Are you sure vampires won't find peace once their dead?"

He shook his head.

I whimpered, trying to sit up. "This is why I can't leave you."

His eyes glowed now as he smiled at me. Like he was preparing to say goodbye. "No, this is why I need you to leave me. I need you to go and do great things. Be a good man. With your redemption comes my soul's liberation. And if not, I will haunt the ever-loving hell out of an Ecclesiast named Sylas."

"I don't understand."

"It is necessary," he said pointedly. "I came to save you, as I said. So that my soul may rest in peace. Dying for you is the greatest thing I could ever do. But you must carry the standard onward. If you forgive and let go of this anger, I might be saved. That was my mission. I want to move on. But I have to save you first."

I smiled. "Those are nice stories, Cecil." I swallowed against the pain and fading light. "Remember after Django took your blood?"

He looked at me, confused and still panicking.

I went on, "I knew then you'd do anything for me. You wouldn't leave no matter how I treated you or what I chose to do." I smiled weakly at him. "Why? Just for your redemption?"

He reached both hands through the sun, fire kindling on his flesh. He grimaced and groaned. His hands caught my face. "You were desperate. Alone. I wanted you to need me. You were so damaged and hurt. I saw how you fought to rise above how you'd been treated, but I also saw the savage killer in you. Like the one I had been. I wanted to save you. Will you leave me to save me?"

He suddenly cried out in pain, fire exploding up his arms from where the sun touched him. He fell back into the shadows, clutching his limbs.

"I can't!" I begged him to stay, to be stronger than I was. To keep saving me. "I won't let you die."

He leaned back, eyes half-closed, and laughed weakly. "You've never saved anyone but yourself, Ezekiel. This time, it's fine if you don't. Just leave me and save Ezra."

I stood up. "Spades and snakes, sunflower," I cursed.

I marched to the windlass in the center of the small sloop and shoved my metal shoulder between the cogs. I cranked it until it held on with an iron grip.

Untying the bandages, I ripped at the stitching and prosthetic flesh. Then, I closed my eyes and twisted. I ripped that arm off, tearing open the parts of me that latched it to my torso. I know I screamed and screamed, ringing the rafters and shaking the catwalks. But, by all that is holy, I ripped that arm off. Silver free, I stood up, kicking the arm away. Just in the nick of time, too. The hangar began to collapse from imbalance. The sun burst into the room through the new openings, blazing everything in light.

"This way!" I grabbed Cecil's arm and dragged him, burning and ashen, towards the hangar's underground storage. The door proved almost too heavy to lift. I couldn't hold it, so after throwing Cecil down, I fell in after him. The hatch slammed onto me as the docks above collapsed onto it. Seventeen stone steps to the underground greeted me.

No more screaming. No more breathing. My ribs collapsed, my legs were broken, collarbone shattered. Nothing moved, but everything hurt like hell fire when I came to rest at the bottom of those steps.

"Why?" Cecil cried, falling next to me. "Ezekiel, why!"

Above, the hydrogen exploded, no doubt ignited by a falling airship. Smoke slowly seeped into the cellar, and I could feel the fire bearing down through the floor.

"I did it to…save a good man." I couldn't breathe. I gasped, but nothing happened. Looking down, I saw bones sticking out of my legs. A rib protruded from my middle. I didn't even notice my legs were backwards and twisted all wrong. "Cecil…drain me. There isn't much left, but it will get you out of here."

My armless wound drained me faster than I could count the fluttering thumps of my heart.

"You have to hurry. Now. Go and find my son. Raise him well. To be like you." I tried to laugh. "He can be your redemption. Maybe he was all along. I will…never be a man worthy of your soul." I couldn't see anymore. "Not after all I've done. I know my worth. I died a long time ago. I just didn't know it. You didn't. You have always been alive because you have always had hope for redemption. I…died the day I was buried in The Château d'Oubli."

I tried to move my remaining arm to indicate my neck for him to drink, but I couldn't so much as blink. If I did, I'd never open my eyes again.

His face broke. "But I wanted *you* to live." I felt him gently cradle my destroyed body in his arms, pushing my bloody hair out of my face.

"Cecil, you promised me you wouldn't make me do anything I didn't want to. Remember? All I can give you is my blood. Take it. Go." I smiled, taking in the dark underground and remembering how we'd met. "This is just like the second time we got holed up together, sunflower. I saved you by accident. I didn't mean to."

Cecil looked around the darkness and the stone walls. It was like the solar adamant cave where we had saved each other's lives for the first time. Where we had gained power over one another. It seemed a millennia ago.

"Fine," he whispered. "I'll find Ezra. But you have to come, too."

Silence.

"Ezekiel?"

# Epilogue: The King of MidWest

The sunlight blazed inside the majestic cathedral, blinding the hundreds gathered inside. Every wooden pew was filled with an excited civilian. Every side aisle was packed with standing watchers. The nave overflowed, too, and even the transept was crowded as a cattle pen. Incense permeated the air from swinging censors and hymns finished in loud, celebratory cheers as the ceremony ended.

"By the power vested in me by the might and grace of God and this great empire," the Arch Father announced, "and as you have sworn yourself before this congregation, I crown you High King of MidWest, Emperor of the American Empire, and Duke of the Hawaiian Islands as seen by the people there who pay homage to you as lord, gifted their sovereignty and freedom."

He held the crown above the young man's glossy blond hair. "Do you swear to uphold the laws of God and America as given to you by the people?"

"I swear so to do," the young man replied, beaming so hard his eyes watered.

"Do you swear to balance justice with mercy, seeing all people in your kingdom and lands as equals, deserving of fairness and a voice?"

"I swear so to do," he said again. He tried to hide it, but the boyish smile pulled at his eyes and mouth, making him glow.

"So shall it be as here witnessed by you all," the Arch Father said.

With that, he placed the orb in the boy's hand and the crown on his head. He raised his arms for silence. "Rise, Ezra, High King of MidWest. God save the king!"

"God save the king!" the people screamed in joy together. The applause made the boy smile even wider, showing white teeth behind his dark lips. He looked over at his mentor, who was hiding in a dark corner of the church, swathed in a flouncy coat with a high collar and an overly wide-brimmed hat. His violate eyes sparkled behind red glasses.

"Oh, what a day, Cecil!" Ezra sang as he spun around his guardian that night at the festivities. "Do you think Father would be proud of me?" He drank deeply from his golden goblet before his guardian could answer. "I'm to dance with Princess Esmeralda tonight. Is she pretty? What if when we're dancing, she has a berry seed stuck in her teeth? Do I tell her?"

"If she is pretty, you will no doubt sweep her off her feet," Cecil replied dryly, trying to hide his own gladness. "I heard she likes men with a drinking problem and the mental age of a twelve-year-old."

The boy pulled his blond hair over his shoulder and examined it. Deciding facial hair was more important, he looked into the back of his golden goblet to check for any hairs on his chin. No hairs showed on his dark skin.

"At least I'm her type. That makes it easier for me." He smiled and winked, returning the jibe with good humor. "So, I'll be off. Don't wait up. Or whatever it is you do."

He ran off before he could be stopped. Cecil shook his head and meandered out onto the marble veranda out the back doors. The night air smelled of smoke as the sky lit up with fireworks for the empire's one hundredth anniversary of freedom and for the crowning of their new king. Stretching out before him, the prairie land gently curved with golden waves. He stared into the darkness, knowing soon the sun would be up. The revelries had gone on all night. Good. The empire and Ezra deserved it. After the years of proving Ezra's bloodline and the fights they'd battled over political nonsense, despite a signed letter from Queen Camille, they had finally made it.

He drank in the night air with a deep, unnecessary breath, loving the smell of life on it. He'd done it. He pulled the letter from the Ecclesiast out of his pocket and read it one more time. The churchman had absolved him and told him, if he so desired, it would be safe now to walk into that sunset. Not yet sure, Cecil hesitated.

*He has a good council and a loyal court,* he told himself. *I found the prince who did not exist and put him on the throne. France will not attack. There is peace for now. I have done what I was asked to do.* Something tugged at his heart. *Then why do I feel so incomplete?*

A familiar scent wafted up on the prairie wind to him. A scent he had not come across in over eighteen years. A scent he loved. Someone watched him from the night shadows out in the fields of sunflowers. He spun around. There, outside the light of the gathering, a man in all white, trimmed with gold, loomed like a shadow. An over-plumed hat obscured his face. He inhaled deeply, taking in the familiar scent. Leaping over the marble railing, he ran out into the prairie.

Seeing me under the gaudy attire, his eyes shone with surprise and a kind of sorrow. His embrace took me by surprise. Had I done the wrong thing in hiding from him these twenty years?

The ache in my heart answered that question. I had to thank him for raising you, my son, and for saving me…for everything. But I had no words. I couldn't stop myself. It felt like being under his spell all over again. I threw myself at him, returning the embrace with all my might.

A sob almost broke from my lips. "I had to stay away," I stuttered. "My change was horrible. I thought the hunger would never stop. I was a monster. The tether broke and I was alone."

Cecil didn't let me go, crushing me harder against him. "I told you it would pass and we'd be linked again. But you didn't believe me."

I melted into his arms just a moment more before pulling away. "I never trusted you, sunflower."

We walked farther away from the crowds into the purpling horizon. Cecil told me how DeMarque had found Ezra after the battle with my mother and Jethro. He'd kept him for some weeks, tracking down the queen's letter about her being with child so he could present the child to the court.

"Wise man," I mused, letting my hand brush the thick stems of the sunflowers filling the field.

"He found me by sending out two letters to post boards," Cecil went on. "One for a hunter for a vampire and the other were letters for a private tutor for the young prince. I wasn't far as I had to wait for that churchman to arrive back in town and tell him my tale. I saw the inquiry after being hunted down and sought out DeMarque."

"What came of the Grande Mancer?" I asked, curious about the man who had saved my son.

Cecil smiled fondly. "He had a wife and some children. He never spent much time far from Palais Kansouri, but had his own battles to fight."

"Had?"

The vampire nodded. "The geomancy took him about a dozen years ago. I believe one of his sons, who bears his name, is a Warden for the Creed, and strongly advocates to make geomancy illegal. His daughters, I'm not sure. They did not stay in the palace after he died."

This news hit me oddly hard. I hadn't known the man well, but he had saved Ezra. And vampires felt everything more deeply than mortals.

"Ezra is a wonderful young man," Cecil told me after a moment of silence.

"I've seen his work in the nearby cities," I replied.

"He was the good that came from you, Ezekiel. He has his mother's heart and imagination and your endurance. And stubbornness." He laughed. I laughed, too.

Something had been burning on my mind the last eighteen years as I'd watched Cecil raise my son. "I was never your mission, was I?" I had known it to be true for years now. Maybe I even knew it from the start. It broke my heart, but I needed him to say it. "It was Ezra all along."

The vampire stood close to me, not meeting my eyes. "It was the hardest thing I've ever done," he began softly. "Not knowing when my salvation would come. All I knew was that I had to save the prince, and through that victory, I would be saved. I didn't know what I was doing, who needed to live, who needed to be saved. Who was the man I was to put on the throne? 'Find the king's son, the prince. Put him on the throne and soon enough, a good man will rule. This will save your soul,'" he quoted. "I had to decide everyone was worth saving."

I swallowed, looking at the ever-brightening horizon. "It wasn't me."

There is nothing hard about confronting your own mortality. But confronting your own uselessness is a bleak affair.

"Don't think you were worthless, Ezekiel," Cecil whispered, taking hold of the back of my neck and pulling me into a second embrace. I felt his breath catch as he tried to hold all the broken pieces of my soul in place.

"But there was a better way," I said.

"There is always a better way," he agreed. "But we have to make the choices and choose the actions before us. The only sure thing is that we always had a choice."

I had damaged people along the way. There were many things I could not repair. And now, I had eternity before me. When Cecil had saved me in that dark, fiery hole, I'd thought I'd go on for a millennium. See the world. Raise my son. But the world was done with me. I had outlived my welcome already, and I didn't want to do anymore damage.

We stood in silence, watching the people from a great distance.

"Even if you weren't my salvation," Cecil said, "I wanted to save *you*."

"I know."

I let him take my hand and lead me away from the city and the castle.

"Where have you been?" he asked.

I had to step high over the tall grass. "The Château. I wanted to liberate everyone. But when I got to it, I saw it wasn't right. That place made us into the evil they told us we were. None of them were guilty when they went down there. But when they accepted that there was no hope, no way out, they became what they were told they were. Just like me."

Cecil hummed gently. "You didn't deserve that life, Ezekiel. None of them do."

"I know. But they do now. They made that choice, to succumb to the role they were told they deserved."

"What else could they have done?"

I raised my head. "They could have fought. They could have defended the flame inside: their innocence, protected the thing that made them good. But they chose not to. They decided there was no help coming, so they would not help themselves."

"Like you?"

"Like me. I learned the only way to survive in such a place was to take a beating. So I did. I thought I wasn't like them: I wasn't scheming, hurting others, stealing, killing. At least, not like they did. I thought I was better than them. Of course, that wasn't true. But when you gave me the chance to rise above the pain I blamed them for, I took it. I soared to greater heights of madness and revenge than they ever will. I thought I was better than them, but I wasn't. Given the chance, any living creature will dole out the pain they feel they've unjustly born. I am done here." I was satisfied. "Shall we?" I asked.

"You don't have to do this," Cecil whispered. His violet eyes were bright with unshed tears.

I led us both out into the vast prairie. The grass waved between the stalks of tall sunflowers in the early morning breeze, long and fresh, plump and green. Wild mustangs nickered as we approached, but didn't seem to mind us. I sat in the grass, leaned up against a boulder, and faced the east. Any minute now, the sun would rise just over the horizon.

"You're going, aren't you?" I asked.

"But *you* don't have to," he weakly begged again. "You have centuries ahead of you. You have a boy who is king now. You can watch him grow old and have children of his own."

I laughed coarsely. "We went over this eighteen years ago. Don't make me repeat myself."

"Is this it?" he asked, pointing to a thick leather journal I had opened to pen some final words.

I nodded. "Everything. Written down for him to see one day. I hope that he—"

"He will understand," Cecil consoled me. "I can put it in his room," he offered.

I nodded and wordlessly handed the tome over. He was only gone a moment before reseating himself next to me, facing the east.

The sky grew pink, darkening to a dangerous red as the sun rose. With the first rays, my head began to burn. It hurt. I smelled my flesh and hair start to smolder. Beside me, Cecil didn't even wince.

"Do you think your soul is saved?" I asked.

"We're about to find out," Cecil said.

# About the Author

Abi works part-time as a freelance ghostwriter, editor, and audiobook narrator, hoping to one day make these passions her full-time job while she hunts for the next bohemian adventure. She has published works of fiction, poetry, academia, and even won awards for her short stories in science fiction and horror. Her novel *The Trial of Two* was recently named as an Honorable Mention in Writer's Digest for the 2021 self-published awards and won first place in dark fantasy in The BookFest Awards. Abi is also a proud mom of two…ferrets! She currently resides in Kansas.

She is one of nine children--all who share the creative spark.

Find Abi online at: www.abigaillinhardt.com

**Also by Abigail Linhardt**

Season of the Runer Book I: The Trial of Two

Season of the Runer Book II: Sojourn

Season of the Runer Book III: The Eldritch Hunt

Why They Killed: A Waksha Virus Novelette

These Darker Streets

www.ingramcontent.com/pod-product-compliance
Lightning Source LLC
Chambersburg PA
CBHW020936310726
48980CB00007B/803/J

* 9 7 8 1 9 5 7 1 7 5 0 5 8 *